I0831427

PREPPY GYRL COUNTRY CLUB

College Dorm Diaries of the Pretty Church Girl Crew:

Book 1

Church Girl Dropout: Beauty, Brains & Lipgloss on His Bed

by LaToya N. Ausley

Printed in the United States of America

First Printing, 2017

ISBN 978-0-692-91775-6

Black Teen Girl Books & Bubblegum
www.preppygyrl.com

I dedicate this book back to God. For the girls of today that will become the ladies of tomorrow with distinction. Keep God first, stay submitted to the One True God and try your best to make wise decisions based on the Future You! With Love, Hunny Bunnies!

Table of Contents

PREPPY GYRL COUNTRY CLUB

College Dorm Diaries of the Pretty Church Girl Crew:

Book 1

Church Girl Dropout: Beauty, Brains & Lipgloss on His Bed

by LaToya N. Ausley

Urban Privilege

Oh! Yes! It! Is! A beautiful day. Why, you ask?! It's the last day of school!! Anddd, it's not only the last day of school, honey bunnies, but it's our last day as high school seniors at St. Martin High School. Oh how I will miss those steps where all the clicks would hang out after school. I'm so going to miss our parking lot and how the traffic would jam in the morning as everyone rushed to try to apply that last lipgloss, while fixing their knee-high socks and grabbing their books out of the backseat before rushing to their lockers before the bell rang.

As J.D. waited in her car in the school parking lot for her friends to arrive, her phone rang . . . "Hey, hun! Did you want something from Pink Java?" said Emory.

"Hmm, yeah, can you get me a small peppermint mocha latte?"

"Just a small?" asked Emory.

"Yes hun, I can't do all that extra stuff that you get in yours everyday," said J.D.

"Alrighty, the line is not that long today for whatever reason, so it shouldn't take me that long to get to the school," said Emory.

"It's probably because the public schools are out today," said J.D.

Emory exclaimed, "Oh, that's right, I wish we had today off! Ok," said Emory as she pulled up to the drive thru window to place her order, "I am at the window, I will see you in a minute."

Emory pulled into the school parking lot next to J.D.

"So you have the top down today huh?" J.D. said.

"Oh yeah, it feels so good out here and it's only 70! When I was at Pink Java, guess who asked about you? Well, he thought that I was you, I'm like, huh, you are talking about my friend with the pink Ivy Kennington, not me," Emory said as she laughed.

"What!! The college guy that goes to UC?" asked J.D. "He just will not stop! Geez! He is so irritating anddd . . . how do you get a blue Ivy Kennington mixed up with a pink one? I mean, the least that you can do is remember my car?! Ugh!" exclaimed J.D.

"I know, right," said Emory. "Where are Fah'ry and Brooke?"

"Brooke said that she was around the corner and hmm, I haven't talked to Fah'ry since yesterday after school," said J.D.

"She's probably with Chaston," said Emory.

"Why would she be with Chaston this early in the morning?" asked J.D. "Oh that's right, public schools are out today! Oh gosh, I hope that she doesn't make us late playing around with Chaston. I hate being late," said J.D.

"Me too, it is so embarrassing and tacky! Here comes Brooke!" said Emory.

Brooke pulled up next to J.D. "Hey hun!" said J.D.

"Where is my latte, girl?" said Brooke.

"It's in my car. Don't be acting like you are the wicked step sister!" said Emory as Brooke laughed.

"I am not!!! I see you have your top down, Emory! I started to let mine down too but I didn't want to mess up my ponytail. Once my new cheer bow comes, I will be able to wear my ponytails with no problems," said Brooke as they laughed together.

"Ooh, you ordered a new bow?" asked J.D. "What kind did you get?"

"Yup, I ordered this plaid style with a dark purple, pink and lavender like the color of my car!" said Brooke. "I can't wait!"

"Ooh that sounds cute!!!" said J.D. and Emory.

"It's almost time for us to go in! Where is Fah'ry?" asked J.D.

"Oh, she called me when I was on my way here and said that she was at breakfast with Chaston but she said that they were at a restaurant close to the school," said Brooke.

"Here she comes now, I can hear her music already," said Emory.

"Yeah, she thinks that she has sounds!" said Brooke. As all the girls laughed, Fah'ry pulled in the parking lot next to the girls in her light yellow IvyKennington with her music blasting.

"Hey y'all," said Fah'ry. "What's so funny?"

"Oh, we were just talking about your love for LOUD music!!" said J.D. "So I see that you have your top down too."

"Oh yea! It's almost summa, we gotta let da top down and let our hair blow in the breeze!" said Fah'ry. "What time is first period today?"

"NOW . . ." said J.D. "We have to go before we get tardy slips from Sister Catherine and I haven't had any all year," said J.D.

As we walked into school together, it suddenly dawned on me that this was really the last day at St. Martin! However, I am so excited that I will be spending the next 4 years at Brighton University with my best friends!

Ring!!! the school bell rang.

Emory yelled, "Come on you all, we can't be late!"

Fah'ry sighed, "Really Emory! That is just the first bell, plus, it's the last day of school! I mean, what?! Are we going to get in trouble?!" she laughed.

"Well," said Emory, as she looked at Fah'ry and rolled her eyes, "it is important to me to be on time, ALL THE TIME!"

"Ok, ladies," said Brooklyn, "no attitudes today, ok? Emory is right, we need to be on time, no matter the situation. We must be ladies of distinct character!"

Fah'ry spoke under her breath, "Yea, yea, yea . . . ladies of distinction."

A loud voice was echoing down the hall . . . "Fah'ry, pull those socks up and button that blouse, young lady!"

"Ugh!" said Fah'ry, as she pulled up her socks. "I can't wait to get out of here! I hate these uniforms!"

"I know that it is hard for you as a fashion designer to wear the same thing everyday and look like everyone else but it's almost over friend," said J.D. "It's the last day of school hun! Let's go to class and enjoy this! You know that Sister JoAnn is going to crack us up with her hums after every word."

"Bahahaha, true!" said Fah'ry.

"There goes Emory and Brooke. They saved us seats. You know Tierra will try to sit there just because they are holding the seats. She is so conniving!" said J.D.

"Girl, I am not worried about Tierra," said Fah'ry. "She only tries that with you because you let her. She knows that I will . . ."

"O - kaay!" J.D. laughed, "we know, we know!"

"What took you all so long?" Brooke asked.

"You know!" exclaimed J.D.

"What?" said Fah'ry, as she laughed.

We all said at the same time, "YOU AND SISTER CATHERINE IN THE HALLWAY! Hahahaha," as we laughed loudly.

"Ok, ok," yelled Sister JoAnn, "settle down!" And the class got silent. "I understand that it is the last day of school and you are leaving for the L.O.C. retreat, but you must conduct yourselves as ladies of distinction. Please be sure that your desks are clear of all garbage and remember to take your journals. The bus will be arriving at 9:00 AM promptly," said Sister JoAnn.

As she began to try and teach a lesson, the intercom came on. "Yes!" said the entire class. As the speaker grew louder, Mrs. Thompson, our principal, announced that the buses had arrived!

"Ok, class, make sure that you have everything . . . journals, pens and overnight bags and don't you forget that . . ." said Sister JoAnn. ". . . WE ARE LADIES OF DISTINCTION!" we all said together as a class. Sister Jo Ann smiled as we said goodbye and headed to the bus.

"Ooh, it feels good out here, I am ready for da summa!"

"I'm sure you are Fah'ry," said Emory.

Fah'ry looked at Emory with a weird look. ". . . And what is dat supposed to mean?"

"I'm just saying, you need to be careful with Chaston. I mean, I understand that you all have been together since you were babies," she snickered, breathing hard as they walked to the bus, "but he hasn't been the best boyfriend," said Emory.

"Look, yes, we have had some problems but what couple doesn't? Especially when you are with the one," said Fah'ry while entering the bus.

"Hello," said Emory to the bus driver. The driver nodded.

Fah'ry laughed, "Girl, did she just nod at you?"

"So, J.D., where are you sitting?" asked Emory.

"In the back, hun," said J.D.

"Ok, I am going to sit with you. This is going to be a long ride and I don't feel like listening to Fah'ry talk about Chaston alllll the way there."

"Well hun," she took a deep sigh, "she loves him and until she gets tired, there isn't anything that we can say to change her mind," said J.D.

"I know," Emory said with a sound of disappointment. "She deserves so much better. I pray that a smart and Godlay man finds her at Brighton." They both started laughing.

"Did you just say Godlay? You are so funny!"

"I'm so serious, God has some great things in store for her."

"And how do you know, did you have a dream?" asked J.D. She laid her head back and closed her eyes in an attempt to relax on the ride.

Emory looked over at the seat across from them and noticed that Fah'ry and Brooke were in a deep conversation. She thought to herself, *I bet she is talking Brooke's ear off about Chaston. I should say something but I'll choose my battles wisely.* She laid her head back and closed her eyes. After so long, Emory couldn't do the relaxing thing like everyone else, especially with Fah'ry and Brooke's conversation ringing in her ears. "J.D., are you sleep?" Emory asked.

"No, just thinking."

"You are lying," she said as she smacked her lips. "Why do you sleep so much?" asked Emory.

"What are you talking about Emory? I was just thinking!"

"Jordan Dakota!" Emory exclaimed. "You can't lie to me! You have been sleeping like this for some months now. Did you think that I didn't notice? Like, uh no. We have been best friends since first grade. I pay attention HUN!" Emory emphasized.

J.D. laughed, "It's nothing." She laid her head back again and closed her eyes. Emory looked over at Brooke and Fah'ry as she interrupted their conversation and silently pointed at J.D., gesturing her continuous sleeping. Brooke and Fah'ry shrugged their shoulders at Emory and they kept chatting.

Emory tried once again to relax but she started having a dream and it woke her up. "J.D.," said Emory as she tapped J.D.

"What's going on Emory?"

"Oh nothing, like, I am so excited about Brighton!" said Emory. "I can't wait until I take all these chemistry classes! I really want to invent something that changes the world! I know that my Dad wants me to go to seminary but I believe that God can and will use me in the Chemistry world."

"Yes, hun," said J.D. "You have wanted this ever since Mr. Weber's 4th grade class and guess what hun? You will become a chemist. Just stay focused on your goal. That's bold of you to choose a different major other than what your dad expects. There are many that can't do that," said J.D.

"Well, I just think about the fact that I have to take those classes and be in college for umpteen years! I figure, I have to love what I am studying, especially when those classes are hard. I love my dad and I respect his opinion and I know that he wants what's best for me but I love Chemistry. I want to make an impact on the world through it," said Emory.

"Wow, that's profound!" said J.D. They started laughing together.

"I am so serious," said Emory. "Speaking of majors . . . did you make a decision?"

"Yeah, I am going to major in Biology. I really want to be a Neurologist like my mom," said J.D.

"Are you sure? Like, you don't sound so sure. I thought that you wanted to design clothes? I remember when we were kids, you would sit for hours and draw patterns and put pretty colors together. You love that stuff friend!" said Emory.

"Well, that is not going to make me any money or give me a promising future. Plus, how many fashion majors do you know that are well off and have national popularity? Especially black girls our age, all that you see are people trying to get their clothing line out. It's just too much of a hustle and I ain't a hustler," said J.D.

"Bahahaha, did you just say ain't?" Emory said.

"I guess it just slipped out," said J.D., laughing. "And let's not even talk about Intellectual Property laws and fashion. Ugh! There is very little trademark protection in design. So do I really want to create pieces and the next person bootlegs me? I am sorry, I mean, knocks me off!" said J.D. "No thank you, I'll take my happy self to Brighton and be on the road to becoming a doctor."

"It sounds like you've done your research but I know you and you still don't sound sure or happy," said Emory.

"I'm good hun," said J.D. She looked over at Brooke and Fah'ry and said, "So, Fah'ry are you talking about Chaston, hun?"

"No J.D.," Fah'ry said.

"She is talking about our grammar school cheer days! She's over here reminiscing and doing all the cheers!" Brooke laughed hysterically.

"Let's hear one Fah'ry," said J.D.

"Naw, y'all ain't ready on this bougee bus," said Fah'ry.

Tierra jumped in the conversation, ". . . Yeah Fah'ry, let's hear it." Tierra started clapping her hands to make a beat: one-clap, one-clap, one-clap, one-clap.

"Ok ok ok, let's do it like we did at St. Joseph's on the way to the basketball games, Brooke!" said Fah'ry. Fah'ry stood up and put one knee on her bus seat and started one-clapping. One-clap, one-clap, one-clap. "Are you ready Brooke?" she clapped and laughed.

"Oh my goodness, Fah'ry!" Brooke laughed and started clapping her hands with Fah'ry.

"Come on J.D. and Emory!" They started one-clapping and stood up in their seats and before you knew it, the entire bus was one-clapping on beat!

Then Fah'ry started to cheer-chant with the clapping beat. "It all started out at the basketball game when the coach told BROOKE (shouting) to do her thang, she said Ah go, go heeeead. Go, go go, go heeeead," as Brooke danced and all the girls shouted, "AYE!" Fah'ry sang, "You ready Emory? It all started out at the basketball game when the coach told J.D. (the girls shouted) to do her thang, she said, AYE, go, go heeeead. Go, go, go, go heeeead," as J.D. danced and all the girls shouted, "AYE!"

"Ok Emory, J.D. took your turn," Fah'ry shouted to the beat, "let's go!" Everyone kept one-clapping as Fah'ry kept cheer-chanting.

J.D. yelled as she one-clapped, "Come on Emory, it's fun!"

As everyone cheered Emory on, Fah'ry started . . . "It all started out at the basketball game when the coach told EMORY to do her thang, she said AYE, Go, go heeead. Go, go go, go heeead," as Emory danced and all the ladies shouted, "AYE!" They laughed and cheer-chanted all the way to the L.O.C retreat destination! Of course, every girl on the bus got a chance to dance, even the bus driver!

St. Martin High School

Senior Finale

Twin Day

Pajama Day

School Spirit Day

Fashion Show Day

Rep Your College Day

Senior Picnic

Senior Prom

Senior Trip

Graduation

Last day of school - 1st period dismissal for retreat

L.O.C. Seniors Only Retreat

The Smart Girls Only Party

"Oh wow, look at those cabins!" said Brooke.

"And look at dose boats!" said Fah'ry.

"Ooh, I hope that we get a chance to take a walk over there. I so love the water!" said Emory.

"So where are we supposed to go? This place is huge," said Fah'ry.

"Let me check," said J.D., as she rumbled through her bag to find the check-in papers. "Ok," said J.D., as she flipped the papers in her hand to read while they were walking. "It says that we are to check-in at the Scholar Prep building," said J.D.

"So where is dat?" said Fah'ry. "It's probably dat building over by the water."

As J.D. scanned the paper and they followed the crowd, she said, "Yes, we are going the right way, that's the building!"

As the girls entered the building, they all looked at each other with discreet but surprised looks on their faces. "Ok, let's keep our composure honey bunnies. We have to find this check-in desk," said J.D. as they finagled their way through the crowd of high school seniors. "It's probably down this hall where the big fountain is . . ." said J.D. as the other girls were looking around, as they continued to follow J.D.

"It looks like that's the line," said Emory. "Everybody is just standing, so I would assume so."

As the girls stood in line, they finally had a chance to sort of huddle and talk.

"Um, how did we not know that guys would be here?" said Fah'ry.

"I know right!" said Brooke.

"Emory, you ok?" asked Fah'ry.

"Uh huh," said Emory, as she quickly drew her attention back to the girls' conversation.

"Shoot! And Chaston asked me if it was gon be some guys here! Now, he's gonna think I was lying to him," said Fah'ry.

"Girl, stop!" said Emory. And all the girls laughed at Emory's unusual use of words to mock Fah'ry. "You don't know what God will do here or maybe your Boaz is here," said Emory.

"Girl, who is Boaz?!!! (as the girls were laughing) . . . And anyway, I already have a good guy, God has sent him already. So I don't know what you talmm bout!" said Fah'ry. She smirked.

"So, you think that Chaston is God sent?" asked Emory, "Tuh!"

"Ok ladies, we are next to check in," said J.D.

"You good Emory?" asked Brooke.

"Yes," she said as she once again quickly drew her attention back to the girls' conversation.

"Hello, I will need to see your student ID's," said the registration lady. The girls passed her all of their ID's. "You are in cabin 2030, right next to the docks," said the registration lady. The girls were so excited and giddy to get their room assignments! As they said in unison, "THANK YOU!" to the lady, they hurried to get to their cabin!

"Did she give you the keys?" asked Brooke, as they stood at the cabin door.

"Yeah, I have them." J.D. put her bags down to open the door.

"Wow, oh my goodness, this place is dope!" said Fah'ry. "Look at the view Emory! You can see the lake from the room, come up here girl!"

"Are you serious?" Emory said, as she ran up the stairs. "Oh my goodness, this is beautiful," said Emory, as they stared out of the window. "I have to have this room! I love how it overlooks the dining room! I love being up high," said Emory, as she walked around and eventually put her bags on the bed.

"Girl, let's go see da rest of this house, cuz this is a house!" said Fah'ry as they laughed and raced down the stairs.

Brooke yelled, "Check out the room down here!" They all headed towards Brooke's voice.

"Where are you?" said Fah'ry.

"Just go past the game room, it is to the right of it!" said Brooke.

"Wow!" said J.D. "This is pretty cool! The room is a movie theater!"

"Look at that big ol' tv!" said Fah'ry. "And that big bed with all da candy and nacho boxes in the glass door in the wall! Y'all know I love nachos!" said Fah'ry. She opened the glass door to the candy bar to look around. "Ok, ya'll, I gotta have this room!" said Fah'ry, as she put her bags on the bed.

"I want to see the bathroom!" said Brooke.

"I know there's one down here, we passed it on the way in here!" said J.D.

"It's probably upstairs in the luxury suite, hehehe," said Fah'ry.

The girls ran back upstairs.

"Yup, here it is!" said Fah'ry.

All the girls walked in the bathroom and all at once said, "Ooh!"

"There is every lipgloss color you could imagine!" said Fah'ry, as she went through the colors.

"Ooh, look at the eye shadow palettes!" said J.D. "I'm super excited! I have to stay up here honey bunnies!" she said, as she smiled unusually.

"I'm going to check out the other bathroom to see if there's a makeup table too!" said Brooke. "Yay!" she said as she yelled upstairs to the girls. "There's one down here too!" She went and put her bags in the movie theater bedroom.

They all met up in the living room and finally sat down.

"Ok come on now, fashion magazines?" said Fah'ry, as she flipped through them. "These are all the top local and international fashion mags! I am done!!" said Fah'ry.

"How unreal is it that guys are here?" said Emory. "I mean, I thought that it would only be our school here, didn't you all?"

"Yea, this is supa crazy. I thought it was gon be our same ole boring all girl school getaway to pray!" Fah'ry snickered. "But I don't know what this is."

"Yeah, they looked liked the guys from St. John," said Brooke. "I remember some of them from our grammar school. Didn't you see Chris when we were checking in Fah'ry?" said Brooke. "Do you remember, he was in grammar school with us and he transferred?"

"Girl no, I was not paying attention to those guys!" said Fah'ry. "Y'all know I ain't into da catholic school boys."

"Well, it was a lot of them at check in," said J.D. "They were all over the foyer! I saw a couple of cuties, if I must say so myself. Ya'll know I can spot a basketball player!"

"Hahaha!!" exclaimed Brooke. "Yeah, J.D, you and those basketball guys," said Brooke. "Speaking of spotting people, Emory, I saw you staring at that tall, light skinned boy with the baby face and curly hair."

"Uh huh, me too!" said Fah'ry, laughing as she covered her face.

"I was not staring!!!" said Emory. ". . . Wait, was I staring? Oh my gosh, I hope that he didn't see me staring?! Wait," she laughed, "was I really staring?"

They all answered, "GIRL YES!!!" And they all started laughing.

"What time is it? It seems like we have been on this couch forever," said Brooke. "Do we have to go anywhere? I know that most retreats have ice breakers and stuff the first night? I hope we didn't miss it?"

"I know, right, because we been chillin in dis cabin!" said Fah'ry.

"And I hope that we are not late because I hate being late?!" said Emory.

"It's 7:30 pm," said J.D, "let me go and get the agenda."

J.D. flipped through the L.O.C. retreat packet. "O . . . dahdahdahdah . . . Ok, there isn't anything scheduled for tonight besides a parTY!!! It starts at 10!!"

"A party!!!??" the girls yelled.

"I am so glad that I packed some dope outfits and not no joggers!" said Fah'ry.

"Ooh, I must get started on this face!" said J.D. "I know just the look for tonight. Simple and GORRRGEOUS!"

"Can you do mine too?" said Emory.

"Of course, you might meet Boaz tonight!" All the girls snickered.

Fah'ry yelled as she laughed, "WHO IS BOAZ??"

The girls headed to their rooms to get ready for the party.

"I didn't even call my mom to let her know that we made it here," said J.D.

"I need to call my dad too," said Emory.

J.D. picked up her phone and called her mom and there wasn't an answer and she got nervous. She called again and there wasn't an answer and now her heart was beating fast. So she called her grandmother . . . "Hey Grandma, have you talked to my mom today?" J.D. asked.

"Yeah, I talked to her earlier this morning. What's wrong?" said her grandma.

As she talked in a low tone, J.D. said with fear, "She's not answering."

"Well keep trying my dear, I know it worries you and I wish I could do something but you know I can't. I'll try to call over there. Where you at?" said her grandma.

"I am at my high school retreat. Let me try and call again, grandma. I will call you back." J.D.'s heart was racing and her stomach was in knots as she tried to call her mom again but their was no answer. She started to panic and just held the phone in her hand and prayed to God. *How am I going to get home from all the way out here? God please let my mom be ok, let no weapon formed against her prosper. Please please please, let her answer the phone Lord.*

Emory walked in the room from putting her clothes together for the party. "Are you still on the phone with your mom J.D.?" Emory looked concerned.

"No, I called my grandma first, I had not talked to her today."

"Oh ok, I know that you call your grandma everyday," said Emory.

"Yeah, I'm about to call my mom now though," said J.D.

"Oh ok, I'll see you downstairs, we are having a little ice cream in the kitchen," Emory said.

"Ok," replied J.D. She rushed to call her mom again and every digit she dialed, her heart beat faster, her stomach turned and her hands shook. Her mom finally answered. ". . . Mom, are you ok?" All she could hear in the background was what she feared. Her mom was on the line but there was a confrontation going on with her.

". . . J.D., call the police!!!" her mom urged.

"I don't care about that little b**** calling the police and give me this phone you stupid b****!!!" said the guy in the background. And the phone went dead.

J.D. tried to call back home several times but there was no answer. She thought to herself, *I need you Lord, I am tired of this.* J.D. called the police to be sent to her home. She then took a deep breath and called and notified her grandma of what was happening. She tried to call home again and her mom answered. "Mom, are you ok?" asked J.D.

"Yes, he's just mad that a guy said hello to me in the gas station and instead of him confronting the guy, he waits until we get in the house to fight with me. But you know that I will not let any man just hit on me. I bust his head with the lamp and the police came just in time because I would have really hurt him. I refuse to let him continue to act stupid."

"Where is he now?" said J.D.

"He's gone to jail, they arrested him," said her mom. "Let me call you back J.D., they want me to fill out these papers because I pressed charges this time."

"Ok, Mom." J.D. took a deep breath, thanked God and went downstairs to have ice cream with the girls . . .

"J.D., do you have a secret boyfriend or something?" asked Brooke.

"No hun, why'd you ask that?"

"Well you were on the phone a long time, I'm just saying."

"Yea," said Fah'ry, "we thought you were getting all boo'd up on the phone!"

"Uh no, now you all know that you would be the first to know if I had a boyfriend . . ." She pushed her chair back from the kitchen table and stood up to leave the table. ". . . It's hard to find a good guy anyway, you can't trust them," said J.D. "But really, I was talking to my mom and grandma. Anywho," she looked at her phone, "it's almost 9! We have to get ready for the party. Emory, did you still want me to do your makeup hun?"

Emory pushed her chair back from the table. "Of course!"

The girls all headed to their rooms to get ready for the party. As they were going up the stairs, J.D. said, "So, what kind of look do you want?"

"Hum, I am thinking something like a doll face." said Emory.

"Cool, you'll look so cute with that!" J.D. was clapping her hands as they ran into the bathroom. ". . . Wait a minute!!! I just thought about it, you don't wear makeup!!!"

"I know!!!" said Emory. "I just wanted to try something different. I mean, we are almost college girls, right???"

"Oh yeah," J.D. replied with a side eyed look of suspicion at Emory.

Meanwhile downstairs . . .

"Girl, we need to turn some music on!" said Fah'ry.

"I know right!" said Brooke. As she turned on the speakers . . . "Ooh girl, turn that up! I gotta hear dat bass! Dat makes the windows rattle!!!" said Fah'ry.

"So what are you wearing?" Brooke said. "I know that you have something cute that you don designed."

"SOOO, I designed these jeans at the fashion league and I have been waiting to wear them. I am supa excited!"

"What's the Fashion League?" Brooke asked.

"It's a program for aspiring fashion designers. They teach us how to sketch, sew, design patterns and everything."

"Oh, I knew that you were doing the fashion classes but I never knew the name of it. That's the class that's downtown with that famous designer that you were talking about, right?" said Brooke.

"Yeah," said Fah'ry.

"Is it expensive?" asked Brooke.

"I don't know, my dad paid for it. I just asked him to put me in it. It's really cool dough. How about you? What you wearing tonight?" Fah'ry said.

"I don't really know. I have like 3 outfits out."

"Let me see what you got?" said Fah'ry. She went over to the bed to look at the clothes that Brooke laid out.

"Girl, first of all, why do you have a cheer bow with your clothes for tonight? Not tonight,'" said Fah'ry as they laughed, "ok Brooke? Can you pleaseeeee leave the bow out?" asked Fah'ry.

"Nope, you know my bow is a must! It means a lot to me."

"Ok ok ok, well if you insist, then I would say the outfit with the bow is dope! Not that you asked but hey, I can't help it," said Fah'ry.

"I know, speaking of, let's hurry up and get ready so that we can go upstairs because you know that J.D. will be in that makeup all night," said Brooke.

"Oh yes, she'd be don created some new color combo!" said Fah'ry as their favorite song came on and they started to sing.

The girls were on their way to the Prep building for the party. And J.D. was having a tough time walking with the girls to the building. All the girls were fly in their clothes but J.D. was thinking to herself . . .

I don't know how long I am going to make it. Ok ok, as she looked at the other girls as they walked . . . I can do this, just look confident and ignore the pain, as she coached herself through *Ugh . . . Oh my gosh! I am not going to make it!*

"Ok, ok, J.D. you can do this!" she whispered to herself. She looked at Emory and she was walking with so much grace. She looked at Brooke and she was gliding like she was on ice skates and Fah'ry was walking with so much confidence that it made it look so easy.

I have to get this, especially before I get to this building. Ok, 1-walk 2-walk, as she coached herself through . . . *Ouch! Sssss, my feet are burning and my legs are wobbling.*

"Wait a second y'all," J.D. said, as the girls were walking and talking . . . "I think that I have a rock in my shoe," said J.D. All the girls stopped while J.D checked her shoes. She shook both of them. "Ok, I'm good now,"

"Dose are some pretty shoes, I need to get me some! Did dey have some in tan?" asked Fah'ry.

"Thank you hun, yes I saw some but I'm not telling you where I got them, hahaha."

"It's cool!" said Fah'ry.

As the girls continued walking to the party . . . *Alright, ooh that ground felt good,* J.D. thought to herself. *We are almost there. Come on J, you can do it!* she encouraged herself. *I knew I should have worn my flats but Noooo, I'm out here trying to look like everybody else. I feel too sexy. Ugh!! I feel too grown and I hope these boys don't look at me like a hoe. I knew I should have worn my flats.*

The girls arrived at the party (to their surprise) . . . and their eyes were wide and they were in astonishment as they entered the party . . . "This is so not real!" said Emory.

"I know right, dey don't have no lights on and this music is rockin!" said Fah'ry.

"I know and where are the chairs?" said J.D.

"Chairs! Girl, ain't no chairs at no real party!" said Fah'ry.

The girls were all in a group as they looked around and saw the groups of girls in huddles talking, people standing on the walls watching people dance, the football guys posted everywhere, the preps were talking to everybody and the basketball players were searching for the hottest girls.

"Come on Brooke, let's go dance?!" shouted Fah'ry.

"Girl it's not really anything good on!" said Brooke, smacking her lips.

"Come on Emory!"

"I'm not going out there! I don't want these guys humping on me," said Emory.

"Really Emory, you are not going to go to hell for dancing. You don't have to dance with no guy, just dance with me! Come onnn???" said Fah'ry.

A popular song came on and the entire party ran to the middle of the floor to dance.

"Ayee!" said Fah'ry as all the girls ran to the floor to dance.

As Emory was dancing, she thought to herself, *Ooh I feel so free. I love dancing.* As Emory danced, a crowd started to form around her and a guy started to notice her. *What am I doing?* she said to herself. *I have to stop. I mean, I'm just dancing. What's wrong with that? Naww, this doesn't feel right,* said Emory to herself.

As Emory kept dancing, a guy started dancing on her and more guys came and started dancing on her friends . . . *Ok this is too much. I feel horrible!! I need to stop. This is not right! Mannn,* she said to herself.

J.D. started to move closer to Emory as she danced. ". . . I am about to get from out here!" said J.D. "My feet are hurting."

"Yeah, mine too," said Emory.

Emory and J.D. went and stood on the wall and watched the party, laughed and chatted. "I saw your guy over there by the concession when we came in," said J.D.

"What guy?" Emory laughed.

"You know I know!" said J.D.

"Know what, J.D.!?"

"That you've been crushing on him since we checked in earlier. I saw y'all staring at each other in the line. He is fine though," they laughed.

". . . And why you watching me, I saw that guy dancing all on you!" said Emory. "He was cute too."

"Yeah, and I don't know where he came from!!" J.D. said. "We just started dancing! He had on this cologne that really smelled . . ."

"What y'all talking bout?" said Fah'ry.

"That boy that J.D. was dancing with," said Emory.

"Oh yeah, I saw y'all!" said Brooke.

"Y'all would make a cute couple," Emory said.

"I don't know about all that but he is cute." said J.D., as she smirked and scanned the room for him.

"I'm going back out there to dance while y'all all scanning the place. If I see him, imol tell him to come over here J.D.!" said Fah'ry.

"Uh, no, don't do that!!!" J.D. blushed.

"Let's go back out there, Brooke!!" said Fah'ry.

Brooke and Fah'ry went back to dance and Emory and J.D. continued to talk by the wall. "I'll be right back, I'm about to go to the restroom," said J.D.

"I'll go with you," said Emory.

As they got to the restroom, Emory started fixing her hair and J.D. took her shoes off.

"Your makeup still looks soooo cute," said J.D.

"Oh, thank you!"

"Those shoes are so cute on you. You look very pretty in those!" said Emory.

"Thanks, hun." J.D. thought to herself, *I am just glad to get these shoes off of my feet! Whew!* as the cool floor soothed her feet.

"Are you ready?" asked Emory.

"One sec hun." She put her heels back on. "Ok, I'm ready!"

As the girls were walking back into the party, Emory asked, "So are you going to dance with him again?"

"If he comes over to me. I'm not going to look like a hoe and go up and start dancing all on him. I'm not going to stalk and sweat him. BUT I hope he does come back and dance with me because he is so cute," said J.D., as they laughed together.

Walking into the party, J.D. and Emory heard the crowd chanting, "AYE AYE AYE!" They ran into the party and there was a huge crowd in the middle of the floor. Emory and J.D. rushed to see what was going on. J.D. went silent as she watched but rocked with the beat to shield her hurt.

"Girl Brooke is out there getting it!!" said Emory. "And she's dancing with the cute guy. I guess he dancing with everybody tonight!'

"I know right"' said J.D., as they rocked to the beat.

Yeah, I guess he's dancing with everybody, she thought to herself. "I'm going over here," said J.D., as she walked away feeling so hurt.

"I'm going, too," said Emory.

The girls headed back by the wall and watched Fah'ry and Brooke dance as they chatted and laughed.

As they were standing there . . . "Hey, how you doing?" said a guy.

"I'm fine," said J.D., as she thought to herself . . . *Ooo this is not the time. Ugh!*

"So what school you go to? You look like a St. Martin girl." As he continued to talk to J.D. . . .

"Hello, how are you? My name is Bryce."

Emory was trying to hold her smile. *Oh my goodness, my heart is beating so fast and I hope that I'm not turning red,* she thought to herself. "Hi, I'm Emory."

"So what school do you go to?" asked Bryce.

"St. Martin," said Emory.

"What school are you at?"

"I go to St. John," said Bryce.

The conversation grew silent and they watched the crowd dance as he stood next to her.

"This is crazy, right?" said Bryce. "I would not have expected a party at a retreat!"

Emory smirked, "Yea it totally caught me off guard."

As J.D. was still captured in conversation with the uninteresting guy, she bent her head back behind Bryce to avoid him seeing her and she smiled at Brooke with excitement.

"So why aren't you out there dancing with ya girls?" asked Bryce.

"Oh, I don't dance," Emory said.

"What!!! You don't dance???" he said as he chuckled.

As they laughed together Emory replied, "Nope."

"Now is it that you don't dance or you can't dance??" questioned Bryce with charming humor.

"Umm . . ." as Emory began to speak, Bryce quickly interrupted.

". . . I'm just kidding," said Bryce, as he chuckled. "Don't get all mad, I was just playing."

Emory snickered, "Cause you know I was about to say . . ." said Emory, and they laughed together.

"So why aren't you out there dancing?" asked Emory.

"Well, I saw you," said Bryce, as he moved in closer to Emory because of the loud music.

Oh my goodness, is he really this close? she thought to herself. *I hope my face is not turning red. And I don't know what to say to him. I mean what do I say? Come on Emory, think of something.*

"So, what college are you going to?" asked Emory.

"Oh, I am going to Brighton," said Bryce.

"Really! My friends and I are going there," said Emory. Her heart started beating really fast and butterflies were in her stomach.

"Wow, so you're going to Brighton," said Bryce.

"Yup," Emory said as they both tried to hear each other over the music.

Bryce moved in closer to Emory to speak closer to her ear. "Is that your girl next to us?" said Bryce. "Cause she looks like she is going to smack him," he chuckled.

"Yeah," said Emory. "She doesn't like random guys coming up to her."

"Aw ok," said Bryce. "So how does she meet guys then?"

"Well, she would rather talk to someone that she is familiar with like somebody at church, school or in the area that she lives in."

"I can understand that in a way but ya'll go to an all girl school? So she must know a lot of people out of school?"

"She's good, just very particular," said Emory.

"I got yah," Bryce said. "So what made you choose Brighton?"

"They have a strong science program and I have always wanted to go to California," said Emory.

"Science, huh?" asked Bryce with an impressed look. "So, you're a smart girl?"

"Of course," said Emory. "I have a 5.0 GPA; I rank number 1 in my class," she said proudly.

"Ok ok, I see you, so that means that you are Valedictorian, right?" said Bryce.

Emory smiled. "Why, yes I am!"

"So, do I get some cool points for guessing that?" asked Bryce.

"Um we will see," said Emory.

"Aw man," he chuckled, "now you know that was a good guess, come ooon???!" said Bryce.

Emory laughed.

"So what kind of science are you studying?"

"I will be a Chemistry major. I want to create something that will touch the world. I believe it is where God has gifted me. I've loved chemistry since I was a little girl. So, I am so excited about studying what I love! What about you?" Emory asked, as she looked him up and down checking out his tall physique, well groomed hair and face.

"Well . . ." Bryce took a deep breath, "I chose Brighton because of their seminary program."

"Oh ok," said Emory.

"Yeah," said Bryce.

"So what do you plan to do with your degree?'

"Whaatt!!! You didn't change the subject? Most girls, when I tell them that I will be studying Theology, they quickly change the subject."

"So tell me more!" said Emory. "Why seminary? Are you planning to be a pastor?"

Bryce smirked, "Now I don't know that part yet, but I do want to travel to many nations and teach the Bible, maybe in a university."

"Oh ok, that's cool," said Emory, as she started to think . . . Oh my gosh! Seminary school! This has got to be a dream . . . as she tried to snap back into the conversation with Bryce.

"Yeah, I'm pretty excited about Brighton too," said Bryce. "I love the campus especially the dorms," said Bryce.

"The DORMS!!!" Emory emphasized. "You like the dorms? They were alright to me but nothing spectacular. I mean I am not too thrilled about community shower stalls and just having a sink in the room."

"A sink in the room!!" exclaimed Bryce.

"Are we talking about the same Brighton?"

"There's only 1," said Emory, "from my understanding."

"Yeah, we don't have a sink in our room. Well, we have one in the bathroom and oh, in the kitchen!" he chuckled.

"In the KITCHEN!!" said Emory.

"Yeah," Bryce said. "We are staying in Xander Hall. The tall building that they just built. Ohhhh, you must be talking about Anderson hall and all those dorms over there."

"Yeah!" said Emory. "I never knew that there was a new building! When we went to visit in October, I did not see a new building!"

"Yeah, they finished Xander and Sebastian Hall about a month ago," he said with sarcasm. "They are like suites and 4 people can stay in them instead of those little old school dorm rooms."

As Emory had this astonished look on her face, she leaned over to J.D. and interrupted her conversation with the uninteresting guy. " - Wait!! J.D, did you know that Brighton had new dorms with suites??"

"Suites!!" said J.D. "Um, no hun! I only know of Anderson!"

"Nope, Bryce just told me that they have new dorms and that they finished them a month ago," said Emory.

"Huh?" J.D. said, "Wait a minute, a month ago? How did I miss that??"

"Yup," said Emory. "He said that the rooms have kitchens and bathrooms in the rooms!" said Emory.

"Huh?" said J.D.

"Yeah," said Bryce, "they are dope. They gave us a tour when they opened."

"That was a month ago, you were there a month ago?" asked J.D.

"We have to go every so often for Academic Athletic Prep."

"Sooo, you're an athlete?" asked J.D. "What sport do you play?"

"Yes, I am, I play basketball and so do my roommates."

"Awww, ok," said J.D.

"So, you know who your roommates are already?" asked Emory.

"Yeah," said Bryce. "We got our room assignments in January"

"JANUARY!" Emory and J.D. said together. "They told us that we wouldn't get our room assignments until summer break!" said Emory.

"Naw," said Bryce. "I have been back and forth to Cali at least 5 times this school year."

"Wow!" said Emory.

"I am going to have to find out about why we didn't know about these new dorms," J.D. said.

Emory laughed and looked at Bryce. ". . . She loves researching, that's why she's saying that. She's probably going to be researching all night."

As they all chuckled together, J.D. said, "Well, hey, I love research! I like being informed and looking at the why because there is always a why. Well, it was nice meeting you Bryce. Emory, I am going to go and get Brooke and Fah'ry off this dance floor so we can head out, it's getting late and I don't want to play around with these night animals on the way to the cabin." J.D. walked to the dance floor as she started to search for them.

"Oh, that's right!" said Emory. "I so forgot that we were in these woods!"

"Yeah that's true, it's probably some bears out there," he laughed.

"Stop playing!" she said, as she hit Bryce in his chest. "That is not funny!"

"Ok ok I'm sorry!" he said. "But it was really nice talking to you. You are very interesting."

"So are you," said Emory, as butterflies started again in her stomach and it became hard to swallow.

"So . . . will you dance with me before you go? I know that you don't dance butttt I'd thought I'd ask."

All the girls suddenly came to where Emory and Bryce were.

". . . Emory, you ready?" said Fah'ry, "oh, how you doin, I'm Fah'ry," as she looked Bryce up and down.

"Hi." He shook Fah'ry's hand. "I'm Bryce."

"It is nice to meet you," said Fah'ry.

"Hello and I'm Brooke."

"Hello, it is nice to meet you, Brooke."

"Well, it was nice meeting you again," the girls said as they started walking towards the door.

Emory stayed by Bryce as the girls walked out. She said, "This was cool."

"Yeah," said Bryce, as they both had looks of disappointment that the night was ending. "So you didn't dance with me?" said Bryce.

"Naw, maybe next time."

"Oh, so there may be a next time? So, does this mean I can talk to you later?" he said.

She smirked, "I guess so."

"Awww man, let me get my phone out right now,"

As they laughed, he said, "Ok ma'am, I am ready to record when you are," as he played around and disguised his voice as a customer service person.

As Emory was laughing, "7-7-3-5-5-5-2-3-1-6," she said.

"Ok, I got it. Let me save it," said Bryce.

"Yeah," said Emory, as she smirked.

As Bryce walked her to the door where her friends were, he said, "Well it was really nice meeting you Emory," as he stared into her eyes.

"Yeah, you too," said Emory, as she stared into his eyes.

"See ya . . . !" Fah'ry said in a loud voice, as they started walking out the door to the outside.

"Emory did you want me to walk you to your cabin?" Bryce asked. Emory paused. . . *Yes, yes, yes!!!* she thought to herself. "No thanks," she said, "but thanks for offering."

"Sure," said Bryce, "see you around."

Emory gave him a cute wave goodbye as she walked out the door to catch up with her friends . . .

"Girllll he is too cute!!!" said Brooke.

"Did you get his numba?" asked Fah'ry.

"I hope so, they talked allll night!" said J.D.

"Nope!" Emory said. "I didn't get his number."

"Whatttt!!" said J.D.

"Girl he look too good to let him get away," said Brooke.

Emory started laughing, "Naw ya'll I gave him my number."

"What, why didn't you get his numba too?" asked Fah'ry.

"If he wants to talk to me, he will call me," said Emory.

"O-kayyy," said J.D. "We don't chase guys, they find us!"

The girls continued to laugh and talk on their way to their cabin.

As the girls got to their cabin, they quickly kicked their heels off and flopped down on the comfortable living room couch, turned on the big screen television and they grabbed some juice.

"I am so hungry!" said Brooke. "I wonder if they will deliver pizza here?"

"I hope so cuz I'm starving!" Fah'ry said.

"I'll check," said J.D. "I have my phone right here."

As J.D. called to order the pizza, the girls started to talk about the party.

"Emory, so what was up with you and . . . what's his name?!" asked Fah'ry.

"Yeah!" said Brooke. "You were with him all night! Come on!! So . . . what did he say???"

Emory smirked and started glowing. ". . . He is really cool and I couldn't stop staring at him, he looked so good! I was trying to listen to what he was saying," she laughed, "but I kept looking at his hair, his face and oh my goodness, his lips!! I really wanted to kiss him!"

J.D. chimed in as she finished the phone call. "Yes hun! I thought he was going to kiss you a couple of times the way he kept getting all close to your ear!"

"Bwhahahaha!!" exclaimed the girls.

"I know, I was like, is he really this close to me?" said Emory. "Ooh and I still can still smell his cologne on me," she said, as she sniffed her shirt.

"You are hilarious," said Fah'ry snickering.

". . . And guess what?" said J.D. "He is going to Brighton!"

" Whattt!!!" they said.

"Yeah," Emory smirked, "Isn't that crazy?!!

"And he was telling us that Brighton has these new dorms that are like suites that him and his friends are staying in," said J.D.

"New dorms! What? I thought that Anderson Hall and the other ones around them were the only ones?!" asked Brooke.

"Nope!" said Emory. "He said that they finished the new dorms about a month ago."

"So how does he know?" asked Fah'ry.

"He said that he's been there a couple of times this year for some academic athletic thing," Emory said.

"He look like he play basketball," said Fah'ry.

"Yup!" said J.D. "And he said that he and his friends had their room assignments already."

"How did that happen??" asked Brooke.

"I don't know," said Emory.

"Yeah me either," said J.D., "but I am going to look it up tonight!"

"Ok so don't try to talk about Bryce and I all night," said Emory.

"What about you Brooke?!!!" they laughed loudly.

"Yeahaaa, we saw you out there!" Emory said.

"Uh huh," said Fah'ry. "That boy had you all on the wall andddd he picked you up!"

"We were just dancing!" said Brooke. "I had so much fun!"

"Yeaahh, me too - " said Fah'ry. She quickly interrupted the conversation. " - Ooh I forgot to call Chaston! I haven't called him since we got here!"

"Has he called you?" asked Emory.

"Naw," Fah'ry said, as she ran downstairs with her phone. "I'll be right back!!" Fah'ry called several times and there was no answer, so she left a voicemail: "Hey Chaston, I keep trying to call you and I don't know why you not answering the phone. I was just trying to let you know that I made it to the retreat. Well, call me when you get this message. Love you."

Fah'ry just sat on the bed in worry as she thought about the many things that he could be doing and with whom at 2 in the morning. Fah'ry took a deep breath and headed back upstairs with the girls. As she was walking . . . *Let me try again, she thought to herself. She tried 3 more times but there was no answer. Ugh, why he ain't answering his phone?* she said to herself. Her heart started racing and she became overwhelmed with worry. As she sat back down on the couch with her friends, her phone rang and her heart jumped.

"Hello?" said Fah'ry. "Oh, hey grandma. Oh, I'm sorry I forgot to call you when we got here. Yeah, I know that you were worried and I couldn't answer my phone where we was at cuz it was too loud. But I'm ok. Ok . . . Love you too."

All the girls were laughing and talking on the couch. "What y'all laughing at?" asked Fah'ry.

Emory laughed. Brooke said, "She's still talking about Bryce!"

Fah'ry smirked, "Girl you still talkin about Bryce! So, I meant to ask you, why didn't you kiss him since you said you wanted to?"

"Because I felt like that was inappropriate. Like, I had just met him," said Emory. "That is way too soon to be kissing a guy. Why'd you ask?" asked Emory.

"Oh, I was just wondering," said Fah'ry. "I mean, you said that you wanted to kiss him, why didn't you just do what you felt?" she asked.

"First of all, I don't know him like that," said Emory. "I also know that kissing leads to other things and I'm not trying to go that far. I really don't want to have sex with anyone until I am married."

"Me either hun," said J.D.

"Yeah me too," said Brooke. "I don't have time to be worrying about getting pregnant or catching a disease. I have some goals that I have to complete. I don't need anyyy kids," and they all smirked.

"Yea I feel the same way," Fah'ry said. "It's just so hard."

"Wait, what do you mean?" asked Brooke. "I thought you did, with Chaston already?"

"Well, remember when I went over his house that day his mom and dad was at work?" said Fah'ry. "So I went over there knowing that it might happen and I was so scared but apart of me was like whateva. I mean we have been together forever and we have been talking about marriage anyway. So I figured why not and I was just tired of him asking and saying that he was tired of all that grinding and stuff. I just was like whateva but deep down I knew that I should have not went over there and I knew I was about to do wrong and I was ready to deal with the consequences. I knew that God would not be happy but I had in my mind that He would forgive me. I was really trying to wait until marriage and I ain't gon lie, a part of me wanted to as well. I mean we love each other, so I figured we would finally get a chance to share our love on a new level. So I was thinking, at least I made it through high school a virgin. Other girls been having sex. So, we are getting ready and I get in his bed and I see a garter on his bed post!!!"

"What!!" J.D. said, "like a prom garter??"

"Yes girl!" Fah'ry said. "So I'm like, 'Who's is that??' He's like, 'Aw man, my sister told me that if you found out that you would kill me!!' So I put my clothes on so fast and hopped in my car and left."

"That was nothing but God!" said Emory.

"Wow! I know," said Fah'ry.

"So, what did he say about the girl's garter?" asked J.D. "I mean, how did he get it?"

"Ok so he said that one of his momma co-worker's daughter didn't have a prom date and his momma asked him to take her," said Fah'ry.

"Ok, but why didn't he tell you if it was just a charity case!?" said Emory with an attitude.

"That is what I said!" Fah'ry exclaimed. "Anddd I was thinking how did I not know that he went on prom with another girl?! We talk all the time and I never suspected a thing," she said in a confused voice. "I mean my heart dropped to the floor. I just would have never thought that he would lie to me."

As she started to cry, her friends came over to her side of the couch and hugged her. "It's going to be ok hun," said J.D.

As Fah'ry wiped her tears she kept trying to talk but the tears wouldn't stop. "That's why . . ." she cried and tried to talk. "That's why," she sniffled, ". . . I figured I would have fun tonight maybe there is someone better for me," she said as she wiped her tears.

The Retreat (Boys, Boys and More Boys!)

Beep! Beep! Beep! J.D.'s alarm went off. She quickly turned it off so that she didn't wake up Emory. She headed to the bathroom to prepare herself for the day. J.D. grabbed her phone and went downstairs to the balcony that overlooked the lake. She silently opened the balcony door and crept outside.

Good morning Lord, J.D. said. *I thank you for waking me up this morning and allowing me to see another day. I ask you to forgive me of any sins that I have committed knowingly and unknowingly. I ask that you would cleanse me from the top of my head to the soles of my feet. Lord I am so scared. Please help me. Please help my mom and protect her. I ask that you cover her in the blood of Jesus. Lord, please don't let him do anything to my mom. Please keep him away from her. I ask that his car doesn't work and he has no way to get to her. And Lord, if he is there, please let the neighbors hear them arguing and call the police. In Jesus' Name, Amen.*

She sat in silence as she looked at the water and clouds. *Lord please don't take my mom away . . .*

Fah'ry came upstairs and went to the refrigerator for juice. As she sat down on the couch and started thinking, she noticed J.D. on the balcony and went onto the balcony. "Hey what you doin up so early?" asked Fah'ry.

"I was praying and just enjoying the water," said J.D.

"Yea, I love this place," Fah'ry said.

"Yes hun, this place is dope!" They both started laughing.

"Dope!!!" Fah'ry said. "You don't use the word dope!"

J.D. smirked, "I know. That's just not me huh?"

"Um no!" said Fah'ry and they laughed.

"So are you cool?" J.D. asked.

"Girl, I don't know, I guess," said Fah'ry. "I mean what am I supposed to do? I love him. We've been together forever. He's the only boyfriend I have ever had. I just don't know what to do. I never thought he would lie to me and I never thought he would ever want to be with another girl," she said as her eyes started to water.

"I know," said J.D., "but you have to stop crying over him. You deserve better. You can get another boyfriend and he's not all that cute anyway. Did you not see all those guys trying to talk to you last night?" asked J.D.

"I know," said Fah'ry, "but I don't care about those other guys. I just want us to be ok."

"Fah'ry, you have to stop this hun," said J.D.

As J.D. gave Fah'ry tissue for her eyes, Fah'ry looked at her phone. "It's almost time to go. Let me go and get ready," she said. As she walked away, she thought to herself . . . *Aw shoot, I forgot!* "J.D, do you have some body wash? I forgot mines," Fah'ry said.

"Sure," said J.D. "It's in my bag upstairs on the bed."

"Thanks," said Fah'ry.

As Fah'ry went upstairs and went through J.D.'s bag, she woke Emory up as she rumbled in the bag looking for the body wash.

"Hey there Fah'ry," said Emory. "What time is it?" asked Emory.

"It's about 7:45," Fah'ry said as she went downstairs to take a shower.

Emory sat up in her bed . . .

Our Father, which art in heaven, hallowed be thy name. Thy kingdom come, thy will be done on earth as it is in heaven. Give us this day, our daily bread and forgive us our trespasses as we forgive those who trespass against us and lead us not into temptation but deliver us from evil. For thine is the kingdom, the power and the glory forever and ever. Amen. Father God, I ask that you would place a hedge of protection around me and my family and friends.

Then she immediately grabbed her phone and thought to herself . . . *He probably called after I went to sleep last night.* She scrolled through her phone but she didn't see a call from Bryce. "Let me turn my phone off," said Emory. "Maybe there's bad reception here . . ." Her phone restarted but there were no missed calls or voicemails. Emory's heart dropped.

She thought, *I thought that he said that he would talk to me later? Ugh! It's whatever. I need a latte!* She headed downstairs to make some lattes and yelled, "DOES ANYONE WANT A LATTE?" Emory ran downstairs and knocked on the bathroom door. "Fah'ry, do you want a latte?"

"Yea!" Fah'ry yelled through the bathroom door and continued to take her shower.

Thank you, God, thought Fah'ry. *This shower feels good.* She grabbed the body wash. . . *Aw, I need one of those poof things or something for this body wash!* she thought. *Well, I'm going to make this work with this towel.*

I thank you Lord for today. Please forgive me of anything that I have done wrong. Can you please let Chaston and I get better? I don't know what's going on? Why won't he answer my calls? It's been 2 days. Please let him call me today. And God can you take care of my grandma and dad? In Jesus Name, Amen.

I hope my hair didn't get too wet, she said to herself. *I couldn't ask J.D. for body wash, a poof and a shower cap. She would be looking at me like, what! Ahh, this shower should last me for a couple of days.* She gathered her things to leave the bathroom. She shook her bag over the toilet. *Let me make sure that nothing is in here,* she said to herself. *I don't want anything crawling out in front of anybody.* She double checked the bathroom before she went to her room to get dressed.

"Brooke!" said Fah'ry. "Girl you still sleep?"

"Uh, yeah Fah'ry, I'm still sleep," said Brooke with sarcasm.

"It's 8:30, we leaving at 9," said Fah'ry. "I'll be upstairs, Emory is making lattes."

"Is she?!" Brooke said with excitement. "Ok, I am about to get ready." Brooke grabbed her bag and quickly put an outfit together and laid it on the bed. As she was rushing to get ready . . . *Thank you God for today,* she prayed as she fumbled through her bag looking for her toothbrush. *Please forgive me of my sins*, as she looked for her slippers. *I ask for your protection and please keep my mind stayed on you*, as she ran into the bathroom. *She turned on the shower. God, I don't know why my mom treats me like this. I am so tired of being treated like this. God, what did I do to her*? she prayed with frustration . . .

All the girls met up in the kitchen as Emory served lattes. They grabbed their pink tumblers and headed to the Prep building for the day. As they were walking over, J.D. swung her purse close to her so that she could reach in her purse without dropping her latte. She grabbed the paper out . . .

"So how is today supposed to go?" Brooke asked. "Is it all day?"

"I bet it is," said Fah'ry.

"Let me see," J.D. said as she looked at the itinerary and sipped her drink. "It looks like it's over at 3 and it looks like we will have classes all day and . . . lunch is at noon." The girls enjoyed the quiet scenery as they walked over to the building.

Emory thought to herself with butterflies in her stomach, *I don't know what I'm supposed to do if I see Bryce? I thought he would call? I thought he liked me? I wasn't expecting him to be my boyfriend or anything. Ok ok ok, maybe I was? I mean at least I thought we were getting a relationship started,* she said to herself. *I hope we are not in these classes together. Well, I do want to see him. He looks so good! He seems so right for me.* "Ugh! I need to stop," she sighed out loud by mistake.

"Emory you good?" asked Fah'ry.

Um, No! she thought to herself. "Yeah, this latte just went too fast!" Emory emphasized with slight frustration.

The girls arrived at the Scholar Prep building and J.D. took a second look at the itinerary to check for the first class for the day. "Ok, hunny bunnies, I think our first class is upstairs," said J.D.

"How long is the class?" asked Brooke.

As J.D. looked over the papers . . . "It's over at 10, so about an hour."

"Let me call my mom right quick," said Brooke.

"Yes, I need to call my mom too," said J.D.

Brooke stepped away from the girls just a bit to call home. She thought to herself as she dialed the phone . . . *She's probably not going to answer anyway. But I might as well try. I hate looking like the one who's mama doesn't care. I mean, I have not talked to her in weeks. I could be anywhere doing anything and she could care less. I'm going to call,* Brooke said to herself. *But please God, don't let her say anything to hurt my feelings.*

She looked at her phone and dialed in fear. The phone rang but there was no answer. She let out a sigh of disappointment. *Huhhhh, I guess she's still not talking to me,* she thought. *I mean, what did I do? I guess she's still mad about graduation.* Brooke let out another sigh of disappointment and walked back over to her friends who were huddled together chatting as they waited for the first retreat class to begin.

"Did you talk to your mama?" Fah'ry asked. "What did she say?"

"She didn't answer," said Brooke. "She's probably at the beauty shop."

"Oh ok," said Fah'ry. "Yo mama stay fly."

"Yes!" said Emory. "Every time I see her, her hair and nails are always done."

"And her clothes be too cute!" said Fah'ry in admiration.

Brooke smirked, "Yeah she's been like that ever since I was little. We would go to the beauty shop every Saturday to get our hair done and then go shopping, get something to eat and then she would take a nap for the rest of the day, and then she would prepare her mind for church on Sunday."

"You got yo hair done every week?" asked Fah'ry.

"Naw," said Brooke. "She did but I got my hair done about every 3 weeks. That's too often to put heat on my hair, especially since I would get my hair pressed."

"And you still do," said Fah'ry. "Girl, I don't know why you won't get a perm. At least you will be able to put some gel on your sides and have a slick ponytail," said Fah'ry.

"Um no," Brooke laughed. "I am not putting any gel in my hair! I don't care who's wearing it. My beautician told me not to use gel because it dries your hair out and she made sure I slept with a bonnet on my head. I don't know how she knew when I wasn't sleeping with that bonnet or oiling my scalp everyday! I think my mom was telling her," Brooke snickered.

"Yea, I try not to put gel in my hair either," said Fah'ry.

"Fah'ry what do you need gel for? You have good hair. All you have to do is wash your hair and it curls up really pretty," said Emory.

"O-Kay!" said Brooke. "I wish I had good hair. I would have had so much more fun as a kid on those hot summer days. I used to get in trouble for getting my hair wet! Especially when I had just gotten my hair done."

"Bwhahaha, I remember that!" said Fah'ry. "When we would be outside getting wet, you would have like 2 plastic bags on your head and Ronzo would always throw water right on your head!!" Fah'ry laughed, ". . . And you would start crying and be like . . ." she mocked Brooke as a kid, "'My mama is going to whoop me!' She talked supa proper even when we were kids," Fah'ry continued to laugh.

"Girl you know that my mom did not play when it came to my speech. I used to feel so out of place at those ski lodges and tea parties but I loved my ballet and jazz classes! At least there were some black girls in those classes! I guess it wasn't too bad being around Caucasians, some of the girls were really cool. Their houses were so big and pretty! I used to love swimming in their backyard. I didn't have to worry about swimming in that dirty pool at the park around our house," said Brooke. "The only thing was that they would always look at my hair funny and I never knew why until one day, my friend Morgan whispered to me and asked me if my hair was real."

Emory and Fah'ry laughed.

"I am so serious!! Stop laughing," Brooke said as she laughed with her friends. "I'm serious, she's like, 'I thought it was fake because I've never seen a black girl with long hair.' "

"So what did you say to her?" Emory asked.

"Oh, I just laughed and I asked her if she thought that I would keep weave in my hair all of this time. She was like, 'I don't know, I just thought that you had it in really nice.' "

The girls laughed. "That's hilarious," said Fah'ry. "Now, I've always wondered why you always wore your hair in a bun wrapped up but I knew that it was real," smirked Fah'ry.

"Fah'ry, please tell me that you know why I wear my hair in a bun?" asked Brooke.

"Well, I kind of thought it was because you cheer," said Fah'ry with curiosity.

"It is now but I started wearing my hair up when we started high school and my mom used to make me take the bus before I got my car. I guess or she claimed that she wanted me to learn how to take the bus and be aware of my surroundings," said Brooke. "But I also know that between her working and getting her Masters degree, she didn't have time to pick me up or drop me off at school. So, I used to have to ride on the 63rd St. bus and those girls from the projects would get on the bus. I already had on this catholic school uniform and my hair was long!" exclaimed Brooke. "I didn't want those girls to think that they could mess with me, so I never smiled or at least I tried to look tough and I wrapped my hair up, just in case one of those girls tried to fight me."

"Wow! Girl, why didn't you say something?!" said Fah'ry. "My dad would have picked you up! We live right down the street from each other," Fah'ry said with concern.

"Yeah!" Emory said. "My mom or dad could have picked you up too! I mean, they both would pick me up and drop me off. We had to pass by your house to get to the school."

"I didn't want to be a burden and make my mom look like she didn't care about me," said Brooke.

"Well I can see where you are coming from," Fah'ry said. "But why would she let you ride the bus with all those project girls?"

Emory quickly interrupted, ". . . So, Brooke, did you say that you got your nails done with your mom too?"

"Oh no, my mom did my nails and toes. She said I had to wait until high school to get my nails done at a shop," said Brooke. "She frowned upon fake nails or fake anything for that matter."

"Oh, so that's why when we go to the nail shop, you never get acrylic nails?" asked Fah'ry.

"Yup," said Brooke.

"Wow, I never knew that," said Emory.

As Brooke smirked Emory looked around and then looked at her phone, ". . . Where is J.D.?"

"I think she's still on the phone," said Brooke. "She said that she was going to call her mom." Brooke looked over in the corner and gestured to J.D. that it was time to go. As J.D. noticed Brooke, she tried to call her mom again several times. "Oh, hey Mom, I tried calling you a couple of times but there wasn't an answer," said J.D. "Is everything ok?"

"Yes J.D., I am fine," her mom said. Suddenly, J.D. heard a man's voice in the background and her heart filled with fear.

"Good morning J.D.!" he yelled in the background.

J.D. thought to herself, *What is he doing there? I thought that he went to jail?*

Her mom responded to his yelling in the background. "He got out of jail this morning and came here knocking on the door. I went ahead and let him in. It's the God thing to do. He is my husband and I have to do what God would want," her mom said. "We are just about to have breakfast. I have to go into the hospital today, I have a couple of patients to see. If I am not here when you get home tomorrow, he can let you in the house."

"Oh, I have my keys, he doesn't have to let me in," said J.D.

"Ok," said her mom.

"I have to go to class Mom, I will call you at work," J.D. said. As she hung up the phone and walked back towards her friends, she thought to herself . . . *That is so stupid, with anger in her heart. I thought they were done! I thought that this would be the last time! I don't understand how she could be a Christian and a doctor and live like this,* she thought to herself with confusion. *God, when will you end this?* she asked, while finally making it back over to the girls.

"Are you all waiting on me hunnie bunnies?" J.D. asked with a big smile on her face.

"I swear you must got a boyfriend that you're keeping from us," said Fah'ry.

"No hun, I told you that I don't," she said with a simple smirk. "I was really talking to my mom."

J.D. grabbed the retreat schedule for the day and scanned it. ". . . Our class is in Lecture Hall B," said J.D.

"Lecture hall??!!" Fah'ry asked. "Are we in college already??"

"I don't think it will be boring if it was anything like that party last night," said J.D. "Come on before we are late."

The girls arrived in Lecture Hall B and looked for the perfect seats. "I don't want to sit all the way in the front and I don't want to sit in the back with the slackers," J.D. snickered.

"Let's sit right here," Fah'ry said, as she chose middle seats. As the girls were getting settled, a man and woman walked in the room.

Lecture Hall: Sorority Girls, False gods and College Majors

"Hello high school grads!" said the couple. "Welcome to the Love On Campus retreat! I am Dr. Wellington and this is my wife, Dr. Mackenzie Wellington."

"Hello everyone," she said with a smile. "We hope that you all enjoyed last night's activities!"

Dr. Wellington chimed in, ". . . Yeah, she is talking about the party!!!"

"The entire class laughed at his candid approach. "The purpose of the L.O.C. retreat is to prepare you for the transition from high school to college," she said.

"Today is designed to educate you on several aspects of college and what is required for maximum success on campus," Dr. Wellington said. "You will have lecture style classes all day and a lunch break at noon."

"So just a little about us," he said. "We started L.O.C. about 7 years ago in an effort to minister to high school students who are on their way to college. We want to see you all successful both in and out of the classroom," he said. "So, with that said, we will be covering the do's and don'ts of relationships and friendships!"

"Oh yes," Dr. Mackenzie said, "we will be all in your business this weekend!" she said, as she smiled and heightened her voice. "We have an entire class dedicated to this subject. Why?" she asked. "Well, we were college sweethearts and we have some ideas of what you all will face on your journey."

"We are here to help you in any way that we can. So, please ask questions," he said. "If you see us around, don't hesitate to stop us. Does anyone have any questions?" Dr. Wellington asked.

Fah'ry raised her hand. "How long have you all been married?"

"We have been married for 10 years," Dr. Mackenzie answered.

Bryce raised his hand. ". . . Yes sir?" Dr. Wellington said as he acknowledged Bryce's hand.

"So what advice would you all give us as we embark on this new journey?" asked Bryce.

Dr. Wellington answered, "First, make sure that you are diligent in maintaining your relationship with God. This is very important and quite frankly, the most important. So, my suggestion would be that once you get comfortable on campus, find a church nearby that lines up with your beliefs or find a campus ministry right on your campus. This will give you some accountability and help you to continue to grow in your relationship with Christ. This alone will help you to make good decisions, at least more than you would if you did not have a close relationship with God. It is imperative that you grow spiritually just as much as you are about to grow academically and socially. Did you have anything to add honey?" he asked.

"Sure," she said. "It is also important that you set goals, become great planners, practice and perfect becoming very disciplined and STAY focused!" Dr. Mackenzie said. "Oh and of course, watch the company that you keep. It could determine your success or failure in college and honestly in life. We will talk about this subject in detail in our class on connections and why Christians should not join Greek organizations," she said. "That's later today and many of our students love that course. Did anyone have any other questions?" she asked as she looked around the lecture hall.

"Ok!" Dr. Wellington said. "If there aren't any more questions, we will get started. Be sure that you have your Journey Journals with you as you go to each class. The first class is actually held in here, so you all don't have to leave until the next course," he said. "Have a great time!" The class got loud from the various chatter and rumbling through bags to pull out their Journey Journals and writing utensils.

"We will see you all later," Dr. Mackenzie spoke over the noise as she and her husband walked out of the class.

Emory thought to herself, *Oh my gosh, Bryce is in this class,* as she looked for her journal in her bag and tried to calm herself down. *Ok, I have to stay focused. Do not look over there!* she said to herself. She took a quick glance over in his direction. *Who is that girl he's sitting next to? And they look like they are having a deep conversation. She's pretty too,* she thought as her face started to turn red. *Stay focused . . . I must stay focused . . .*

"Good morning everyone! I am Professor Robinson." She put her books and laptop on the podium with excitement. "Welcome to The College Journey course! We will explore how to choose the right college for you and provide you with an opportunity to evaluate whether or not you have chosen the best college for you. Let's start by finding out where some of you all are going and why you chose that particular college," Professor Robinson said.

J.D. raised her hand and started to speak as she was acknowledged by the professor. "I am Jordan and I am attending Brighton University in the fall. I chose Brighton for its academic prestige and I have always wanted to live in California," said J.D.

"Wonderful!" Professor Robinson said as she looked around the room to notice any others that may raise their hand. "Yes," she nodded in the direction of Emory.

"My name is Emory and I will be attending Brighton. I chose Brighton because of their Chemistry program."

"That's awesome!" Professor Robinson said. She acknowledged Brooke.

"I am Brooklyn. I am also attending Brighton University. I chose Brighton because of its overall reputation. I love the campus and all of the extra-curricular activities and organizations."

"Great point Brooklyn!" the professor said. "We will be covering some of those points in the lecture!"

She acknowledged more students and looked around. "Anyone else before we get started?"

Fah'ry slowly raised her hand.

"Yes ma'am?" Professor Robinson said.

"I'm Fah'ry. I am going to . . . Polk State University. I chose PSU because it is a historically black college and I would like to be around more African Americans in my learning and social environment. I think that I will have more professors that are dedicated to seeing me successful in college and after graduation."

"Excellent point of view, Fah'ry!" said Professor Robinson.

What!!! J.D. said to herself as the girls looked at each other in awe and looked at Fah'ry puzzled.

I can't believe this, Emory thought.

Fah'ry ignored their obvious looks of confusion and started to doodle in her notebook.

"You all can take a look at the screen up top for notes if at anytime, you feel that I am moving too fast," said Professor Robinson as she moved over to the podium. "Let's get started . . .

College Journey Journal

"The key to choosing the best college for you is based on a few key factors such as: the school's academic reputation, are they accredited, do they offer your major, is the degree program at the school a certified program (this is common for Teaching and Psychology majors along with other health fields), would you like to attend a big or small university, would you like to be close or far away from home, do you want to go to school in the city, suburbs or a rural area (secluded), do they have good food, do they have nice dorms or apartments, do they have student organizations and sports that interest you, do you like the weather climate, is it always hot or would you prefer change in seasons, would you prefer a private or public school, do you want diversity or would you like to attend a Historically Black College, do you want to attend an ivy league, prestigious or research college/university, is the school environment safe (check their campus crime rate; the admissions office will have the most current info), will the school's overall environment make you happy and provide you with an enjoyable college experience, are you following your friends or a significant other? These are things that you should consider in choosing the college that is best for you. If you choose a college based on your own preferences, you will find that your experience will be enjoyable, successful and memorable!

"The college experience is just as important socially as it is academically. Choose carefully and try to take your time in making your decision, one that is based on your preferences."

College Search Website Resources

www.colleges.usnews.rankingsandreviews.com

www.collegeboard.com

(Be sure to use the college matchmaker tool)

Always go to the college's website to get specific information about the college.

www.fafsa.ed.gov

(Apply for federal grants and loans)

www.fastwebscholarships.com

(Scholarships)

www.bls.gov

(Occupational Outlook Handbook)

-Career and salary info

www.collegeboard.com

(BigFutures)

Assists with finding a college major

"The following pages are designed for you to journal and write down all the pros and cons of each college you research. You can also take notes as you visit colleges and browse them online to notate whether each school is meeting your preferences. You will also want to think about which qualities of a school you will compromise on. For example, if you would like to attend a college that has really nice dorms and you go to visit the campus and the dorms are old but they a winning football team. Are you able to live with this as a compromise? On the following pages, you will find quick preference guides to assist you in your college journey note-taking. Once you get the hang of it, you can take college search notes on your own in the notebook. Happy searching!

"This is the end of the lecture," Professor Robinson said as she closed her laptop. Remember to jot down those websites that were given! I am available for a few minutes before the next class, if anyone has any questions," she said. "Have a wonderful day," Professor Robinson said as the class walked out.

J.D. walked up to her. "Thank you, this was great information. It really made me think more about my college choice and the reasons that matter."

"Oh, you are welcome," the professor said as she smiled. "What is your name again?"

She said, "My name is Jordan," as she shook Professor Robinson's hand.

"Well it is nice to meet you, Jordan." She smiled and J.D. walked out of class to catch up with her friends.

"We have 5 minutes before the next class," said J.D.

"Where is it at?" Emory said.

"It shouldn't be that far, it's Lecture Hall D," said J.D. as the girls were walking to class . . .

"Um Fah'ry, what was that in class??" Emory said with concern. "We are going to Brighton together . . ."

"Right!" Brooke said with disappointment. "You could have at least told us."

"I know, but I didn't know how to tell ya'll," said Fah'ry with sincerity. "I kept trying to find a good time to say it but I couldn't. Me and Chaston decided awhile ago to go to Polk."

"But Fah'ry?!" J.D. said with disappointment, "we have been planning to go Brighton together since we were freshman," said J.D. "You worked hard for those A's that you received. Brighton is a prestigious school and very hard to get into."

"Yeah Fah'ry, why are you throwing that away?" Brooke asked with concern as they walked in class.

"I just think that it is the best thing for me," said Fah'ry.

"Right," Emory said with sarcasm as they sat down in the new lecture hall.

"Good morning all! My name is Dr. Keisha Prink. I am a lawyer and I have my own Law firm that specializes in Intellectual Property. I became a lawyer after switching my major about 3 times. I finally realized after a lot of wasted money and time that I should go to law school."

J.D. raised her arm with her pen in her hand.

"Yes," Dr. Keisha said as she called on J.D.

"How did you know after all those changes in majors that you were supposed to be a lawyer?"

"Great question!" Dr. Prink said. "Well, she sighed, I had to be real with myself. I had to take a closer look at my strengths, weaknesses, likes and dislikes. Once I did that, I realized that I was studying the wrong thing."

Fah'ry raised her hand ". . . So, what were some things that you realized that helped you decide?"

"Sure," said Dr. Prink. "I realized that I was very strong at writing, researching and I loved reading and even helping others. J.D. raised her hand. "Yes," Dr. Prink said.

"So, what were some of the majors that you had?" asked J.D.

"Oh geez!" Dr. Prink said. "When I first entered college, I was a Biology major but I quickly discovered that Biology was not for me! I ha-Ted Math!" she emphasized. "I then became an education major. I thought that I was going to be a school teacher but that was ruled out when I realized that I didn't work that well with children. My internships in education turned out to be the worst for me. I became really discouraged and I didn't know what to study. So, I just picked the easiest thing for me that would allow me to graduate. I chose Sociology and I got straight A's in all of my classes. However, because I had changed majors a couple of times, I had to wait an additional year to graduate in order to fulfill the graduation requirements as a Sociology major. I was sooo behind because I waited too late in my undergrad college years to declare Sociology as my major," she said. "Even after graduation, it was extremely difficult for me to find a good paying job with a Sociology degree. I ended up getting a job doing something totally different from what I studied."

Brooke raised her hand and Dr. Prink called on her with a hand gesture.

"Did you make a lot of money?" Brooke said.

Dr. Prink laughed subtly. "Well, let's just say this, I was making about 30 thousand a year and my friends from college who were Biology majors were making about 70 thousand a year. I also had friends that actually studied Education and they were making more money than me," she said.

Wow! J.D. thought to herself and raised her hand again.

"Yes ma'am?" Dr. Prink said.

"So how did you become a lawyer?" J.D. asked.

Dr. Prink smirked, "I decided to go to graduate school. Believe it or not, I changed majors twice in grad school." The entire class looked at her in awe but with interest. "After changing majors twice in grad school, I knew that I was not going in the right direction," she said. "I was getting good grades but I just couldn't see myself really having a career in what I was studying that really spoke to who I was. I decided to take a break from grad school once I realized that I was in the wrong major once again," Dr. Prink said. "I ended up going to see a college advisor that recommended that I take this College Prep Assessment and the results changed my life! I found out that I was not focusing on my strengths or the things that I liked at all!" she said with her hands dropping to her side. "Based on the results, I did some further research into majors and I realized that I had many qualities and strengths that were very similar to the backgrounds of attorneys. So, I decided to apply for Law school!" Dr. Prink said with a smile.

J.D. raised her hand again with hesitation. Dr. Prink peeked over and saw J.D.'s hand slightly up. "Yes? Are you raising your hand?" Dr. Prink said.

"Um yes, J.D. said in a low voice as she cleared her throat. "With all of your college major changes . . . What would you saaay was the problem? I mean, why couldn't you find the right major?" asked J.D.

"Good question hun! "Professor Prink said with excitement. I did not know anything about myself. I knew that I was smart and that is how I was able to get A's in my classes regardless of what major I had BUT that was not enough. I needed more understanding of who I was in order to make clear choices about my future. I could not make good decisions about my academic field of study without knowing at least some of my strengths, likes and even weaknesses. This was critical for me because I was wasting a lot of money AND, she emphasized . . . Time!" J.D.'s hand went up once again. Dr. Prink smiled and acknowledged her.

"So, what do you actually have a degree in?" asked J.D.

"Of course," Dr. Prink said as she started to prepare the podium for her lecture. I have a Juris Doctorate degree which is a Law degree and I have a Ph.D in Fashion Business."

Oh, J.D. thought as she raised her eyebrows with interest. *Fashion Business!* she thought to herself.

Fashion Business! Fah'ry thought as she wrote it down in her notebook.

"Does anyone have anymore questions?" Dr. Prink asked.

Fashion Business! Brooke thought to herself as she started to look it up on her phone.

"Ok, great!" Dr. Prink said, "If there aren't any other questions, let's get started on Choosing a College Major," Dr. Prink said as she turned the lights off to show her presentation on the screen.

Fashion Business? Emory thought to herself. *I think that I saw that word in a dream?? Lord, please help me remember why I saw those words?*

"Alright everyone, be sure that you have your journals ready because we have a lot to cover," said Dr. Prink.

Choosing a Major

"Choosing a college major is more important than choosing a college or university. If you randomly choose a school without an understanding of your area of study, it can become the beginning of wasting a lot of money. The key is to get a return on your college investment. College is an investment and it is important that you eliminate as many risks as you can. To choose a college without a major is risky, some may argue that you should explore and enter school undecided, I say, go in with a plan and a goal in mind. The risk is higher in the case of entering school as an undecided major; chances are, you will choose a easy, fly-by major. It is better to plan and work that plan at a school that caters to your area of study.

"The most important section in this notebook is the College Major Prep Assessment. The assessment is designed to help you to identify your strengths, weaknesses, likes and dislikes. This is the foundation of identifying majors and possible careers. It is important to get as close as possible to doing what you love and are skilled at in regard to a profession. Once you have identified these things along with careers that interest you, it will be easier to measure whether or not your strengths and weaknesses work for your ideal career choice.

"Now that you have some careers in mind, you can identify the college majors that are required to prepare you for your chosen career. It is vital to your academic success in choosing a realistic major and career. If you desire to be a doctor and declare Pre-Med as a major but you hate math and science, this is unrealistic and will cause college to be quite miserable for you. This notebook will allow you to identify this problem early enough to avoid a possible change in major to replace an unrealistic major declaration. It also decreases high chances of transferring from one college to another along with repeating courses. The goal is to identify a major by eighth grade so that you can properly prepare and build a quality academic portfolio throughout high school. Your academic portfolio will include what is required for you to accomplish your career goal, even as a high school student.

"Your chosen field of study can prepare you to exit college with great salary potential or the lack thereof. There are many majors that have starting salaries that are double that of other majors. It is important that you choose your major, not just based on your strengths and likes but also on your desired lifestyle and the current industry demands of the world. For example, if you care more about learning a skill in college organizing knowledge to give back, it may not be as important for you to make a lot of money right out of college. On the other hand, the most common reason for attending college is to gain knowledge in an effort to get a great job and make money and as a result, be able to live a comfortable lifestyle. I urge you to choose your college major wisely.

"This leads to my next point. Do not take the easy route! It is very common in college for students to quickly hear about the easy and difficult professors. Once you know this, it is easy to choose the easier professor and in many cases, get the easy "A". In some cases, this is not avoidable and based on your major, you will have to take "Professor Doom". Be careful in this area, do not let the campus gossip intimidate you. In cases where "Professor Doom" can't be avoided, take the class, work hard and get the hard earned "A" or "B". It is better to get a hard earned "B" than an easy "A".

"Be careful in making quick decisions in regard to change of major. Often, students will change their major based on class difficulty, time that classes are offered or something that is absolutely irrelevant like wanting to take more classes with your friends. Be aware of this! If you have chosen the right major and you are serious about your career goal, do not change your major. If the classes start to get difficult (they will), you will have to work hard, remain focused and possibly adjust your study time. For example, increase your study time and limit your social life. This will start to happen towards the end of college when you are taking a lot of classes within your major or it could remain difficult the entire time you are in college based on major. It is very true that some majors are more difficult than others and require more study time. You will learn all about the easy and hard majors once you arrive on campus and this is when you will need to be focused and not change your major based on difficulty.

Changing Majors

"I have spoken extensively about not changing your major. Of course, there are always exceptions. Let's say, you created a wonderful plan in this notebook but once you get to college, you take a couple of electives and you learn something new about yourself and new subjects start to interest you. If, and only if, you start to feel a true need to change your major, just go back to the steps in this notebook on searching salary potential for your new career and the requirements to get information on your new career destination. If you are ok with the new change based on salary potential and course requirements, go for it.

Double Majors

"It is a great idea to declare two majors, often called a Double Major. I highly suggest this for all students. This allows you more flexibility in your career choices once you graduate from college and it also makes you more marketable to potential employers. Furthermore, a reason for declaring a double major is when you choose areas of study that don't seem as promising financially but you receive a wealth of knowledge and skill. Many areas of study are not as promising financially right after college unless you receive that big opportunity that places you in connection with celebrities that will endorse your skill and talent. It is great to go to school to study what you love but always be realistic. If you love fashion or entertainment, I would suggest studying it, perfect the gift that you have but always have a back up plan that will still allow you to have a great career while you wait for that great opportunity. If you desire to have your own clothing line or become a celebrity stylist, keep in mind that for the average person, it takes time. Of course, build on what you love to do but at the same time, that double major is working for your benefit. For example, you love fashion, you attend a college with a great school of fashion, declare a major in fashion; my suggestion to you would be to also major in education, business or other areas that will allow you to get a great position while designing your clothing line as you wait to hit it "big". By choosing fashion and education, you can set a goal of becoming a college professor that teaches fashion. There are many careers that filter from the study of fashion and this is why it is important to explore who you are, what you love to do, what it will take to get there and what will the end result be. There are many college graduates without jobs who are very lost. It is most often based on choice in major. If you study hard and contribute to an area of study that will benefit the current trends in society, you will become a commodity and will be desired professionally.

Be Consistent In Your Major

"For many, it seems common to explore various majors, for example, study one major in undergraduate school and a different major in graduate school. This is a great concept, as I took this route. It is also marketable to be a specialist at the seemingly small things. For example, if you study Sociology or English in Undergraduate school and you are not sure what you'd like to study in graduate school, it is best to choose the same major you studied in undergraduate. In cases like these, it is better to be an expert at a subject than the "jack of all trades", meaning you have a little bit of knowledge in many areas. Picking a college major is not easy and deciding to change your major can be difficult. If you have a realistic plan and know what it will take to accomplish your career goals along with and understanding of the end return on your college investment, you'll be just fine. Just remember, It is important that you choose your college major wisely! It can cause you to make money or waste money!"

The girls were walking out of class and were standing in the hallway as it began to get crowded and quite loud. "So where are we going to eat at?" said Fah'ry.

"I think that everyone is eating here somewhere," said J.D. as she pulled out her retreat packet. "It looks like they have several restaurants."

"Let me see," said Brooke as she and Fah'ry looked at the paper!

"Ooh," said Fah'ry. "Let's go to dis seafood place!"

"Yeah, that sounds really good!" said J.D.

"Ok, let's go there then!" said Brooke.

"Emory, you cool with that?" said Fah'ry. "Cuz you can get real picky," she said as the girls snickered.

"Um yeah, I am fine with that," Emory said as she stared at every crowd of guys coming down the hall.

"We need to get going so that we can get a good seat," said J.D. The girls walked through the tight crowd of students to get to the restaurant.

I have not seen Bryce, Emory thought to herself. *Who was that girl that he was talking to? I shouldn't be worried about him,* she thought. *I have to get him off of my mind.* Emory tried to focus on the girls' conversation.

"Oh, this was not far at all," said J.D.

"Hello, how many?" said the waitress.

"Hi, 4," said J.D.

"Ok, right this way," said the waitress.

"Here are the menus, let me know when you are ready to order."

"OK, thank you!" said the girls as they were looking over the menus.

J.D. looked up and saw a group of tall guys walk in.

"UHM, there is Bryce," said J.D. mumbling but looking down at her menu.

The girls looked up from their menus and took a glance at them. "Ooh wee!" they all said under their breath.

"They all look good!" said Brooke.

"I know!" said J.D. as they laughed.

"Let me stop looking over dere," said Fah'ry. "I am faithful to Chaston but the one with that khaki hat on is too cute!!"

"Oh, not Fah'ry!" said Emory. "You're looking at another guy?"

"I know, right!" J.D. said.

"I am just looking, that's allll!" said Fah'ry.

"The one with that varsity jacket though!" said J.D.

"And Bryce is bow legged!" said Brooke.

"Yeah, I saw that at the party!!" Emory said with impression.

"Are you all ready to order?" asked the waitress as she smiled with the girls as they giggled.

"Um yes, I'll have the lobster and shrimp scampi and water with lemon," said J.D.

"I will have the lobster feast and a peach lemonade," said Brooke.

"Ok, I will have da steak and crab and a water with lemon," said Fah'ry.

"Hum, I'll have the Fillet Mignon with asparagus and mashed potatoes and can we have an order of calamari and grilled shrimp sticks as an appetizer?" said Emory.

"Ok got it," said the waitress. "Anything to drink?"

"Oh!! Yes," said Emory. "I'll have a blue raspberry lemonade."

"Thank you, ladies. Your food will be out shortly," said the waitress.

"I'm about to go wash my hands," said Fah'ry.

"I'll go with," said J.D.

"Yeah, I need to go to the restroom anyway," said Brooke.

The girls head to the restroom. ". . . Emory, you not coming?" asked Fah'ry.

"No, I am going to stay and watch our drinks," said Emory.

"I will go when you all come back." Emory pulled her phone out of her purse and called home. "Hey Mom!" said Emory. "Hey hunny!" said her mom. "Are you having a nice time?"

"Yes," Emory said. "It is a really nice place, the cabins are amazing and oh, the classes have been really cool so far as well. I am so excited about this next class!" said Emory.

"Oh, how exciting!" said her mom.

"Yes! It's about sororities, fraternities and campus life."

"Now Emory, you know that we don't believe in that," said her mom

"I know, Mom."

"How are the girls?" asked her mom.

"They are good, we are having so much fun! Where is Dad?"

"He just went in his study to prepare for tomorrow's sermon," said her mom. "I'll page the intercom to his study and transfer you."

"K, thanks Mom."

"Love you hunny, see you tomorrow," said her mom.

"Ok, love you too."

The call transferred. ". . . Hi sweetheart," said her dad.

"Hey Dad," said Emory.

"How's it going?"

"I am having a great time! Thank you for letting me come," said Emory.

"Of course, sweetheart. You have done really well in school and we are so proud of you. You have shown yourself to be trustworthy, so we know that you will make good decisions while you are there."

"Thanks Dad."

"Will you be back in time for church in the morning?"

"I don't know but I am sure that I will make the second service," said Emory.

"Well enjoy yourself sweetheart, I am going to get started on tomorrow's sermon."

"Ok, love you Dad."

"Love you too sweetheart! Oh, and Emory, I know that there are boys there, so conduct yourself as a young lady."

"Ok Dad," she smirked. *Oh my goodness, does his prophetic gift ever turn off?* she thought.

"Who were you talking to?" asked Fah'ry.

"That was my mom and dad," said Emory. "Let me go to the bathroom before the food comes."

As Emory went to the restroom she ran into Bryce . . . *Oh, um, there he is,* said Emory as she walked towards him. Her heart started beating fast and she thought . . . *What do I say?* They got closer to each other as they walked towards each other from opposite directions. *Ok ok, think of something,* Emory thought. They got closer to each other but were walking very fast to get to where they each were going. They looked into each other's eyes as they walked towards each other . . . "Hello," said Bryce as he continued to walk.

"Hey," said Emory as she noticed that he didn't stop.

Bryce continued to walk to his destination and Emory kept walking to the bathroom. *Ooook, all he said was hello?* she said to herself. *Wow, he didn't even stop. He acted like we didn't just have that long conversation last night at the party. What was that!!*

Emory went back to her table. "Oh, the food is here already?" asked Emory.

"Yeah, we were trying to wait on you before we pray and eat," said J.D.

"Ooh this looks good too, I am starving," said Emory.

"So Fah'ry, said J.D. I don't think it's a good idea to go to Polk with Chaston. The table went silent. "I don't think that you should give up a great opportunity at Brighton to be at the school with him," said J.D.

"Yeah, Fah'ry, I mean, you are already having problems with him," said Emory. "Do you think that it will get better in college? That's all new girls and a lot of freedom," asked Emory.

"I know!" said Fah'ry "That's why I am going. Dat whole campus will know that I am his girlfriend."

"I hear you but I think that you are making a big mistake," said J.D. as she ate her shrimp.

"Well, I am going and I'll get the same education. Plus, if I go to Brighton, I will be all the way in California. That's too far from him, I will never see him," said Fah'ry. "Christmas breaks and all, that is not enough for me."

"So, you're giving up your scholarship, too?" asked J.D. "Brighton gave you a full scholarship. You're going to give up free tuition to go to another college and pay??" asked J.D. with concern.

"I didn't think about all that but yeah," said Fah'ry. "I've already signed all of the papers to start. I can get financial aid also."

"Ok that doesn't make sense, Fah'ry!" said Emory. "You have to pay those loans back!"

"Yea, but that's years later," said Fah'ry.

"Yeah, but you are taking on unnecessary debt," said J.D.

"You really need to pray about this friend," said Emory.

"Yes, seriously," said J.D. as she placed the tip on the table. "It's time for us to go back. I think that the next class starts at 1," said J.D.

"Yeah this next class is going to be gooood!" said Emory.

The girls made their way to their next class. "Ok, this ain't no lecture hall," said Fah'ry.

"Um no, absolutely not," said Brooke as she looked and walked slowly around the place with the rest of the girls.

"I guess we can sit here on these couches," said J.D.

"Ooh, and they have a bar over there by the door!" said Brooke.

"I wonder why they have those beds in here?" asked Fah'ry.

"I know, right!" said Emory. "And those little tables look like altars or something?? I only worship the one true God and that doesn't look like an altar from the Bible. I know a fake when I see it," said Emory.

Fah'ry walked over to the altar to get a closer look. "Girl, it's blindfolds and all kinds of stuff on here!!" said Fah'ry.

"Don't touch that Fah'ry!!" said Emory

"Yeah, I don't know what kind of class this is??" said J.D. with skepticism.

"Yeah, I am about to rebuke the devil in here," said Emory. All the girls started laughing. "You all are laughing but I am so serious!" said Emory. "We have to be careful of what we let in our spirits, especially through what we hear," said Emory.

"You know you right! Preach!!" yelled Fah'ry. "Naw, but you're right! Let's see, I am sure it's not what it seems."

"I agree hun," said J.D.

"Good afternoon everybody!" said the Wellingtons. "We told you that we would see you later," they said as they grinned.

"Yes, we are your instructors for your last class of the day," said Dr. Makenzie Wellington.

"There's one more," her husband whispered to her.

"Oh, I'm sorry," she said. "There is one more class after this on study skills and habits but we promise that this class is really cool."

Dr. Wellington chimed in, ". . . Yeah because we are teaching it!"

They chuckled at him. "This class is called Campus Life!" she said. "We will cover several topics dealing with your life on campus. We will not hold back!!" she said.

"Yup!" Dr. Wellington said. "Get ready!!"

"Yes, we will talk about relationships and friendships, good and bad decisions, sex and soul ties, drinking and parties, sororities and fraternities and how to manage your spiritual life as you embark on this new journey," she said. "We want to see you successful on this next step and you will need some information and tools to take with you to make the best decisions and stay on track as best as possible! So we will start with the most popular topic outside of sex!"

Dr. Wellington said with excitement, "Sororities and Fraternities!! Let's go," he said as he grabbed the mic and walked towards the altar with the blindfolds.

As Dr. Wellington stood at the altar, Dr. Makenzie walked around and passed out handouts.

"You will need these handouts in order to follow along as we teach the Greek section," Dr. Makenzie said. J.D.

started to look over the handout as Dr. Makenzie continued to pass the rest of the papers out to the rest of the class.

"Oh MY-Goodness!!" she said.

"What??" Fah'ry asked with curiosity.

"Look at this paper! Page 7 is crazy!" J.D. exclaimed.

Emory picked up her handout and flipped through the pages. She stared at the paper but tried to keep reading. "The blood of JEE-SUS!" Emory said.

"O-Kay!" Fah'ry said. "This some hoodoo voodoo stuff!"

Brooke laughed, "Let me see what you all are talking about!"

"Ok, so who can tell me? What is religion?" Dr. Wellington asked the class.

Emory raised her hand. "Yes ma'am?" he said.

"A set of beliefs," said Emory.

"Ok!" he said. "Give me a little more!"

Fah'ry raised her hand. "Yes ma'am?" Dr. Wellington said.

"I would say dat it is also the way in which you carry out your beliefs," said Fah'ry.

"Ok great!" He said. "Great answers!"

J.D. raised her hand. Dr. Wellington pointed to her. "I believe that it is a set of beliefs and includes a deity as supreme in those beliefs," said J.D.

"Yes," Brooke chimes in. "I mean what's a religion without a god?"

"ABSOlutely!!" he said with excitement as he clapped his hand once. "We are about to show that the sororities and fraternities that so many admire are religions instead of social organizations. Let's look at the Oxford dictionary and see what religion is," Dr. Wellington said. "Ok, according to the Oxford dictionary, religion is:

Number 1. The belief in and worship of a superhuman controlling power especially a god or gods.

Number 2. A particular system of faith and worship.

Number 3. A pursuit or interest to which someone ascribes supreme importance.

"Now," he said, "let's look at some of the origin of the text. It says: 'Of life under monastic vow, from French or Latin meaning obligation, bond, reverence... From Latin... To bind' " Dr. Wellington said with emphasis. "Now that we know what religion is, let's look at some things that we do in our religions. I want you to think about some things that you do at church."

J.D. raised her hand. Dr. Wellington pointed to her. "Pray," she said.

"Ok!" he said.

Brooke raised her hand. He acknowledged her. "Worship," Brooke said.

"Be more specific," he said.

"Like singing praises and dancing," she said.

"Excellent!" Dr. Wellington said.

Emory raised her hand. "Yes ma'am?" he said.

"Well, we learn the Bible and its teachings. We are taught by a leader how to live according to the Bible. I mean it tells us what to do and not do, who God is and Bible history. Like rules and laws," Emory said.

"Ok, DOCTRINE! Excellent!" Dr. Wellington said in a raised voice. "So, let's look at some practices that are common amongst various religions. According to Wikipedia:

Some things that are common practices in the average religions are sermons, rituals, initiations, commemorations of gods or goddesses, symbols, works of service, singing, dancing, funerary and matrimony services, sacrifice, prayers, meditations and mythology.

It goes on to state that 'Religion as a word is used interchangeably as the word faith, meaning a set of beliefs'. Is everyone with me so far?" Dr. Wellington asked.

The class responded with a low tone of "yes" as they waited in anticipation.

"Ok awesome!" he said. "We will now go a little bit deeper." Dr. Wellington said, "According to Baird's Manual of American College Fraternities, he found that there were 3 commonalities amongst all of the collegiate fraternal organizations. They are secrecy, rituals and a lifetime commitment. He goes on to state that rituals and altars go together. You can't have one without the other!

"Now there is a video by Taleva Durham and she does an excellent job of dissecting the Delta ritual book or rather doctrines. She states that within Greek organizational rituals, there are 3 components. Oaths, prayers and hymns! Can you all see religion yet?" Dr. Wellington asked. "Does it sound like church yet?

“Let's take a look at the definition of ritual," he said. "A ritual is . . . 'The prescribed order of performing a ceremony, especially one of a religious type or church'!! Are you all hearing this?!" Dr. Wellington asked rhetorically.

"Since Baird mentioned that rituals and altars go together, let us check out what an altar is . . . 'An altar is a table or flat top block used as the focus of a religious ritual, especially in making sacrifices or offerings to a deity'. As you can see, rituals and altars do go together. Remember, there are 3 components in rituals. What are they?" Dr. Wellington asked.

Emory raised her hand. "Yes ma'am?" he said.

"Oaths, prayers and hymns." Emory said.

"ExcellenTAY!" he said and the class laughed as he excitedly walked around the class. "Now that we have some of the basics down, let us try and find some of these practices in sororities and fraternities. Why am I standing at this weird looking table or rather . . . Altar?" Dr. Wellington asked. "Well, when you take your oath to become a member of a particular sorority or fraternity, you must kneel at that altar! The question is . . . Whose altar is that? Remember, an altar in biblical days was used for worship and had a sacrifice and an offering! So when a person kneels at this altar, where is the sacrifice? Because there must be one! Right?" Dr. Wellington asked.

"So, what's an oath?!" Dr. Wellington asked. An oath is a solemn promise usually invoking a DIVINE witness regarding one's future acts or behaviors. So . . ." Dr. Wellington paused. "Who is the divine witness?

"Thus far, we have talked about rituals, altars and oaths. Where are the prayers, hymns and meditations? Alright," he said as he went to the podium to reference the handout that was given at the beginning of class. "Please refer to your handout for this next section," Dr. Wellington said. "If you misplace this document, you can download a copy at www.dontgogreek.com.

"OK, the things that you want to hear! All the strolling, singing and dancing that looks so cute and quite frankly makes many of you want to pledge . . . Have you ever paid attention to the words that they are saying? What is a hymn? A hymn is a religious song or poem typically sung as praises to God or gods. If you take a look at your document, you will see examples of sororities' and fraternities' hymns, prayers and meditations. All are listed in their ritual book. So ladies and gentlemen," Dr. Wellington said. "Who are they praying to? Who are they singing praises to? The Almighty God??" he asked. "Let us see!

“Turn to page 7, it lays out Delta's national hymn in detail. If you read here, let's take a snippet of it, 'O Delta Sigma Theta, we rejoice in thee.' How about this one," Dr. Wellington said. "'To the O Alpha Kappa Alpha, we pledge our hearts and minds and strength to foster its teachings, obey thy laws and make thee supreme in service to all mankind.' What?!" Dr. Wellington said in astonishment. "How about this hymn?! 'To the only Sigma Gamma Rho, I pledge my life . . .' What?!" Dr. Wellington said. "I think that we found that sacrifice that we were looking for at the altar!!! It is the member and it could be and will be you if you decide to join a sorority or fraternity!!

"Does it sound like a religion yet? A church yet? We have altars, rituals, oaths, sacrifices, prayers, hymns, meditations, teachings and laws! Let me mention also, according to Taleva Durham's video on the truth about Greekdom, Delta Sigma Theta does have a statement of faith in their ritual book or rather book of doctrine! A statement of faith explains in detail what a particular religion believes. Every church has one," he said. "Ask your pastors, when you all go back home for a copy of your church's statement of faith.

"You might say, I am not convinced that it's a religion. Ok," he said. 'What are we missing?" he asked.

Emory raised her hand. "Yes?" Dr. Wellington said.

"A god or deity," Emory said.

"Absolutely!" he said with excitement as he clapped his hands once.

"Now, we all know that frat and soror mean brother and sister. In the Christian Faith, we call our fellow believers, brothers and sisters in Christ because we believe the same God is our Heavenly Father. Is it the same for these organizations? Do they have the Almighty God as their parent? Whose making them brother or sister with one another?

“Here is the missing piece. Delta Sigma Theta pays homage to or has as their god, the goddess of wisdom, Minerva. The AKAs pay homage to the organization and makes it the actual god. The Alphas pay homage to or have as their god or reverence the Great Sphinx of Giza and the list goes on for what are called the Divine 9 organizations. I would say that this is a religion, wouldn't you?" Dr. Wellington said. "How about a fake church?!!

"So, what does scripture have to say about this? We will go through a couple and we will dismiss you." Dr. Wellington said. "First and foremost, what does God say about having idols and other gods before Him? In Deuteronomy 5:7, God tells us that we shall have no other gods before Him. Joining one of these organizations, you are taking on another god. So, can you be Christian and Greek? I don't think so!" Dr. Wellington shouted. "Don't take my word for it. In Matthew 6:24, it states that no man can serve two masters, for either he will hate the one and love the other or else he will hold to the one and despise the other. You can't serve God and mammon. Yes, this scripture speaks of money as the other master but can be applied to anything that we have allowed to be our master.

"So, what about those oaths? What does God say about them?" He said, "In Matthew 5:33-37, the Bible tells us not to swear an oath at all. "Just say yes or no and anything beyond that is from the evil one'. Those are not my words," Dr. Wellington said, "but they come from the Holy Bible." As he looked around the class, the students were taking notes in their journals enthusiastically.

"What about the whole brother and sister thing?" he asked the class. "Well," he sighed, ". . . In these organizations, it doesn't matter what religion you are, anyone can pledge. Once you take that vow, you become brothers and sisters with those members! What does the Bible say about this? 2 Corinthians 6:14 tells us not to be unequally yoked together with unbelievers, meaning bound together, in covenant.

"Do you recall the Latin origin of the word religion? It meant . . . To bind! I encourage you to do more biblical research on other questions that you may have. I am going to leave you with this last definition and question," Dr. Wellington said as the class stared at him. "Is all of this worship? Let's see!

Number 1. The feeling or expression of reverence or adoration for a diety. Number 2. Adoration or devotion comparable to religious homage shown towards a person or PRINCIPLE!

Dr. Wellington shouted. "So, are sororities and fraternities a religion? I pray that you have your answer now ladies and gentlemen! If you have further questions, my wife and I are available to answer any questions that you may have."

The class packed their items to go to their next class but the line was extremely long with students that had questions.

"I am going to wait here," Emory said to her friends.

"Girl, that line is too long, we will be late for our next class," Fah'ry said.

"I know but I want to ask him one question," Emory said.

"Well, I have to call home real quick," said J.D. "I'll be in the hallway by the window."

"Ok," the girls said as they waited in line.

"Hey Granny," J.D. said.

"Your mom kept trying to call me and I kept saying hello but all I could hear was arguing. I kept trying to hear what was going on but the phone went dead. I tried to call back a couple of times but there was just a busy signal," her granny said. "Maybe you can try but it was an hour ago and she still hasn't called back."

"Ok, I'll call," J.D. said and hung up quickly. *Lord, please, please, please let my mom be ok,* she thought as she dialed home. *This line is still busy,* she thought with worry. She kept trying but there was no hope of an answer. J.D. felt overwhelmed and her body got very hot and she fainted in the hallway with all her books scattered on the floor. Her friends ran out in the hall when they heard the commotion.

"J.D.!!" they yelled in her face but there was no response . . .

The Proof Is In The Pledge

AKA pledge and the blatant contradiction to the Holy Bible is provided below:

Are you considering pledging to a sorority? Yes, the colors are pretty, the community service is great, the connections can be beneficial to your potential career and Ooh, those parties and the reputation of being known as a Pretty and Smart girl! It is quite fitting for a good girl! Right? Well, maybe not so much when it requires you, as a Christian, to pledge your heart, mind and strength to another god. Let's take the blindfolds off of you and show you why you shouldn't join a sorority. It is very simple. Check it out!

The AKA Pledge

To thee o Alpha Kappa Alpha, we pledge our hearts, our minds, our strength to foster thy teachings, obey thy laws and make thee supreme and service to all mankind. O Alpha Kappa Alpha, we greet thee.

Scriptures on what God says about what was said in the pledge:

Deuteronomy 6:5-6

Matthew 22:37

Mark 12:30

Luke 10:27

This is the greatest commandment given in the Bible.

* There is an idol in your heart and you put it there by the words that you spoke. There can only be one supreme. In this pledge, AKA is the false god. There are indicators by the usage of words like thee, thy and supreme. There is also reference to thy teachings and thy laws. These are religious words and AKA is being referenced as a being as opposed to an organization. In addition, at the end of the pledge, the statement is made that "O AKA, we greet thee." This is acknowledging the presence of something. What is that something that you are acknowledging? This pledge is said at every meeting and is private. Who are you greeting when you say this at the end? You may want to say that AKA is not a false God but the proof is in the pledge. The use of words like thee and thy are words that elude to sacred or holy. If that is not enough, the use of the word supreme being referenced to AKA places it in a high place. There can only be one supreme and that is the almighty God and beside Him, there is no other. We should not allow any other to take God's place. There is no room for two. You should not have any other gods before the one true God. To acknowledge something else as supreme is doing just that. You are placing it higher than the one true God. To be supreme means that it is superior to all others. If you are AKA, the fact that you profess these words out of your mouth often, you are professing that AKA stands in a superior place in your life, particularly in your heart, mind and strength which are areas that should be dedicated to the one true God, our Father in Heaven. What about those teachings and laws mentioned in the pledge that are being professed? Doesn't that sound religious in nature? Teachings in law? Doesn't that sound similar to the Bible and how we reference it as the

law and its teachings? These are words that define doctrine, which are a set of beliefs taught by a church or organization. The word doctrine derives from Latin, meaning teaching, learning and teach. In totality, the pledge that you are saying is professing that you pledge to make thee supreme, in this pledge, the thee is the being, AKA. This sounds like you are a part of another religion and you have professed it out of your mouth. So, you can't be Christian and greek. You must renounce one of them! That false God has to go and if you haven't pledged yet, don't do it! Do not let that idol in! You can only be deceived when you don't have knowledge to defend what is being presented to you. The blindfold is off!

Idol- an image or representation of a god used as an object of worship.

Renounce- refuse to abide by or recognize any longer.

Deuteronomy 6:5-6 AMP

5. You should love the Lord thy God with all your heart and mind and with all your soul and with all your strength; your entire being. 6. These words which I am commanding you today shall be written on your heart and mind.

Matthew 22:37-38 AMP

37. And Jesus replied to him, you should love the Lord your God with all your heart and with all your soul and with all your mind. 38. This is the first and greatest commandment.

Breakdowns and Broken Hearts

"Call the ambulance!" The students in the hall shouted as they gathered around J.D. as she lay on the ground. Her friends were on their knees around her.

"Y'all need to get back!!" Fah'ry yelled to the crowd of students. "J.D." She leaned in closer to her face. "Can you hear me?" Fah'ry said as her voice trembled.

Emory was staring at J.D. on the ground. *Lord, what am I supposed to do??* she said in prayer.

Brooke quickly got up to push the crowd back as Fah'ry stayed close to J.D. "Can you all please back up?" said Brooke. "She needs air."

The crowd didn't move and as Brooke started to get frustrated, she heard a guy's voice. "Ok, I need everyone to move back!" Bryce said with authority. "Logan, can you go and get Dr. Wellington?" Bryce said to his friend as the crowd moved back.

Suddenly, as Emory was staring at J.D., she was reminded of a dream. *Oh my God!* she said to herself. *I saw this in my dream a couple of months ago! I saw J.D. fall but I also saw her get up!* Emory said to herself. *And I didn't think anything of the dream! I ignored it!* she said to herself in disappointment. *What do I do God?* Emory asked. She began to feel calm and heard and felt in her heart . . . *Touch her head, pray my words of healing and watch. Huh?* Emory said to herself. *God?? Is that you?* she thought.

Emory kneeled down at J.D.'s head and touched it and began to pray that no weapon formed against her would prosper. "You shall live and not die to declare the works of the Lord!" Emory said. "By his stripes you are healed!" Emory decreed. "The Lord said in his Holy Word that I shall decree a thing and so shall it be established. I decree and declare that you wake up, J.D.!" Emory said with authority as she felt a weighty feeling on her. She paused and watched and so did her friends. J.D. started to open her eyes and move her legs to get up.

"Here comes the Ambulance!" Bryce said as he directed them to J.D. as she sat in a chair with her friends surrounding and consoling her.

Logan brought J.D. a cup of water as the paramedics walked up. "I need everyone to give us space," said the paramedic. "How are you?" the paramedic asked J.D.

"I'm ok," said J.D. as she sipped her water.

"What's your name?" he asked.

"Jordan Posh," she said.

"Well Jordan Posh, you have some wonderful friends," he said as they placed her on the stretcher. The girls followed the paramedics out of the door. The paramedics placed her in the ambulance and adjusted the stretcher to a sitting position as they checked her vital signs. "Ms. Jordan Posh," the paramedic said with care. "It looks like you experienced exhaustion. Are you stressed or worried about anything?"

"No, I don't think so," said J.D. as she looked at her friends stared at them and their conversation with concern. "Have you been getting enough sleep?" he asked.

"I think so," J.D. said in a low voice.

"Ok, well things look good," said the paramedic. "BUT, you need to get some rest and if you are worrying about anything . . . you have to keep it to a minimum, ok?" the paramedic said. "Nothing is worth you worrying about that it costs you your life," he whispered to her as he placed his hand on her shoulder.

J.D. paused and took in his advice.

"Thank you," J.D. said.

"Not a problem," he said.

"So can I go to my next class now?" J.D. asked.

"No ma'am," he said. "We are taking you to your cabin to rest for the remainder of the day."

"I can't miss class!" J.D. said with concern.

"You'll be fine," said Dr. Makenzie Wellington as she walked up to sign the paperwork. I will be riding with you over to the cabin," she said.

"We will meet you at da cabin," said Fah'ry.

"Ok hun," said J.D. The ambulance drove away to take J.D. to their cabin.

The girls started walking to their cabin and they felt someone running from behind them. "Emory! Wait a sec!" yelled Bryce "Is your girl ok?"

"Yeah, she's fine," said Emory. "We are on our way back to the cabin to be with her."

"Oh ok, that's good to hear," said Bryce as they stared at each other and Emory just waited. *Hurry up and say what you are going to say,* Emory said to herself. *I don't have the time to play games with him.*

"You did a great job out there," said Bryce.

"Thanks," said Emory with her hands in her pockets.

"I have to get to the cabin," she said. "I'll see you around," Emory said as she walked towards her friends to go to their cabin.

"What did he say?" asked Fah'ry.

"Nothing much, he just said, 'Oh you did a great job out there.'" she mocked his words. "I don't have time to chase him."

"His friend Logan was cute too," said Brooke.

"Oh yessss," Emory said with impression and the girls laughed. The girls arrived at their cabin and J.D. was being taken inside of the cabin. The girls put their books down on the dining room table and they sat on the couch while J.D. was getting settled.

"We should probably order something to eat," said Emory. "I know that we are in for tonight."

"Yea, we should see if that seafood place will deliver," said Fah'ry.

"Yes, it was good," said Emory. "I'll call in a few. Let's go upstairs with J.D."

Thank you, God for protecting me, J.D. said as she prayed quietly. *I don't know what happened out there today. Well, I do know. I know that I have not been sleeping because of all of the fighting at home. I just try to stay up so that I can protect my mom. I just keep the phone in my room under my pillow so that he can't take it from her when it's time to call the police. God, my body is so tired and sore from all the fighting,* she sighed. *I don't know how to just sit in my room and hear them fighting, all the bumping and glass breaking and not jump in to help my mom fight him. I guess I didn't know that it was .* . . . and the girls came in the room and interrupted. J.D. sat up in the bed. "Hey hunny bunnies!" she said.

"Hey, how are you feeling?" Emory asked.

"I am ok." J.D. said.

"Cool," said Brooke.

"We tried to call your mom a couple of times but the line was busy."

"Oh ok," J.D. said. "She's probably at the hospital and her phone doesn't work well there."

"Oh," Brooke said.

"I don't remember what happened in that hall," J.D. said as she put her hand on her head to fix her hair. "All that I remember is getting really hot and it going black all of a sudden."

"Girl you scared us," said Fah'ry. "But Pasta Emory was out dere laying hands!"

The girls laughed as they all crowded in the bed with J.D.

J.D. smirked, "What do you mean?"

"Girl, Emory was on dat floor praying for you."

Emory laughed, "Fah'ry you were right there with me!!"

"And Brooke was da security!" said Fah'ry. "She was like 'I need everybody to get back!'" The girls laughed hysterically!

"Oh no, that was Bryce!" said Brooke.

"Bryce!!" J.D. said with curiosity. "What was he doing there?"

"Girl he was da one that kept the crowd back while the ambulance came!" said Fah'ry. "Him and his friend."

"Yes that's true," said Brooke.

"Really??!!" said J.D.

"Yes, he was the cute guy that brought you that cup of water," said Brooke.

"OHHH," said J.D. "I remember, he was the guy with the varsity coat on at the restaurant!"

"Yup," said Fah'ry. "I think his name is Logan."

"I think so too," said Brooke.

"So did you get a chance to talk to Bryce, Emory?" J.D. asked.

"A little," said Emory.

"Oh good," said J.D. "Well, you all know that I love you sooo much! Thank you for being there for me," she said as she started to cry.

"Awww, we are friends forever," Emory said as they all hugged J.D. together.

"Ok can we go and hang out?" said J.D.

"Um no, girl you will be resting tonight!" said Fah'ry.

"So what are we going to do all night?" asked J.D.

"WATCH MOVIES!" they all said together.

"Yea, we can watch in our room," said Fah'ry. "We have dat movie theater in our room."

"Right!" Emory said with excitement. The girls ran downstairs to Brooke and Fah'ry's room to get comfortable for movie night.

Fah'ry headed to the snack bar in their room to prepare the snacks while she was calling her dad. "Hey Dad."

"Hey Fah'ry. What's up?" he said.

"Oh, I was trying to get some clothes for the London trip," she said.

"How much?" he said.

"Like 500 hundred dollars."

"Alright, just call me when you get back and I'll bring it," her dad said.

"Ok, thanks Dad. Emory did you want hot peppers with your nachos?" yelled Fah'ry.

"Yes, that's fine."

"I want popcorn!" yelled Brooke.

"How about you, J.D.?" asked Fah'ry.

"Yea, I'll have nachos with hot peppers," said J.D.

"I'll get the sodas," said Emory.

"Y'all want some candy, too?" asked Fah'ry.

"Yes! If it's chocolate," they said.

"K, I'll bring it over," said Fah'ry as she passed out the snacks and started the movie.

"Let me go to the bathroom," said J.D., "before you start the movie."

J.D. closed the bathroom door and called home. The phone rang and he picked up. "Hey, J.D.," he said.

"Where is my mom?" she said.

"One second," he said.

"Hey Mom, are you ok?"

"Yes J.D., just watching movies," said her mom.

"I tried calling earlier but the line was busy."

"Oh ok," said her mom. "I'm alright J.D.," her mom said.

"Are you sure?"

"Yes, J.D."

"I got sick today and fainted."

"What? What happened?" her mom asked with concern.

"The ambulance guy said that it was exhaustion. He said that I needed to rest."

"Did you eat?" her mom asked.

"Yes, I had eaten lunch, but I'm better. The girls and I are hanging out in the cabin."

"Ok, J.D. call me if you need me."

"Ok Mom."

"Love you," her mom said.

"Love you too, Mom."

"See you when you get home."

J.D. headed back to the room with her friends. "You ready?" asked Fah'ry.

"Yes." J.D. flopped down on the bed to watch the movie.

The girls were enjoying the movie and J.D. noticed that Brooke was wiping her eyes secretly. *Is Brooke crying*? J.D. thought . . . She kept watching the movie but looked over at Brooke again and her tears were uncontrollable. "Brooke," J.D. said with concern. Brooke looked at J.D. with puffy eyes and tears. J.D. and the girls jumped up to go to Brooke's seat. "What's the matter?" asked J.D. "Why are you crying, hun?" J.D. asked as she hugged her.

"What's wrong Brooke?" asked Fah'ry.

"Oh, it's nothing," said Brooke as she wiped her tears.

"Here you go," Emory said as she gave Brooke a tissue.

"Brooke, what is going on hun?" asked J.D.

"Yea, girl it's something because you would not be crying while we are watching a high school movie," said Fah'ry.

"I was just thinking," Brooke said as she tried to clear her face of her tears. "I guess I got a little emotional while watching all of the prom stuff," Brooke said.

"What, is it Josh?" asked Fah'ry.

"No," Brooke said as she held her tissue tightly in her hand. "I'm not worried about Josh. I am really over him. I just don't understand," said Brooke.

"What do you mean?" asked Emory.

"Ok, well, do you remember when we went on prom?" Brooke said. "Well, Josh came to pick me up in that cheap car and he didn't even wash it to make it look nice and sparkly, you know . . . I know that we were having problems before that but he could have picked me up in a clean car. It made me feel like he was doing me a favor by taking me. We did not really talk on the way to prom. I know that we had just broken up last week but we talked and I thought that we were fine."

"But Brooke, you and Josh have broken up so many times," said J.D.

"I know and I am always the one calling him to try and make up. It's because of me that we kept getting back together. I mean, why didn't he ever call me and try to make up? I feel so stupid looking at all the prom dates in the movie, knowing that I could have had a better time."

"Why do you feel stupid dough?" asked Fah'ry.

"I feel stupid because the week of prom, I had not heard from him. I started getting worried because he was not calling me back. I am like, I know I am not going to be one of those girls that doesn't have a prom date," said Brooke. "So I called his house all times of the day, everyday, trying to catch him at home. His mom would always say that he wasn't there. He ended up calling me back like the day before prom."

"Are you serious?" asked Emory. "I thought that you all were fine."

"Oh no," Brooke said. "Prom was horrible! I couldn't wait to leave! You all saw how he was dancing with everybody at prom?! I mean, it was my prom, not his. He didn't know anyone but you all. It was the worst! He danced all night and never came to ask me to dance or even sit down and eat with me."

"Oh my goodness, hun!" said J.D. "How did we miss all of that?"

"You all were dancing and eating. I couldn't talk about it then," said Brooke.

"You should have said SOMEthing, friend," Fah'ry said with sympathy.

"Right," said Emory.

"I really thought that you were happy. I saw you taking pictures and talking to people," said Emory.

"I know but I smiled to stop from crying. And I was talking to the teachers all night or at least standing with them. I really don't remember anything that happened at prom."

"Awww friend," Fah'ry said as she hugged Brooke. "I am so sorry that you had to go through that."

"Wait, we all went to the hotel after prom!" said J.D. "We all were all laughing and everything."

"Yeah, I actually thought that things had got better after prom. My cousin got that hotel room for me. I know that I'm not supposed to have sex before marriage and I was trying to wait. But, I thought that maybe if we had sex, our relationship would get stronger and we wouldn't keep breaking up," said Brooke. "So much for that! My period came the morning of prom."

"What!!!" Fah'ry said. "Why didn't you tell us?"

"I don't know," said Brooke. "I didn't want to be the first one of us to have sex. I wasn't going to say anything. So, after we all left the hotel, he dropped me off at home."

"That was God!" Emory said. "I am glad for you that your period came!"

"I know!" said Brooke. "So, remember I told you all that I was cramping really bad the day after prom?" asked Brooke.

"Yea, the day we went to the water park and you didn't come," said Fah'ry.

"Yeah, well, I didn't have cramps," said Brooke. "Josh never came to pick me up."

"He stood you up!!" said J.D.

"Yes, so technically I have not seen or talked to Josh since he dropped me off after prom."

"He is SUPA stupid," said Fah'ry.

"Yes, and on top of all of that, my mom did not come and see me off to prom."

"What do you mean?" J.D. said. "I thought that you said that your mom had a class that night?"

"No, we got into an argument while I was getting dressed for prom. I promise, I don't remember doing anything to her. I just know that she started snapping on me for something small. So she got mad and left. I just knew that she would come back. She wouldn't dare miss me going on prom," said Brooke. "But she never came back."

"Wow!" said Emory.

"I know right," said Fah'ry.

"Honestly, I was wondering why she didn't cancel her class to see you off to prom. I mean, I know that college professors have busy schedules but my sister's professor cancels class all the time," said Fah'ry.

"I know that you were hurt, hun. I could not imagine having my mom missing my prom," said J.D.

"Yeah, it was tough," Brooke said. "But, you know, she started snapping on me like that around our sophomore year. I would be in my room with the door closed and she would just bust the door open and would say things like: 'I know you are not love sick about Josh!' Or 'You need to get up out of the bed!' She would holler and be so mean to me. And she would stop talking to me for something small. I hated how she made me feel. Then, she started to accuse me of having an attitude and I really did not," said Brooke. "Then, she started to threaten that she was going to put me out."

"For what?" asked Emory.

"I don't know," said Brooke as she teared up. "She just always had something to say about my attitude or me laying around, accusing me of being love sick. So one day, I got tired of her threatening and telling me to get out and so when she said it, this time, I packed my things and left."

"Huh?" said Fah'ry. "Where did you go?"

"I called my dad and he got me an apartment," said Brooke.

"So you were living on your own in high school?" asked Fah'ry.

"How did we not know?" asked Emory.

"Yes, I was living on my own at 16. I didn't say anything because I didn't want my mom to look bad or it to look like I had the messed up family.

"Wow, so have you been back home?" asked Fah'ry.

"No, actually prom was one of the first times in a long time that my mom and I talked. I would say, it had been about 6 months."

"6 months hun?" J.D. asked. "You didn't talk to your mom for that long?"

"Nope," said Brooke. "I used to hope that I didn't get one of those white envelopes in Sister JoAnn's class! We all knew what those were but no one ever said anything."

"Yea, dat's true." said Fah'ry. "It meant that yo parents were behind in tuition and you were about to get kicked out of school."

"Uh huh," said Brooke. "I really thought that she would stop paying my tuition and I would have to go to public school but she kept paying my tuition," said Brooke.

"Oh, I know," said J.D. "When my mom was in school to be a doctor, she wasn't working and could not pay my tuition. I was out of school for 2 weeks!" said J.D.

"When was this?" asked Emory.

"Freshman year," said J.D. "You all thought that I was sick but the school had kicked me out for past due tuition."

"Oh my goodness!" said Brooke.

"Yup," said J.D.

"Dat's crazy how they will put us out of school if dey don't get their money," said Fah'ry.

"I know," said Brooke.

"So do you still have your own place?" said Fah'ry.

"No, my dad told me last week that he might be going to prison and that I couldn't stay there anymore because he would not be able to check in on me."

"What in the world??" said Emory. "Prison!"

"Yeah, so I packed my bags up and I had to leave," said Brooke.

"So, it's been a week," said Fah'ry. "Did he go to prison?"

"No," said Brooke. "I saw him drive past me on my way to school the other day.

"So he lied???" asked J.D.

"I don't know but I honestly think that he wanted to move his girlfriend in there," said Brooke. "It's whatever . . ."

"So where are you going to stay?" asked J.D.

"I have some money saved up for the London trip. I was going to use a little of that for a hotel until we leave. We don't have long and we will be gone all summer, so I figured I'd be ok," said Brooke.

"You don't have to do that," said Emory. "I'll ask my mom and dad if you can stay with us."

"Thanks Emory, but it's only a couple of days. I will be fine," said Brooke.

"Ok, well let me know if you change your mind," said Emory.

"Can you go home?" said Fah'ry. "I know that you and your mom weren't talking at prom but we've had graduation since then," said Fah'ry.

"Wellll . . . No, I did not talk to her at graduation," said Brooke with shame on her face.

"Something else happened, Brooke?" said Fah'ry.

"Yeah, we were actually talking the day of graduation and we were downtown looking for me a dress for graduation. She didn't want to pay for the dress I chose because she felt that it was too expensive. She picked a cheaper dress that I did not like. I guess she got mad and said that I had an attitude and that I was ungrateful. So she walked out the store and we got in the truck. I am thinking that we are going to try another store because I still need a dress and graduation will be starting soon. Well, she pulled up to the bus stop and told me to get out," said Brooke.

"You lying!!!" said Fah'ry as the other girls placed their hands over their mouths in awe.

"What Brooke??" said J.D. "That is really sad."

"Yeah," said Emory. "So how did you get the clothes that you had on at graduation?'

"I had 20 dollars and I took the bus to 63rd and Halsted. Now you all know that I don't shop on Halsted but I had to find something quick. I went in one of those stores and found a pink collared shirt for 10 dollars and that pink glitter belt that I have . . . It was on sale for 3 dollars."

"Oh wow!" said Fah'ry. "You got dat belt from off Halsted??"

"Yes," said Brooke. "It was all I could find in 30 minutes. I walked to my granny's house and changed there. I had a pair of gray slacks and some black quarter length boots. My cap and gown had not gone to the cleaners because I did not have time to do it. My granny ironed my gown and gave me 50 dollars for a taxi because I left my car at my mom's house to go shopping downtown. Anyway, I am in the taxi and I realize that I have not written my Valedictorian speech. I asked the taxi driver for paper and pen. He gave me this little piece of hot pink paper. I prayed and asked God to give me the words to say to our class and I wrote the speech in the taxi," said Brooke.

"Where was Josh?" asked J.D. "He still was not answering my calls from after prom. I called his house so much that day, his mom asked me if something was wrong. I'm like, 'Yes! My graduation is today.' She responded like, 'I don't know what's wrong with that boy.'"

"So she knew that he was ignoring you?" said Emory.

"I would say so," said Brooke. "So she asked me what time was my graduation and when I got out of the taxi, I saw her car. I thought that Josh may have rode with her. I was so hot and embarrassed in those boots and pants! You all had on pretty dresses and heels. That's why I kept my gown on. I had to cover up those clothes."

"Oh MY GOSH! You are making me cry," said Emory. "This is too much!!" she shouted with concern.

"Brooke how did you get through all of this?" asked J.D.

"I prayed and tried to be as strong as I knew how to be. But I prayed a lot and I know that God comforted me every time."

"Amen!" said Emory.

"So, did Josh come?" said Fah'ry. "I don't remember seeing him but it was SUPA crowded."

"Nope!" said Brooke. "All that I could do was look in the crowd continuously. When I got up to give my speech, I kept looking in the crowd for my mom. I just knew that she would show up. I looked all over that audience for her," said Brooke with tears in her eyes. "I would have never thought that she would miss my graduation! That hurt me so bad," she cried. "Here I am, Valedictorian, and I am giving an inspiring message and blessings for the future of our entire class and my own mother was not there."

Brooke put her hand over her eyes to stop the tears. All the girls were wiping their tears and consoling Brooke. "It's going to be ok hun," said J.D.

"And then I am looking for STUPID Josh in the audience, too but all I saw was his mom smiling at me while I spoke. Her smile meant a lot but it wasn't my mom. My dad gave me 3 dozen of roses but I wanted my mom. My family was there, but I just wanted my mom. I had the applause and I was Valedictorian but it meant nothing. I honestly don't remember seeing any of you, who I sat next to or any songs we sang. I don't even remember walking across the stage. I just wanted to see my mom's face in that crowd," said Brooke as she kept wiping the tears.

The Holy Girls, Holy Spirit, and the Prophet

"Oh my gosh!" yelled J.D. as she looked at her phone and jumped out of the bed.

"What!" said Emory as she jumped up in worry.

"It's 9!!" said J.D. "We are supposed to be at the Prep building for the close-out at 10!"

"Aw man!" said Emory as she ran to her duffel bag to pick out clothes for the day.

"Fah'ry!!" J.D. yelled downstairs.

"Are you all up hun?"

"No!" yelled Fah'ry in a raspy voice.

"Well, it's 9," said J.D.

"Oh shoot!!" Fah'ry said as she jumped out of the bed.

"What's wrong?" Brooke asked as she pulled the covers from over her head.

"We are late," said Fah'ry. "It's 9 and we gotta be at da Prep building at 10 o'clock."

"Oh! Ok!" said Brooke. "I don't have a clue of what to wear!" Brooke said as she walked into the bathroom. Brooke looked in the mirror. "Look at my eyes! They are so puffy!" She headed upstairs to J.D. and Emory's room.

"Where you going?" asked Fah'ry as she ironed her shirt.

"I need J.D. to do something with my puffy eyes!" said Brooke.

"Good morning y'all," said Brooke to J.D. and Emory.

"Hey hun," said J.D. as she unwrapped her hair.

"Hey there," said Emory as she walked to the shower. "How are you feeling?"

"I'm a little better," said Brooke. "All that crying last night has made my eyes really puffy. J.D., can you do my makeup? Nothing extravagant, just a natural look but I need these puffs covered up! I wish I would have thought about it last night. I would have put on my cucumber mask but I didn't think about it."

"Yes, that would have naturally helped," said J.D. "But, sure, I'll help. Let me finish my hair and I'll be ready."

"Ok, thanks," said Brooke. "I am going to hop in the shower right quick and by that time, you should be done with your hair. Fah'ry should be out of the shower by now," said Brooke.

"Oh shoot!" said Fah'ry. *I forgot to ask J.D. for her body wash,* she thought as she took a shower. *I hope Brooke left hers in here. I wish I had some shampoo. I would really wash my hair. Ooh, here is da body wash! Pomegranate?"* Fah'ry thought as she looked at the bottle. *What does this smell like?* as she sniffed the bottle. *Ooh, this smells too good! Thank you, God so much for this shower,* Fah'ry prayed as she tried to lather up the body wash with her towel. *Dis smells so good! as she used the wash everywhere. Hopefully, this shower will last me for awhile. Oh, I should be good since we are leaving for London on Tuesday!*

Brooke knocked on the door. "Fah'ry, come on! I have to get in the shower too!"

"Ok!" said Fah'ry. "Here I come." *Let me brush my teeth,* Fah'ry said to herself. She brushed her teeth 3 times. *Let me rinse dis toothbrush really good,* she said to herself. She opened the door and Brooke rushed in with her clothes. Fah'ry left out and Brooke closed the bathroom door.

It smells like my body wash in here, Brooke said to herself. *Did she use my body wash?* She paused and thought. *I doubt it, we probably have the same kind . . .*

"Since I am ready, I am going downstairs to make lattes," said Emory.

"Ok," said J.D. "I'm almost ready. I'm just waiting on Brooke."

"Alright, well I'll be downstairs," said Emory.

J.D. sat on the bed and picked up her phone. *Ugh, I don't even want to call home,* J.D. said to herself. *It's always something,* she said with sadness. *Let me call or I'll be worried all day about her.* The phone rang and her mom picked up quickly.

"J.D.!" her mom said with urgency in her voice. "Call the police! I keep telling him to leave and he won't give me my car keys! Give me my car keys!!" her mom yelled.

"No, so you can whore around with those rich doctors," he said. "You think they're better than me!" he yelled as he got closer to the phone.

"Mom!" J.D. yelled. "Is he in your face?!?!"

"Just because they got all dem degrees and I got a high school diploma, don't mean nothing!!" he said in a rage. "You know what!" he said. "I'm gonna kill you and him!"

"What are you talking about?" her mom said. "You are just insecure! Are you threatening me?" her mom yelled as the phone dropped and went dead.

"Ugh!" J.D. said as she called the police to go to her home. She called back home and her mom answered. "Hello!" she said in a loud and angry voice. J.D. could hear the tussling over the phone.

"Mom!" she said with fear. "The police are on the way!"

"Get your hands off of my hair!" her mom yelled.

"J.D. don't hang up!" her mom said. J.D. heard the knock on the door through the phone. The knock got louder. "It's the Chicago Police!" the man said. "Ma'am, open up!" J.D. listened hard through the phone.

"Is everything ok?" the officer asked.

"It's just a misunderstanding," her husband said.

"Is that so?" said the officer. "Ma'am, are you ok?" he asked. "Did he hit you?"

"Yes," her mom said.

"Was it open or closed hand?" the officer asked.

"It was open," her mom said as her husband interrupted.

"Sir," the officer said. "I need you to be quiet."

"Ma'am, do you want to press charges?" the officer asked.

Please say yes, J.D. said to herself.

"No," her mom says. "I would just like for him to leave."

"Ok man," the officer said. "She wants you to leave. Just go somewhere else for awhile and cool off." The officer continued to talk to them.

"J.D.," her mom said. "I am going to call you back."

"Ok," J.D. said in disappointment as she hung up the phone. *That is so stupid!!* she said to herself. *Does it really matter if it's open or closed hand? And I don't understand why she didn't press charges?? Lord, please take care of my mom? Please don't let him kill her,* she prayed with tears in her eyes. *I need my mom,* she cried and looked for worship music in her phone and started to pray in tongues. Suddenly, there was a knock on the door. "Come in," J.D. said as she wiped her eyes before Brooke entered.

"Hey, are you ready for me?" Brooke said.

"Yeah, I'm ready, hun. Just worshipping before we go over to the Prep building."

"I can understand that," said Brooke. "I need to be doing the same. What's on the agenda for today?"

"I don't know," said J.D. "I didn't get a chance to check the itinerary this morning with all the rushing."

"Yeah, I hate rushing," said Brooke as she leaned her head back to get her makeup done.

"So are you feeling better?" asked J.D.

"I guess so," said Brooke. "It felt good to get it out. I just couldn't hold it anymore. It hurts still. I just can't believe that my mom would leave me like that and miss the most important times of my senior year."

"I know," said J.D. as the worship music continued to play. "I know it's hard, hun but all you can do is trust God to heal your heart."

"I know, but it's so hard when she hasn't said sorry at all. How could she not be sorry?" said Brooke.

"Yeah, that's hard. Well, you know that we are here if you need us," said J.D. as she wrapped up doing her makeup.

"Let's get downstairs," said Brooke. "I know that they're waiting on us. Thank you friend," she said as she looked in the mirror at her face.

"No problem, hun."

"Are you beauties ready?" asked Fah'ry as they all laughed.

"Don't forget your lattes," said Emory. "I left your tumblers on the counter."

"Oh thanks," they said as they grabbed them and walked out of the door.

The girls entered the Prep building. "J.D., did you look at the itinerary for today?" asked Emory.

"No hun, let me check." J.D. looked through her bag. "I don't think I have it," said J.D.

"Ok, now we gone have to ask somebody what's going on," said Fah'ry.

"They should have one around here somewhere," said J.D. "Let me go to the front desk and see if they have a copy." J.D. walked to the front desk and grabbed a copy of the agenda. She turned around and saw the tall guy with the varsity jacket.

"Hey." He smiled at her. "I see that you are doing better today."

"Um, yeah, I feel great," said J.D.

"I know that you don't know me but I'm Bryce's friend, Logan." He reached his hand out to shake her hand.

"Hi Logan. I'm J.D."

"It's nice to see you smiling J.D.," said Logan. "You had us all nervous yesterday for you."

"Yeah, it was pretty scary," said J.D. as she smirked.

"Well, it was really nice meeting you J.D.," said Logan as it was his turn at the front desk.

"Likewise," said J.D. as she walked back towards the girls. *Ok, he was cute,* she thought to herself.

And he didn't even ask me for my number? That's weird. "Ok hunny bunnies," J.D. said, "it looks like we have a close out session in the sanctuary," as she looked over the agenda. "Annnd, it looks like that's all for today.

"Oh ok, sanctuary??" asked Fah'ry. "Are we going to church?"

"I have no clue," said J.D., "but we need to go over there now."

The girls started walking to their final class. "So, J.D., were you just talking to the guy that brought you water yesterday?" said Brooke.

"Yea, that's Bryce's friend. His name is Logan," she said.

"What did he say?" the girls asked in excitement.

"He just said it was nice to see that I was doing ok," said J.D.

"That's it!!?" Emory said.

"I know right, that's what I said. He was all formal and everything," J.D. said.

"He was cute though. Did he ask for your numba?" asked Fah'ry.

"Actually, he did not," said J.D.

"Are you kidding?" said Brooke.

"I know right?" said Fah'ry. "Guys are always trying to get yo numba,"

"Nope, he didn't ask," said J.D.

"Maybe he has a girlfriend?" asked Emory.

"True!" They said as they laughed.

"Yeah, he's too cute to not have a girlfriend," said J.D. "Anywho, here is our class."

As the girls walked in, they tried to find seats. "Wow, it's crowded in here," said Fah'ry. "Dis looks just like a church!"

"Ooh, I can't stand sitting in the back of a church!" said Emory.

"Yeah, we should have gotten here earlier," said J.D. "Well, these are all the seats that are left."

As they sat down, Fah'ry's phone rang. *Oh, how interesting, he gone call now,* she said to herself. *Should I leave out and answer?* she thought. *I haven't talked to him all weekend.* She ran out of the sanctuary to answer his call. "Hey Chaston," she said with butterflies in her stomach.

"What's going on?" Chaston said.

"Nothing, at my high school retreat still," she said in a sweet voice. "I called you a couple of times," she said.

"Yeah, I had practice, did some running around for my mom and slept if I wasn't just chilling," he said. "Hold on for a second," Chaston said. He clicked over on the other line and placed Fah'ry on hold for a very long time. "I can't believe this," she said as she looked at her phone. *He just gone leave me on hold,* she said to herself as her feelings were hurt. She hung up the phone and went back into the sanctuary.

"Good morning, ladies and gentlemen!" Dr. Wellington said as he and his wife stood in front of everyone. "As you know, today is the last day of the L.O.C. retreat. We pray that you have had a great time this weekend. Every year, we close out the retreat with a worship service to edify you spiritually for your next journey. After service is over, you all can dismiss yourselves. Most of your buses will arrive about noon. We will have our worship team come up now and afterwards, Apostle Noah York will come up to minister. The worship leaders walked up to the microphones while Dr. Makenzie Wellington prayed. The worship music began to play and the students stood up and lifted their hands as they gave honor to God. The worship songs began to touch the hearts of many of the students as the glory of God entered the room.

Oh God! Emory said as she cried and lifted her hands. Fah'ry started to walk to the front of the room and she placed money on the steps of the altar as an offering of thanksgiving to God for his presence in the room. Many students started to do the same as Fah'ry, and gave offerings at the altar spontaneously.

Brooke thought to herself, *I really want to dance. I feel something pushing me to dance.* As she looked around, she became fearful. *I don't want all these people looking at me,* she said to herself. She cutely clapped her hands and swayed with the music. Suddenly, one of the worship leaders started to sing, "When the Spirit of the Lord comes upon my heart, I will dance like David danced!!" The students in the audience started to dance and move into the aisles dancing.

Oh wow, said Brooke. *I guess that was you God, prompting me to dance.* Brooke moved into the aisles dancing and slowly made her way to the front and started to dance as graciously as a ballerina before the Lord.

As the Spirit of God moved throughout the room, Emory started to watch various students and their reactions.

J.D. started to feel like a weight was on her. *What is happening?* she said to herself. *I can barely stand up. Why does my stomach feel like this? I praise you God!* J.D. said, *I don't know what's going on but I give you all the glory! You are the Living God!* she said. As J.D. continued to praise God, she started to speak in tongues. "You are Holy, Lord!" she cried out. She then thought to herself, *Wait a minute, this doesn't sound right. I sound like I am speaking another language.* J.D. started to get scared. *It's weird but something is different,* she thought to herself as she continued to pray in tongues.

Apostle Noah York started to speak to the students in the audience. "The glory of God is here!" he said. "His presence is here!" he proclaimed. "God inhabits the praises of His people. Keep worshipping! God is pleased! For I hear the Lord say, you are a chosen generation, a royal priesthood! I have plans to prosper you and not harm you. I knew you before I formed you in your mother's womb! I know the thoughts that I have towards you! They are good and not evil! For I am doing a new thing in you! I am pouring out my Spirit on this generation and I am distributing my gifts to you to serve my people and build them up! Let no one look down on you because you are young! Draw nigh to me and I will draw near to you! As you move forward, seek me with your whole heart and you will find Me, says the Spirit of the Living God!

"Young lady with the pink shirt." Apostle York pointed to J.D. "Can you come up?" he asked. J.D. walked up to the front. "And I hear the Lord saying, while you were in the back wondering what was happening, the Lord says that I was filling you with the gift of tongues. Diverse kinds of tongues and even the ability to interpret tongues. The Lord says that what you spoke with before was your mom's tongues. You mimicked her tongues and God says now, I am giving you the real thing. I am also anointing you to sing songs that I will give you. Many will receive my Holy Spirit as you minister in singing and help usher people into my presence, says the Spirit of the Living God."

The students started to clap and Apostle stood in silence as the minstrels played. Emory thought to herself, *I know that he's going to prophesy to me. I always pray and worship God. God knows that I have been crying to hear a word from Him.* Apostle York walked towards Emory. *Here he comes,* she said to herself. *Let me get ready. Look humble and get ready to receive!* Emory said to herself.

Apostle York looked at Emory as he was walking towards the girls and gestured to Fah'ry. "Can you come up?" he said. "As I saw you sitting there, I saw dollar signs all around you. The Lord says that you have an unusual desire to give to people and even to Him. It's a gift and it's not just money. You are a compassionate person and will give all that you have to help another. You've been like that since you were a young girl. The Lord says that you will accomplish all that you set out to do. Just trust in the Lord with all of your heart and lean not unto your own understanding, In all your ways acknowledge Him and He shall direct your path. I see this building with pink lights." Fah'ry started to look confused. "Do you know what I am talking about?" Apostle York asked her. Fah'ry shook her head "no". "Well, God is going to show you," he said. "You are going to touch the world." Apostle paused, ". . . Aww, God said that you are not going to want to hear this!" Apostle York moved the mic from his mouth and whispered in her ear. "God says, now is not the time for a companion." Fah'ry's heart dropped. *No Chaston?* she immediately thought to herself. "I have great plans for you, said the Lord."

The audience clapped as she walked to her seat. *Is he going to call on me now?* Emory thought. *God please don't let me leave here without speaking to me. I need to hear from you. What do you want me to do with my life? Are you going to use me as your vessel? What are these dreams? Am I a prophet? Do I have a spiritual gift? I can't sing or play an instrument! How can you use me to help your people?* she thought.

As the music subsided, Apostle York started to speak. "Ok, I am going to try and move on. Clearly, the Lord wanted to speak to many of you. Today I am going to teach about spiritual gifts, what they are and why you will need them. Turn to 1 Corinthians 12 and put a marking at Romans 12 also," he said.

Ok, Emory said to herself, *I guess you don't have anything to say to me Lord,* as she put her head down in disappointment. She looked at her Bible and started reading with the rest of the group.

As Apostle York started to teach for awhile, he looked over in the direction of the girls. "Young lady with that bow on your head," he gestured to Brooke. "The Lord says that there are some people that are close to you, very close to you but they are not good for you. He says that you need to get away from them. There are some around you that you think are your friends but they are not. God says that He is going to give you some new friends. So let them go. There is an administrative and business anointing on you. God is going to give you wisdom and you will have the opportunity to manage large Fortune 500 corporate accounts. Says the Spirit of the Lord." All the audience clapped as he walked around and ministered to other students.

Fah'ry leaned over to Emory. "Girl you hear him? He's prophesying to Bryce."

"I see," said Emory. *Everybody except for me,* she said to herself.

Apostle York went back to his teaching after he prophesied to Bryce. He started to list the gifts of wisdom, gift of knowledge, prophecy, tongues, discerning of spirits, healing and miracles, interpretation of tongues and he moved on to the gift of faith. As he did so, he saw a light shining on Emory. "Sweetheart in the back with the glasses and long ponytail," he said as he spoke to

Emory. Her heart jumped. "It seems that your dreams are very real. The Lord says that you need to sleep with a pen and journal by your bed every night.

Apostle continued with his teaching on spiritual gifts.

Okaaay, that's all he's going to say? she said to herself.

Pretty Scars

The girls were on their way to their bus to head back to the school parking lot. J.D. and the girls were walking and she saw Logan walking towards her. "Hey J.D.," Logan said as the crowd of students boarded their buses.

"Hey, is it Logan?" J.D. said as if she didn't know his name.

"I don't normally go up to girls and try and get their number and all that," said Logan. "But, I would like to get to know you. You are gorgeous and you have a captivating spirit."

"And so," J.D. said in a curious voice.

Logan chuckled, "So, I want to know, who is J.D.?"

She smirked and looked to the side as the last few students boarded their buses. "What school do you go to?" asked J.D. with sass.

Logan chuckled, "Dang! I go to St. John's."

"Oh ok," said J.D. as she looked at his broad shoulders and tall physique.

Ooh wee! she said to herself. "So, who are you?" J.D. asked. "Who is Logan?"

He put his hand in his pocket and gave her his business card.

Oh!! J.D. said to herself. *A business card!* She read the card briefly as Logan was checking how long he had to run for his bus.

"So, can I get to know J.D.?"

She grabbed his phone out of his hand and added herself to his contacts. "I have to go," said J.D. "It was nice meeting you, Logan. I'll see you around," she said with a flirtatious smile.

"Of course," he replied as he watched her walk off and her long hair blowing in the wind.

J.D. placed the business card in her pocket as she stepped on the bus. "Girl, what was all dat about?" Fah'ry asked as J.D. sat down in her seat. "Y'all was talking for a long time," she said, being inquisitive.

J.D. smirked. "Fah'ry, stop," she said as she smiled.

"Ok, so tell us what happened?" Brooke asked.

J.D. smiled and couldn't help her warm feelings. "He just said that he wanted to know more about me. He seemed like he really did. And that face! He had me!"

"Hahaha," laughed the girls.

"It was like I felt this connection between us. I kept trying not to look in his eyes! Oh my gosh! And he just kept smiling at me with this look," said J.D.

"Girl, he got you!!" Fah'ry said as they all laughed. "Did you give him yo numba?" asked Fah'ry.

"Yeah I did," said J.D, and all the girls looked at each other.

"What!!" they said.

"See, I told you!" Fah'ry said. "He got J.D.! The pretty boy has attacked!"

"Bwhahaha," the girls were giggling.

"No," J.D. said. "He doesn't," she laughed. "I am cool hunny bunnies!"

"Ok, friend," Emory giggled. "You did give him your number. You never give random guys your number!"

"Well," J.D. laughed. "He seemed different. I promise, I felt a connection," she laughed and looked at her friends in a convincing manner.

"Ok ok ok, we will stop!" said Emory. "It's cool that you like him. At least you know that he comes from a good school."

"Anddd, he did bring you water da otha day!" said Fah'ry.

"True true," said Brooke, "so we at least know that he's a caring guy."

"I would say that he's worth at least getting your number," said Emory.

"Is he black though?" asked Fah'ry.

"He sounds like it," said J.D. "But he does look like he's mixed with something."

"Have you talked to Bryce, Emory?" Brooke said.

"Nope, well, yes, when we left the Prep building yesterday after the ambulance thing. I'm not thinking about him," said Emory. "I can't wait until we leave for this London trip!"

"Yes!" said Fah'ry with excitement. "I have a few more clothes to get and I'll be good."

"Yeah, I need to pick up a few more things," said Emory.

"Girl, like what?" Fah'ry said in a sarcastic way. "You got everything, don't you?"

"Um no," Emory said as she smirked. "I don't have everything."

J.D. grabbed her notes from the retreat and started reading to prevent an argument between Fah'ry and Emory.

What was that about, Emory said to herself.

J.D. was reading her notes from the Choosing a College Major class.

"What are you reading?" asked Emory as she glanced at J.D.'s notes.

"I'm looking at these notes from class and checking the net to see if Dr. Prink's info that she gave us is true."

"Oh ok," said Emory.

"What's going on with you?" asked J.D.

"Nothing, just preparing myself for service today," said Emory. "My mom and dad are expecting me to be in service today."

"Oh, so you're not going to get any rest today?" asked J.D.

"Not really, I'm going straight to church when we get back," said Emory. "Did you want to come?"

I need to, J.D. said to herself. *I hate that house. But I need to go home, just in case something happens,* she thought.

"Thanks hun, but my mom is supposed to take me shopping after she gets home from church. I haven't done anything for the London trip."

"Oh shopping with your mom should be fun," said Emory.

"Yeah, I really want those new jeans to go with my brown sandals. I need like 2 more pair of sunglasses as well."

"You and those sunglasses," said Emory.

"I know, I know, I love sunglasses," said J.D.

"So are you feeling ok?" asked Emory.

"Yes, I am ok hun. I feel better," said J.D. "That rest on Saturday really helped."

"That's good," said Emory. "I am glad that you are better."

Fah'ry looked over at J.D. and Emory's seat. "Emory, can you send me your aunt's number in London," said Fah'ry. "I need to give Chaston the phone numba to where we are staying."

"I'll send it in a sec," said Emory.

J.D. picked her notes back up. *I really want to study Fashion,* J.D. thought as she reviewed her notes from class on college majors. *My mom would be horrified if I tried to study fashion . . . I already know that she is going to say that there is no future in it and that it's a waste of money. But I so love drawing, color matching and all of that. It's so me,* she thought to herself. *But, I know that there is a high risk in majoring in fashion. But, I can't really see myself being a doctor either. Ugh, I just don't know! How can I have this high GPA and not know what I want to do with my life! I feel so behind,* J.D. thought to herself as she concentrated on her notes.

Emory laid her head back against the bus seat and closed her eyes. *I can't believe that he barely prophesied to me,* Emory thought to herself. *Even Fah'ry received a prophetic word and she's wild as ever. Look at her and Chaston and all that perverted stuff that they do. I mean, I don't even have a boyfriend. I'm not letting boys hump all on me at parties. I don't even dance. I haven't thought about drinking or smoking marijuana. I pray everyday and I go to church every Sunday. I'm not sleeping around like some of these girls my age. God, why didn't you say anything to me?* she thought. *What do you want me to do? Why won't you tell me? Do I have a gift? Am I special?* The bus ride home was unusually quiet and most of the girls on the bus were either reading or sleeping.

Now God, I heard you about the companion stuff but I can't leave Chaston. I need him. I don't really have anybody. Fah'ry thought to herself, *My dad is always gone and my grandma doesn't talk that much. He's all I have,* as she looked out of the window at the beautiful scenery with tears in her eyes.

I need to say something, Brooke thought to herself. *I can't hold this in any longer. What kind of friend am I?* Brooke looked quickly at Fah'ry and noticed her staring out of the window. *She already looks like she has a lot on her mind. I am just going to keep it to myself. I don't want to hurt her even more. Chaston has done enough to hurt her feelings.*

Fah'ry started going through her purse looking for her favorite pen. She pulled her sketch pad out of her bag, put her earplugs in her ears, turned up her music and started drawing clothing. *Ok, she looks fine. I am not going to say anything,* thought Brooke. *I need to call this hotel anyway. I hope that they have some rooms available. I wish that I could go home.*

I miss my mom. I just hate being out here like this. It's like I don't have parents at all. Look at all of my friends, Brooke thought. *Their moms love and care about them. My mom doesn't love me. My dad just lies to me and never talks to me. I mean, he is around but I feel like he's a stranger. I don't really know him,* she thought as her eyes watered.

Josh doesn't talk to me me. He keeps ignoring my calls. I try not to even think about it. Maybe I don't look good enough? Brooke thought, *I can't wait to leave for London. I need this getaway. Maybe, they'll miss me then,* as she pulled out her phone to watch cheer videos.

The bus arrived at the school and J.D. looked at her phone. *A missed call?* J.D., said. *I don't know this number.* She put her phone back in her purse.

The girls walked to their cars on the school parking lot, each of them hitting the disarm alarm buttons simultaneously on their IvyKenningtons. As their cars were side by side, each convertible top started to come down slowly as they were walking towards their cars.

"Did you all want to come to church with me?" asked Emory.

"I would hun, but I am going shopping with my mom to get my last little things for London," said J.D.

"Yea, I'm going to my church," said Fah'ry. "I don't like missing it. I like being in a more Apostolic/prophetic atmosphere."

"My church has that," said Emory in an offended voice.

"Oh ok," said Fah'ry. "What denomination is your parents' church again?"

"We are non-denominational," said Emory quickly. "Why did you ask that?

"Oh, just was wondering because I neva hear you talk about any known apostles or prophets coming to your church," said Fah'ry.

"Well, that doesn't dictate whether my church is powerful or not," said Emory with an attitude.

"What time is service?" Brooke quickly interrupted to keep peace between her friends.

"I'm going to the 4 o'clock," said Emory.

"I'll go, I just need to book this room by the airport."

"Are you sure that you don't want to stay with us?" asked Emory.

"I'm ok, it's just two days before we leave." Brooke said, "Let me take care of this and I'll be there," as she opened her car door and sat down.

"Ok, actually, I'm going to stop at Pink Java before church," said Emory. "We can meet up there and then go."

"Cool," said Brooke as she called to book her hotel room.

The girls all got into their matching IvyKenningtons and fixed their hair for their ride with the tops down. They applied their lipgloss and Fah'ry turned her music up loudly.

J.D. pulled her phone out. *Let me see who this was that called me?* she said to herself. *Lord, please let my mom be ok. I hope that this isn't a hospital or anything.* She redialed the number with her heart pounding.

"Hello," the voice said.

"Hi, who is this?" J.D. asked as the girls drove off the parking lot one by one in their pink, purple, yellow and blue matching cars.

"It's Logan," he said in a calming and cool voice.

"Oh hi," she said as she felt butterflies form in her stomach.

"So, what are you up to today?" he asked.

"Well, we just arrived at the school and I'm headed home," she said.

"Did you want me to call you back?" Logan asked.

"No, I'm cool, I can talk," she said. *I couldn't wait to talk to him,* she thought. *I was hoping that he called.*

"Cool, cool," Logan said.

"So, what does the infamous J.D. like to do?" he asked.

J.D. smiled and turned on soft jazz and talked to Logan all the way to her house. She pulled up to her house and parked. *I feel good,* she thought. *He was really cool to talk to. Ok, I need to calm down. It's just one call.*

J.D.'s phone rang as she was getting her bags out of the car. "Hey, Fah'ry," J.D. answered.

"Hey, where is dat restaurant that you was talking about that was downtown by da water?"

"It's on Crayger and Baylor," said J.D.

"I thought that you were going to church?"

"I am," said Fah'ry. "I'm on my way. After I leave, I'm going to take Chaston to dat restaurant."

"Ok, Fah'ry," J.D. said in disappointment. *Why is she taking him out?* J.D. thought. *When is she going to get it? She deserves so much better.* "Oh cool, well let me take these bags in the house," said J.D.

"Ok, talk to you laytah," said Fah'ry.

J.D. walked up the stairs of her house. She took her keys out to open the door but heard her mom's voice in the backyard. She walked quietly to the back and as she got closer, she heard her mom's husband's voice. *Ugh, he's here.* she thought. *I can't stand him!* All of her happiness from earlier left suddenly. She stopped on the side of the house to hear the conversation because she heard the word college. She listened so hard to make out the words. "Well, she will be gone to college soon," her mom said as they talked. "Things should be better. She has her own life to live," her mom said to her husband.

What?? J.D. said to herself. *They are waiting for me to leave? They think that I'm the problem in their marriage? I can't believe her! I would have never thought that she would say something like that?? Not my mom! I don't even want to go in here. I should get my things and never come back,* she thought. *Ugh,* she walked back to the front and went in the house. She went in her room and sat at her desk. She started looking up tourist attractions in London to ease her mind. J.D.'s mom and husband walked in the house. She heard minor arguing. *Ugh, here they go,* she said with frustration. *I am going to stay in here as long as I can,* she thought. *Where is the phone?* She put her finger on the 9 and waited to hear the argument escalate.

They walked past her room arguing but they did not see her. Her mom walked in the bathroom and he followed her. "Are you pulling my hair?!" she asked with anger.

Let me go out here, J.D. said to herself. *Maybe he will stop if he sees me.* J.D. walked out of her room to where they were arguing. "Hey Mom," J.D. said as she looked at them.

"You need to leave," her mom said to him with anger. "You need to leave now!" He continued to argue and stand there. "If you don't leave, I'm going to call the police," she said. He walked out of the door and gave her an evil and dangerous look.

I think he's the devil himself, J.D. thought. *I am glad he's gone.* J.D. went to her room and continued researching.

The house phone started to ring. J.D.'s mom picked up and began to argue with her husband over the phone. She hung up and he would call right back. "Stop calling here!" her mom yelled. She hung up on him and he called back over and over again for hours. I wish he would stop calling, thought J.D. The phone rang again and again. Her mom would pick up and argue with him and hang up. The phone rang again. "Why do you keep calling!" she shouted. "Oh, so you're going to sit here and describe to me how you are going to kill me?" she said loudly." I'm not scared of you," she said and hung up.

Oh God, please help us, said J.D. She walked to the front window and sat there watching out for him to come near their house. *As soon as I see him, I'm calling the police,* J.D. thought in fear. The phone rang again.

"What do you want!?" her mom yelled, "I hope you know that I am recording everything that you say!" as she hung up. Her mom got up and started to pray in tongues. "J.D.!" she said with urgency. "You need to be praying!" she demanded. J.D. got up and started praying in tongues and walking around the house mimicking her mom's prayer posture. The phone stopped ringing and things settled down. Her mom lay down and fell asleep.

Ok, he stopped calling, she thought to herself. *The prayers worked!* She still sat by the window to watch for him. *God, this man is threatening to kill my mom. Please stop him,* she cried. *The phone is not ringing anymore. At least when it was ringing, I knew that he was far away. Now, I don't know where he is,* she thought with fear in her heart. *Please don't let us die tonight! If he has a gun, please don't let it work right.* J.D. looked at her watch. *Wow, she said. I got home at 3 PM and it is now 9:30 PM! This is crazy!* J.D. went in her mom's room to get the phone. *Let me see if anyone has tried to call me.* J.D. saw the base to the phone lighting up. *Wow, the phone is still ringing!* J.D. picked up the phone once the light stopped blinking. She looked at the phone and turned it to the side. *The ringer is off!* she said. *Can't believe that she turned the ringer off! So, he hasn't stop calling. Our prayers didn't work,* she thought. *Ok, I am getting sleepy. I can't sit here any longer. I can barely keep my eyes open.*

J.D. went to lay down for the night. She said her prayers and tried to go to sleep but couldn't. *I can't sleep in this house,* J.D. said to herself. She finally dozed off. She was awakened by a loud noise at the door. *What is that?* she thought as she and her mom jumped up. The noise got louder. "Mom, he's kicking the door down!" J.D. said in fear.

"I'm not worried," her mom said. J.D. looked in her mom's face and saw fear but also felt that she was giving up. *Is she ready to die or something?* J.D. thought. J.D. grabbed the phone and called the police while he kicked the large door down. *What do I do?* "Hello, please come to my house!" J.D. panicked as she spoke with the police over the phone.

He busted in the house and went straight into her mom's room. J.D. followed him into the room. *Whatever is about to happen, I will be right here,* she said to herself. *I don't want to die but I will give my life for my mom,* J.D. thought.

He grabbed her mom by the neck and they started fighting. *Please police hurry up!* She thought. *It's 1 o'clock in the morning, please let one of the neighbors hear us!* J.D. jumped in the fight with her mom. J.D. was able to hold him down for a while and then they started fighting, both him and J.D.

He swung her around the room by her long hair. She hit the glass table and cut her back. She started to yell for her mom as her mom called the police again. "Mom!!" J.D. yelled and cried. "He hit me and swung me around the room by my hair!" Her mom rushed into the front room where they were fighting. Her mom ran into the kitchen and grabbed a large knife. She charged at him quickly and started to cut him.

He ran out of the house bleeding very badly. J.D. held her wounded back and went into the bathroom to check her hair. "This gash is bad," she said, as she watched the blood run down her back as she looked in the mirror.

Fashion Forward Slum

Emory woke up at home and went to sit on their patio. "It feels so good out here," she said. *Lord, I thank you for today. You are my strength and comfort. You are worthy to be praised.* As Emory prayed, a memory came to her mind. "Oh!" she said with eagerness. She looked at the trees and her mom's garden. *I just thought about it,* she said. *I saw this big cobra stand up and open its mouth and hiss at me. Oh, and I was at our old house in Englewood. What was that about?* she thought. She suddenly remembered what Apostle York had prophesied to her. She ran in the house and up to her room.

Emory grabbed her journal and pen and ran back on the patio. She sat on the patio chaise, kicked her feet up and started to write. *Ok God,* she said. *Please help me remember the dream.* As she wrote, parts of the dream would come to her mind. As the wind blew softly, the leaves on the trees moved with grace and the sun shined brightly upon her face as she thought and wrote. Emory finished her writing, closed her journal, placed her pen on top of it and laid her head back as she stretched out on the chaise.

She looked up at the clouds and smiled as she tried to identify what each cloud looked like. *I remember being in the park with my mom as a little girl,* she thought. *My mom would get a blanket, some fresh bottles of water, my comb and brush and she would braid and bead my hair for summer camp. I would stare at the clouds and try to make out the shapes as I lay on the blanket while she braided my hair,* she thought. *Man, I hated getting my hair braided! It hurt so bad,* she thought and smirked. *I always wondered why she would braid my hair outside on the park hill by the tennis court,* she thought to herself. *I know now though. It was so hot in that house in the summer and the fans did not help. The lights didn't work that well. Even when they were on, it was still dim in the house. Turning the lights only made it hotter. Lord, I am happy that you gave us a new home,* Emory said. *I don't miss anything about that neighborhood. I am glad to be away from the city.* She started to think . . . *I couldn't even play in the sand long in the park because I had to watch for the glass in it from the drunks from the previous night throwing their beer bottles in the sandbox. Lord, thank you, I can go to a clean park now and walk a path without stepping on glass or coming out of my house and seeing potato chip bags and all sorts of garbage on the ground. I am grateful,* she said. She looked at her phone and saw the time. *I guess I drifted, haha.* She called the girls.

"Hey J.D.," Emory said. "Did you want to go to breakfast on my dad's yacht this morning?"

"Sure hun, let me get dressed," said J.D.

"No rush," said Emory, "I have tennis lessons first anyway. We can go after that," said Emory.

"So what time should I meet you at the dock," asked J.D.

"10 is fine," said Emory.

"Are the girls coming?" asked J.D.

"Yes, I talked to Brooke already but Fah'ry is not answering. She's probably on the phone with Chaston. She never clicks over when she's on the phone with him," said Emory.

"Of course," said J.D. "I'll try to call her. I'll see you in a little," said J.D.

"Ok, don't forget to put on sunscreen," said Emory. "Breakfast will be on the top deck. There's a large umbrella at the table for shade but it's so unpredictable," said Emory.

"I will," said J.D.

"Let me get to practice. My tennis instructor hates when I am late," said Emory.

"Ok," said J.D., "see you later," as she smirked.

J.D. called Fah'ry and she picked the phone up right away.

"Hey J.D.," Fah'ry said.

"Hey hun, we are going to breakfast in a little, did you want to go?" asked J.D.

"Where are you all thinkin?" asked Fah'ry.

"We are going to have breakfast on the boat," said J.D.

"Emory's dad's boat!" Fah'ry said with skepticism.

"Y'all know I get sea sick every time I get on dat boat."

J.D. laughed, "That's because you always stay downstairs and watch tv in the room. That's the lower part of the boat," said J.D. "You can feel the waves more. Just don't go downstairs."

"Emory said that we were eating on the top deck since it's so warm," said J.D.

"And why you call me and ask?" said Fah'ry. "She could have called me herself!"

"She said that she tried to call you," said J.D.

"I ain't get no call!" said Fah'ry! "I been in da house all morning."

"Well," said J.D., "she said that she called you. We are meeting at the harbor at 10."

"Oh, it's 8," said Fah'ry. "Ok, I'll get ready and meet y'all there," said Fah'ry.

"Ok, see you later," J.D. said. "Fah'ry please be there at 10 or before. You know that her dad is going to leave exactly at 10."

"Ok, J.D.!" exclaimed Fah'ry. "I will be there on time! Let me find something to wear!" said Fah'ry.

"Talk to you later," she said.

"K" said J.D.

Fah'ry got her clothes together and laid them on the chair in her room. *I need to iron these shorts,* she thought. Fah'ry went to get the iron as she walked past her grandmother and uncles sitting in the living room on the old raggedy couch. She walked across their view of the t.v and all that she could hear was them smacking their lips.

Geez, no one ever says hello or good morning around here, she thought as she walked to the kitchen to get the iron. She opened the refrigerator door to get something to drink. "Ugh," she said as the roaches crawled quickly out of the refrigerator. She looked for the drink with the tightest lid on it. *It's only pop in here,* she thought as she stood with the door open. *I need some water!*

She grabbed the bottle of pop and suddenly heard a voice shout. "Aye, don't drank my pop!" her uncle said.

"Ooh," Fah'ry said with anger. She threw the pop back in the refrigerator. She grabbed the iron and walked back past them.

"Tell yo mama to buy you some groceries," he said.

"Shut up talkin to me!" Fah'ry said with an attitude. She walked into her tiny homemade jail size room and put the broken door against the opening as if she was closing her door. She laid the towel on the floor as her ironing board. She plugged the iron in and grabbed her canary yellow shorts off of the broken brown chair. She sat on the floor and started to iron her shorts. "Ugh!" Fah'ry sighed as the roaches crawled out of the iron and brown spots from dead roaches mixed with water leaked on her pretty yellow shorts. "Ugh! Ooh wee," she mumbled. "What am I going to wear now!??" She turned the iron upside down and beat it against the floor in anger and to try to get all the roaches out.

She looked in her duffel bag in the corner of her room that served as her dresser drawer and pulled out a pair of dark denim shorts that didn't require ironing. She laid her clothes and underwear on the broken chair away from the wall to protect them. Fah'ry picked up her army blanket and pillow off of the floor, which served as her bed. She looked in her book bag for her soap, deodorant, toothpaste and towel that she secretly kept there for cleanliness. She pulled a green pan from behind her duffel that was also hidden. She removed the door from the opening and walked past her grandma and uncles as they were glued to the tv.

She heard all these noises in the kitchen and was afraid to walk through it to get to the bathroom. *I hate those stupid rats!* Fah'ry thought to herself. *It's like 5 of dem in dere! And they are big! Maybe if I walk in more, they'll run.* Fah'ry took a deep breath and walked in the middle of the dark kitchen with no working light. "Thank you, God," said Fah'ry as the rats got silent.

Fah'ry walked in the bathroom and turned on the dim light. She held her breath. *I hate this smell!* She looked around the small bathroom for a gallon of water. She started to feel the urge to use the bathroom. *I know that I am supposed to pee in the bucket but I hate that!* she said to herself. *Everyone in da house pee is in that bucket. I'll wait until grandma goes to empty it to use it. I just feel like some germs or bacteria gone jump in my private area. So, grandma will just have to holler at me for putting pee in the toilet,* she said to herself. Fah'ry grabbed a couple of newspapers from the top of the broken-down sink. She placed the newspaper inside and around the toilet. She made a bowel movement and peed.

It would be nice if this tub worked, she thought as she peeked behind the dirty shower curtain, *if grandma get all these crates and dirty buckets out of this tub.* She looked up at all of the holes in the ceiling. *How did this happen?* she wondered. *I don't remember it being any other way since I was born.* She looked on the floor and could see outside from the holes. *There's the gallon of water!* She looked past the broken and rusted sink pipes. *They always trying to hide the water.* She felt accomplished that she had found the hidden water.

She finished using the bathroom and grabbed a plastic bag from the designated area crate for them. She pulled the newspaper from the dry and rusted toilet. She folded the paper correctly so that a turd wouldn't fall out. She held the paper tightly to let the pee run into the dry toilet. Fah'ry placed the feces filled newspaper into the plastic bag. "Let me double tie this bag," she said. She walked outside with the bag and placed it in the garbage. *I'm just doing what I've seen dem do,* she thought, *I don't feel like hearing grandma mouth.* 'Who boo booed in the piss bucket' as she mocked her grandma's voice. She went back in the bathroom to grab the gallon of hidden water. *I am glad it's warm outside,* she said. *Cuz all dis pee in this bucket would be froze. I hate da winta! You can't even come pass the kitchen cuz of how cold it is in here.*

Fah'ry walked back past her family in the living room. Her uncle smacked his lips.

"Where you get dat wata from?" her grandma asked with an attitude.

"Out of the bathroom," Fah'ry said.

"Put that back," her grandma said. "Look in yo mama room for y'all own wata!" Fah'ry rolled her eyes and walked towards her mom's room. I'm not gonna even look at him, Fah'ry said to herself as she tried to ignore her uncle pull his penis out and pee in the pop bottle in the living room in front of everyone.

She looked in the normal places for the gallons of water. "I don't see nun," she said. All I see is her urinal and wash up bucket. *I hope I don't have to go to the park,* she thought with worry. She started to smell a strong bleach smell. Grandma is cleaning up the bathroom already!

"Fah'ry!" Her grandma yelled. "Why did you put this piss in the toilet!"

Fah'ry ignored her fussing. "I hate that bleach," said Fah'ry softly. "She uses bleach for everything," she said as she coughed from the strong smell of bleach. She looked on her mom's dresser and saw a note. You need to go to the park and fill those empty gallons up with water, Fah'ry read the note. "Ugh! Why do I have to go over there?" she said with anger. "I feel like I'm stealing water! Why don't she ever go and do it herself? She has like 5 empty jugs!!" Fah'ry said in a whispering voice. *Now that I have my car, she just gone add more jugs to fill. It's bad enough that I used to have put a jug on each side of my handle bar on my bike and fill the jugs with water from the park water fountain. It was almost impossible to ride my bike back home with 2 full gallons of water,* she reminisced. *What time is it? I need to go fill these jugs while the park is still empty and no one recognizes me,* she thought.

Fah'ry jumped in her car and drove to the park to fill the empty jugs with water from the public water fountain. "I need to hurry up before somebody sees me," she said. She looked around to make sure the park was empty. All of a sudden, she saw a lady coming towards the fountain with a buggy full of empty jugs. *Here comes Agnes. Let me hurry up and go!* Agnes walked up with a skull cap on, a winter coat down to her ankles and a long stick that she carries and the buggy in the other hand. *It's 90 degrees!* Fah'ry thought to herself. Agnes just stared at Fah'ry. *I guess she's in one of her moods. She not speaking today,* thought Fah'ry. She filled her last jug and quickly got in her car.

Ooh, I remember when I used to be so scared of her when I was younger. I would be so scared to walk pass her house as she would stand in front of it and yell and talk to the air. She would turn into like 4 different people in a matter of seconds, Fah'ry smirked as she drove back home. *All the kids in the neighborhood called her the voodoo lady. Ha,* said Fah'ry! *Her whole house was covered with trees and broken branches like a fortress. You couldn't even see her house. Her garage had little children on it that she had drawn in red and the paint dripped like blood. Man, I was I scared of her! I would walk all the way around the corner, out of the way, to get to my house that was a couple of houses down,* she reminisced. *Until that one day! My mom sent me to the water fountain to fill those jugs.* Fah'ry shook her head from side to side. *It was about 6 in the morning and I was the only one out. I heard this buggy sound behind me and I turned around and it was Agnes! She has on all of those heavy winter clothes in da summa, a buggy full of empty jugs and that shabby dog. I was so scared and I couldn't run!! I had my bike and I couldn't go back home without those jugs filled,* she smirked. *I looked at her with fear in my eyes and she looked at me . . . I'm like, oh my gosh, she's about to put a voodoo spell on me! I kept my head down and didn't look at her while I filled the jug. I looked up to put the top on the jug and she stared at me. I was so frightened,* thought Fah'ry! *Then and out of nowhere, she said . . . 'Hello' in the nicest voice! She then asked me, 'what's your name?' I was like 11 years old. I finally had to face my fear of Agnes. From that day, we would have short conversations at the water fountain at 6 in the morning as we both sneaked water. I would say hi when I was outside playing,* she smirked *And all of my friends and family was puzzled at why I was speaking to the voodoo lady and wasn't running anymore.*

Did I just drift like that? Fah'ry laughed, took the keys out of her car and took the 5 jugs of water in the house.

Fah'ry walked in the house and put the gallons of water in the designated place in her mom's room. She grabbed a gallon and walked past her family to get to the kitchen. Her grandmother smacked her lips and rolled her eyes at Fah'ry. *I'm just gonna ignore them,* Fah'ry thought to herself.

"So she went and got all dat wata," her uncle said to her grandma and uncle loud enough for Fah'ry to hear. "Yea, they think they betta than everybody!" her other uncle said in a loud voice.

"Huh!" Fah'ry sighed loudly. "Let me hurry up and get ready." She paused at the threshold of the kitchen door to wait for the rat noises to subside. She put one foot forward and stomped her foot in hopes that the rats would scatter. She walked to the aluminum foil covered stove and picked up the hidden pot that her mom used to wash her face. Fah'ry filled the pot with water and turned on the stove to warm the cold water up. She quickly went to her room and grabbed her green wash up pan. She went back to the kitchen and poured the boiling water in the pan. *This is not enough water,* said Fah'ry. *I can't wash up with this.* She poured almost the entire gallon of water in the pot. *I know my mama gone be mad that I used all dis water but I'm not a little girl anymore. I need a gallon for the suds I make after cleaning myself and a gallon to rinse off good. I ain't trying to leave no soap down there,* she thought while she poured the second pot of water in the pan. *I've done that before and it burns like crazy.*

Fah'ry walked to her room slowly with the steamy pan in her hands. She put her broken door up to the opening for privacy. "This water is too hot!" said Fah'ry after picking up the steaming wash cloth. "I gotta hurry up! I don't want them to leave me for breakfast." She poured water from the gallon to cool her pan of water. "Oh well," she said as she looked at the empty jug. Fah'ry picked up a bottle of rubbing alcohol that was by her pan neatly next to her deodorant and apple body spray. She picked up the cotton balls that were on a paper towel on the floor to keep them clean from the dirty carpet filled with the aroma of urine from the dog. Fah'ry took the cotton balls and poured the rubbing alcohol on it and rubbed her legs and arms free of dirt. "I am glad that I am old enough to do this myself now," she mumbled as she scrubbed her ankles with the cotton ball. "My momma used to take forever to do this when I was little." She picked up the warm towel from the wash pan and washed her face first. *I have to wash up in the same order,* she thought. *Face, privates, underarms and feet.*

Fah'ry put lotion on to moisturize her eczema covered chest, neck, back and face. She put her fly clothes on and fixed her off-the- shoulder shirt that she designed at the Fashion League. "Ooh, this shirt is too cute!" she said as she looked down at her outfit because she didn't have a mirror in the house. Fah'ry sprayed her apple body spray on her clothes. Let me spray a little more cuz I don't want to smell like this house. Fah'ry took the pan of dirty bath water and poured it out on the side of their house as she was taught as a little girl. "Ooh, it stinks ova there," she said, trying to hold her breath. Fah'ry went back to her room.

"Did you pour that wata in the right place?" Her grandma asked with a mean tone.

"Yea," said Fah'ry. She put the broken door back up and they all smacked their lips.

"What she closing the doe foe?" her uncle said in a confrontatinal tone to those in the living room loud enough for Fah'ry to hear. She put her soap, deodorant and all of her personal items behind her duffel bag of clothes so that no one used them. *Let me put my soap way back here,* she said. *I don't want nobody using my soap.* She pulled her toothpaste and toothbrush from her purse. She unwrapped the tissue from around her toothbrush that covered it from infesting it with crawling roaches. She realized that she didn't have enough water to brush her teeth. "Oh shoot," she said. "I have to open another gallon of water!"

She went to her mom's room and opened another gallon of water. She poured just enough on her toothbrush to rinse it off before brushing her teeth. She thought, *I know grandma gone fuss about this water in the toilet but o well,* as she spit the toothpaste in the toilet from brushing. She put the gallon of water to her mouth and put a little water in her mouth to rinse the toothpaste out. She put the gallon back and walked to her room. *I don't understand why my mama gets to go to the health club every morning and take a shower and I don't,* she wondered.

She took her purse off of the nail on the wall that the clothes hung on as a closet. She took her car keys out and put her purse on her shoulder. Fah'ry walked towards the kitchen to get to the back door. She approached the kitchen threshold and walked in with confidence. "AHHH!!!" Fah'ry screamd very loudly, frightened and disturbed.

"Girl what you screamin foe?!" her grandma hollered from the couch.

"Dat big ole rat just jumped on me and scratched my legs up!!!" Fah'ry screamed and cried loudly as her car keys lay on the floor.

Pretty Girl Mask

Fah'ry ran to her car hysterical. She took her phone out of her purse to call Chaston. She dialed and there was no answer. "Come on," she cried. She called him a second time but there was still no answer. "Ooh!" she exclaimed. "Where is he??! He neva answers the phone!" Fah'ry said with frustration. She let her top down on her canary yellow IvyKennington, put her sunglasses and lipgloss on, checked her leg for scratches from the rat and turned her music up loudly. She drove off speeding and headed to Lake Shore Drive. "I need to hurry up and get to dis harbor before they leave me," said Fah'ry as her curly hair blew in the wind.

She started to cry as the love song played loudly in her car. "I don't understand why he treats me like this," sobbed Fah'ry. "I really need him! It's like he only calls me and comes around when it is convenient for him," she cried and the lake breeze dried her tears.

God, I know you said that now is not the time for a companion but I can't do that. I can't leave Chaston, she cried with fear. *I know that you were talking about him when Apostle York prophesied to me. I just can't be alone. I need him by my side,* she prayed as she wiped her tears.

Fah'ry picked up her phone and called Brooke. "Hey Brooke," Fah'ry said.

"Hey there," said Brooke.

"Are you at the harbor yet?" asked Fah'ry.

"Nope, I'm almost ready," said Brooke. "I need to find this hotel key," she said. "I thought that I left it on the nightstand," said Brooke as she looked around for the key while holding the phone.

"Aw ok," said Fah'ry.

"Let me call you back," Brooke said as the hotel phone rang.

"I'll just see you on da boat," said Fah'ry.

"Ok," said Brooke as she rushed to answer the room phone.

"Yes," Brooke said to the hotel receptionist.

"We are trying to run your card for your stay. How long is your stay?" the receptionist asked.

"2 nights," said Brooke.

"Ok," the receptionist said as she typed.

"I am going to charge your card 350 dollars," she said. "Is that ok?" the receptionist asked.

"Yes, that's fine," said Brooke. "Oh, am I able to come down and get another key?" asked Brooke. "I seem to have lost my room key."

"Sure," the receptionist said.

"I will have one ready for you at the desk."

"Ok, thank you so much!" said Brooke with relief. She grabbed her car keys and purse and left out of the room. She put the Do Not Disturb sign on the door so that the housekeepers would know not to enter her room. She walked to the elevator and pressed 1. *I hope my ears don't start popping,* Brooke said to herself. *50 floors down is a long way,* she said. Brooke looked at her outfit in the elevator mirror. *This shirt doesn't look right by itself,* she thought as she twists and turned in the elevator mirror to see if she looked right. *I can't wear this tank top by itself,* as she looked at her breast. *I feel uncomfortable,* she thought. *My cleavage is out too much.* Brooke got off of the elevator and walked past the pool and jacuzzi to get to the front desk.

"Hello," Brooke said to the receptionist as she stood at the front desk.

"Hi," said the receptionist. "Ooh, that's a pretty cheer bow!" the receptionist said with a smile.

"Thank you!" said Brooke. "Room 5032," said Brooke as she took the new set of room keys from the receptionist.

"You are welcome," she said. "My daughter cheers and wears those bows all the time. She loves them!" the receptionist said with passion.

Brooke smiled and giggled. "I do too! Who does she cheer with?" asked Brooke.

"Legacy," said the receptionist.

"Oh, I used to cheer with them. Actually, that was the first team I joined!" Brooke said.

"Really!" said the receptionist.

"Yes," said Brooke. "I learned how to tumble and coordinate routines there. It's a very good program," Brooke said.

"Oh, that's great to hear because I am spending a lot of money for her to be on that team," said the receptionist.

"Yeah," Brooke said as she smirked. "Cheering is an expensive sport! Well, it was nice talking to you," said Brooke.

"Likewise," said the receptionist with a smile.

Brooke walked to her car in the hotel garage. She let the top down on her lavender IvyKennington and popped her trunk. She rambled through 5 bags of clothes to find her plaid collared shirt to go over her tank top. "Oh, here it is!" she said. She fixed the bags of clothes neatly back in the trunk. She put her shirt on in her car, put her purple lipgloss on, fixed her hair bow and headed to the harbor for breakfast with her friends. Brooke grabbed her phone to call Emory as she approached Lake Shore Drive expressway.

"Hey Brooke!" Emory said as she picked up her phone on the first ring.

"Hey, are you at the harbor yet?" asked Brooke.

"No," said Emory. "I'm about to leave out now. My tennis lesson went longer than expected."

"Ok good," said Brooke. "I am just leaving the hotel."

"No, you're good," smirked Emory. "Anyway, my dad got an emergency call from the church. So, he'll be at the dock around 11:00," said Emory.

"Cool," said Brooke. "I can stop speeding. You know that your dad will leave at the exact time that he says."

"Yeah," Emory smirked. "He is very serious about being on time."

"So, um, girl, let me get out of here. I am going to try and get my car washed first. My mom is supposed to be taking her car in and we usually get them washed together," said Emory. "Hopefully, they can take me first."

"Oh, yeah, well you need to hurry up," said Brooke.

"I'll see you at the dock," said Emory as she yelled, "Mom!" loudly while hanging up the phone.

I wish I could hang out with my mom like that, Brooke thought to herself. *Shoot, I wish I could just talk to my mom.* Brooke put her phone on her lap and she started to think about all of the good times that her and her mom had shopping, beauty shop and nail salon trips as a little girl. *I have no clue what happened,* she pondered. *God,* she thought as her face turned red, *I really feel like she doesn't like me,* as the tears rolled down her face. *What did,* she sniffled, *I do to her? Why doesn't she talk to me? How can she go so long without talking to or checking on her child?*

Her phone started to ring on her lap. She looked down and saw J.D.'s name lighting up on the screen. *It's J.D., ugh, I don't feel like talking to her and hearing all that hunny bunny stuff.* Brooke let the phone ring and ignored the call. *J.D. acts like she always has it together,* she thought. *She never talks about anything personal in her life. Yeah, her mom's a doctor but something is not right about her husband. Every time I see him, he looks high. I have seen enough in my family. I know when someone is high or drunk. Let me stop, that's not right for me to think that,* thought Brooke. *I'll just see her on the boat.*

J.D. placed her phone on the bathroom sink. *I guess Brooke is ok at that hotel,* thought J.D. *She's not answering, which is weird. She always answers my calls. I'll try her again when I get in the car.* J.D. turned her back slightly towards the mirror to look at the scar on her back from last night's fight. She put peroxide on it and placed a large bandage on the scar. J.D. put her pink polo style shirt on and grabbed her car keys and purse. She walked to her mom's room as she sat in her bed reading the Bible.

"Mom," J.D. said. Her mom looked up at her as if she was being disturbed. "I am about to go to breakfast with the girls on the boat," said J.D.

"Did you pray and read your word this morning?" her mom asked.

"Yes, I was up at 6 this morning."

"Ok," said her mom.

"Are you going to be ok?" J.D. asked her mom with concern.

"Yes, J.D., I'm fine, God will take care of me," her mom said.

J.D. kissed her mom on the cheek, "Ok, see you later mom," as she left out the broken door hanging from its hinges. "Excuse me," J.D. said to the repair men as they prepared to put up a new door with stronger locks.

Lord, please keep my mom safe. Please keep him away from her, she prayed with fear. J.D. walked to her car and quickly put her sunglasses on to shield her eyes from the bright and hot sun. "Ooh, it's hot out here! I need to take this hot shirt off!" She sat in the hot car seat and her back pressed lightly against the seat. "Ouch!" she said. "This scar is stinging! I guess I couldn't wear a tank if I wanted to, with this stupid scar," J.D. said with anger.

She put her pink lipgloss on, pulled a second music player from her glove compartment and turned the air conditioning on. She took the first music player and placed it in the cup holder. She turned on the music player and set the playlist to all of the R&B and popular songs that the radio stations were playing. *I know that my mom doesn't allow me to listen to worldly music but I get tired of listening to those church songs,* she thought. *Now, I just have to remember to change the player back to the gospel one. Just in case she rides with me somewhere. I hate hiding my music! Why can't I be like a normal teenager? I want to put posters of singers and all that on my room wall,* J.D. said in frustration. She turned her R&B music up loud and drove off with a smile in her light pink IvyKennington.

Emory called J.D. She quickly turned her music down. She glanced at her phone as she was driving. *Ooh,* as her heart was beating fast, *I thought that my mom was calling me! Whew!* "Hey Hun," said J.D. as she answered the phone.

"Hey, are you gone yet?" asked Emory.

"I just left home," said J.D.

"Ok cool," said Emory. "I am about to leave the car wash with my mom. I was just checking to see how far everyone was from the harbor. I'm at the car wash downtown anyway, so I'm like 10 minutes away," said Emory.

"Yeah, I'm like 20 minutes away," said J.D. "I just got on Lake Shore Drive."

"Cool," said Emory. "I'll see you in a sec."

J.D. turned her music back up and enjoyed the beautiful lake scenery on the side of the expressway.

Emory went to check out her car from the car wash. The washers pulled her and her mom's car up at the same time. "Ooh, hunny," her mom said. "Your car looks so pretty. They did a great job!"

"Yeah, they did," Emory said as she walked around her car to check how clean it was.

"Ok, mom, I have to go! Dad is supposed to be at the yacht at 11! And you know how Dad is about being late!"

"Ok hunny, yes, make sure you get there on time," her mom smiled. Emory kissed her mom and hugged her. "See you later," Emory said. "Love you!"

"Love you too," her mom said.

"Oh Emory!" her mom yelled to catch her attention as she jumped in her car.

"Yes, Mom?"

"Tell your dad, I love him."

Emory and her mom laughed together. "I will," said Emory. She put on a second coat of her iridescent lipgloss and drove off in her light blue IvyKennington. *I should let the top down but I don't want to mess my hair up,* she thought. *I really wish that I could have told my mom about that dream I had last night. I saw all these snakes in a pool of water with me while I was having fun in the water. She would probably say it's nothing anyway. She'd probably just tell me to pray,* she thought with feelings of disappointment. *Maybe, I can try and tell Dad?* she wondered. *Maybe not, he'd probably tell me to just be careful of who I'm hanging around. Ugh,* she sighed.

Emory pulled into the harbor and saw all of the girls' cars in the parking lot. Everyone got out of their cars to hug one another. "You guys ready?" asked Emory. "We have to move fast because it's almost 11," said Emory.

"Girl, I can't walk that fast," said Fah'ry. "I got these heels on! These rocks all in my shoes!" Fah'ry kicked the rocks out of her sandals as they walked up the wooden dock to board the boat.

"You should have worn flats," said J.D.

"Yea, but me and Chaston supposed to go to the show after dis," said Fah'ry.

"Oh, what are you all going to see?" asked Brooke.

"I think we are going to see that new fashion documentary."

"Oh yeah, that's right!" said J.D. "I want to see that too! It came out Friday."

"Maybe we can go tonight," said Emory.

"Yeah, tonight is the only time that we have to go," said Brooke. "Our plane leaves early in the morning for London."

"Well, let's go tonight," said J.D.

"Y'all wrong," said Fah'ry.

"You can go!" said Emory. "You'll have to just be watching it twice."

"I'm cool with dat," said Fah'ry. "What time y'all talkin about?"

"Like 7," J.D. said. "I think that's a good time? That way, we still have time to get rest for that long flight in the morning," said J.D.

"That works for me," said Emory.

"Yea, I'll meet y'all there," said Fah'ry.

The girls walked upstairs to the top deck of the yacht and took their seats at the bar style table. *Ooh wee,* Fah'ry thought as she sat on the bar stool. *Why do I keep itching down there,* she thought, *this is really irritating.*

OB/Gyne Fears

Ever since I left that retreat, I've been itching, Fah'ry said as she sat on the stool at the breakfast bar. *I think I'ma have to go to the doctor,* she thought as her mind wandered while the other girls were laughing and talking at the table. *Ugh!* she said while squirming in her seat. She tried to stay engaged in the conversation with her friends. Fah'ry laughed. "I know right," she said. *I have no idea what they talkin bout,* she thought. "Huh?" Fah'ry said.

"What kind of latte do you want?" asked Emory.

"Oh, the mint is fine," said Fah'ry.

"I am so excited to use this new machine that my dad bought me!" said Emory. "I can make 6 flavors of latte at the same time!"

"Girl, you need to think about opening a coffee shop," said Fah'ry. Emory passed the girls their pink tumblers filled with her specially made lattes. Fah'ry took a sip. "Girl, this is gooood! It tastes just like Pink Java!"

J.D. sipped out of her tumbler. She took her time and enjoyed the flavor. "Yes hun, this vanilla bean is really good."

"Why, thank you," Emory said while washing her hands at the sink on the top deck of the yacht. Emory sat down with the girls and drank her latte.

"What kind did you make?" asked Brooke. "This one is a white chocolate with a little mint," said Emory.

"Ooh that sounds gooood!" all the girls said together.

"You are a true Barista," said Brooke. "It comes so natural to you. You should really think about the coffee shop idea," said Brooke.

"Aw, thank you!" said Emory. "I never thought about it. I just love making them." She moved her pink tumbler aside to make room as the chef brought out the girls' plates. "Breakfast for the ladies!" the chef said while putting each girl's plate in front of them.

"Mmm, smells good," said Emory.

"Yes! The omelette is so fluffy," J.D. said.

"Thank you, Chef," said Emory.

"You are welcome," he said. "Enjoy," he said as he gave a subtle nod of respect.

The girls placed the cloth napkins on their laps.

"Emory, are you praying or should I?" asked J.D.

"You can," said Emory.

"Lord, we thank you for this food. We ask that this food be nourishing and strengthening to our bodies. We ask that you purify this food and bless the hands that prepared it. In Jesus' Name, Amen."

"Amen!" the girls said.

"Ooh, I always get these forks mixed up," said Fah'ry.

"Yeah," Brooke said while eating her fluffy ham and cheese omelette. "I just try to remember that the deeper fork is the salad fork and the other one is the entree fork," said Brooke.

"That's a good way to remember, hun," said J.D. as she cut her pancakes.

"Yeah, that is," said Fah'ry as she removed the strawberries from the top of her pancakes.

"You remember that stuff from that etiquette class? I remember where to place the napkin when I am done and how to eat the soup right," smirked Fah'ry "but those forks be looking the same."

Brooke smirked. "Yeah, I remember. That was one of my favorite after-school classes at St. Martin."

"Awww, you're going to make me cry," said J.D. "I miss St. Martin already."

"I don't!" said Fah'ry. They all laughed together.

"I'm sure," said Emory. "Hahaha, you and Sister Catherine were so close!!"

"Yea, she got on my nerves," said Fah'ry. "She always was watching my socks!"

"Hahaha," laughed the girls. "Sock watcher!"

"I hated those hot knee socks," said Fah'ry. "It's like she looked for me everyday just to check to see if my socks were down."

"Yeah," Brooke laughed. "It did seem like she was looking for you."

"It would have been cool if we didn't have to wear those uniforms," said Fah'ry. "I hated all those vests, skirts and sweaters everyday. I mean, really, did we have to wear the same thing everyday?! And, we all looked alike, wearing the same clothes," said Fah'ry with sass.

"Yeah, wearing the same thing as everyone in an all girl school was too much," said J.D. with her fork in her hand. "They could have given us some free uniform days or something."

"I know! That would have helped." said Fah'ry with sass while sipping her latte.

The chef walked up to the breakfast bar. "Are you ladies done?" he asked.

"Yes," the girls said as they sat back in their stools for the chef to reach their plates.

"Thank you, Chef," they said.

"My pleasure," he said with his normal subtle head nod. "Are you all ready for your London trip?"

"I think so," said Emory. "Any suggestions? I know that's your hometown," said Emory.

"Well, you ladies love fashion," he said with the plates in his hand. "You must visit Oxford St," said the chef. "You all will love it! I know that you all love to shop."

The girls smiled and at the same time, they replied. "Oh yeah!!"

"I can't wait," said J.D. "When I was researching, it did say that London was one of the Big Four fashion capitals in the world."

"Oh, and don't forget to get pictures in front of Buckingham Palace!" the chef said. "Take a lot of pictures and be careful young ladies," he admonished them with his strong accent.

"We will!!" they said with huge smiles. "Thank you, Chef."

"I will see you all when you come back," he said as he began to walk off with their plates.

"Oh no, Chef!" Emory said as she thought about what he said. "After the trip, we will be leaving for Brighton!"

"Well, I guess I'll see you ladies on the first college break!" he said with a smile. "Enjoy your first year of college! That's an order," he said.

"Hahaha, thank you Chef!!" they said as they took their sandals off.

"I heard that Oxford St. has every store you can think of!" said Fah'ry.

"Yes, that's true," said J.D. "It's like a mile long. It's the biggest shopping district in London," said J.D.

"I am so ready," said Emory. "I talked to my aunt yesterday and she said that she will meet us at the airport."

"You never gave me her number," said Fah'ry. "I need to give it to Chaston tonight when we go to the show."

Emory grabbed her phone off of the table and started typing. "I just sent it to you," said Emory.

"I can't wait to go to see the Royal Ballet!" said Brooke.

"Yeah, I think that's going to be nice," said J.D. "I've always wanted to go to the Royal Ballet."

"Yeah, I pulled up some stuff on the Art Musuem there, I really want to see Aubrie Donovan's work," said Fah'ry. "Her style of abstract art is amazing!"

"I saw that Musuem as one of London's top tourist attractions," said J.D.

Here she goes, thought Brooke. *She has the answers to everything.* "Fah'ry, I'm glad that you found that Fashion & Finance internship," said Brooke.

"Yea, my Fashion League teacher had some great things to say about it," said Fah'ry. "She was able to get us the last slots for the summer internship."

"I'm excited about it," said Emory. "They have a Chemistry and Beauty track. I can't wait! I ordered my books already."

"Me too, hun!" said J.D. "I picked the Pattern and Color Design track of study. The University of Fashion at London is a prestigious school of fashion. How did your instructor get us in Fah'ry?"

"It is. She is friends with the person over the internship admission committee," said Fah'ry.

"Well, I'm happy that your Fashion League instructor had favor," said Emory.

"Yea, I'm glad that my dad paid the money to put me in it," said Fah'ry. "I thought that he was going to say no because of how much it costs but he paid for it," said Fah'ry. "I love it. The Fashion League has taught me so much. My instructor said dat when I come back from London, I'll be ready for my own line of clothes. She said that if I do well in the internship, I should be well prepared." She pulled on her curly hair as she was talking. "All my clothes are packed and I'm ready to go!!"

"I know, right," said Brooke.

I don't know how I am going to do this, J.D. thought. *How am I going to leave my mom for the entire summer?* she pondered as she looked through her bag for her sun tan lotion. She started to rub it on her arms. "It's starting to get hot on this top deck," said J.D.

"Yeah, the sun is at its peak," said Emory. "We can go downstairs to the tv room if you all want."

"The breeze is nice but this sun is hot," said Fah'ry. She walked over to the corner to look over into the water and saw a slide starting at the top deck and spiraling around into the water. "Ooh, when did y'all get dis slide?" asked Fah'ry while peeking over the rails.

"That's the surprise!" said Emory. "I was hoping that you all didn't see it until after breakfast!" The girls ran over to look at the new slide that was connected to the yacht.

"This is the perfect day to go for a swim," said J.D. "but we don't have swimsuits!"

"No worries," said Emory. "My mom and I went shopping for swimsuits for everyone last night. I got everyone's favorite color in different styles," said Emory. "We can go to the tv room, they are laying on the bed."

"Are you serious?!" said Fah'ry. "The first hot day in Chicago and we are going swimming in the Lake! Dis is supa cool!"

"Yeah, I talked my dad into getting the slide," said Emory as the girls were walking downstairs to the bottom room on the yacht.

"Ooh, this is too cute!!" said Fah'ry as she picked up her yellow polka dot swimsuit.

"Yes hun, this pink one is gorgeous," said J.D. as she held her swimsuit in the air to get a better look at it.

"Purple and pink plaid!" said Brooke as she put the high waisted boy shorts up to her waist to measure the size. "Thank you, friend," said Brooke.

"Yes, thanks hun!" J.D. said.

"This is so sweet Emory," said Fah'ry.

"I figured, let's have some fun. High school is over," said Emory. "I'll be right back. I need to tell my dad that he can drop the anchor. This is a good place on the lake for us to swim," said Emory.

"How deep is the water?" asked Brooke.

"It's like 20 feet," said J.D.

"Um, I'm not getting in that much water," said Brooke. "The slide looks fun, but I'm not sliding in water that deep."

"Come on," said Fah'ry. "It's not that bad. You'll float right back up."

"Yeah hun," said J.D. "We will all be right there."

"Nooo thank you," said Brooke. "I am not getting on that slide. That's too much water," she said as she sat on the couch.

Emory walked back in the room. "Ok, everything is all set. My dad lowered the anchor," said Emory.

"Brooke, why aren't you getting dressed?"

"Um, that water is too deep," said Brooke.

"Awww, come on Brooke."

"Nope, I can't do it."

I told her we will be right there," said J.D.

"Yeah," said Emory, "it's really fun."

"I'll pass," said Brooke with a serious face.

"Well, ok, if you want, you can still hang out on the deck and relax on the recliner by the top of the slide," said Emory.

"Cool, I'll do that," said Brooke.

"That way, you'll still get to wear your swimsuit," said Emory.

"I think your phone is ringing," said J.D.

"Mine?" Emory said with a puzzled look. Emory went to pick up her phone from off of the bed. "Well, it stopped," she said. "I'll see who it was once I change."

"I'll be back," said Fah'ry. "I'm going to change into my swimsuit." She went in the bathroom to change. *It's not itching as bad as it was but I know I have to go to the gynecologist,* she thought, *I can't keep waiting. I'm just so scared of that doctor,* she thought. *I have never been and I heard the girls at school say that it hurts. I don't want the doctor all in my personal. What if it's a man? What if they make me not a virgin anymore? I'm so scared,* she thought as she folded her yellow shorts up in her bag. *I thought Pap smears were for girls having sex? Ugh!*

Fah'ry walked back to the tv room where the girls were getting ready. "Where can I put my clothes Emory?" asked Fah'ry.

"You can put them on the bed or couch," said Emory. Fah'ry placed her folded clothes on the couch and put her flip flops on.

"Are you all ready? Emory asked.

"Almost," said J.D., "I need help with this halter top," as she tried to fix the straps herself.

"I'll help, I'm done getting ready," said Emory. She walked over to J.D. and stood behind her to help tighten her straps. "What happened to your back?!!" asked Emory. "Why do you have this big bandage on your back friend??" Emory asked with much concern.

Oh shoot, J.D. thought as her heart raced. *I forgot about this stupid scar,* she thought.

"Oh, I was rearranging my closet and I forgot to push the box back and when I was putting clothes on the bottom rack, the box fell on my back," said J.D.

"Oh ok," Emory said as all the girls paused to hear J.D.'s explanation.

"Yeah," J.D. said, "I tried to stack too many boxes up there."

"It looks like it hurts," said Emory.

"It's not that bad," said J.D.

She went to the mirror to put her pink cover-all over her swimsuit. "Ok, I am ready," said J.D. The girls walked out of the room and back upstairs to the deck in their pretty swimsuits, flip flops and towels on their arms.

I wish I had good hair like Fah'ry, Brooke thought as she watched Fah'ry twist her hair in a bun so easily. *She looks so pretty with curly hair,* she thought. *I would look so much better with good hair. I wish I was mixed. I mean, Fah'ry doesn't have any naps in the back. But, her skin is not the prettiest. She has spots on her back and neck,* she thought.

"Ooh," said Fah'ry as they all entered the deck, "It is supa hot in this sun."

"I wish I had my sunglasses," said J.D. "We have to protect our eyes from the UB Rays from the sun."

"Girl, you always researching something," said Fah'ry. "You need to be a lawyer!"

J.D. smirked, "A lawyer! Nah, I'm too quiet for that," said J.D.

The girls placed their towels and items on the recliner chairs and walked to the entry to the slide. They started to laugh and look down at how far down the slide goes. ". . . Who's going first?" asked Emory while laughing.

"You can!" laughed J.D.

"It's your boat!! Hahaha," laughed Brooke as she sat on the recliner. "I know you all are not scared!! 'It's only 20 feet of water,'" she mocked their words.

"I'll go!!" said Fah'ry. "I ain't scared!"

"Ok, wait, let me grab my phone to take a picture," said Emory.

Fah'ry stood at the top of the slide. "Oh geez!" she said. "I'm not going to look down!"

The girls were laughing hysterically as they watched Fah'ry. "Gone head hun," J.D. yelled with lots of giggles.

The music changed on the deck to one of Fah'ry's favorite songs. "Oh that's my song!" said Fah'ry. "Turn that up!!" she said loudly. "I'm ready now!" she said with excitement. Fah'ry sat down and went down the spiral slide and plunged into the lake. "Ooh wee!!" Fah'ry yelled. "This wata is cold!" The girls looked down and laughed with Fah'ry. "Come on y'all!" Fah'ry yelled up top as she swam.

"Ok, I'm going," said Emory. She sat at the edge of the slide and pushed herself down the spiral slide. "Woo Hoo!" she screamed as she went round and round until she dropped into the water. "Wow!" she laughed as she cleared the water from her eyes.

"I told you it was fun," said Fah'ry as she swam over to Emory.

"Come on J.D.!" they yelled as they kicked their feet to stay afloat.

"Ok, here I commme!" J.D. screamed as she plunged into the water. "This is so fun," said J.D. The girls swam and splashed water on each other for hours.

Brooke watched from over the deck and laughed with them from afar. She controlled the music and laid back in the seat and enjoyed the lake breeze. She took pictures of the girls and all of the beautiful boats and yachts that passed by.

"Hi!!" The girls said to the people on a small sailboat passing by.

"Emory, your phone is ringing!" Brooke yelled.

"Who is it?" Emory yelled.

"I don't know, it doesn't have a name," said Brooke.

"Ok, here I come," said Emory. "Answer it!" she yelled to Brooke. Emory got out of the water and started to dry off. Brooke answered Emory's phone. "It's Bryce!" Brooke yelled.

"Ok ok ok," Fah'ry yelled from the water.

J.D. laughed at Fah'ry while swimming.

Emory giggled, "Y'all stop!" She walked up to the top deck to take the call. "Hello," Emory said with butterflies in her stomach.

"Hi Emory," he said.

"Hi Bryce."

"What's going on?" he asked.

"Nothing much, just hanging out with my friends on my dad's yacht." Her voice trembled and she took a hard swallow.

"Your dad's yacht?" he asked as one who is impressed. "So you are a princess huh?" he said as he chuckled and spoke.

She giggled. *Ooh it's hot,* she thought.

"Well I was calling to see what you were doing tonight?"

"Um, I don't think I'm doing anything," she said while walking to the deck railing.

"Did you want to go to the movies?" he asked.

"Sure, that's fine," Emory said as her heart beat fast and her palms started to sweat.

"Tonight is the best time anyway," she said. "I'm leaving for London in the morning for the summer," she said.

"Oh London," he said with disappointment in his voice.

"Yeah, our flight leaves at 6 am."

"Oh, so why are you going there?" he asked.

"My friends and I are going for a Fashion & Finance internship," Emory said.

"That's cool," said Bryce in a charming voice. "I'm sure that will be enlightening. So, you're into fashion huh?" asked Bryce.

"Yeah, we love fashion."

"So are you staying in a hotel or something?" he asked.

"No, my aunt lives in London. We will be staying with her," Emory said.

"That's nice, no hotel costs!" said Bryce.

"Yeah, I'm really excited! We've been counting down the days to leave."

"Make sure you get pictures of Buckingham Palace and go on Oxford St." he said.

"You've been?" she asked with surprise.

"Yeah, my team and I went in high school. It's a cool country. I didn't want to leave."

"Aww, you're making me excited!" Emory said in a sweet voice.

"So how about you?" she asked. "What are your plans for the summer?"

"Oh, I'll be back and forth from Cali. I have to be at Brighton for basketball training."

"Sounds like work," said Emory.

Bryce chuckled, "Sort of." The Conversation went silent for a brief moment. "Did you want me to pick you up tonight?" asked Bryce.

"Its ok, we can meet at the movies," she said. "I'll probably be out and about."

"Cool, I'll meet you at 7. We can decide then, what we will see," said Bryce.

"That's fine," Emory said. "Well, I'll see you then,"

"I'll call you when I get to the parking lot," Bryce said.

"Ok, I'll talk to you later," Emory said.

"Absolutely," said Bryce.

Emory hung up the phone and took a deep breath. *I can't believe he called,* she thought to herself.

"Dang!!!" Fah'ry said. "Y'all was on da phone for a long time."

The girls laughed as they sat on the recliners and drank icy lemonade.

"Sooo, what did he say hun?" asked J.D.

"He asked me to go to the movies tonight," said Emory. "We are supposed to go at seven. I'm going to meet him there," she said.

"Wait, we are supposed to be going to the movies tonight at seven, remember?" said J.D.

"Oh." Emory put her hand on her head, "I totally forgot, I am so sorry!"

"It's alright," said J.D. "Just have fun."

"Yea, we'll be together all summer," said Fah'ry.

"That's true," said Brooke.

"I had so much fun," said Fah'ry.

"Yeah, me too," said J.D.

"I was a little scared in that watah dough," said Fah'ry. "I kept feeling like a shark was going to come and get us!"

The girls started to laugh at Fah'ry. "Girl, ain't no sharks in that water," said Emory as she smirked.

"It was fun dough!" said Fah'ry. "I have to get ready to go so I can meet Chaston for this movie. But I will see y'all tonight for the movies too," Fah'ry said. She gathered her things to prepare to change.

I really need to tell her, thought Brooke. *Am I really a good friend to keep this from Fah'ry?* thought Brooke.

"It looks like my dad is pulling in anyway, so I guess we will all be leaving," said Emory. The girls gathered their things and walked down stairs to the television room to take showers and change into their clothes.

"J.D., your bandage came off," said Brooke. "Ooh, that is a really bad cut," Brooke said.

"We have some bandages in the bathroom, I'll show you where they are," said Emory.

"Ok thanks," said J.D. *Please don't let them ask me anything else about this scar,* J.D. thought.

The girls showered and got dressed to leave the yacht as Emory's dad pulled into the dock. "Are you all ready?" Emory asked after all of the girls had showered and were dressed.

"Yup," they said.

Emory's dad came out of the steering room of the yacht. "Hi girls," he said. "Did you all have a great time?"

"Yes!" they said all together.

"It was awesome," J.D. said.

"Yes, it was amazing," said Fah'ry.

"Yes, thanks Dad," Emory said.

"Yes, thank you," said Brooke.

"Not a problem," he said. "Don't forget, we will be having prayer in the morning before you all leave for London."

"Okay," they said all together. The girls said bye to each other as they walked off the dock and to their cars.

Ooh that was close, thought J.D., *I almost forgot about that scar,* as she got in her car. *I am kind of glad that we are going to the movies tonight, I really don't want to go home,* thought J.D.

Brooke pulled off to go back to the hotel. *Really should have got in the water,* Brooke thought. *They looked like they were having so much fun. I wish I could go home. I really want to talk to my mom,* she thought as she drove.

I need to call this doctor, Fah'ry thought as she let the top down on her car. *I am so scared but I half to push my self to go to this doctor's office. I just don't know what's going to happen! I mean, how big is that thing that everybody talks about that the doctor puts in you,* she thought.

I can't wait to tell my mom that Bryce called me and that we are going out tonight, Emory thought as she helped her dad close up the yacht.

Fah'ry was on her way to the doctor's office and her phone rang. "Hey Brooke," she said.

"Hey," said Brooke. "I have to tell you something. Please don't be mad at me," said Brooke. "Do you remember when we were at the retreat?"

"Yea," said Fah'ry as she tried to brace herself for what Brooke had to say. Brooke paused. "What is it?" asked Fah'ry as she got closer to the doctor's office.

"Ok, so remember when you were talking about Chaston going on prom with that other girl and you didn't know," said Brooke.

"Um yea," said Fah'ry as her heart pounded. She turned her music down to listen.

"Well, I knew that he went. Josh told me that his cousin saw him at prom with her."

"Huh?" said Fah'ry.

"I know, I'm so sorry," said Brooke. "I really wanted to say something but Josh told me not to get in the middle," said Brooke with sincerity. "I wanted to say something so bad. Please don't be mad?" asked Brooke.

Fah'ry sat in silence to really think about what she was saying.

"Ok," said Fah'ry.

"Are you going to be ok?" Brooke asked her.

"Yea," Fah'ry said as she walked into the doctor's office. "I will call you back," said Fah'ry.

"Ok," said Brooke.

I can't believe her, Fah'ry thought to herself. Her heart felt betrayed but she was trying not to think about it. *I have enough to think about. I don't know what's wrong with me and my health. I don't know what this doctor is about to do in there,* she thought. She walked up to the front desk to sign in. She took a seat and waited to be called. Her hands were shaking as she tried to look at magazines to ease her mind. The nurse opened the door.

"Fah'ry Kanary," the nurse said into the waiting room.

Fah'ry got up and walked with the nurse to the exam room. *Oh help me Lord,* she thought.

"You can have a seat right here," said the nurse. She gave Fah'ry a gown. "You can change into this," she said. "Please take everything off. Both top and bottom underwear," the nurse said.

"Ok," Fah'ry said as she held the gown in her hand.

"The doctor will be with you shortly," she said. The nurse left out of the room and closed the door quietly.

Fah'ry started to change into her gown. *They want me to take off all of my clothes,* she thought as her legs shook. *They could have at least let me keep my bra on.* She sat on the exam table with her gown on. *It is freezing in here,* she thought while rubbing her arms. *Please hurry up! I am ready to get this over with.* Her short brown legs dangled off of the exam table. She kept taking deep breaths. "Ugh, this is taking forever!" she sighed. Suddenly, there was a little knock at the door. "Come in," said Fah'ry.

"Hi there, I'm Dr. Patel."

"Hi, I'm Fah'ry." After that the doctor started to ask her questions about her health and sexual activity. "No," said Fah'ry to the question about her being sexually active. "No," Fah'ry said to the question about her ever having sexual intercourse.

"Ok," The doctor said as she asked her final questions. "So, what brings you in today?"

"Well, I used this body wash and I've been itching ever since."

"Ok, let's take a look." The doctor reclined the exam table. "Ok, place each foot on the stirrup on each side," Dr. Patel said. Fah'ry's legs shook out of control. "Is everything ok?" Dr. Patel asked her. "Just relax your legs."

"I'm just nervous," said Fah'ry. "This is my first time."

"I understand, it's Ok," said the doctor as she put on plastic gloves. "I don't think that I will have to do an internal exam but we will see," said Dr. Patel.

"Um and," said Fah'ry. "I was molested by my uncle, so this is very scary."

The doctor stood up from her chair to listen to Fah'ry. "It is ok," said Dr. Patel. "I understand. I hear many stories like this all the time," she said. "This will be over in no time. Just relax and think about something good," she said.

"Ok," said Fah'ry as her voice trembled. The doctor started the exam.

"Yes," she said as she took a look. "I don't need to do an internal exam."

Whew, Fah'ry thought.

"It looks like you were just irritated from the body wash," said Dr. Patel. "In the future, do not use those scented body washes and soaps on feminine areas. They were not made for that. Companies just make money off of creating all of those scented soaps. All you need to do is use regular bar soap with as little scent as possible," Dr. Patel said. She started to show Fah'ry how to properly wash herself. "Ok and I am all done," she said with a soft voice. She took her gloves off and threw them in the garbage. "Did you have any more questions or concerns?" she asked.

"No, thank you so much," said Fah'ry.

"Oh, you are welcome," said Dr. Patel. "Be sure to schedule a follow up with the receptionist for next year. I'll need to see you every year for your annual check-up from now on," Dr. Patel said with care. "You can leave the gown on the table and the nurse will get it. Have a wonderful day," she said as she walked out of the door.

"Thank you, you too," said Fah'ry. She quickly changed back into her clothes. *Whew, thank U God. Let me hurry up and get out of here,* said Fah'ry.

Fah'ry got in the car and called her mom. "Hey ma," she said. "I just left the doctor."

"You just left the doctor," her mom said with a mean tone.

"Yea, I was itching in my private area . . ."

"What do you mean you were itching?!" her mom said in a scolding voice. "So, you are out there having sex, huh! And now you have caught something," her mom said.

"No, I'm not having sex," said Fah'ry. "I used some fruity body wash at the retreat and it irritated me."

"Uh huh, whatever Fah'ry. I got to go," she said. Her mom hung up the phone quickly.

I can't believe that she just accused me of having sex like I'm all out here, thought Fah'ry with hurt in her heart. She turned her music up and drove off to meet Chaston for their date. *I can't wait to leave for London tomorrow,* she thought. *I won't haf to deal with that house at all.* She drove for a while and was soothed by the music. She picked up her phone to call Chaston.

"What's up," he said as she heard a lot people in the background.

"Um, are you on your way?" she said.

"On my way where?" he said nonchalantly. "Chaston," she said as her heart dropped, "why are you acting like this?" she asked. "We are supposed to be going to the show."

"Oh," he said as he laughed and talked to the people in the background. "I'm not going to be able to make it," he said as he slurped on a drink and laughed and played on the other end. "I have something else to do today," Chaston said.

Fah'ry tried to listen hard on the other end. She heard the sound of girls around him. "Who is dat?" she asked.

"Nobody," he said.

"Well, you know that I am leaving in the morning," she said with slight tears in her eyes.

"Yeah, I know," he said. "Aye, I don't want to do this anymore," he said.

"What do you mean, Chaston?"

"I don't want to be in this relationship anymore," he said with no feeling.

"Why? What is wrong?" asked Fah'ry as she started to cry. "What did I do?" she cried and pleaded. "What ever it is, we can make it better. We can work this out!" she said in a crying voice. "We have been together for too long to let this go now," she said.

"Nah, Fah'ry. I just don't want to be in a relationship with you anymore," he said with no feeling.

"What did I do to you??" asked Fah'ry.

"Nothing really," he said. "We have been together for so long and all I know is you," he said. "I want to know what it's like without you."

"And what does that mean Chaston!!" she said with anger.

"Like I said, I am done," Chaston said. Fah'ry sat on the phone in silence as she was shocked. "Fah'ry," he said, "I gotta go."

"Ok," she said. She hung up the phone and cried non-stop. She tried to concentrate on the road as she drove. *God, I can't believe this! I need him! Please don't let this happen?* she said. *He is all that I have. No one else cares about me.* She drove to the lake front and parked her car. She just sat there and all types of thoughts came to her mind. *I can't make it without him,* she thought. Her phone rang and she quickly looked at it thinking that it was Chaston calling to change his mind. *That's just J.D.,* she thought as she looked at her phone. She ignored the call and turned her phone off.

Why is Fah'ry not answering? J.D. thought. She always answers her phone. J.D. called back and the phone went right to the voicemail. *That's really weird,* J.D. thought. *Maybe her battery is dead, I know she said that they were going to the movies. I will try her again in a little bit,* she thought. J.D.'s mom walked in her room and sat down on her bed.

"Hey Mom," J.D. said.

"We need to talk before you leave," she said.

"Ok," said J.D. as she turned from her computer to listen to her mom.

"J.D. I love you so much." Her mom said with watery eyes. J.D. started to get scared. "I just want you to know that if anything was to ever happen to me, I love you," her mom said with tears in her eyes.

"What's wrong Mom? Why are you saying this?"

"Things are getting really bad between us and I don't know what he will do," said her mom. "I also wanted to tell you that I am pregnant," her mom said. J.D. just stared at her mom's face as tears rolled down J.D.'s face.

Ooh! I Can't Wait to Leave for College!
I Hate this House!

A baby! J.D. thought to herself. *This is crazy! Now we are really stuck in this mess. I am about to go to college and she's about to have a baby. I've been the only child all of this time,* J.D. thought. She tried to cover her tears as her mom sat on the bed.

"Before you leave for London, make sure all of the laundry in the house is done, the bathroom is cleaned, the dishes are washed and scrub that living room floor rug," said her mom. "Oh, and when you are done, the grocery list is on the counter, go to the grocery store in

Hyde Park . . . and stop at the bank and deposit these checks. You can take my car because I want you to stop at the car wash and put my clothes in the cleaners," her mom commanded.

"Ok," said J.D. with furious emotions in her heart. She started to sort the two big bags of clothes to prepare them for the washer. *I'm supposed to go to the movies tonight,* she thought to herself. *How am I going to finish all of this?*

She went to her mom. "Mom," she said. "I'm supposed to go to the movies tonight."

"Ok, so what are you saying?" her mom asked.

"Do I have to finish tonight? she asked with hesitation to avoid sounding disrespectful and challenging.

"Well, you're not going to be able to do it all tonight anyway," her mom said. "The bank is closed and so is the car wash." J.D. stood there listening with anger.

"Ok," J.D. said. "Mom, my flight leaves for London early in the morning. "I know," her mom said quickly. "So, you'll need to get up early enough and plan to get it done before you leave," she said.

"Ok," J.D. said as she tried to keep a straight face and not roll her eyes. J.D. went back to preparing the laundry. *So I'm supposed to get up and do this before I leave,* she thought, *Ugh,* as she threw the clothes in the basket in frustration.

She started to think and plan how she could get all of the commands done before she left. *I'll just get up at 4 in the morning to go to the grocery store, drop the clothes off at the cleaners,* she thought . . . *and then go to the bank, they should be open by then,* J.D. thought. *I'll bring the groceries home and put them up before the milk and meat gets warm. I'll just go back out to the car wash and I should be back in enough time to get to Emory's house for prayer before our flight leaves,* she thought. *And I'll finish this laundry before I go to the movies, then I will just fold the clothes when I come back tonight, wash the dishes and scrub the rug last. That way, it will be dry by the morning,* she strategized in her mind as she struggled to carry the heavy laundry basket to the elevator of her high-rise building.

"I hate this!" J.D. mumbled. "She could at least do some of this stuff. I hate this building! She thinks that this building is nice just because we live on the lake and can see the water from our windows. Shoot, this ain't nothing but the projects," she ranted. "How does she make all of this money and choose to live here. How can you be a doctor and marry a man with a high school diploma? And a crackhead at that," she grumbled as she put the clothes in the washer. *All these project people in here! This is just a fancy project! Look at these little bars on these windows! Projects!! I'm tired of these girls in here saying that I think I'm all that and I think I live in a penthouse! Ugh! And how many times is he going to overdose on drugs and she take him back! I'm glad I'm leaving for the summer and since she's pregnant, I guess they won't be fighting,* she thought.

"Ugh!!! What time is it? I need to get this crap done so I can go to the movies." *Now what is she doing while I'm doing all of this like a step daughter?? Nothing!! She gets to watch tv and chill until he calls and talks stupid and threatens to kill her. I'm tired of all of these orders of protection! They don't work, he just came and bust a big project door down and he had an order of protection on him then. That stuff don't work!!* she ranted. "Ugh!! He's an idiot! I hope he drops dead! I hate him! Ooh!!"

J.D. looked at her phone. Fah'ry hasn't called me back yet, she thought. That's weird. J.D. called Fah'ry again and there was no answer. J.D. left a message. "Hey hun, call me."

Fah'ry was still sitting in her car on the lakefront crying. "God please help me!" Fah'ry shouted in the confines of her car. She picked up her phone and saw several calls from J.D. *I just can't talk right now,* she thought to herself. I don't want them to know that I'm crying over him. She continued to cry. *They'll just say that I need to get over him. They don't understand. We have been together for 6 years. He's the only boyfriend I've ever had,* she thought as the tears rolled down her face. *I have been faithful to him. I have never cheated or given anybody else my numba. We were supposed to get married when we got older. I just can't do this,* Fah'ry thought with pain in her heart.

No one in my house cares about me. They don't pay attention to me. They can care less about what I'm doing. My mom is so busy getting her Ph.D., she doesn't have time for anything but those books. She's never home. Chaston is the only one that acted like he cared about me. Now, he's leaving. She put her hands on her head and leaned back in her car seat. Fah'ry picked up her phone and called Chaston again. *I know I shouldn't be chasing him but I need to know why he really just broke up with me,* she thought.

"Hello," Chaston said on the other line.

"Hello," Fah'ry said with a worn out voice from crying. "Chaston, what's wrong?"

"Nothing," he said as Fah'ry heard a loud movie playing in the background. Fah'ry heard the movie sound get lower and it sounded like he was walking.

"I mean, why are we breaking up?" she asked. "We can work things out," she pleaded.

"No Fah'ry, I don't want to," Chaston said with no care or concern about her feelings. "Let me get a large popcorn, two fruit punches and a bag of that candy," he said in the background of the phone call. Fah'ry's heart dropped as she heard him place an order for movie theater items.

I feel like I'm getting stabbed in the heart, she thought as the tears kept coming. "Chaston, we've been together for a long time. Why should we throw that away? We are going to college together," she said.

"Fah'ry, look," he said. "You ain't on nothing. I'm tired of waiting on you," he said. "You keep playing around and all you wanna do is kiss. I'm tired of all that," Chaston said. The movie sound got loud again. "I gotta go," he said in a low voice.

"Ok," Fah'ry said. Fah'ry just stared at the water in front of her, let her car seat back and thought. Her phone continued to ring as it got closer to the time that her and her friends were supposed to meet at the movies. A call from J.D. and then a call from Brooke. She looked at all of the calls but ignored them. She jumped at every call hoping that it was Chaston, but only to be let down. *He'll probably call me when he gets home and thinks about me,* she thought..

Brooke called J.D. "Hey hun," J.D. said.

"Hey, have you talked to Fah'ry? I keep calling her but she's not answering," said Brooke.

"No, I haven't talked to her either," said J.D. "I've been calling since earlier."

"Well, she was supposed to go to the movies with Chaston after we left the boat today," said Brooke. "You know how she gets when she's with Chaston," said Brooke.

"Yeah," J.D. smirked, that's true.

"Well, the movie starts at 7, so we might as well leave out," said J.D. "We tried to wait on Fah'ry to call."

"Yeah, well I'm leaving the hotel now," said Brooke.

"Ok, I'll leave out in like 10 minutes," said J.D. "I need to finish folding these last few clothes."

"Ok," said Brooke. "It looks like it's just us two anyway because Emory is going out with Bryce tonight," said Brooke.

"Oh, I totally forgot!" J.D. said. "Ok, let me finish this and I'm on my way."

"Ok that's fine, I'll meet you in the parking lot by the movie entrance."

"Ok, see you later."

Brooke got in her car and headed to the movies. *I really want to go home,* she thought. *I miss my mom. Maybe I should call? Nah, maybe not,* she thought. *I don't want to call and she says something to hurt my feelings.* She continued to drive and ponder while enjoying the Chicago summer breeze with her car top down. *I don't even know what I would say. What . . . I wanna come home?? I mean, she put me out. I didn't do anything,* she thought. *She should be calling me. Does she even care where I'm living? She hasn't even called to see how my graduation or prom went. I just want to go home at least before I go to London,* she thought. *Maybe I should? Should I be the bigger person?*

Brooke started dialing the numbers to her house and then hung up. *I can't do it.* She put her phone in her lap as she drove. *All she's going to do is say something to hurt my feelings. I think that prophecy that Apostle York gave about some people that were really close to me, I needed stay away from was talking about her. I don't know,* she thought. *Maybe it was someone else that he was talking about?? I'm going to just try.*

Brooke picked up the phone and called her mom. She took a deep breath and dialed. The phone started ringing and she became nervous. The phone rang a long time. I should hang up, Brooke thought. Her mom finally picked up the phone. "Hey Mom," Brooke said with hesitation and nervousness.

"Yeah Brooke," her mom said with an attitude. Brooke tried to ignore her mom's cold response. "I was just calling," Brooke said as she was lost for words.

"Ok," her mom said and there was a long period of silence.

"I'm leaving for London in the morning and I'll be gone all summer," said Brooke.

"Oh, ok Brooke," her mom said as she took a long loud sigh.

Really, Brooke thought to herself. *I guess I'm getting on her nerves.* ". . . Well, I was just calling to let you know that I was leaving," she said as her eyes watered.

"Ok Brooke," her mom replied.

"Ok," Brooke said and her mom hung up the phone. Brooke started to cry, *I will not be doing that again,* as she wiped her tears. She turned on music from one of her old cheer routines and reminisced about the times when her mom would come to her cheer practices and competitions. She started to smile and subtly do the old cheer moves as she drove. "Aye!!" she said as she turned her music up louder. She started to drive faster and enjoy the ride.

J.D. pulled into the movie parking lot. She grabbed her phone from the passenger seat and called Brooke.

"Hey," said Brooke.

"Hey hun," said J.D. "I am here."

"Ok, I'm pulling in now," said Brooke. She pulled into the movie parking lot in her light purple IvyKennington convertible. She swooped around the parking lot in each lane looking for J.D. "Where are you?" Brooke asked with one hand on the steering wheel and the other holding the phone to her ear.

"I'm right by this silver truck," said J.D.

"Oh, I see you," said Brooke as she hung up the phone. She sped into the parking space next to J.D.'s light pink convertible IvyKennington. They both let their car tops up and turned on their alarms.

"You look cute hun," said J.D. with her white collared shirt on, little dark denim shorts, leather brown belt and matching sandals and a light brown classic purse.

"Aw thank you," said Brooke. "So do you. I love those sandals! They are so classic," said Brooke in her summer dress and heeled sandals and her hair in a bun with a matching cheer bow. The girls walked towards the entrance.

"Aye!" A loud voice shouted behind them. "Aye shawty!!" The voices grew louder. J.D. and Brooke kept walking and ignored the guys behind them. The guys walked faster to catch up to them. "Shawty thick with them shorts on!" he shouted. They finally caught up to the girls. One guy on J.D.'s side and one guy on Brooke's side. "How you doin?" he said to J.D.

"I'm fine," J.D. said with sass as she continued to walk.

"Dang, you walkin fast," he said. "Can I call you sometime?"

"No," said J.D.

"Shawty mean joe!" he said to his friend that was talking to Brooke.

J.D. kept walking towards the movie door entrance while Brooke was giving the other guy her phone number in the parking lot. *I don't know why she always does this,* J.D. thought as she waited for her to finish. *Sometimes she acts so desperate. These dudes are stupid and they sound like they can't read.* Brooke caught up to J.D. and they walked in to purchase their movie tickets.

As they were walking towards the counter, they saw Chaston walking out of the theater with his arm around another girl.

"Um," said Brooke, "that's not Fah'ry," She stared in shock as they walked closer towards them laughing and cuddling as they walked.

"Oh and he's all in her face," said J.D.

Brooke picked up her phone to call Fah'ry.

"Hey Chaston," J.D. said to make her presence known.

"Oh, what's up J.D., what up Brooke," Chaston said as he kept his arm around the girl and walked off.

"She is still not answering," said Brooke with concern. "Why isn't she answering?

"Something is wrong," said J.D. The girls left the movie theater and jumped into their IvyKenningtons and headed to Fah'ry's house.

J.D. called Fah'ry again but there is no answer.

Fah'ry was still on the lakefront laying back in her car seat. She went from staring at clouds to staring at stars. She looked over at her phone and saw it ringing and ignored it. "I don't want to talk to nobody," said Fah'ry. *It's late and he still ain't called. I can't believe this!* She laid her head back and her mind wandered. *Maybe he'll call me in the morning after he sleeps on it,* she thought. "Lord help me!!!" she cried out loud. "I'm not going to be able to make it!!!"

Where is Fah'ry? (The Crisis)

J.D. and Brooke arrived at Fah'ry's house. They walked up the three little stairs to get to the front door. Brooke knocked on the door several times but there was no answer. "Oh, I forgot," said Brooke. "I have to knock on the window in order for someone to hear us," she said. Brooke knocked on the large window and walked back to the porch steps. J.D. walked around the corner to look for Fah'ry's car in her normal parking space. She walked back to the steps with Brooke.

"I don't see her car," said J.D. to Brooke with concern. Brooke knocked on the large front window a bit harder. The large burgundy door opened and Fah'ry's grandmother answered with a mean look on her face.

She just looked at Brooke and J.D. as she cracked the door open to hear them.

"Hello," J.D. and Brooke said together to her grandmother.

"Yea," her grandmother said.

"Um, is Fah'ry here?" asked J.D.

"Fah'ry ain't here," her grandmother said with a rude tone. "I ain't seen Fah'ry since dis mornin," she said.

"Oh ok," said Brooke. "Thank you! Can you tell her that we came by?"

"Ok," her grandmother said as she slammed the door. The girls walked off to go to their cars that were parked on the next street over.

"Girl, her grandma looks so mean," said Brooke.

"I know," said J.D.

"You know what?" said J.D. "I have never been in Fah'ry's house. Have you?"

"Um," said Brooke. "Now that I think about it, no," Brooke said with a confused look on her face. "Actually, now that I am thinking, even when we were little, she would always come to my house and play," said Brooke. "We would play on her back porch and backyard all the time. She had the biggest backyard in the neighborhood," said Brooke. "We used to make up dances and all of that on her back porch and played with our dolls but she never invited me in her house. Wow, I never thought about it until you asked," said Brooke.

"So, she didn't invite you to her sleepovers?" asked J.D.

"Well, um, the sleepovers were always at my house," said Brooke.

"Oh, ok," said J.D. as they arrived at their parked cars.

"I don't know where Fah'ry is," said J.D. with concern. "I hope that she is ok."

"Yeah," said Brooke. "It's not like her to not answer her phone. I know it has something to do with Chaston," said Brooke.

"Of course," said J.D. "Especially since we just saw him at the movies with another girl. She was supposed to be with him at the same time that we saw him."

"Yea, he is so wrong for that," said Brooke. "And then, he spoke to us like he didn't care if we told her."

"I know!" said J.D. "He had his arm around the girl and everything!"

"I can't believe him!"

"TRIFE!!"

"And Chaston is nottt that cute anyway!" said Brooke.

"Exactly!" said J.D. as they stood at their cars and talked.

A shiny silver car with loud music and sparkling tire rims pulled up beside them. "What's up SHAWTY," the guy yelled from the passenger window. J.D. continued to talk to Brooke and ignore them.

"Y'all some pretty girls, huh," he said. "Y'all look like some private school girls or somethin," he said with red eyes. Brooke snickered as she looked over at him. "Why you laughing," he said. "It must be true," he said as he smiled. "That's your pink car?" he asked Brooke.

"No, the purple one is mines," said Brooke.

"Yea, y'all some private school girls," he said as the car sat double parked." Aye, I need a good girl in my life," he said. "So what's up?" he said to Brooke. "Can I take you out?" He got out of the car to get closer to Brooke.

I can't believe this girl is talking to this thug, J.D. thought to herself. *Can't she see that he is high?!! Why is she wasting her time talking to a guy like this? He's not the type of guy that we would even consider having a conversation with,* J.D. thought. *I mean, I can smell the weed all the way over here!*

Brooke started to give the guy her phone number. "Aye," he said as he walked back to the car. Brooke turned towards him in the sleek silver car. "Y'all know that girl with the car like ya'll's?" he asked. He looked over at the driver to ask him about the car. "It's a yellow car," he said. "She parks over here all the time. He looked back at the driver to hear what he was telling him. "She got puffy curly hair," he said.

"Yeah, that's our friend Fah'ry," said Brooke. He turned to the driver. "Her name Fah'ry. My buddy be seeing her go in and out the house but she don't talk to nobody around here. I don't never see her even talking to or hanging with the girls over here," he said.

"Yeah," J.D. said as she giggled.

"Her mom doesn't allow her to hang out over here even though she lives around here," said Brooke.

"Oh she bougee huh," he said.

"No, not really," said Brooke. J.D. started her car to indicate that she was about to leave.

"I'm going to call you tonight," he said. "So answer yo phone." Brooke giggled and got into her car. "And tell yo girl Fah'ry, my guy said what's up."

Brooke smiled at him. "Yeah, ok," she said as she started her car and the guys drove off.

J.D. got back out of her car and walked to Brooke's car. "It is getting really late and I still have some things to do before we leave in the morning," said J.D. "I am about to go home and I will try to call Fah'ry again. Don't know what else to do."

"Yeah, I have a long ride to the hotel," said Brooke, "and I need to finish packing. I will keep trying to call as well."

"Cool, I will see you in the morning," said J.D. "Make sure that you call me when you get to your hotel room so that I know that you made it in safe."

"I will," Brooke said. "See you tomorrow." The girls pulled off in their pink and purple IvyKenningtons for the evening.

Meanwhile, Fah'ry was still sitting in her car on the lakefront. "I don't even feel like going home," Fah'ry said. *They don't care about me. I've been gone all day and it's 10 o'clock at night and no one has called to check on me. Why should I go home? My mom is probably studying at school or sleep. She ain't thinking about me. I need this time alone anyway. I feel much better by myself,* she thought. *Yeah, I'm going to stay right here. Let's see if someone calls and checks on me.* She turned her music on to love songs and lay back in her car seat.

She let the top up on her convertible and locked the doors. *I'm sure that Chaston will call me in the morning. He knows that I am leaving for London early. He's not going to let me leave for the summer without saying goodbye,* she thought. Her phone started to ring. *It's Brooke,* she said. *I just can't talk right now. I don't feel like trying to explain what happened and being looked at like I'm stupid for loving him. I just can't deal with that right now. I'll call her back when I'm on the way to Emory's house for prayer before our flight leaves.* Fah'ry's phone rang again. *It's J.D.,* she thought. She ignored the call and leaned her head back again in her car seat. *If I tell them that he broke up with me, they'll all have too much to say. I don't feel like the embarrassment,* she thought. *And all Emory is going to say is 'I told you'.* Fah'ry's phone rang again. *It's J.D.,* she said. *Should I answer it?* She decided to pick up the phone. "Hello," said Fah'ry.

"Hey hun," said J.D. "Are you OK? We've been trying to call you all day!"

"Yea, I'm fine," said Fah'ry.

"We went by your house tonight because we didn't know if something was wrong," said J.D. "Girl, where are you?"

"I'm just driving and thinking," said Fah'ry. "Oh ok," said J.D. "Well, I have something to tell you hun. It's not good but I wanted to tell you right away. Fah'ry's heart started to beat really fast. "What?" Fah'ry asked with anxiety in her heart. "What is it J.D.?"

"Well, when we were at the movies tonight, we saw Chaston there with another girl," J.D. said with sincerity. "They were all hugged up and everything." There was a brief moment of silence on the phone. Fah'ry's heart dropped immediately. *Don't even know what to say,* she thought to herself. *Wow, ok.*

Fah'ry said to J.D., "I'm about to call him right now! Let me call him right now!! He see y'all?"

"Actually, yeah, he spoke to Brooke and I while he was hugging the girl," said J.D.

Fah'ry started to sweat. "Oh ok," said Fah'ry with anger and embarrassment. "Let me call you back," she said as she rushed to get off of the phone.

"Ok, I'm sorry you had to hear something like this," said J.D.

"It's ok," said Fah'ry. "Just wait until I talk to him," she said. "I'll call you later," Fah'ry said as she hung up.

J.D.'s phone rang while she was doing the last of the chores at home.

"Hello", she said.

"Hi J.D.," Logan said.

"Hi," she said as she started to blush.

"So what's up?" he said. "What's been up with J.D.?"

She smirked, "Nothing much. Nothing much. Just getting ready to leave in the morning."

"Leave?" Logan said. "Yeah, my friends and I are leaving for London in the morning.

"Wow, really," he said. "How long will you be there?"

"We are spending the summer there for an internship at one of the fashion universities," she said.

"Oh," he said in amazement but disappointment. "That is cool, it sounds like you all will be having a nice summer."

"Yeah, we have been planning this trip since the beginning of the school year," she said.

"So, you're into fashion?" asked Logan.

"Yeah, I guess you can say that," said J.D. "I love matching and mixing colors as well as making different patterns and textiles."

"Really, that's different," Logan said.

"Yeah, so my internship will be focused more on pattern design and color creation. The cool part is that all of us were able to pick our own area of fashion interest within the internship. So, we will be together in the program but studying different aspects of fashion."

"Cool cool," said Logan. "So, are you studying fashion at Brighton?" he asked.

"No," she said. "I will be a biology major."

"Oh," he said.

"Yeah, I plan to go pre-med."

"So you're going to be a doctor huh," he said. "I'm impressed," he said in a calm and cool voice. They both laughed.

"Yeah, I would like to be a pediatrician. I should be able to do well and have a great starting path for internships and things like that because my mom is a doctor," she said.

"That's cool," he said. "What kind of doctor is your mom?"

"She is a neurologist."

"Oh, so she's working on people's brains huh?" he said.

"Yeah," J.D. giggled.

"So how weird is that?" Logan said.

"What do you mean?" asked J.D.

"Well, you said that you loved fashion but yet you are studying to be a doctor," he said.

"Oh, yeah, I just believe that there is no future in fashion. I mean no real future, where I would have stability and make a lot of money."

"I hear you but will you be happy being a doctor knowing that you love doing something else?" he asked. "Is money really everything?"

"Great question," said J.D. "I would love to do what I love but that's not going to pay the bills or allow me to have a stable life. I don't want to be poor. I hate poverty! If I pursued fashion, I feel like I would have to hustle to try to be successful with it," she said. "And I can't stand a hustler mentality."

"It sounds like you already have made up your mind," said Logan. "You make many great points but I am a firm believer also that if you do what you love and put your all in to it, you can be just as successful," he said with a convincing tone.

"That's true," she said. "It's a huge risk though. The chances of wasting money on a degree that will not really benefit you is highly likely," she said. "Didn't you hear Dr. Prink in the lecture hall at the retreat?" she asked.

"I did," he said.

"That's just one perspective though," he said with a strong stance.

J.D. started to think about what he was saying. "So, I saw your business card," she said. "What are you majoring in at Brighton?"

He chuckled, "I plan to major in political science and minor in Mandarin as a second language."

"A political science major?" she asked.

"Yeah, I plan to go to law school," he said.

"Oh nice!" said J.D.

Wow, a lawyer, she thought to herself.

"Yeah," he said in a boastful but playful way. They both shared another laugh together. "Seriously though, I would like to become a sports attorney. My plan is to represent professional athletes," Logan said. "So, we've been on the phone for a while tonight," he said. "I haven't heard your phone beep."

"What is that supposed to mean?" she said.

"I'm just saying, if you were my girl, I would be on the phone with you this late at night," he said. "So, since I haven't heard your phone beep, I'm assuming you don't have a guy or he's a horrible boyfriend," said Logan.

J.D. smirked, "Nooo, I don't have a boyfriend," she said. "So, how about you?" J.D. asked.

"Me," he said. "Oh no, I don't have a boyfriend," he said as he laughed. "I don't do that kind of stuff, I believe in one man and one woman!" he exclaimed as he chuckled.

"Real funny," she said. "You know what I mean!"

Logan laughed again. "Nah, I don't. We broke up about 6 months ago," he said.

"Oh ok," she said. "I haven't had a boyfriend in about a year."

"Wow, that's a long time," he said.

"Yeah, I know." They continued to talk on the phone until about 3 AM.

"So, can I come and see you before you leave?" Logan said.

"Um, my flight leaves at 7 AM and I am supposed to be at my friend's house for prayer at 6," she said.

"Cool, I'm going to meet you at the airport," he said in a serious but calm voice.

"Are you serious?" she asked with butterflies in her stomach.

"Yeah, why not!" he said. "I would like to see you before you go."

She smirked in amazement, "Ok." J.D. changed the subject.

"I am serious, I want to see you before you go," Logan said. "What's the airport and terminal?"

"We are leaving from O'Hare, terminal five," she said. The conversation went on and on until about 5 AM.

In the meantime, Fah'ry was lying in her car seat contemplating what to say to Chaston. "I can't believe that he is with another girl," she said with shock. She dialed the phone, ". . . Lord please help us to work out," she said. The phone rang continuously but there was not an answer. *He must be with her,* she thought. Fah'ry turned her music on to try and keep her mind off of him. *Ugh, this is too much! What am I going to do now?* She started to have all types of images in her head of what he and the girl could be doing. *Oh God,* she thought in anguish.

Fah'ry called Chaston again. *Please pick up,* she thought. *I just need to get this out. I just want to ask him why . . . Why did he take that girl to the movies and he just broke up with me earlier? He had to be going with her already.* She started to think back to try and remember if anything seemed strange or started to change in their relationship. *He did stop answering my calls, especially at night,* she thought. *And then, it took him a couple of days to call me back at the retreat . . . And . . . Every time I would talk to him, he would put me on hold for a long time,* she thought as she pondered. *How could I miss that? How could I be so stupid?* Fah'ry said. As more thoughts came to her mind, more tears started to flow. Fah'ry cried until she fell asleep in her car.

Meanwhile, it was 5AM and the girls were getting their last luggage loaded into their cars to meet at Emory's house for prayer before their flight left.

Brooke called J.D. as she was driving from the hotel. "Hey hun!" said J.D.

"Hey, did you leave out yet?" asked Brooke.

"Yeah," J.D. said. "I am on my way."

"I kept calling Fah'ry last night but she never answered," said Brooke with concern.

"Yeah, I actually talked to her last night," said J.D. "She said that she was just driving and thinking. She seemed like she had been crying but you know with Fah'ry, it's hard to tell if she's hurting," said J.D.

"Absolutely," said Brooke. "So did you tell her about us seeing Chaston?" Brooke asked in a whispering tone.

"Yes, I did," said J.D. in a confident voice. “I wasn't going to keep that from her and let her look stupid!"

"So what did she say?" Brooke asked curiously.

"Oh, she was sooo mad!" said J.D. "She got off the phone with me right away to call him."

"Ooh I know that she probably went off!" Brooke said.

"Yeah," said J.D. "I'm almost at Emory's. Let me see if Fah'ry is close,"

"Ok, I'll see you there. Girl, I am so excited! We have been waiting on this day all of our senior year! Can you believe that this day is finally here?!!" Brooke said with excitement.

"I know!" J.D. replied with the same intensity.

"Ok ok ok, I'll see you in a sec!" Brooke said as she pulled up to Emory's house.

J.D. hung up with Brooke and immediately called Fah'ry. The phone just rang but actually woke Fah'ry up in her car. J.D. called again but Fah'ry did not pick up the phone. Fah'ry looked at her phone and ignored her friend's call.

She looked at the beautiful sunrise on the lake and started to think about Chaston and all the hopes and dreams they had planned together. "It's almost 6 AM," she said. She scrolled through the phone to see if he had called her back from last night, to no avail. She did not see any missed calls from Chaston. Fah'ry's heart started to beat fast. *He probably stayed all night with her,* she thought.

I'm going to call him right now, she thought. *I don't care what time it is! Shoot, I can't sleep and I feel like crap,* she said. Fah'ry called Chaston and the line went right to the voicemail. "Ok," she said with tears in her eyes. *The only way a phone does that is if he sent me to the voicemail. I know that he's up, he's an early person,* she thought. Fah'ry called him again and the phone went immediately to his voicemail. She waited 10 minutes and called him again. *Maybe his battery is dead,* she thought as her stomach started to form knots in nervousness. She attempted to call him again but the same thing happened. "Chaston, this is Fah'ry, can you call me back when you get this message?" she said on the voicemail with a broken heart. When she tried to call him one more time, her other line started to beep. She quickly looked to see if it was him returning her call but to her disappointment, it was Brooke.

"Ugh!" she said. *They are probably calling me to see if I am ready,* she thought. She ignored the call, turned on love music, laid back in her car seat and the tears started to flow once again. *God, I need you! I am hurting really really bad! Why did we have to break up now? I thought that he loved me! I can't do this life without him! I feel so stupid! I can't believe I'm chasing him!*

All of the girls were at Emory's house laughing and talking until it was time to leave for the airport.

"Girl, I love your living room!" said Brooke. "This teal couch is so pretty and it matches so well with the cream and caramel accents.

"Oh, thank you," said Emory. "That's all my mom," Emory said. "Her interior decorating business has grown really fast. She actually just got a call from Apostle York's wife for services."

"Really!" J.D. and Brooke said in amazement. "Apostle York is really popular! He's on every church channel you find," J.D. said. "My mom watches him every morning."

"Yeah," said Emory.

"Sooo, what happened with you and Bryce last night?" Brooke asked.

"Yes hun," J.D. said as they giggled and were all ears.

Emory quickly walked to open the mirrored balcony door to the swimming pool. "Ok, let's go out side by the pool, this air is too cold in here." They went outside to the reclining lawn chairs to sit by the pool in the backyard. Emory talked as she pulled her hair in a ponytail. "Gosh, I was up all night talking to my mom about Bryce," said Emory. "So, he was the perfect gentleman! He opened my door and he brought me a box of fine chocolates! It was so cute! It was in this pink bag with a blue ball, the same color as my car!" she said.

"Awww," they said as they listened.

"How did he know that you like chocolate?" asked Brooke.

"I don't know, I don't remember ever telling him that I liked fine chocolates," said Emory with a curious smile. "So, we went to dinner on a boat! Now, you all know that I love boats and the water!"

"Are you serious!?" asked J.D. with amazement in her voice.

"Yes!!" Emory said. "It was a beautiful night and then we watched the fireworks as we ate dinner! Then," she emphasized, "we took this river walk to a movie theater. I never knew that there was a movie theater by the river!" said Emory.

"Me either, girl!" said Brooke.

Emory kept checking the time as she talked. "Ok and so, the entire time that we were at the movies, he never tried anything. I couldn't believe it," said Emory in astonishment. "I was at least expecting him to put his arm around me at the movie but he was the perfect gentleman! I am still in awe! Anyway, I will save the details for the plane," she said to tease the girls.

"Hahaha," they all laughed.

"So, did you all kiss at the end of the night?" asked Brooke.

"Yes hun, at least tell us that part," said J.D. with curiosity.

Emory nicely changed the subject. "So, how was the fashion documentary?"

"Oh, girl, we didn't get a chance to see it," said Brooke.

"Yeah!" said J.D. "We stumbled into some drama at the movies last night."

"What!" Emory said. "What happened?" Emory asked with concern.

"Well, we saw Chaston at the movies with another girl last night," said J.D.

"Yes," Brooke interrupted, "and he was all over her!"

"Huh?" Emory said as she looked confused. "I kept telling Fah'ry that he was trife," said Emory in disappointment. "I never understood why she kept giving him so many chances anyway. He's not that cute and he's definitely not that smart."

"Yeah," Brooke said in agreement.

"Did you all tell her," asked Emory?

"Yeah, you know I did," said J.D. "I kept calling her yesterday a couple of times but she did not answer. But, I finally called her late last night and she finally answered the phone," said J.D. "She said that she was just riding and thinking," said J.D.

"Riding and thinking??" Emory said with suspicion. "What does that mean?"

"Yeah, I know," said J.D. "I thought the same, but I figured that she was just chilling or getting her mind free from whatever because I had not told her about us seeing Chaston yet."

"Aww, so have you talked to her this morning?" asked Emory.

"No," said J.D. "I tried calling her twice this morning but there was no answer."

"Yeah," said Brooke. "I tried to call her a couple of times as well this morning."

Emory jumped up and grabbed her phone. "It's 6:30, where is she? We have to leave in about 10 minutes!" said Emory. She called Fah'ry herself but there was no answer. She stood up and started to walk into the house as she called again. "Fah'ry, where are you? It's almost time for us to leave for London. Call me back, I'm getting worried," said Emory on the voicemail. Emory's dad called them all into his office for prayer before their flight. The girls got on the elevator and went downstairs to her father's study office.

Fah'ry looked at the missed call from Emory. *Oh God, I can't do it,* she cried! *I don't want to feel like this! I don't feel like telling them another thing that Chaston has done to hurt my feelings. They are just going to look at me like I am stupid for giving him all these chances. I don't want to be crying all on the plane and ruining their trip because I am sad and hurting. I am going to call him one more time and then that's it, I'm not going to keep chasing him,* she said. She picked up the phone and called.

"Hello," he said with a raspy voice.

"Chaston, my friends told me that they saw you with another girl last night at the movies."

"Yeah," Chaston said. "She ain't my girl or nothing, we were just chilling."

"Chillin?" Fah'ry said with hurt. "You just broke up with me yesterday but you go to the movies with another girl the same night? That don't make sense Chaston!"

"Look Fah'ry," he said. "You ain't my girl, so why you worried about it," he said smartly.

"What!!" Fah'ry said furiously.

"You, you ain't on nothing and I'm tired of waiting on you," he said. "I gotta go," he said and hung up the phone.

Fah'ry looked at the phone and started to cry uncontrollably. *I can't believe this! I can't believe he just talked to me like that! It's like I meant nothing to him after all of these years,* she cried. She leaned her head back on the reclined car seat and lay in silence and stared at the lake waters. Several calls started to come in from her friends but she ignored them. *I just can't make it,* she thought. *I don't want to live anymore.*

The girls started to put their luggage in Emory's dad's truck. "Did you all talk to Fah'ry yet?" her father asked.

"No Dad," Emory said. "I keep trying to call her but she's not answering."

"Yeah, me too," said J.D. and Brooke.

"Well, we have to go," he said as he put the last luggage in the truck.

"Maybe, she's just running late and will meet you all at the airport," Emory's mom said as she got in on the passenger side of the truck. "Just keep trying to call," she said to the girls. The girls got in the truck and put their purses on the floor as they sipped their lattes in their pink tumblers. J.D. tried to call Fah'ry as the truck pulled off as she looked in the rear view mirror at their pink, purple and blue IvyKenningtons neatly parked in the large circular driveway.

There's a yellow one missing, J.D. thought with concern. She just let the phone ring until the voicemail picked up. "Fah'ry, where are you hun? We are on our way to the airport," she said with sadness. "Are you meeting us there or something? Our flight leaves at 7:30 AM," she said. "Call me back, OK, love you."

Fah'ry's Demise

The girls arrived at the crowded airport and Emory's dad made sure that all of their luggage and boarding info was all set. Emory's dad and mom waited with the girls for a awhile. They gave their final pep talks of responsibility, hugs and reassurance of the summer being great.

"Yeah, I know mom," said Emory. "It just won't be the same without Fah'ry. I don't understand where she could be? What would cause her to miss our London trip?" Emory asked her mom with concern.

"I don't know hunny," her mom said. "You all have about 20 minutes," she said. "There's still hope that she will show," said her mom.

"I know," Emory said with a pout as they all sat on the airport bench and each girl continued to try to call Fah'ry on the phone.

"But mom, she's not answering," she said. "That's not like her. And when J.D. and Brooke went by her house, she wasn't there. No one knows where she is!" said Emory.

"Well sweetheart," her father said. "Did you all want to stay here? You seem very concerned."

The girls looked at each other in sadness and confusion with no answer. "Hunny, I don't think that they should miss their trip," said Emory's mom in a soft and sweet voice. "They've waited all of their senior year for this trip. They can't miss this internship either. This is important and Fah'ry also knows that," her mom said. "This internship is more important to Fah'ry than any of the girls. Fashion Design is her major, right?" her mom looked over and asked Emory.

"Yes," Emory said. "Her Fashion League instructor was the one who had favor to help us get spots when they were all filled."

"See," her mom said. "I don't think that Fah'ry will miss something this important for anything," her mom said. She got up to embrace and console all of the girls. "It will be OK," she said with sincerity.

"We have to head to a meeting at the church," her dad said as he finished hugging them. "We are about to go. You ladies make sure that you make wise decisions and be watchful," he admonished. "Have fun and get all that you need during your internship! You never know what doors God will open so do your best and stay focused."

"Yes," her mom said. "Call us as soon as you land. Emory, your aunt will be waiting at the airport."

"Yeah, I talked to her as well," said Emory.

"Ok, ladies, have a great summer!" her mom said with excitement.

"Ok!" the girls said in unison.

"Yes, and don't forget to call us when you arrive," her father said in a stern voice. "And try not to worry about Fah'ry, she will be ok," he said.

Emory's parents turned around and walked towards the airport exit. "Byeeee!!" they all said.

They started to gather their carry-ons and walk towards the boarding area. As they were walking, they heard a voice yelling J.D.'s name. "J.D.!" the voice yelled through the airport. "Wait!" the voice said.

The girls turned around quickly to see . . . "Is that Logan?" asked Brooke with surprise.

"What is he doing here??" laughed Emory.

"Yeah," J.D. said as she blushed. "He said that he was coming to see me but I didn't think anything of it. I mean I didn't take him seriously!" she said.

Logan ran up to her huffing and puffing. "Man," he said as he tried to catch his breath. "I thought I had missed you. The traffic was crazy. I know that you said that your flight was leaving at seven but I figured I would still try," Logan said.

"Yeah," J.D. smirked. "Actually, I thought it was seven also but it was 7:30 instead. So, I'm glad that you came anyway," she said as she placed both of her hands in each of her pockets and twisted from side to side.

"Yeah, me too," Logan said as he smiled and took a deep breath.

"J.D.!" Emory yelled. "It's time to board!" J.D. looked at Logan and they stared at each other as if they were going to kiss. He pulled a pink box out of his pocket. "Um, here, this is for you," he said with a slight nervousness.

"Aww, thank you!!!" she said. "What is it?" she asked in excitement.

"I think that you will like it," said Logan, "but don't open it until you get on the plane."

"I - ok," said J.D. laughing. They both laughed together and shared a moment where nothing else mattered in the world but them.

"I know that you have to go," he said. "Like I said, I just wanted to see you before you left," he said in his normal cool and calm voice. "And to give J.D. a hug." They held one another quickly and J.D. ran off to board the plane.

"Have a great summer!" he said.

"Thank you!!" she yelled while running to board.

Fah'ry was still sitting in her car on the lakefront. She looked at the time. *They just boarded da plane,* she thought to herself as the tears started to roll down her carmel brown face. *I gotta stop cryin,* she said as she looked at her puffy eyes in the car mirror. *I don't want to go home,* she thought to herself as she laid back in her car seat and reclined the seat all the way out. *My friends are gone. How did I miss my trip? God, help me! I can't go home. My grandma doesn't care what I do. She lets me do whatever I want. My mom is probably at the health club takin ah showa or at school studying already. I've been gone all night and she has not called to see where I am,* she thought as her eyes watered. *Me and Chaston are over and my friends are gone. I don't have anyone now,* she thought. *I really need somebody. I need some help.*

Fah'ry thought about who she could call for help but couldn't think of anyone. She started to think of all of the personal talks that she had with Sister Catherine in her office. She suddenly remembered a moment when she was on her office couch. She started to look for her purse on the floor. Fah'ry grabbed it and rumbled through her purse for a card with a blue and gold shield on it. *Here it is,* she thought. *Thank you, God.* She started to dial the numbers on the card. "Please answer," she said anxiously as it rang.

"Hellooo," said Sister Catherine.

"Hi Sister Catherne," said Fah'ry in a crying voice.

"Oh, hi Fah'ry!" she said with happiness and surprise. "What's wrong?" she quickly asked as she could tell by her congested voice.

Fah'ry started to cry and attempt to talk. "Chast-on broke up with me, my momma don't care a-bout me, I missed my fl-ight to London for my su-mmer internship, my friends are gone and I don't have No-body," she cried. "I just don't know how I will make it! I don't wanna live anymore!"

"Fah'ry, don't say that," said Sister Catherine. "Where are you?"

"I'm on the lake," she said. "I been out here all night," said Fah'ry.

"What!" Sister Catherine said. "Where did you stay?"

"In my car," said Fah'ry.

"Oh no, all night!??" Sister Catherine asked with heightened concern.

"Yea, I just didn't want to go home."

"Where are you on the lake?" she asked.

"On the north pier side parking lot," said Fah'ry.

"I'll be there," said Sister Catherine.

"I'm about to go home," said Fah'ry.

"Ok, what's your address? I'm on my way. I'll meet you at your home," said Sister Catherine in a serious voice. "Fah'ry, I am worried about you . . ."

Fah'ry pulled off of the lakefront in her light yellow IvyKennington and headed home in despair. *I hope nobody says anything to me in dat house,* she said to herself. *I don't feel like nobody pickin a argument wit me. I'm goin straight to my room and lay on my stupid made up bed on da floe until Sister Catherine comes. And, I know it's hot in nere,* she said. *I need to stop and buy a fan or somethin.* She rode in silence as she dreaded going home.

Fah'ry arrived at home and parked on the side of her house. *I betta go through the front,* she said. *If I go through the back, I gotta dodge nem rats in na kitchen.* She walked through the door and a wind of hot air and urine smell hit her. *Ugh,* she sighed as she walked into her room. Her uncles sat on the living room couch glued to the television.

Fah'ry put the broken door up to the opening as if to close the door. She laid her three blankets on the floor, turned on the small tv that sat in the chair as a stand and sat down on the floor and put her back against the wall as if it was a headboard. She turned the fan towards her and watched television. Her mind kept wandering as she flipped through the channels. She thought about her and Chaston as she came across television shows with couples on them. "Ugh," she sighed as she changed the channel. *It's so hot in here,* she thought. "Dis fan is not workin," she said while turning the fan on high.

She attempted to lie down to get her mind off of Chaston. "This not gone work," she said while tossing and turning. *I just need to go to sleep,* she thought. She pulled the covers over her head and tried to fall asleep again. *Ok, I gotta do somethin,* she said to herself as an encouragement. She could not stay up with all of the overwhelming thoughts. She laid down and forced herself to sleep. Fah'ry dozed off for a few but the loud car music, motorcycles and people laughing and loud talking out of her room window prevented her from peaceful sleep.

She got up to see if there was something to drink in the refrigerator. Fah'ry opened the broken door and her uncle smacked his lips. "I don't know what you smakin yo lips foe," said Fah'ry in extreme frustration.

"I can do what I wanna, you lil b****!" her uncle said.

"Yea ok," said Fah'ry. "That's why you going to hell," she said.

"Aye," both of her uncles became furious, "we don't care nothin about God!!" Her uncle got out of his seat and walked in her face. "Aye, f*** God!" he said as he foamed at the mouth. "You and yo mama holy self can kiss my a**!" he said as her other uncle agreed.

"Dat's why ima tell grandma when she get home from work!" she yelled in anger.

"Aye, you think I care!" he hollered.

"I can't wait for you and yo mama to get outta here!" her other uncle shouted.

Fah'ry tried to ignore them and walk to the refrigerator. "Move outta my way!" she said as her uncle stood tall over her with a crippled hand and partially blocked the kitchen threshold. She opened the refrigerator to look for something to drink but there was only soda in the refrigerator and old French fries in a greasy brown paper bag. She gazed through the refrigerator and ignored her uncles' taunts. *Ugh, I hate this lunch meat and I don't want no hot dogs,* she thought.

"Aye!" her uncle said as he watched her in the refrigerator. "Don't drink my pop neither!" he shouted. She picked up the other soda, which she knew was her grandmother's soda. "And don't drink dat either!" he shouted. "Dat's Mama pop!" Fah'ry threw the pop back in the fridge. "And don't even think about eatin our meat!" he said. Her other uncle shouted, "Yeah! Dey need to get they own house! Yo mama supposed to be so holy and all dat school ain't got her nowhere!" he said.

"SHUT UP!!!" Fah'ry yelled in their faces. She walked past her uncle who was standing in the way of her getting to her mom's room. *Ugh, I hate that smell*, she thought. I will never forget that smell. Ugh, she sighed as her mind drifted to the upstairs bedroom with her uncle at age 7. *Gross,* she thought as she shook her head quickly to come back to reality. Fah'ry walked into her mom's room to find the worship song that she always listens to. She noticed a letter on her mom's dresser.

"*Fah'ry, I will be gone for two days on a case study assignment," the letter read. "I will be back tomorrow, love mom.*"

So, she wasn't even here last night, Fah'ry thought. She turned up the worship music in her mom's room and started to pray and bind the devil as she saw her mom do and was taught in church. The worship music was really loud due to the small living quarters.

Her uncle started to yell. "Turn dat stupid music down!!" Fah'ry ignored him and started to pray in tongues and bind the devil intensely. Her uncle turned on his secular music and turned it up as loud as he could. After Fah'ry was done warring, she left her mom's room to go to the corner store next door for something to drink.

She walked outside as all of the shiny cars with loud music rode past on the busy street. A sleek, shiny silver car with silver tire rims pulled up beside her. The driver looked over through the passenger side and said . . . "What's up Fah'ry," he said smiling.

She looked over at the guy in the car and was confounded. *How does he know my name?* she thought as she ignored him and continued to walk into the corner store. Fah'ry grabbed a cream soda from the large fridge full of juices and sodas. She walked down the potato chip aisles to find a bag of hot chips. "Oh, here they are," she said. She picked up the bag of hot chips and grabbed another bag of chips to mix together with them. She walked up to the register to pay for her items.

"Hey Fah'ry," the foreigner said with an accent.

"Hey Abe," she said. She looked at all of the candy and chocolates behind the counter covered with glass. I am so hungry, she thought. *I have not had breakfast or anything.* "Can you give me one of those chocolate bars?" she asked the guy behind the counter.

He slammed the candy bar on the counter and gave her the total. "No tax," Abe said, "just give me the two dollars," as he gestured with his hands.

"Oh ok, thank you," she said. She tried to grab all of her items off of the counter but it was too much to carry. "Um, can I have a bag Abe?" she asked. He gave her the unopened brown paper bag. Fah'ry turned to walk out of the door.

"Hey Fah'ry!" the young lady said in excitement.

"Hey Keke," said Fah'ry as she smiled.

"Why you don't neva come outside?" Keke asked.

"I don't really have the time," she said.

"I know you go to private school and everything but you can hang out with us sometime," said Keke with a sassy tone. "You ain't been outside around here since we was little."

"Yea, I never have the time with school and all of my afterschool activities," Fah'ry said.

"Well, it's summa now," Keke said. "What you doin tonight?"

"Um . . ." Fah'ry was lost for words. "Nothing, I don't think."

"Well, come around my house lata," she said. "I steal live in da same house on da corna," said Keke.

"Ok cool," Fah'ry said as she started to walk out of the store with her.

"Don't be lyin either," Keke said as she switched out of the store with her tiny shorts on, belly top, gym shoes on and slick, short ponytail.

Fah'ry laughed at Keke. "No, I'll be there," she said. *As long as my mom doesn't know,* she thought to herself as she walked back into the house. *My mom would kill me if she found out I was hanging out over there. She was very serious about me not hanging out over here, especially with those girls,* she thought. *Oh no,* she thought. *And she always told me that I should be careful of those girls because they would be jealous of me because of how I looked with my long hair and pretty face. But, then again, she would never know if I went over there,* she thought.

Fah'ry went back into her room and put up the broken door. She picked up her phone and noticed a missed call from Sister Catherine. She immediately called her back. "Hi Sister Catherine," said Fah'ry.

"Hi Fah'ry," she said. "I am pulling up."

"Ok," Fah'ry said. "I'll be out." *Let me hurry up and meet her on the front porch,* she thought. *I don't want her to think that she can come in. And Lord knows I hope she doesn't ask to use the bathroom,* she thought. She walked outside and stood on her front steps to wait for Sister Catherine

Sister Catherine walked around the corner towards Fah'ry and gave her a huge hug. "Are you feeling better sweetheart?" Sister Catherine asked.

"I don't know," Fah'ry said as she shrugged her shoulders with watery eyes.

"Come on," Sister Catherine said. "Let's take a ride."

Fah'ry ran in the house to get her purse and phone. She met Sister Catherine at her car and opened her sleek car door. *Wow, this is a nice car,* she thought to herself. *Sister Catherine is riding nice.* They pulled off and started to take a slow peaceful ride towards the expressway.

"Now, what's wrong sweetheart?" Sister Catherine asked. "You can't keep letting this boy get to you," she explained with sincerity. "He is not the only boy around, there are plenty of boys that would love to be with you," she said. "His little dusty self," she said and they both laughed together. "I'm serious," Sister Catherine said. "You have your entire future ahead of you. You are on your way to one of the most prestigious schools and you are crying over a little boy. You are worth more than that. You should not want to lose your life over any boy, he is not worth it," she explained with love.

"Now, I know that your family situation is not the best and your mama is never around but you have to put your trust in God. You have to find a way to get strength and not worry about all these people. This is why you are depressed and all in your car sleeping and everything," she said sarcastically. Fah'ry giggled. "Now, you are going to have to stay busy to keep your mind off of all of these depressing things," she admonished. "If you sit around crying, it will continue to get to you. Fah'ry, I mean it," Sister Catherine said as she looked her in her face with a serious tone. "You must stay busy. Now, you have missed your internship opportunity for London messing around with this boy. Now, what are you going to do?" she asked.

"I don't know," said Fah'ry.

"Well, you need to find another one here in Chicago or something. Don't just sit around and do nothing all summer. You are going to have to fight those depressing thoughts or they will get the best of you," Sister

Catherine said with concern. "You can't be scaring me like that, on the phone saying that you are contemplating suicide," she said.

"I just don't know what else to do," said Fah'ry with a confused face. "Chaston broke up with me and now all of my friends are gone for the whole summer!"

"Stop saying that!" Sister Catherine said. "You can live without him! You have to believe that yourself! And you could be in London with your friends but you decided to miss your flight," Sister Catherine said. "Now, you have to make a decision to do something productive with your summer. I love you Fah'ry and I want to see you do well. You are a smart girl," she said. "Come on, who graduates Valedictorian with all the problems you have going on at home?"

Fah'ry immediately thought to herself, *Yeah, it was a three-way tie between me, Brooke and Emory. I can understand Brooke, but Emory should have been Salutatorian,* Fah'ry drifted for a moment while Sister Catherine was giving her wise advice.

"Girl, it's a miracle that you haven't lost your mind but God has been with you and you have to know that. He has been watching over you the entire time. So, don't let this little time in your life alter the rest of your life," Sister Catherine said. "You must make it and you have what it takes to make it!"

Fah'ry continued to listen to Sister Catherine as they rode on the expressway and listened to talk radio. Fah'ry felt her phone vibrating in her purse and she grabbed it to see who was calling. *Oh, this Keke,* she thought. *Should I go over there when I get back home?* she contemplated. *My mom's note did say that she won't be back until tomorrow, so she'll never know that I went to her house,* she thought. *And grandma doesn't care, it's not like she's going to ask me where I'm going. Yeah, maybe I should. I'm not doing anything else today. What will it hurt?* she thought as she continued to listen to Sister Catherine.

Welcome to the Neighborhood

Sister Catherine dropped Fah'ry off at home and gave her final encouraging words before she drove off. Fah'ry went back in the house and put her purse on the nail on the wall that served as a closet in her room. She walked towards the kitchen and stopped at the threshold to listen for the location of the rats. She walked into the kitchen with caution and looked for something to eat. *I am so hungry,* she thought as she stood with the refrigerator door open. *It's nothing in here,* she thought. *I don't want no hot dogs or sandwiches.*

She looked on the stove to see what was in the big pot. *Grandma is home from work, let me see what she made for dinner,* she thought as she peeked in the pot. *Yuck! That is gross! What in the world! This pot stinks with this dirty water in it. And look at this dirty towel with holes in it!* She started to get the creeps as she saw the floating dead roaches in the water. *This is gross,* she thought as her grandmother yelled.

"Don't mess with my dish water!" she said in a grumpy tone.

Fah'ry thought, *DISH WATER!* She looked over at the right side of the kitchen that was covered with black table cloths that covered up what appeared to be the kitchen sink and counter. She looked at the cloths in curiousity. *I wonder what the sink looks like,* she thought. *I wonder what color is the counter?* Fah'ry opened the kitchen cabinet that was above the covered sink. She picked up a cup and roaches quickly ran out. "Oh my gosh!" Fah'ry said in disgust. She slammed the cabinet door and sat on the run down brown couch on the other kitchen wall to get herself together. *Ooh wee! That is so nasty,* she thought. She glanced at the bottom of the covered-up sink and counter and was able to see outside on the ground. *Oh wow, that's how the rats from the alley are coming in here.*

She got up and walked in the living room towards her room. She stopped to speak to her grandmother who was sitting on the couch. "Grandma," she said, "did you know that there were holes in the kitchen under the counter?"

"Yea," her grandmother said. "I got to get somebody to patch those holes up."

"Aw," Fah'ry said and walked into her room. She took some money from her purse and put it in her pocket. *I need to go and get something to eat but I betta leave my purse here,* she thought. *I don't feel like those girls looking at me like I think I'm all that, just because I have this purse on.* She walked through the living room to get to the front door. "I be back," she said out loud. "I'm going across the street to get something to eat." *I need to call my dad,* she thought. *I only have like five dollars left.*

She walked across the street and into the small box style restaurant that was take-out only. *This place is so hot and small,* she thought. *It's like only room for these two video games in here. I hope a lot of people don't start to come in here. I don't feel like all of that cursing and everything,* she thought. She stepped up to the plexiglass window with bullet holes in it and placed her order.

"Yeah?" the Arab man said.

"Can I have a pizza puff and fries?" Fah'ry said. The Arab guy yelled behind him in his native language. *What is he saying?* she thought as she stepped away from the order window and stood on the wall filled with gang slang and other writings. *It is so hot in here,* she thought. A group of girls walked in the small restaurant talking loud and cursing. They laughed with each other and continued to curse at one another as common language. They placed their orders and took up most of the restaurant inside and also covered the entrance of the doorway as they stood around. *I hope don't none them try to start something with me,* she thought with fear. *Lord, please let them hurry up and finish with my food.*

One of the girls started to stare at Fah'ry. "Is dat yo hair?" the girl asked. All the girls in the restaurant stopped talking and looked over at Fah'ry.

"Yea," Fah'ry said as she stood by the corner wall.

"You got some long hair," the other girl said. Fah'ry smirked at her to show laughter. "You got Indian in your family or somethin?" she asked.

"No," Fah'ry said.

"Dose some cute shoes," the girl said as she looked Fah'ry up and down. "You go to Pershing?" the girl asked.

"Naw," said Fah'ry. "I go to St. Martin."

"Oh, dat's a private school," the girl said.

"Yea," Fah'ry said with a smirk.

"Oh," the girl said. "I be seeing you going in dat house across the street. "Dats yo yellow drop top?" she asked as she looked her up and down. One of the other girls quickly interrupted.

"Dang PooPoo, you all in dat girl business. I wouldn't tell you sh**!

"Shut up b****," the girl said while laughing. "I can ask her what I want!"

The Arab yelled, "Pizza puff and fries!"

Ooh, thank you, Fah'ry thought as she walked up to the closed-up counter to get her food from a small window opening. *Please let them move out of the doorway,* she thought. *I hope one of them don't try to start anything.* She headed towards the door and the girls slowly moved out of the way to let her out the door.

"She probably stuck up," one of the girls said as Fah'ry walked outside.

I'm just gonna ignore her, she thought. She walked across the busy street and went back into the house.

She went into her room and put the door up to the opening and sat on the floor with all of her blankets that served as her bed. Fah'ry enjoyed her meal and tried to watch television on the small TV fixed on the broken chair. *I can't watch this,* she thought as she changed the channels over and over again. *Everything on here is about love,* she said. *I have to find a way to stop thinking about Chaston. It's hot outside, I bet he's out enjoying hisself and I'm stuck in here crying over him.* She picked up her phone to call Chaston but he did not answer. "Ugh," she sighed in disappointment.

She started to dial her dad. "What's up Fah'ry?" he said.

"Hey Dad," she said. "I need some money for these shoes and purse that I saw."

"How much Fah'ry? he said.

"Like 250," she said.

"Ok, give me bout a hour and I'll be ovah there," he said. "Why you not in London?" he asked. "Y'all was leaving this morning?"

"Yea, they did leave this morning," she said. "I missed the flight. Long story."

"Ok," her dad said. "Well I'll be over there in a little bit."

"Ok, thanks dad," Fah'ry said with a smile. She laid on the floor and turned her music on while eating.

She picked up her phone again to call Chaston. "He just ain't gone answer the phone at all," she said with frustration. "Ugh!!!" She grabbed her sketch book and favorite pencil and started to design clothes on her sketch pad. Fah'ry designed for a couple of hours while listening to music and her mind was occupied.

Ok, I'm getting tired of sitting here in this hot house, she said as she put her pencil down. *I can't go nowhere because all my friends are gone. I guess Chaston was really serious about us breaking up cause he not answering my calls at all,* she thought. Fah'ry sat in her room with her back against the wall and listened to more music. *I don't know what I am going to do for the rest of the day. It's only 2 oh clock! I don't have nothing to do,* she started to think as she felt depressing thoughts start to come to her mind. *I gotta do something to keep my mind off of all of this,* she said to pep talk herself.

She suddenly thought about seeing Keke in the corner store this morning. *Well, she did invite me to come and hang out by her house,* she thought. *My mom won't be back til tomorrow anyway, so she will never know that I went over there.*

Fah'ry called Keke with hesitation. "Hey Keke," said Fah'ry.

"Who is dis?" Keke said with sass.

Fah'ry smirked, "Dis is Fah'ry."

"Aw, hey," Keke said. "Girl I didn't know who you was, sounding all proper."

"Hahaha," laughed Fah'ry. "What you doin?"

"Nothin," Keke replied as loud music played in the background. "You comin ovah here?" Keke asked.

"Yea," said Fah'ry. "Let me put some clothes on and I'll be over there."

"Ok, I'll be here," said Keke. Keke hung up the phone immediately.

Ok, Fah'ry thought. *She didn't say bye or anything.* Fah'ry looked in her corner duffel bag for clothes. She pulled out her soap and toiletries along with her green wash up pan. She went to her mom's room to get a gallon of water and headed to the kitchen to warm up water for her wash up routine. *Maybe Chaston will call me lata tonight,* as she poured the hot water in her pan. *He gotta miss me. Maybe I should stay home, just in case he surprises me and comes by,* she thought. *I just don't know,* she thought in confusion. *I need to get out of here. But what if he comes and I'm gone? I'm just gone go anyway,* thought Fah'ry.

She washed up and put on a light pink collared shirt and a knee length skirt with a pair of brown leather thong style sandals. She sprayed her hair with water and it immediately curled up. Her phone started to ring and she quickly ran to the phone. *Aw, I was hoping that was Chaston,* she thought.

She answered. "Hey Dad," she said.

"Aye Fah'ry, I'm outside," he said.

"Ok, here I come!" she said as she grabbed her purse and car keys. She ran through the two doors in her house to get outside. Fah'ry walked up to her father's car window. He let the window down. "Hey Dad," she said.

"What's up Fah'ry," he said with his dark sunglasses on. He passed her the money and she placed it in her pocket.

"Thanks Dad," she said.

"I gotta go Fah'ry," he said. "Just call me later," as he put the car in drive.

"Ok," she said as he drove off. *He don't never talk to me,* she thought. Fah'ry walked to her car and drove around the corner to Keke's house. She drove past several abandoned buildings and vacant lots. *Wow,* she thought. *I've never been dis far down the street,* she thought. She looked at the groups of guys standing on the corners and the packs of girls walking in the middle of the streets like mobs. She saw families sitting in kitchen chairs on the sidewalk of their homes playing cards. *Man, it seems like everybody sits on da porch.*

Fah'ry pulled up in front of Keke's house and parked her yellow IvyKennington. She walked up the two flights of stairs and into the house.

"I'm bout to get ready in a minute," said Keke as she quickly walked past Fah'ry.

"Ok," said Fah'ry. She looked around to find herself a seat.

"I'm bout to iron my clothes and get in da shower," Keke yelled into the living room.

"Ok," replied Fah'ry. *Now, why isn't she ready?* she thought. *It's 3 o'clock and she's just now putting clothes on? What has she been doin all day?* Fah'ry sat back in the chair and watched the music videos that were playing on their television. An hour passed and Keke was still ironing her clothes. "Girl, my clothes gotta be crisp," said Keke. She grabbed an empty spray bottle and added water and flour to the bottle. Fah'ry stared at Keke in silence but curiously. "Girl, dos my starch," said Keke.

"Oh," Fah'ry smirked.

Keke finished ironing and went to shower. She turned the music up loud in the house and took her time in the bathroom. Fah'ry continued to wait for Keke to get dressed. *It's like 4 o' clock,* Fah'ry thought as she continued to watch music videos over the loud music in the bathroom. *She is takin too long. I could've stayed at home until she got ready.* "Ugh," she sighed. Keke came out of the bathroom and went into the kitchen. *Finally,* Fah'ry thought with relief.

She switched past Fah'ry to grab her head scarf. Fah'ry stared at Keke put her scarf on her head and tied it tightly as she stood in front of the television. "I'll be done once dos gel dries," said Keke.

"It's alright," said Fah'ry.

"My ponytail gotta be slick," said Keke. "You got good hair. I gotta gel my hair down to make dese sides slick," Keke said with sass.

Fah'ry smirked as she continued to watch her prep time. Keke started to sweep and mop the house. *Is she cleaning up?* Fah'ry thought as she peeked in the back where she was sweeping. She looked at the videos in irritation as she waited. Keke came out of the back with small, tight shorts, a halter top with her back out and a pair of white gym shoes. Her ponytail was slicked to the side and her legs were thick and shiny.

"I'm ready," said Keke as she rubbed the baby oil in on her legs.

"Ok," said Fah'ry as she stood up and stretched. The girls walked down the stairs to go outside. Fah'ry noticed two kitchen style chairs on the porch.

"You hungry?" said Keke.

"I'm ok," said Fah'ry.

"Ok, cus I'm bout to go cross da street to Devo's," said Keke.

What is that? Fah'ry thought as she followed Keke across the street. *It's a lot of people in a crowd over there,* she thought as they walked. There were about 10 guys huddled together standing on the corner of Devo's. *I hope don't none of dese guys say anything to me,* she thought. She walked through the crowd of guys with as much confidence and courage as she could pull out of herself. *What's all of these potato chip bags they got with forks in them,* Fah'ry thought. All of the guys that were standing around had a bag in their hand as they talked. Keke switched through the crowd of guys with confidence and entered the small store.

"What up Keke?" a guy said, "You thick as he**," as he watched her walk.

"Aye, who is dat?" another guy said. "Who is yo friend Keke? The guys watched Fah'ry and Keke from behind as they entered the store. "What up," the guy said to Fah'ry as he ate from his bag with low, red eyes.

I betta say something, thought Fah'ry in fear. "Hey," said Fah'ry.

"What's yo name?" he asked.

"Fah'ry," she said. She tried to move closer into the crowded store next to Keke.

"Let me get ah a bag of chips with cheese and meat," said Keke at the counter.

"You want hot peppers?" the old black man said as he tried to move the crowded line along.

"Yea," said Keke. "You want one Fah'ry?" asked Keke.

"Yea," said Fah'ry. *I guess I'll try it,* she thought to herself. She stepped up to the window and tried to repeat what Keke said to place her order. *What did she say again?* She thought but couldn't remember. "I'll have what she ordered," said Fah'ry to the old man behind the counter. More people entered the store and ordered the same thing. The guy passed the orders out as fast as they came in. Keke and Fah'ry received their chip bag with the white plastic fork sticking out and walked back to Keke's house.

They walked up the stairs and Keke sat down on the porch in the kitchen style chair. *Oh, I guess I'm supposed to sit in the other chair.* Fah'ry sat down and they ate their chips with cheese and meat out of the bag on the porch. Several cars with loud music and shiny tire rims started to pass by the porch. After an hour, Fah'ry kept seeing the same cars driving by over and over again. *Ok!* she thought sarcastically. *How many times are dey gone pass here,* she thought.

"Dey hittin da block today," Keke said. "Muggfu*****s got dey cars washed!" Keke said with excitement. "Girl you see his car? He got money," said Keke.

Fah'ry laughed at Keke. They sat on the porch for hours and watched the guys in their sleek cars and loud music drive through the neighborhood. *I came over here for this,* Fah'ry thought as she looked at her phone. *Chaston still ain't called me back,* she thought. A silver car with silver tire rims rode by, immediately stopped and pulled up behind Fah'ry's car.

"Girl, his sounds be bangin!" Keke said with excitement. "Everybody love him," said Keke. "He is so fine! Is he comin up here?!" Keke said with surprise. "He don't neva come ovah here."

Oh gosh, Fah'ry thought as he got out of the car. *Dat's the guy that tried to talk to me the other day by my house and knew my name.*

Captured Heart

"What up Swerve!" said Keke in a rowdy tone. She sat in the chair on the porch slurping her blue sno-ball as she stared at him go straight for Fah'ry.

"What's up Keke?" said Swerve. He walked up the porch stairs and grabbed a chair and sat next to Fah'ry. "What's up Fah'ry?" he said as he put his keys and phone down. "Hey," said Fah'ry. *Who is he?* she thought nervously. How does he know my name? She glanced at him and quickly looked back at the cars passing by. *He is cute though. Wow!* she thought. *I didn't know guys looked like this over here. Ooh, I'm so wrong. I am faithful to Chaston,* she thought.

"So, when you start comin around here?" he asked.

"I don't really," she said.

"Yea, cus I ain't nevah saw you ovah here," he said.

"I just came to visit today," she said.

"I be seeing you drivin your lil yellow drop top with your private school skirt on," he said as he tapped her leg.

Fah'ry smirked, glanced at him and quickly turned away. *Ooh wee, he look too good,* she thought.

"Is Keke yo cousin?"

"No, a friend from when we were little. How do you know my name?" she asked in a sweet voice while crossing her legs at the ankles.

Swerve chuckled. "I know everybody! I been watchin you girl." He chuckled and they both shared a laugh. "Naw, yo girl told my guy."

"Who? My girl? I don't know anybody over here," said Fah'ry. "We saw yo girls by yo house one day and my guy stopped to holla at them," he said. Fah'ry smirked.

"My friends?!" Fah'ry asked with curiosity as she gestured pointing to herself.

"Yea," he said in a convincing tone. "The ones with the cars that look just like yours." He tapped her leg again. "As a matter of fact, one car is a light purple and da otha one is light pink. Uh huh," he nodded his head up and down while smiling. Fah'ry laughed at him with no restrictions. "Oh yea, my guy got the one with da purple car numba," he said proudly.

"Brooke?" Fah'ry said as she smiled at him.

"Yup Brooke," he said as if he knew her.

"I can't believe her," she said in amazement.

"Yup," so I asked her your name and she told me.

"What!" She smiled. "I can't believe Brooke! Why didn't she tell me?? That's crazy!"

Keke sat in the chair listening but acted as if she was looking at the cars drive past her house. "So, what grade are you in?" Swerve asked.

"I just graduated," said Fah'ry. "I'm going to Polk State University in August," she said.

"So, you got two months to kick it huh?" Swerve said.

Fah'ry smirked, "I guess so." *I wonder what grade he's in,* she thought. *He might not even go to school, so I'm not going to ask him that.*

Swerve's phone started to ring. He took the call and talked briefly on the phone. He stood up and tried to rush the person on the other end off of the line. "Let me call you back," he said in a stern voice. "I be back," he said to Fah'ry. "You gone be here when I come back?" he asked while smiling at her.

"Um, I don't know," she said as butterflies started to form in her stomach.

'Well, I'll be back to see you," he said. Fah'ry gave him a sweet smirk as they caught each other's eye. Her heart jumped quickly as they stared into each other's eyes for a quick moment. *Oh my gosh, what is happening?* she thought. *My heart is jumping and butterflies? Oh no, I feel horrible! I am not supposed to feel this way about anyone but Chaston.* Swerve walked down the porch stairs and got in his shiny silver car, turned his music up and drove off.

"Girl, how you know Swerve?" asked Keke. "He is fine as he**! Ehbody want him wit his bo-legged self! Girlll, he got that white boy curly hair anddd he he light skinned?? But he too tall for me, doe!" said Keke.

Fah'ry smirked at Keke.

"Girl, I don't know him," Fah'ry said in defense. "I feel so bad," she said.

"Why?" asked Keke. "You betta holla at him!"

Fah'ry smirked. "Naw, I actually got a boyfriend."

"And . . . !" Keke said.

"I'm faithful to him," said Fah'ry.

"Oh ok," said Keke. "I didn't know you were going to college?"

"Yea," said Fah'ry. "I'm going to Polk State with him. Well, I actually received a full scholarship to the fashion university but I turned it down."

"What!" Keke said as she patted her matted head to scratch without messing her hair up.

"Yea, I didn't really want to leave him, so I decided not to take the offer. I haven't told anybody about the full ride scholarship offered to me, not even my mom," said Fah'ry.

"Girl, I would have been happy to take that scholarship," said Keke.

"I know, but I wanted to be with him in college. I couldn't be away from him that long," said Fah'ry.

"Dang, y'all sound like y'all married!" Keke said. "How long y'all been together?" she asked.

"Well, long story," said Fah'ry.

"Do you wanna go walk?" asked Keke.

"Sure," said Fah'ry. They got up and started to walk around the neighborhood as Fah'ry talked about her and Chaston's relationship history. They passed corner after corner with crowds of guys standing around.

"What up Keke?" they said as they approached a new group of guys.

"Hey," Keke said as she switched by them.

"Aye, who is dat?" A guy asked as the crowd was filled with marijuana smoke.

"My friend," she said with sass. "She got a man, so leave her alone." They continued to walk through the neighborhood as Fah'ry told her story about Chaston for almost two hours. "Girl, he is bogus," Keke said in response to Fah'ry's story. "Why you faithful to him?"

Fah'ry tried to explain why. "Naw," said Keke. "I would treat his punk a** just like he treating you." Fah'ry listened to her raw opinion as they walked.

They approached another crowd of guys. "What up Keke?" they said. "Girl, you thick as he**!" a guy said.

"Shut up, Dre!" she said.

"Who is dat," he said as he walked towards Fah'ry. "What's up?" he said. "What's yo name," he said with the aroma of marijuana.

"Dre!" Keke said with a loud voice. "Leave her alone. She got a man, she don't want you."

"I was just sayin 'hi'," he said. "Can she speak for huh self?"

Fah'ry smirked. "Hi, I'm Fah'ry."

"What up Fah'ry."

"Dre, where yo brotha at?" Keke said.

"I don't know! Probably on da block," he said.

"Tell him to call me," said Keke as they moved on walking to the next street. She suddenly came to a stop at a particular street. "We can walk down dis block instead of dat one," Keke said. "I don't mess wit da 3Ks like dat."

Fah'ry just listened, learned and followed Keke around the neighborhood as she unconsciously explained gang boundaries. *What in the world,* Fah'ry thought. Her heart started to beat fast in fear. *I am so pass my house. I need to go home. My mom would kill me if she knew I was over here. Please let her turn around and go back to her house.* They continued to walk the neighborhood for another 30 minutes or so.

"We can go back to da house," said Keke. "It's almost dark." They arrived at her house and sat back on the porch in the chairs. "Ooh, my feet hurt," said Keke as she took her gym shoes off.

"Mines too, and I got these sandals on," said Fah'ry. "My feet are so dirty," she said as she pulled off her expensive brown sandals to look at the bottom of her feet. *Ooh, smell just like outside,* she thought to herself. They sat on the porch and continued to talk and laugh.

"So you really ain't wit Chaston no moe," Keke said.

"Yea, we just having problems right now," she said.

"Girl, from what you said, y'all broke up," said Keke. "Girl, forget him. You betta talk to Swerve cus here he come!!" she said teasing Fah'ry.

She laughed at Keke and tried not to stare at him pulling up and walking up the porch stairs towards her. "What up Keke?" Swerve said.

"Hey," she said.

"I told you I was comin back, Fah'ry," he said with a smile. She gave him a cute smirk. As he talked to her, his friend pulled up and came on the porch and started to talk to Keke. Fah'ry tried to think of things to talk about but couldn't. They spent a lot of time listening and laughing at Keke. Every now and then, he would lean in close to Fah'ry and ask her questions about herself. *Why am I getting these butterflies,* she said feeling puzzled inside. *I don't understand. What's going on?* she thought. Fah'ry hung out on the porch with Swerve, his friend and Keke until midnight. *Oh my gosh,* she thought. *Twelve oh clock! I need to go home!*

Fah'ry eventually went home. She threw her dirty clothes in her designated duffel bag for her dirty clothes. Her grandmother and uncles were in a deep sleep. She took her phone and used it as a light to help her see in the kitchen. She stopped at the threshold of the kitchen. "Ugh!" These rats are making too much noise, she said to herself. "Shoot, I'm thirsty and I gotta use the bathroom. But I ain't going in nere," she said as she tried to creep one foot in the kitchen. *Aw naw, they gettin louder,* she thought. Fah'ry went back to her room and laid down on the floor filled with blankets as her bed.

She laid in the dark and started to think as she stared at the ceiling. *I remember my mama telling me when I was a little girl, that if I threw my broken bed away in faith, that God would bless me with a new one. Man, I was like 10 years old and I'm 18 and I still don't have a new bed or dresser. Where is God? I mean I did what she said. I want a pretty girly room,* she thought. *She always promised me a canopy bed but I still ain't got dat,* she said with an attitude. *Ugh, oh well.*

She turned over and grabbed her phone. She started to dial Chaston. *It's 1 o'clock in the morning, he should be at home.* The phone rang and he picked up after several rings. "Hey Chaston," she said in a low voice. The phone went silent. "Hello," she said to make sure that he was still on the phone.

He took a deep sigh. "What's up?" Chaston said with an annoyed voice.

Ok, she thought. *He gone act like I'm getting on his nerves?* she thought. "I was just trying to see what was going on," she said.

"What do you mean?" asked Chaston.

"What I mean, is why you haven't been answering my calls?" asked Fah'ry.

"I told you that I can't do this anymore," he said. "All I know is you, we been together since I don't know when, like elementary school, I want to know what life is like without you," he said. "Yeah and I told you, you ain't on nothing, I don't have time to keep waiting on you. I'm tired of doing all that kissing," Chaston said calmly. Fah'ry just listened and tried to hold back her tears. The phone went silent again after he finished talking.

"Chaston," she pleaded. "We don't have to break up. We can work this out. It will get better," she said.

"No it won't, Fah'ry," he said. "I don't want it, plus you ain't gone do nothing."

"Chaston, we about to go to Polk together," she said. "We are in the same dorms and everything. Are you just going to throw that away? Our plans for the future?" The phone went silent again as he clicked over his line. "Wow," she said. *Did he just click over without telling me to hold on?* she thought. *I feel horrible! I should not be chasing him like this! But I love him,* she thought to herself.

"Hello," he said as he clicked back over to her. "Yeah," he said. "Fah'ry, I know that we had planned to go to Polk State and everything together but I'm not on that anymore," he said.

"Huh?" she said in anguish and fear. "So, what am I supposed to do?" she asked him.

"I mean," he chuckled, "enjoy yourself, but we will not be a couple," he said with arrogance.

Really, she thought. *I can't believe that he is talking to me like this.* His phone started to beep again. "Who's calling you at almost 2 o'clock in the morning?" she asked.

He sighed loudly. "I got to go," he said. "Let me take this call."

"Chaston," she said with a hurt tone.

"Yea, Fah'ry," he said with an irritated tone.

"You know what, never mind," she said in a disappointed tone.

"All right," he said and hung up the phone.

Fah'ry balled up in a fetal position and cried herself to sleep. She woke up the next morning, said her prayers and just sat up against the wall on the floor in her room. "God, please help me?" she said as she leaned her head back on the wall. *I feel so bad. I just don't know what to do with myself. I feel so lost. I miss my friends,* she thought. *I miss high school. I don't have a boyfriend anymore. I can't go to Polk State with him treating me like this! I'm just going to give it a little more time and see if he changes his mind. I mean, we've been together forever. I know he's going to start missing me,* she thought. *I wish I could talk to my mama. Well, she will be home today but then again, she probably will be too busy anyway,* she thought. *Grandma doesn't talk to me like that and all of my cousins just always have something to say negative like I think I'm better than them, so I don't want to go around them anymore. I hate feeling like that. I hate when they make comments like that. I've never acted like that, just because I go to private school, does it give them a reason to say that about me? I'm tired of people saying that I'm stuck up and they never give me a chance at all. Just because I am light skin and have long curly hair, everybody always thinks that I'm stuck up and will never try to just get to know me,* she thought. *I guess that's why my mom always told me not to be friends with ugly girls and to make sure I chose pretty girls to hang out with, I guess it makes sense. I really wish I would not have missed my flight. I would be in London right now working on my fashion line and taking all those new courses. Man,* she thought.

She pulled out her sketch book and pencil, turned on her music and started to design clothing. *Where are my color pencils?* she thought and she rambled through her fashion sketch bag. She continued to design clothing until she got tired and hungry. *It is so hot in here,* she thought as she turned on the fan and opened the old rusted window. *Yuck, this window is so dirty! Look at all this dirt and these bugs in here!* She quickly let the window back down and moved the fan closer to her and turned it on high mode.

She opened and pulled the door from the opening to go to the kitchen as her uncles smacked their lips. *I'm not going to even say anything,* she thought and she walked past them. She walked into the kitchen with caution and saw a paper plate with aluminum foil on it. *Ooh, grandma made sausage and eggs before she went to work this morning! I love her eggs!* She started to lift the foil up to put it in the microwave.

"Aye, that ain't yours!" Her uncle yelled in the kitchen. "Mama made that for us!" he said in an angry voice.

"I don't care," said Fah'ry with an attitude as she stood at the microwave. She warmed her food up and went back to her room with no care.

She put her door back up to the opening and set down to watch television. *Ugh, I just can't watch this! Everything is about love!* She turned the television to cartoons and watched those while she ate. Her phone started to ring and she jumped in hopes that it was Chaston. "Hey Keke," she said.

"What up," said Keke. "You comin ovah here today? Girl I saw Swerve at Devo's dis mornin and he was like, 'Where's Fah'ry?' I'm like, 'Sh**, I don't know!' So, he lookin for you girl!" said Keke.

"Really?" asked Fah'ry.

"Yea, he was really askin," said Keke. "And he usually don't even be around here like that. Come kick it wit us," she said.

Fah'ry started to think to herself. *It was cool hanging with her after a while. Swerve is cute too and he stayed over there on the porch and hung out with me all night.*

"Um," said Fah'ry. "I will be ovah there in a little bit."

"Alright," said Keke.

Fah'ry put together one of her prettiest outfits and laid it on the blankets on the floor. She pulled out her green wash towel and toiletries from the duffel bag and laid them on the floor. *Now, Ima have to use all of this water to clean this dirt from off of my feet from last night! I ain't going to the park to get no water! I wish that I could take a shower,* she thought as she washed up. *I smell like outside. Ugh!* She continued with her normal wash up routine. She put her white slacks on, her yellow polo style shirt, brown leather belt with matching sandals and her diamond earrings. Fah'ry grabbed her white cardigan and tied it over her shoulder. She sprayed her pomegranate body spray and covered her clothes with it. Fah'ry got in her car and applied her lipgloss. *Ooh, this eczema looks the worst in the summer,* she said to herself as she looked in the rearview mirror.

She turned her music up and drove around the corner to Keke's house. *I hope this girl is ready and I don't have to wait three hours for her to get ready,* she thought. *That is so rude.* Fah'ry pulled up in front of Keke's house and every time that she heard loud music in a car, her heart jumped. *Is that Swerve?* she thought as she glanced in the rearview mirror.

I'm in Love with a Bad Boy (Soul Tied)

Fah'ry walked upstairs to Keke's house. She found herself a seat. "I'm bout to get in da shower," said Keke.

"Ok," said Fah'ry as she got as comfortable as she could. *This girl, ugh!* Fah'ry thought. *This is so rude. If she knows that I am coming over here, why doesn't she get ready on time!* she thought.

Fah'ry heard loud car music coming down the street. She ran to the window. *Is that Swerve?* she thought as she peeked through the curtain. *Oh, that's not him. Oh no, what is happening to me? I love Chaston. I'm not supposed to feel like this,* she thought. As she waited for Keke to finish in the shower, she secretly jumped up and went to the window every time that she heard the rattling loud sounds in the cars. *Ok,* as she looked at her phone. *It's 3 o'clock, I tried to wait at home an extra hour to give her some time to get ready. Ugh! I hate waiting!* Keke finally came out of the bathroom.

"I'm just waiting on my gel to dry," she said as she stood with her scarf tied tight around her head to mold her kinky hair.

"Alright," Fah'ry said with a smirk.

"You hungry?" asked Keke.

"Naw," said Fah'ry. "I ate already."

"Oh, well you can come to the kitchen," said Keke. "I'm bout to fix me somethin to eat." She grabbed a bottle of generic brand mustard and honey. She mixed them together in a small container.

"What's that?" asked Fah'ry. "Girl, dis is my honey mustard," said Keke as she chopped onions and meat like a chef.

Wow, how does she know how to cook like this?? Fah'ry thought. *It smells so good. How does she cook with all these cheap bottles of mustard, seasonings and meats? My grandma always told me that we don't shop at the cheap grocery stores. But, ooh, her food smells good,* she thought.

"So, you talk to Chaston punk a**?" asked Keke as she flipped her meat over the stove.

"Yea," said Fah'ry with a sad voice.

"Why you say it like that? asked Keke. "Cus, he ain't sh**, from what you told me." She walked quickly and went to open the back door to cool the kitchen down.

Ooh, thank you, thought Fah'ry. *It is so hot in here and my hair is starting to drop,* she thought.

"Yea," said Fah'ry. "I talked to him when I got in the house yesterday. He was acting real funny though. I don't think Ima be able to go to Polk with him though," said Fah'ry with a confused voice. She sat in the kitchen chair swinging her legs and watching Keke multi task at the stove.

"I wouldn't go nowhere with him," said Keke. "Look how he actin already."

"Yea," said Fah'ry with her head rested on the pole of the kitchen chair. "I think that I am going to go ahead and go with my original college choice. Me and all of my friends had planned to go to the same college since freshman year but I decided to go with him instead," said Fah'ry.

"Ooh, I woulda been too mad," said Keke as she sat down to eat at the table. "How you gone change plans on your friends! You ain't sh**," said Keke as she laughed and ate.

Really? Did she have to say that? Why does she have to curse all the time? she thought. She looked at Keke's plate adorned with meat and potatoes covered with cheese and fresh vegetables. *That looks good,* she thought. "How about you?" asked Fah'ry. "Are you going to college in the fall?" she asked with hesitation in fear of being offensive.

"I never really thought about it," said Keke. "I mean, I have, but never really thought that it could happen. Sh**, I just couldn't wait to get out of high school. I might take some classes at Hawker Community College," said Keke. "Girl, I don't know. I'm just trying to chill and make some money. You want some?" asked Keke, as she ate and smacked on her food.

"Um, sure, I'll try some," said Fah'ry. *I wonder if they have roaches*, she thought, *it's not that clean in here,* as she felt the holes in the fake leather chairs. Keke got up to get her a plate and made her a small portion of food to taste. Fah'ry ate with caution and poise. "This is really good!"

"Thanks," said Keke.

"So, do you have a boyfriend?" asked Fah'ry.

"Girl, I ain't faithful to no ni****! Ni***** ain't sh** but hoes and tricks," said Keke with no hesitation as she put the plates in the sink and started to wash the dishes. "I don't have time for dese ni***** to be hurting my feelings." She wrapped up washing the dishes and started to tidy up the kitchen. "You ready?" Keke asked. "We can get ready to go outside."

"Ok cool," said Fah'ry as she followed her down the stairs and onto the front porch. They sat down on the kitchen chairs and started to enjoy the summer breeze. The cars started to drive through the neighborhood as their loud music played the top 20 songs of the summer. Keke would get up and dance provocatively to the sounds.

"Hahaha!" laughed Fah'ry.

"Dey is out here!" Keke said with excitement. They continued to sit on the porch and watch the guys drive around the neighborhood for hours. "Let's go for a walk!" said Keke. "I want to see if I see Swerve and nem," she said. "I'm tryin to ride up on Juicy! He got dat money!" she said with excitement.

Why does she keep saying that? Fah'ry thought. *What's the big deal about his money?* They started to walk the neighborhood as usual and greet everyone as they browsed. They walked for about two hours and headed back to the porch. *Now, I smell like outside again,* Fah'ry thought.

"It's dead over here tonight," said Keke in disappointment. "We shoulda stayed on da block. Everybody was over dere," she said.

I didn't see Swerve, Fah'ry thought. *I have to stop this. My mom would kill me if she knew that I was hanging out over here, let alone looking at this type of guy. Oh God, what is happening?* she thought to herself. The sound of loud music could be heard from a block away. As it grew closer, Fah'ry's heart started to jump.

"Dat's Swerve," said Keke.

Fah'ry laughed. "How do you know?"

"Cuz, his sounds are clear," said Keke. "Some of dey sounds be sounding raggedy as he**!" Shortly after, the silver sparkly car with attractive lights pulled up behind Fah'ry's car. "I told you," said Keke as they laughed together.

Swerve and his friend Juicy walked up the stairs on the porch. *Ooh wee,* thought Fah'ry! *He looks so good!*

"What y'all laughing at?" Swerve asked as he smiled and sat next to Fah'ry. "What's up Fah'ry," Swerve said as he touched her curly hair.

"Hey," she said in a soft voice. *I am so scared,* she thought. *I don't know what to say to him. I don't know anything about being over here,* she thought. Keke lead most of the entertaining conversations for the night. She kept everyone laughing and talking. Swerve started to ask Fah'ry questions about herself close to her ear. *Ok, ooh, he is really close.*

"Do you have a man?" he asked her.

Um, she thought. *What do I say? I mean, Chaston treats me like crap anyway. I want to be faithful to him but he seems like he doesn't want me.* "Naw," said Fah'ry to Swerve. "We just broke up."

"Cool," he said.

Oh man, what did I just say? she thought in anguish. *I am so wrong for that. I am a faithful girl.* Swerve started to lean in closer to her as the conversations on the porch became more isolated to couple's style. *This is getting scary,* she thought. *I love Chaston. I'm not supposed to have feelings for anyone else but him,* she thought as butterflies formed in her stomach. Swerve continued to talk to her very close to her face. Fah'ry started to get nervous as she felt herself letting go of Chaston and opening her heart to Swerve. As he asked her a question, Fah'ry turned towards him and he leaned in and kissed her. They kissed for a long period of time and then there was silence. *Oh no, I am a whore!* Fah'ry thought. *I'm cheating on Chaston! But, I think I like Swerve,* she thought. Swerve and his friend got up to get ready to leave.

"Bye Fah'ry," he said.

"Bye," she said in dreamland. Her heart melted as they pulled off in his car.

"Girl, what the f***??" asked Keke. "Did you just kiss Swerve?""Y'all was kissing for a long time! Hahaha!" Keke laughed. "He** nawww!"

"Shut up!!" said Fah'ry while laughing at Keke. "Girl, it's 1 in the morning," said Fah'ry. "I gotta go home."

"You can stay ovah here if you want," said Keke. "My mama don't care."

"Girl thanks but I gotta go home," she said.

"Ok cool," said Keke.

Fah'ry got in her convertible car and drove home. *Oh, I am so wrong for kissing him,* she said to herself. *I feel like such a whore. Chaston is my boyfriend and I love him. We are going to get back together. We are supposed to go to college together and get married and have children. Those are our plans. I can't let anything come in between that,* she thought as she tried to keep her mind off of Swerve. Fah'ry parked her car and went in the house. She went in her room and put the door up to her opening and laid down on the floor full of blankets. She picked up her phone to call Chaston but there was no answer. *He answered yesterday about this time, what is he doing?* she thought with anxious thoughts. She called him again, but there was no answer. *Oh well, I don't know what to do,* she thought. *Why am I being so stupid? Why do I keep calling him?*

Fah'ry turned over to go to sleep and all she could think about was visions of the kiss that her and Swerve shared. She had pleasant sleep that she had not had in weeks. Fah'ry woke up to a longing for the feeling that she felt with Swerve last night. She started to put her prettiest outfit together again in hopes of attracting his attention.

Fah'ry continued to visit Keke's house and become more acquainted with the people and the neighborhood. The routine of walking around the neighborhood and hanging out on the porch became very familiar to her and her way of life. Swerve and Fah'ry became very close and intimate in their kissing as he visited her on the porch night after night. Her mom was away on an internship for the summer and Fah'ry had free reign to come and go as she pleased at home.

She arrived at Keke's house and saw a crowd of girls sitting on the porch. *Who are all these girls?* she thought as she let the top up on her car. She walked towards the porch as they all stared at her and whispered to each other. *Oh God*, she thought with fear.

Bougee Blunts

Fah'ry walked to the beginning of the porch steps. The group of girls sat on the stairs and continued to have their own conversations. They took up most of the steps where she could not walk through them. "Hey," Fah'ry said in nervousness as they all looked so mean and unfriendly. The girls responded as she stood there. "Is Keke here," she asked timidly.

A girl in the crowd blurted out, "She went to the stoe right quick, she will be back."

"Oh ok, thanks," said Fah'ry. She stood at the bottom of the steps and played with her phone to occupy her time. She heard the girls conversations as they snickered.

"Yeah, her hair long," another girl said while sitting on the steps. "But we got her on the straightness, her hair all curly and everything." The girls tried to bring their voices down as if they were trying not to let her hear them but just loud enough so that she did hear them. They snickered. "Kyasia, you crazy," they said. "What!" Kyasia said. "I'm just sayin! Her hair look like a Afro," said Kyasia while laughing.

Fah'ry ignored them and continued to give her attention to her phone. *Please don't let one of these girls start anything with me,* she thought to herself. *Just ignore them,* she thought. *Where is Keke? Please hurry up!* Keke's cousin came from out of the house and the group of six girls left the porch with her to walk around the neighborhood.

Fah'ry walked up the porch stairs and sat in her regular chair on the porch. She continued to wait for Keke to come back from the store. She looked at her phone. *It would be nice if Chaston would call me right now,* she thought. *I miss him so much.* She sat and let her mind wander on all of the negative things that he could be doing with other girls. *I wish my mom wasn't gone on that stupid Ph.D. thing. I just want to hang out with her and talk like Emory and her mama does,* she thought. She started to feel down and laid her head on the bannister.

Fah'ry waited on Keke for another hour. *Where is this girl at? Ugh! I'll just stay here. It's nothing for me to do at home anyway. I so miss my friends. They are probably having so much fun in London right now. I bet they are loving those fashion classes. Man, I'm supposed to be there.*

She looked up at the sky and then the trees blowing in the wind. *God, please help me through this. I feel like I'm all alone,* she prayed with tears in her eyes. *This doesn't feel real at all. Why am I over here? Ugh! I know I am not supposed to be over here. My mom would kill me if she knew I was over here with these girls anddd in the neighborhood?! Man she gone git me!* She looked down the street for the exciting sounds of Swerve's car to brighten her day but the neighborhood was very quiet. Only a few guys stood on the corner and it was brief. Fah'ry's phone started to ring. She jumped in hopes that it was Chaston. She answered. "Hey grandma," she said.

"Yo mama just called here lookin for you," her grandma said in a low voice. I know you been out but she may call back. I told her that you wasn't here and had went for a ride. So be careful now," her grandma urged her.

"Ok," Fah'ry said. "Thanks grandma." She hung up with a fearful heart. *Please don't let her call my phone while I'm over here.*

Keke finally walked up with four girls. They were dancing provocatively in the middle of the streets while laughing and playing. Keke shouted, "Come on G!" gesturing to Fah'ry. *Is she talking to me,* she thought with confusion. "Yeah, come on," said Keke. "We bout to go on da block."

I'm not a G, Fah'ry thought as she walked down the porch stairs to join them.

"What up," said Keke in a hyper and rowdy voice.

"Hey," said Fah'ry. The girls all stood in the middle of the street and continued to dance while waiting for Fah'ry.

"Dis Lexis, dis Monica, dis Quana and dats Kish," said Keke. And y'all, dis is Fah'ry.

"What up!" Alexis said in a loud voice. All the girls started to laugh at her.

"Don't pay attention to her," said Quana with a smile. She crazy." Fah'ry smirked at them.

"Who you callin crazy," said Lexis. "B****, you crazy," she said as they all laughed hysterically.

"Come on y'all, let's go on da block," said Keke. The girls sang and danced throughout the streets of the neighborhood.

Wow, all of these girls got on short shorts. My mom wouldn't ever let me wear those kinds of clothes. I always wanted to wear some of those shorts. The girls switched with confidence down the street and sang hard core rap songs as if they were the only people around. Fah'ry walked slightly behind them to try and disassociate herself from them. *I'm not doing all that,* she thought. *I can't believe that they are dancing like this.*

Keke started to shout as if she was the leader over the girls. "Freak Hoes, Freak Hoes, Bounce your a** and make your knees touch your elbows!!" These are the words she sang as all of the girls joined in and dropped low dancing. They all laughed and repeated it for the duration of the neighborhood walk.

Wow, this is crazy, Fah'ry thought. *I will not be dancing like that,* she thought as she laughed along with them. *I don't understand how they could dance like that in public. My mom would never let me dance like that, even when I was little, she was so strict on me about dancing like the other girls. I couldn't do all that stuff.*

It started to get dark and the girls headed back to the porch. They passed some of the guys on the corner. "What up," several guys in the crowd said. Several cars with loud music and flashy tire rims started to pull up all of a sudden. The girls started to scatter and have individual conversations with the guys on the corner and at their cars.

What's going on, said Fah'ry. She stood by herself as the girls talked and played and hugged up on the guys. *I don't have anyone to talk to,* she thought. *And I am not about to talk to any of these guys. I guess I'm talking to Swerve??? And I don't talk to more than one guy at a time. I am not going to be known as a whore,* she thought.

A sparkly silver car pulled up quickly and swerved into a parking space right by the other double-parked cars taking up most of the street. *Oh, is that Swerve*? she thought. Swerve got out of his car and left his car music playing loudly. He walked towards Fah'ry as she stood alone.

"You was lookin for me?" he said as he grabbed her and held her tightly while standing several feet above her. She smiled and felt safe in his arms.

I am so glad that he is here, she thought. *I felt so stupid standing there by myself while they all talked to the other guys.* Swerve, much to her surprise, immediately started to kiss on her neck and lips.

"So what's up?" he asked.

"What you mean," Fah'ry said acting as if she did not know what he was talking about.

"You comin with me tonight?" he asked as he smiled and held her tightly.

Ooh, he looks so good and I want to go but I can't, she thought. *I'm not giving myself away for anybody,* she thought. *I am saving myself for marriage and I mean that. I really want to go, though. Ugh!* "Naw," she said to Swerve in a sweet voice as she looked up high to see his face. "I am supposed to hang out with my friends tonight," she said.

"Ok cool," Swerve said. "Hang out with yo girls den," he said with jealous humor. Keke started to walk towards them and the other girls followed behind her.

"What up Swerve? said Keke as she switched by him and looked him up and down. He laughed as he continued to hold Fah'ry.

"What's up Keke," he said.

"G, we bout to go," Keke said to Fah'ry.

"Ok," said Fah'ry. The group of girls started to walk past them down the street as if they were leaving her behind.

"I'm about to go," Fah'ry said to Swerve. He stared in her eyes. *Ooh, I don't want to leave,* she thought. *I really want to go with him.* She kissed him and ran to catch up with the rest of the girls. They walked back to Keke's house and sat on the porch until about 11 PM. *Ooh, it's getting late,* Fah'ry thought. *I need to go home but I don't want to. What if Swerve come over here while I'm gone?* she thought.

"I got some weed, y'all wanna smoke?" asked Monica.

"Who got the blunts?" said Keke.

Weed! Fah'ry thought. *OK, I really need to go home.*

"I don't have none," said Monica.

"We can just walk to the stoe to get some," said Keke.

"How much weed you got? asked Keke.

"Two bags," Monica said.

"Girl, dat ain't enough," said Keke. "How much y'all got on da weed?" asked Keke.

All of the girls started to put their money in. "We can stop at the weed man on the way to the liquor stoe." Keke said.

Weed man? Fah'ry thought. *They are about to go and buy drugs? Oh God, please protect me? Liquor store? Are they about to drink?* she thought in serious fear. Keke collected all of the money and they headed to the store. They stopped at the corner to meet the weed man. The girls played around with the guys on the corner while they were on their way to the liquor store.

Monica walked in the store with confidence and stood at the counter. "Lemme get 20 swishers," she said.

"And get a bottle of dat purple," said Lexis.

"Oh, let me get some strawberry juice for it," said Keke. "I can't drink that straight."

Fah'ry looked at the girls speechless as they moved around the store to get their items. *I'm stuck right now,* she thought. *If I leave, they will think that I'm a scary cat but I know I don't need to be here.* She looked around at the holes in the wall and how crowded the store was with the drunk people and even more girls their age being loud and rambunctious. The store started to fill up quickly as the time approached midnight with guys constantly coming in asking for Swishers and drinks. The girls put their items in their large purses and walked back to Keke's house.

They went upstairs to Keke's room and started to spread everything on the bed. "We need cups for the drinks," said Keke.

"I'll go get them!" said Monica in excitement.

Oh God, what is this? What is about to happen? Fah'ry thought. *I can't be in here with this stuff. What am I going to do? How do I get out of here without looking like a little scared girl?*

Lexis took the marijuana bags out and laid them on the bed and took 15 blunts from her purse. "I need a razor blade," she said. "Keke, pass me that razor blade," said Lexis.

What is she about to do with that? Fah'ry thought as she watched closely. Lexis started to neatly cut the blunts open while Monica poured the drinks for everyone. She put a small red cup in front of Fah'ry. Fah'ry looked down at the cup full of liquor as if she had frozen.

Bullets and Sleepovers

Fah'ry looked at the drink with pressure. *Ooh that stinks,* she thought. "Oh, I'm good." Fah'ry said to Monica.

"You don't drink?" asked Lexis as she prepared the 15 blunts.

"Naw," said Fah'ry with confidence.

"Oh," said Lexis. "Pass me dat other box," Lexis said as she sprinkled the marijuana inside of the cut-up cigar. Lexis started to lick the cigars closed and place them in a neat row.

Fah'ry stared at the girls as they prepared for what they considered to be chill and fun. *That is so nasty,* she thought. *Her spit is all over that blunt. Are they all going to each get their own?*

"Where is da lighters?" asked Keke. She turned the music on and the girls started to laugh and talk. Keke lit the first blunt and took a couple of puffs and passed it on to Lexis. She took a couple of puffs and passed the same blunt to Monica. She took some puffs and passed it to Quana.

I can't believe that they all are putting their lips on the same blunt or whatever it is called, Fah'ry thought. Quana passed the blunt to Fah'ry. "Oh, I don't smoke," said Fah'ry.

"Oh sh**. I'm sorry!" said Quana. She passed it along to Kish while Keke was lighting up another one from the pile.

Wow, thought Fah'ry. *So, they are going to just keep passing?* she thought.

"Ouch!" Kish said.

"Dat's what you get for tryin to smoke dat small a** blunt," said Lexis. "Burning your dam* fingertips! Hahaha!" The girls laugh with their low, red eyes.

So is that why their fingernails look like that? Fah'ry observed and pondered. *I know that I won't be smoking because I am not messing up my nails.*

"Shoot!" Monica said.

"What!!" they all said.

"I just burned my lip!!"

"Here," said Lexis. "Here is some stuff for your lips."

Monica applied the lip balm to her lips and kept smoking. *So those things can burn your lips?* thought Fah'ry. *Oh no, I will definitely not be doing dat! My lips will not be turning black from those things!* Keke's small room was filled with smoke as the girls continued to smoke and squeeze in on her bed. *Look at all of this smoke,* Fah'ry thought. *And they still have like ten to go.* She laughed at their jokes and stories so she didn't look awkward amongst them.

"Y'all," said Lexis. "I think I might be pregnant."

"I told you!" Keke said in a convincing voice.

"So you been lettin Beaver hit it?" asked Quana.

"HaHa!" They all laughed.

"B****!" Lexis heightened her voice. "Obviously, if I'm sayin that I think I'm pregnant."

Pregnant? Fah'ry's mind started to wander. *She's only 17!*

"So are you gonna keep it, if you are?" asked Monica.

"I don't know," said Lexis. "I can't take care of no baby," she said as she sipped from her cup of alcohol.

"G, you betta take yo a** to da chop shop!" Keke said as she puffed the skinny blunt.

"Dat's why I get my three month shot," said Kish. "I ain't got time for dat."

"Ok," said Keke. "And you know I gotta get me some d***!" Keke said.

"Yo a** is too hot KeKe," Monica said as she laughed. "You need to sit down somewhere."

Chop shop? Fah'ry thought. *What is that?* She continued to think about it as the girls kept smoking. *Ohhh!! Gross! Why would she say it like that?*

The girls continued to talk and laugh and the room was saturated with marijuana smoke. "So Fah'ry, you messin wit Swerve??" Lexis asked while puffing on her blunt.

"Yeah," said Fah'ry.

"He** yea," KeKe interrupted. "He be ovah here in huh face every night. Dey be kissing all night."

"Really?" Lexis said as she snickered. "G, you be kissin Swerve??"

"Yea," Fah'ry laughed.

"I don't see how y'all could do all dat kissin," said Keke. "I hate kissin! It's so nasty!"

"B****, so what you do den?" asked Monica with a friendly attitude.

"B***, don't worry about me!!" Keke said. "Worry bout all dem baby mamas Toine got!"

"Don't get me started on Pooh Bear fat a**!!" Monica said and all of the girls started laughing loudly. Fah'ry started giggling abnormally.

"G, you high?" asked Keke.

"Naw!" said Fah'ry as she continued to giggle.

"Yes you is!" laughed Keke. "Yo a** done got contact!" Everyone started to laugh again and continue to smoke and drink.

"I am not high!" Fah'ry said. "I am laughing at y'all."

"Keke, why don't you go make us some of dose potatoes dat you make?" Lexis said.

"We don't have no moe," said Keke.

"I'm hungry!" Lexis said.

"Me too," said Monica.

"Ooh, let's go get some chicken!" Kish said.

"Ooh, dat do sound good," said Keke. The girls started to move their drinks out of the way to prepare to go to the restaurant.

It's 3 o'clock in the morning, thought Fah'ry. *They are about to go out this late?* She followed them out of the door with caution as they walked down the street to the small chicken shack. She looked around in fear as the neighborhood was quiet and dark. *Oh God, please protect me,* she prayed to herself. *I know that I am not supposed to be over here but I just don't want to go home. I hate being there.* The girls quickly ordered their own personal orders of chicken with barbecue sauce to go. They walked graciously with their chicken bags in their hands back towards Keke's house.

I can't wait to eat this, Fah'ry thought. *I haven't had food like this in a long time. My grandma or my mama don't ever cook dinner.*

As the girls were walking, they saw a group of guys on the corner and they stopped to talk to them for a brief moment. Suddenly, a car pulled up and started to yell out gang affiliations and they started shooting at each other. "Pow, Pow, *Pow!!!*" as the bullets flew past Fah'ry's face. The girls started to yell and run as fast as they could to Keke's house.

Lord, what in the world? Fah'ry thought as she tried to catch her breath. *We could have been shot! Wow! Thank you God!*

"Dem moth********* are crazy!" Keke said while breathing hard and opening her chicken bag.

"Dat scared da sh** out of me!" Lexis yelled.

"I know," said Quana. "Dey really need to stop!" The girls sat in Keke's room and enjoyed their barbecue chicken while talking about what had just happened. They hung out until about four in the morning before they started to get tired.

"I'm bout to go to sleep," said KeKe. "Y'all know where all da blankets at. Fah'ry, you still here?" KeKe said with surprise. "I can't believe you still out? You can stay with us if you want to. Grab a blanket before Lexis pregnant a** !" KeKe said with tired humor.

Should I stay here? Fah'ry said to herself. *I really don't want to go out there after they've been shooting. I have never heard a gunshot before! That's crazy! I have to find a way to get home. Naw, I think that I should stay. I would be able to take a shower in the morning if I stay,* she thought. "Ok," she said to Keke. "I'll stay here tonight." She grabbed a blanket and pillow and laid on the floor with the rest of the girls. They talked and laughed until they fell asleep. *My mom is gonna kill me! Please don't let her call my phone!* Fah'ry thought with worry before saying her prayers.

Giving It Up

Fah'ry woke up at Keke's house. All the girls were asleep on the living room floor. She grabbed her phone and took a look at the time. *It's seven!* Fah'ry thought. She dialed her grandmother to let her know where she was staying. *It's Sunday. I gotta get ready for church.* Fah'ry took a long shower while the girls were asleep. *Thank you, God for this shower. I am so glad that I get to be over here and get this shower. Especially now, while I am on my period. I hate being on my period at home and trying to wash up in that stupid pan. Ugh!* Fah'ry got out of the shower and dusted off her clothes from last night.

She crept out of the front door silently and got in her car and drove to church. *God, please forgive me for everything that I have done wrong,* she prayed on the way to church. She decided to call her mom but there was no answer. "Hey ma, I was just calling to say hi, I am on my way to church. I hope your classes are going well. Love you!" She said on her mom's voicemail. Fah'ry enjoyed herself at church.

Afterwards, she drove back to Keke's house. She parked her car in front of the house and the neighborhood was very quiet and peaceful. Fah'ry went in the house and it was abnormally quiet. *Are they gone?* she thought. *Wow!* Fah'ry said. *They still sleep! It's 2 o'clock in the afternoon. Who sleeps this late?*

Fah'ry went downstairs and walked to Devo's to get a bag of chips, cheese and ground beef. There weren't any guys hanging out at all on the corners. *This seems like a totally different neighborhood from last night,* she thought.

Fah'ry sat on the porch alone and ate her food. She looked at every oncoming car in hopes that it was Swerve. *This would be the perfect time for us to be together. It's so peaceful. I miss my friends. Man!* Her mind started to drift. *I wonder what Chaston is doing? Ugh! I gotta stop thinking about him. I am not chasing him anymore.* Her mind jumped back to thinking about Swerve. *So, am I his girlfriend now? I mean, he's never asked me to be but we act like it?* she thought in confusion. *I don't kiss guys that are not my boyfriend. So I guess we are dating?* Fah'ry thought with uncertainty. *He's never taken me out anywhere? So, are we really dating? All he does is come and hang out with me on the porch. I mean, he's never asked me to get in the car with him to go anywhere! I don't know! Ugh! Whatever! I really like him though,* she thought. *I think I love him. I'm just scared. I have never dated anybody like him before, I mean, he's from the neighborhood. He's a bad boy and I just don't want my feelings hurt again. I know he's cute and probably all types of girls are throwing themselves at him. Why is he wanting me?* she asked herself over and over again. *I mean, I haven't done anything with him. I know all of these girls are having sex and everything. I mean he probably can get it anywhere.*

Fah'ry heard loud talking coming from upstairs out of the window. *So they are finally up?* She went upstairs to greet the girls. They were all laughing and playing while folding their blankets. The house was filled with the aroma of breakfast.

"Hey Fah'ry!" Lexis said. "We was looking for you. Where you been?"

Fah'ry smirked. "I went to church," she said.

"Oh, I hope you prayed for me," said Lexis.

Fah'ry snickered. "Of course!" Fah'ry walked to the kitchen where the smell was coming from. "What you makin Keke?" asked Fah'ry.

"Some pancakes, bacon, sausage and eggs." Keke said as she mixed the pancake batter from scratch. "How many pancakes you want?" Keke asked.

"Um two is fine." Fah'ry said.

"Where was you at?" Keke asked Fah'ry.

"I was at church." Fah'ry said as she watched Keke prepare breakfast for all of the girls. She sat and hung out with Keke in the kitchen while the other girls took turns in the one shower that they had. She looked at the time. *Dang, it's almost 4 o'clock! We are just about to eat breakfast and they are just taking showers! Ugh! This is horrible!* Fah'ry thought. *And Keke is going to be the last one to get ready. Ugh! She takes forever to get dressed!*

It's going to be like 7 o'clock! "I'll be back," said Fah'ry to Keke.

"Where you bout to go? Lookin for Swerve!" Keke said in a teasing manner.

Fah'ry smiled. "No I am not! I am going to just sit on the porch." Fah'ry said.

"Whatever," said Keke. "Tell Swerve I said . . . What uuup!"

Fah'ry ignored Keke and went to sit on the front porch. She enjoyed the summer breeze and took a look at the sky and watched the trees blow in the wind. *It is so nice out here,* she thought. Fah'ry looked and looked in hopes of seeing Swerve. *Ugh! Where is he? I'd rather sit down here then wait on all of them to take forever getting dressed.* She sat and continued to enjoy the breeze and hope for Swerve to come down the street in his sleek silver car. *Actually, why don't I have his number? And he never asked for mine? I don't even have a way of contacting him? I don't know! I really really like him though,* she thought. *I barely think about Chaston. I mean, sometimes I do but not as much.* Quana yelled out of the window.

Fah'ry!! Yo food is ready!"

"Ok!" Fah'ry yelled. She went upstairs and sat at the table and had breakfast with all of the girls. They laughed and reminisced about last night.

"Dey was bussin like we wasn't even standing dere!" said Lexis.

"I know!! Muggf****** are crazy!" Keke said as she ate her fluffy pancakes.

"I know!" said Monica. "Dey need to stop! Really!" The girls wrapped up eating their breakfast and just hung out at the kitchen table talking.

"Ooh, I wanna smoke!" Lexis said.

"We don't have enough," said Monica. "We will smoke dat up too fast."

They are about to smoke again? thought Fah'ry.

"I ain't going out!" Keke said.

"Where y'all money at?" asked Lexis as she gestured with her hands. "I'll go. Monica you gone come wit me?"

"Yea, I'll go," Monica said. They both went out to get more marijuana and blunts.

"I'll roll dese from last night," Quana said as she grabbed the razor blade.

"Keke, do you want me to help you wash da dishes?" Fah'ry asked as she sat there with nothing to do.

"Naw, I'm good," Keke said. The girls had all of the blunts ready and were waiting on Lexis and Monica to come back. Keke turned on loud love music and started to sing and dance along. "Dis my song!" Keke said as she sang all of the words.

"I love this song!" Fah'ry said. "Put that on repeat!" *This song really makes me think about Swerve,* she thought. *What if he came up here and we talked and stuff?* The kitchen started to fill up with marijuana smoke and loud talking. Monica and Lexis came in the house with the rest of the items.

"G!" Monica said. "We just saw Swerve. He lookin for you." Fah'ry's heart started to beat really fast.

"We told him that you were up here," Lexis said as she put the marijuana on the table. "He on his way up here."

Oh gosh! Fah'ry thought. *What do I say? I've never really been in the house with him before,* she thought as her hands trembled.

Keke walked up to Fah'ry. "Y'all can go in my room. There are condoms under my sheet. If you feel around, you will feel where they are," Keke said.

"Ok," said Fah'ry as she went into Keke's room and waited for him.

"What up Swerve!" Keke said loudly. "She up dere in my room."

"What up," he said as he looked for the room and smiled.

Swerve walked in the room, closed the door of Keke's room and started to hug and kiss Fah'ry. Her hands shook as she could feel the condoms under the sheet just like Keke said. *I am so scared,* she thought as he kissed and caressed her. *Do I want to give this to him? If I do, what if he acts like he doesn't know me after? What if he treats me like every other girl around here? I know that this is precious. I know that it's only one time and it's over. I can't get my virginity back,* she thought. *I know that I am supposed to wait to get married but that just seems like a long time, plus I love him. I really really like him.*

Swerve laid her down on the bed and started to unbutton her top. *Oh God! Is this really about to happen*?! Her heart beat faster and she started to sweat. *Oh my gosh! This feels so right. And my period is gone. I don't have ah excuse at all. I can't do this. Can I? What if I don't do it right? I know he has had all types of girls to do all types of things to him! Keke nem always talking about all these tricks and stuff that they do. I don't know how to do that stuff,* she thought as Swerve started to unzip her shorts. Fah'ry grabbed him and held him tight and engaged with him more.

"So, we doing all this, we might as well go head," he said as he continued to kiss on her.

Fah'ry smiled, laid back in the bed closer to the pillow and subtly rubbed her yellow manicured nailed hands around the sheet to reach for the condom.

Virginity Victory

I can't do this, Fah'ry thought to herself. *I can never get my virginity back. God would be so mad at me.* Fah'ry lifted her head off of the pillow, buttoned her shirt and sat up on the bed.

"What's wrong?" Swerve asked as he looked at her in disappointment.

"Nothing," she said. "I just don't want to do this right now," Fah'ry said as she fixed her hair and opened the room door.

"Aiight," Swerve said. "Man, dey got da whole house smoked out!"

"Yea," smirked Fah'ry. "They always smoking."

Swerve stood up and fixed his clothes. Fah'ry leaned against the door and stared at him fix his clothes. *What did I just do? How did I get out of that?* she thought. Swerve took a deep breath and looked at Fah'ry. She looked at him. They hugged and kissed. "See you," said Fah'ry with confused emotions. *I swear I don't know how to feel,* she thought. *I am happy that I didn't because I definitely was not ready or planning on that. But . . . Naw,* she thought. *I did the right thing!* She walked him to the door and watched him ride off in his sparkling, sleek silver car. Fah'ry went back upstairs to hang out with the girls in the kitchen.

"You done let Swerve hit it!" Keke said as she puffed on the blunt that was being passed around.

"Keke shut up!!" Lexis shouted. "Mind yo d*** business! B****,"

"I wasn't even talkin to you!" Keke said as she laughed and sang.

Lexis passed the blunt to Fah'ry. "I don't want that!" Fah'ry said with a serious look. All of the girls started laughing loudly.

"I know," Lexis said. "I'm just playin! We know you don't smoke." Lexis passed the blunt to Kish and they continued to smoke marijuana into the midnight hour.

"I need some air!" Keke said as she walked to the porch. The rest of the girls eventually migrated to the front porch as well. They sat on the porch, laughed and talked until they got tired. A used truck pulled up in front of Keke's house.

"What up J.K.!" Keke said.

"Aye, it's a party on da six three," he said. "We all ovah dere!" J.K. said.

"Y'all wanna go?" Lexis said.

"Yea, cuz it's dead around here," Monica said.

Who is this dude? Fah'ry thought. *I have never seen him before.* Fah'ry thought. *He must be a 3K. I only mess with the Diceboys.*

"We don't have a way dere," Keke said.

"And I ain't getting on no bus!" Quana said with an attitude.

"Me either," Fah'ry said. "I don't do buses."

"Y'all can ride with me," J.K. said. "I'm bout to go back ovah dere."

"Ok, let us go get our stuff," Keke said. The girls ran upstairs to get their purses and other items.

"G, if he start some sh**, we gone beat his a**!" Lexis said.

"I know!" Keke said with enthusiasm and aggression. "Cuz I don't know him like that."

What! She doesn't know him? Fah'ry thought. *Then, why are we getting in the car with him? It's really bad over there on the 63 anyway. Those are the projects. I don't really want to go but I don't want to stay here by myself. And I don't want to look like I'm scared either. I mean we are all together.* Fah'ry thought. *And I am definitely not driving my car over there.*

"Aye y'all," Lexis said with urgency and whispering. "I gotta tell y'all somethin."

"Come on G! We gotta go foe he leave us!" Monica said.

"Ok," Lexis said. "I told my cousin that I would hold his gun for him. He was running from the police and ask me to hold it."

"What!" Keke said. "Where is it?"

"It's in my purse," Lexis said. "Should I leave it here? I don't know what to do with it!" Lexis said as she looked concerned at the girls waiting on an answer.

"Girl, you gone have to take it with us," Keke said in fear. "We can't leave it here!" The girls were so confused and in disarray.

"Just keep the purse with you, Lexis," Monica said to try and resolve the fearful excitement amongst the girls.

"Ok ok ok," said Lexis. "Oh shoot! I am so scared," she said as all of the girls ran down the stairs to get in the truck.

"Oh my God!" All mumbled to each other as they squeezed in the truck and looked at each other while Lexis held the purse.

A gun? Fah'ry thought. *Lord please don't let me die. Please don't let this gun go off accidentally. I am glad that I am sitting in the front because if I need to jump out of this truck, I will. Ooh, he smells just like alcohol!* she thought. *Is that why he's driving like that?* J.K. kept stopping and going, fast and slow as he drove to the party. He continued to slam on the brakes.

"What the?!" Keke shouted. "J.K., you drunk??"

"Naw Keke. I'm good. I got y'all," he said.

If he slams on the brakes one more time, I am jumping out of this truck, Fah'ry said as she unlocked the doors. *I don't care if it is 1 o'clock in the morning, I will walk back to the house. This dude is drunk! Ok, we don't have long before we get to the party. I am so glad that we are not going too far.*

"Hurry and get us outta dis truck!" Keke said. "Dis mugg****** is crazy!!"

"Ok!" Lexis said. "We might have to use that thang on him!" The girls started to laugh so loudly that it confused him.

"What y'all laughing at?" he asked as he pulled into the raggedy parking lot of the building.

Oh God! Dis ah house party? Fah'ry thought. *Who's house is this anyway? I should have stayed at the house. I don't know none of these people and we are not close enough for me to just walk back. God, please protect me and please don't let us stay at this party too long. I'm ready to go already,* she thought to herself.

The girls headed into the party as a group together.

"Lexis hold dat purse," Keke whispered.

"G, I am!!" Lexis said. "Now shut up!" she said mumbling under her breath.

"Be cool y'all," Monica said. They walked into the small apartment style residence filled with people all on the walls and squeezed on couches. The music was very loud and it was very dark. The only room that was lit was the kitchen to serve the alcohol.

What in the world am I doing here? I really need to go! Fah'ry thought. *My mom would really kill me if she knew where I was. I feel so bad.* The people in the crowd started to dance all around Fah'ry but she politely moved out of the way and found a place on the couch to sit down. The rest of the girls started to dance but Lexis set next to her with the purse.

One of the guys in the crowd started to yell out happy birthdays for the month and passed out alcohol bottles to the birthday people. Lexis jumped up. "Dis my birthday month!" she shouted. "Fah'ry hold dis!" Lexis said. She passed the purse with the gun in it to Fah'ry while she went and danced and celebrated.

All of a sudden, the alcohol bottles popped open and alcohol was being thrown all over the party. *Oh God! I got dis purse,* Fah'ry thought as she tried to stop her legs from shaking. She set the purse on her lap and did not move. *I am just going to stay still until she comes back and get this purse. She needs to hurry up! What if this thing goes off?* Fah'ry thought. *I am ready to go.* The guys and girls danced and sang to the rap songs in the dark living room. The party was full of marijuana smoke as the people went in and out of the front door.

"Blah!!" A girl started to throw up right in front of Fah'ry.

"Uyy!" Fah'ry said as she quickly moved her legs. *Dis girl almost messed up my shoes!* she thought. "Yea, I'm ready to go!" she said as she rolled her eyes. *They need to come on!* The girls continued to dance as the guys pinned them to the walls and danced provocatively. *Ugh! Look at these dudes.* Fah'ry thought. *They got braids in their head, a bottle in their hand and smoking a blunt. Gross! Dat is so not my type.* Fah'ry thought as the purse with the gun lay on her lap. She looked down at it. *Please don't let nobody bump me?* She thought. *Dang, how many people gone come in here? It is too crowded in here,* she thought as she scanned the room the best that she could using the lights from blunt fires. *Where is the door, in case I gotta run out of here. God please let us get back to the house safe.*

A crowd started to run in the house yelling. "Aye! Get dat thang!!" a guy from the crowd yelled.

"On my mama!" another guy yelled.

"Dey don't know us!" People started to run outside in mobs. Suddenly, "Pop, Pop, Pop!!!"

"Dey bussin!" a girl yelled as the girls lay on the floor. *Oh God, please, please, get me home,* Fah'ry thought as she lay on the floor with her head down and the purse beside her.

"We gotta go!" Keke said.

"Right now!" Fah'ry said as she peaked over at her on the floor.

"Dey still shootin," said Lexis with a confused tone.

"Dey stopped!" Keke said. "Let's go! It's a back door right dere! Come on y'all! Let's get outta here!!!" Keke admonished.

Oh Lord! Please don't let me get shot. The girls quickly got up and ran out the back door. "This is crazy!" Fah'ry said.

"He** yeah!" Lexis said as they walked quickly down the alley.

"Here girl, take this purse!" Fah'ry said to Lexis.

"Hahaha!" The girls started laughing.

"G, you was holdin the purse down!" Quana said.

"Not again!" Fah'ry said. The girls continued to walk quickly through the alley to find the nearest busy street with lights. *Lord please don't let somebody mistake us for somebody else in this alley,* Fah'ry thought. *Please just let us get to a main street.* The girls finally reached a main boulevard and started to walk home. They started to hear the sirens of police cars and ambulances.

"Look how long dey took!" Keke said.

"Cuz dey don't care!" Monica said as she tried to catch her breath. The police cars started to ride past them quickly as the blue lights shined and lit up the street. A police car slowed down to look at the girls as they walked.

"Oh sh**!" Keke mumbled.

Oh God! Please don't let me go to jail. Fah'ry thought as her legs started to shake.

"Just act normal," Lexis mumbled. The girls started to fake laugh and try to hold conversations amongst each other.

The officer hit his siren to get the girls' attention. "Ladies, where are you going at 3 o'clock in the morning?" the officer asked from his window.

"We are on our way home," they said in a jumbled but unison voice.

"Where are you all coming from?" The officer asked as the police car sat in the middle of the street.

"We just got off of the bus. We live around the corner. We are not that far," Kish said.

"All right, you all hurry up and get in the house, it is too late to be out here, it's some dangerous people around. You all are too nice of girls to be out in the streets," the officer admonished.

"Ok!! Thank you!" they all said together. "Whew! Man! Oh my God!" the girls sighed in relief as they watched the police car drive off.

"I ain't neva comin ovah here again," Keke said.

"Me either," said Fah'ry.

"We can't neva have fun without dem actin stupid," Lexis said.

"Man!! My feet are hurtin!" Kish said. "Dis is a long walk!"

"We almost dere," Quana said. "We got a couple moe blocks to go".

"Ooh! Dat's why I don't mess with dose 3K's!" Lexis said.

"Dat be Keke tryin to kick it wit erbody!" Monica said.

"Hey, I justtt be tryin to be cool with all of dem," Keke said. "It don't matter to me if dey 3K or whateva!"

The girls finally arrived at Keke's house. They stood on the porch for a brief moment to cool off.

"What up Juicy?" Keke said as he walked on the porch.

"Aye, y'all heard what happened on da six?" Juicy asked.

"Naw, what happened?" Keke said with the other girls.

"Aye, like five people got shot and Jay died."

"What!!" the girls said as they started to cry.

"I can't believe dis!" Keke said. "We just saw him da otha day."

"Man! He was so funny!" Monica said. "He used to have us laughin all night."

Killed? Fah'ry thought. *It is crazy around here.* "I'm going upstairs," Fah'ry said to the girls.

"G, you stayin?" Keke asked.

"I guess so," Fah'ry said with a sad tone. "It's 4 o'clock in the morning."

"G what!! I can't believe you stayin," Lexis said with surprising elevation in her voice. The girls followed Fah'ry in the house.

"I am tired," Fah'ry said.

"Girl, I really need to lay down," Quana said as she grabbed herself a blanket and pillow. The girls followed suit and laid down on the floor to go to bed.

I want my mom, thought Fah'ry. *I really wish that I could have a nice home. I hate being at that house. I get tired of washing up in that pan and not be able to take showers and not be able to use all of the fruity body washes and stuff like the other girls. I want to just be able to brush my teeth and wash my face the normal way at my own house. I hate having all my clothes stuffed in this book bag and stay over here all the time. I just wish I had my own nice house. Want to talk to my mom. I miss her. I wish she could just call me right now. I know that she's busy though. I know she is getting her doctorate degree and things will be better once she finishes. Well, at least I get to stay here and I'm able to take a shower every day which I really don't get to do so that's a good thing. I'm happy to be able to be fresh and clean and brush my teeth and stuff. I like how Keke's cooking too. Grandma doesn't cook like that. I'm glad that I don't have to eat that restaurant food every day from the restaurant across the street. And I get to see Swerve everyday.*

Fah'ry slept over Keke's house night after night. Her overnight book bag eventually turned into a duffel bag. The summer break was moving rapidly along as they enjoyed its freedom.

Pretty, Popped and Pregnant!

"It's 7!" Fah'ry said as she looked at her phone. *This is going to be a long morning. Ugh! I hate waiting for them to get up. They take forever. I don't see how they can sleep til twelve and one in the afternoon,* Fah'ry thought while sitting on her blanket on the floor. She picked her blanket up, folded it and placed it in Keke's room. Fah'ry rambled through her duffel bag for clothes. *Where is my yellow tee? I need that to go with my denim shorts. I gotta stay pretty. I hope Swerve sees me today. I know he will be like . . . Dang! She pretty!* she thought. Fah'ry ironed her wrinkled clothes silently as the girls slept. *I wish I could be at home like this. I don't have to worry about no rats in the kitchen, no roaches, I can actually drink all of the water that I want, I don't have to wash up in that pan, I can clean my whole body and it's peaceful. Well, I'm not arguing with nobody, either. I want to talk to my mama though. I know that she'll never understand why I am staying over here. Even if I told her. I wonder what J.D. and nem doing? I wish I could call them but I can't call out of the country.*

Shoot, I need to figure out where I am going to go to college now! I am definitely not going to Polk State with Chaston. He's not going to treat me trife at school and be talking to all them girls in my face. I would be stupid to still go away to college with him. Ooh, I'm going to call Brighton as soon as they open and see if my acceptance offer is still open! Lord, please let there still be room for me at Brighton? she thought as she put the ironing board up.

Fah'ry took a long, peaceful shower and got primped and pretty for the day. She silently went on the front porch and enjoyed the morning summer breeze. She talked to God and sat quietly as she watched the neighborhood awake. *I hope Keke cook breakfast. I am hungry. Plus, I love her specially made potatoes. I need to call this school before it gets loud over here.* Fah'ry's phone rang. She jumped in hopes that it was Chaston. "Oh, hey grandma." Fah'ry said.

"Yo mama just called here. I told her you was at the stoe. So you betta come here and call her back," her grandma said in a sneaky voice.

"Ok, here I come." Fah'ry hopped in her light yellow IvyKennington and quickly drove home around the corner. Fah'ry parked her car and went in the house. She sat down on the couch to call her mom back. She talked to her mom for a moment and was able keep the story that her grandmother had told intact.

She hung up from with her mom and called Brighton University in hopes that there was still a place for her. "Welcome to Brighton University," the operator said.

Ooh! I'll be gone in August! I got a month and a couple of weeks! Ok, ok, I need to calm down. I need some money, she thought. "Hello, I was trying to reach the Admissions office," Fah'ry said. She was transferred over to her assigned counselor. Fah'ry was transferred from admissions to academic advising to student life and on to financial aid. She spent about an hour on the phone with Brighton taking care of her collegiate business. "Yes!!" Fah'ry yelled and jumped up and down. *Whew! I got my admissions spot back! Thank you God!! And they have not sent out dorm assignments yet. So I can possibly room with my friends. Ooh! Ooh! I am so excited!* "I get to go to Brighton!" Fah'ry clapped her hands in excitement.

Fah'ry picked up her phone and called her dad. "Hey Dad," Fah'ry said.

"What up Fah'ry," her dad said.

"I need some money," she said.

"What's some money? How much?" he said sarcastically.

"Um like, 150 dollars??" Fah'ry said with uncertainty.

"I'll be over there in about 30 minutes," he said.

"Well, actually I'll be over my friend's house," she said.

"Where is that!" her dad said in slight frustration. She gave him the address to Keke's house. "Alright. Give me like a hour," he said.

"Ok!" Fah'ry said with a grin. "Thanks Dad."

Fah'ry went in her room and grabbed more clothes and underwear for her overnight duffel. She got back in her car and drove to Keke's house. She sat on the porch and continued to enjoy the peaceful early afternoon sounds of the neighborhood. *I bet they are still sleep,* she thought. Fah'ry sat and waited for her dad to come. He eventually came and Fah'ry walked to his car.

"Hey Dad," she said. He passed her the money as she stood on the driver's side.

"Aye Fah'ry," he said with concern. "What you doin over here? Why you over here!" he asked. "It's bad around here. You don't need to be over here," he said.

"Just with my friends," Fah'ry said.

"I gotta go," her dad said in disappointment. "Call me tomorrow."

"Ok," she said as she dropped her head in shame. *Man! I know he's mad at me, but he'll never understand how much staying at Keke's house helps me. I get to take showers, eat home cooked meals, there are no rats and no one is arguing with me,* she thought.

Fah'ry walked back on the porch and sat down. *It sounds like they might be up,* she thought. *Oh! Her heart jumped as Swerve's car pulled up silently. Ooh, I didn't know that he was coming! Why doesn't he have his sounds on?* He got out of his car and stood across the street from her. *Why is he standing over there?* Swerve stood across the street from her for awhile. *Really? He not gone even say hi,* she thought. *Maybe I should go and say something to him since everybody always saying that I don't show him that I like him. I just don't want him to be thinking that I'm sweating him. I'm sure that he has enough girls to do that. Should I go? I don't know? What if he doesn't talk to me? I mean, if he wanted to talk to me, he would have come over here. I'm not about to chase anybody. I did that with Chaston and it felt horrible. Maybe I should just be bold and go over there? I guess I will never know if I don't. Maybe he's trying to see if I really like him. Especially after last night. OK, I'm going to go.*

Fah'ry mustered up the guts to go as her heart beat faster and faster. *Ok, think of something to say,* she said to herself as she walked the short distance across the street. He stared at her as she walked but turned his head. *Oh Gosh! He just turned his head. I should go back. I can't though. I mean, what would that look like? I can't even fake it. I am out here now.* "Hey," Fah'ry said to Swerve.

"What's up," he said as he glanced at her but avoided eye contact.

Dang, it's like he's not even paying attention to me. He usually hugs me or we kiss or something, she thought. He looked around everywhere else besides at her as if he was waiting on someone. *Maybe he has something else going on. I think I should go back on the porch,* she thought. *Say something Fah'ry,* she said to herself. Don't just stand here. She looked him up and down. "You have some nice legs." Swerve looked at her and gave her a dry thanks. *Wow,* she thought. *I should not have said that. That sounded so stupid. Why is he acting like this?* The silence grew louder between them as she stood there. "You going to come by later?" she asked.

"Man, you ain't on nothin," he said nonchalantly.

Huh? she thought. "What do you mean?" she asked.

"You know what I'm talking about," he said. Another car pulled up. "I got to go," he said as he walked to the car.

"Ok," she said with her heart on the ground. *Here we go again.* Fah'ry said to herself while walking back to the porch. *I feel so stupid. I don't even know why I went over there. Ugh! Now he's mad at me,* she said in disgust as she went in the house. *I guess all of this is all because I won't have sex with him. Ugh! Is it really that simple? If I have sex with him, will I have a boyfriend then? Is that what I have to do to have a consistent relationship? Is it all about that? I'm sorry but I just can't do that. I'm not giving myself away to anyone but my husband. I think he's just mad for right now. He'll probably be over here on the porch tonight,* she thought with confidence.

Fah'ry walked in the house filled with the smell of bacon. All of the girls were laying their clothes out and waiting for their turn in the restroom as the rap music play loudly.

"Where you been?" Lexis asked.

"I went home to take care of my college stuff." Fah'ry said.

"Oh ok," Lexis said. "G, you be gone early in da mornin all da time. You be outta here for church every Sunday. You be back befoe we even wake up," Lexis said as she rumbled through her bag for clothes.

Fah'ry smirked. She went in the kitchen and sat with Keke as she cooked. The girls ate breakfast together and headed to the front porch. They sat and watched the sleek cars with rims and loud sounds playing the latest hard core rap music. "Fah'ry can you go with me to da clinic?" Lexis said.

Clinic? I'm not going in no ghetto clinic! Fah'ry thought. "I'll drop you off but I'm not going in," Fah'ry said.

"Ok," Lexis said. "Let me get my purse."

Fah'ry dropped Lexis off at the neighborhood clinic. "I'll be parked right here when you're done," Fah'ry said.

"Aiight," Lexis said.

Fah'ry sat in her car and waited for Lexis. She turned her music on and listened to the Jazz radio station. The saxophone melodies rang loudly to her creative ear. She looked in the backseat of her car and grabbed her fashion sketch bag. "Ooh, I miss designing!" she said as her face lit up. Fah'ry took her pink pencil out and started to design new creations. "Ooh, this is hot! Haha!" She laughed in excitement. *I need my colored pencils for this one. This skirt and blouse are so pretty! I just need to make a matching sweater,* she pondered. Oh, here come Lexis. Fah'ry put her sketch items in the bag and back in the back seat.

"Hey," Fah'ry said to Lexis with a compassionate tone. "You ok?"

"Yea," Lexis said with a somber look. "Girl I'm two months."

"What!"

"Yea," Lexis said. "I knew I shouldn't went over his house. I can't have no baby right now. I made an appointment. Can you take me to the chop shop next week?" Lexis said.

Chop shop? Fah'ry thought. *I'm assuming that she's talking about getting an abortion? I'm not taking her to do that. That is not any of my business. Ok, I have to think of something to say.* "When?" Fah'ry asked as they rode back to Keke's house.

"It's Friday at 1," Lexis said.

"Oh, I have a phone appointment with my college counselor at one that same day. Sorry I can't take you," Fah'ry said.

"It's cool," Lexis said as she put her hand on her forehead in disgust. The girls arrived back at Keke's house to an abnormally crowded porch of girls. "Oh, Kyasia nem over here," Lexis said.

Ugh! Fah'ry said to herself. *Dose them girls that were talking about my hair on the porch. I remember the girl Kyasia. Dem Keke's cousin friends. I do not want to go on this porch.* Lexis and Fah'ry walked onto a porch of thirteen girls loudly talking and laughing.

"What up G!" Keke said to Lexis. "What happened?" All of the girls went silent. "You knocked up? Ain't you?" Keke said with a sure tone. Lexis smirked.

"I already know," Keke said. "I can see it in your face."

"Shut up Keke!" Lexis said. She sat down with the rest of the girls on the porch. The girls continued to talk as the conversation centered around Kyasia's child's father, Diesel and all of their problems.

Wow, Fah'ry thought as she listened. *Her child's father treats her really bad. Why does she stay with him?*

"He's a dumb a**!" Keke replied to Kyasia's story about Diesel.

"I know!" Monica said. "I know dat's yo baby daddy but you need to leave him." Kyasia kept telling stories of her and Diesel's relationship.

I wish these girls hurry up and leave, Fah'ry thought. *I know Kyasia or her friends don't like me. I'm not stupid. I have never done anything to any of them. Every time I see them, they never speak to me. They just ignore me and act like I'm not around. So, I don't say anything to them.*

Diesel pulled up in a large flashy truck and picked Kyasia, Keke's cousin and the rest of her friends up. *Whew! I am so glad that they are gone,* Fah'ry thought to herself as she moved back to her regular seat on the porch. The loud music ringing from Swerve's car saturated the street.

"Ooh, Fah'ry!" they said in a teasing voice. "Here come Swerve!" Fah'ry grinned at them.

"Would y'all stop!" Fah'ry said as she smiled. *He's not talking to me anyway,* she thought to herself. He pulled his sleek silver car over and got out of his car.

"Hey Swerve!" all of the girls said together.

"What's up!" he said as he continued to walk down the street past the porch.

Fah'ry's heart dropped to the ground. *So he's not going to come over here?* she thought. *He's just gone say hi to every body and act like I'm not sitting over here. Even if he is busy, he could have at least said hi to me. No hugs, no nothing! Ugh! Here we go! My heart is starting to feel the same way that it felt with Chaston. I hate this feeling. It feels like someone is just stomping on my heart.* Fah'ry tried to jump back in the conversation with the rest of the girls so that it didn't look like she was hurt by Swerve not acknowledging her personally.

"I'm bout to walk to da stoe," Keke said. "I be back."

"I'll walk wit you," Kish said.

"Bring me back some hot doodles with cheese," Monica said. "And a strawberry pop!" she yelled.

"Bring me some too!" Fah'ry yelled.

"Where y'all money at??" Keke yelled as she walked to the store.

"Girl! Just buy the stuff!" Fah'ry yelled, "I'll give yo money back," as she grinned at Keke.

A young lady walked up to the porch pushing a baby stroller. "Hey Candice!" Lexis said.

"Hey, where Keke at?" Candice asked as she stood by her baby's stroller.

"She went to the stoe," Monica said. "She ah be right back."

"Ok," Candice said as she sat on the porch steps in front of the stroller. She put her baby bag down that she wore in the style of a purse.

"How old is yo baby now?" Lexis asked.

"She two," Candice said as she took the bottle filled with red juice out of her baby bag. She gave the little girl the large bottle to drink.

That little girl looks like she is too big to still be drinking out of a bottle, Fah'ry thought. *And this girl looks like she's about our age, and she has a baby?* Fah'ry thought. Keke and Kish came back from the store and passed out all of the hot doodles and pop to everyone.

"What up Fancy Candy!" Keke said.

"Hey," she said as her daughter started to cry. Keke picked her up and rocked the baby to sleep. She placed her back in the stroller and the girls started to laugh, talk and watch the flashy cars ride by as they ate their hot doodles. "Ooh, my fingers are supa red. I be back," Fah'ry said. She went upstairs to try to wash the redness off of her fingers. Meanwhile, Diesel's truck pulled up.

"Aye Keke! Come here for a minute."

Keke went over to his truck to see what he wanted with her. She talked to him for a brief moment as his truck was parked in the middle of the street and started to back up traffic.

"Ok!" Keke yelled to him as a response while walking back to the porch.

"What he want?" Lexis said in an in inquisitive manner. "Girl, he wanna holla at Fah'ry."

"Oh!" Lexis said.

Fah'ry came back on the porch from washing her hands. "Girl," Keke said in a gossiping yet serious voice.

Fah'ry started to look confused. "Diesel just left from over here and he wanna holla at you!"

"Huh?" Fah'ry said. "Kyasia's baby daddy? Oh no!" Fah'ry said.

"Yea," Keke said. "He was like, 'Who is that'? I can take care of her!'" she said in a whispering but convincing tone.

"I'm not talking to him! And he's not cute!" Fah'ry said with a twisted face.

"Come on G! Talk to him! He got money!" Keke said.

"I don't need him! I got my own money," Fah'ry said in a serious tone.

"Yeah! You should!" The girls said as they joined in with Keke.

"Naw! I'm talking to Swerve," Fah'ry said.

"Dat don't matter!" Keke said. "You ain't got to get serious with him. Just take his money G!" Keke said in a convincing manner as she stood next to Fah'ry.

"Y'all crazy! I ain't talking to him," Fah'ry said.

"Girl you so stuck on Swerve!" Quana said. All of the girls started laughing.

"I know!" Keke said. "He got her on lock! Y'all wanna smoke?" Keke said.

"I got five," Monica said. The girls started to put their money in.

"Fah'ry where yo money at?" Keke said while laughing. "Hahaha! I'm just playin! We know you don't smoke."

"Fancy Candy, you smokin?" Keke said in a sassy, loud voice.

"Yea," she said as she passed Keke the money.

"Ok y'all," Keke said as she counted the money.

The girls started to leave the porch and walk around the neighborhood to go and get their marijuana and blunts. Fancy Candy grabbed her baby bag, threw it over her shoulder and pushed her stroller. She pushed the stroller along with the girls as they walked the neighborhood while singing and dancing provocatively.

Wow, is this girl really out here pushing this stroller with this baby? Fah'ry thought, *Shouldn't she be in the house? It's getting kind of late?* Fah'ry walked behind the girls as they danced in groups in the street. *They are so crazy!* she thought as she laughed at them. She heard a girl on the porch as they were passing by say words to her friends.

"Dey some rats!"

Huh? Rats? I am not a rat, she thought. *I don't sleep around or mess with any of these guys over here like that. I mess with Swerve and that's it! Is that what people think of them over here?* she thought with concern. *Am I hanging with the wrong girls?* she thought.

The girls stopped and received all of their marijuana and other items and headed back to Keke's house. While they were walking, a little mannish boy came up to play with them. "Stop throwing dem d*** bricks in da air!" Keke yelled. He started to laugh and continued to throw them in the air.

Suddenly, the girls yelled, ". . . Fah'ry WATCH OUT!!" Fah'ry quickly moved to the side in an effort to dodge the brick but she moved in the direction of the brick and it hit her in the back of the head. She blacked out for a second as she heard the girls running to her. "G, you ok?" They all asked her as they consoled her while she held the back of her head.

"Let me see?" Lexis said. "It's not bleeding, it's just a knot there. Do you want us to call the ambulance?" Lexis asked.

"Naw, I just need some ice," Fah'ry said as they quickly walked back to the house. *I need to call my mama,* she thought.

The girls got back to the house and Keke made Fah'ry an ice pack.

"You alright?" all of the girls asked as they surrounded her in the kitchen.

"Yea. I'm ok," Fah'ry said with pain in her voice.

The girls sat at the table, turned the music on and started to roll blunts for the night. Fah'ry went in the living room and decided to call her mom. "Hey ma," Fah'ry said.

"Hey, Fah'ry."

"I just got hit in the head with a brick," she said in a sad voice.

"A brick?" her mom said in a surprised voice. "Where are you? Where did you get hit at?"

"Um," Fah'ry said with hesitation. "I'm over Keke's house."

"Keke?" her mom said in an elevated tone. "Who is Keke?" she asked in frustration.

"Keke from when I was little, the one I used to play rope with," Fah'ry said to try and remind her mom.

"The one that live around the corner???"

"Yeaah," Fah'ry said in a fearful tone. *I am going to get in so much trouble,* she thought. *She is going to kill me.*

"You know what!" her mom said in a snappy tone. "That's what you get! You had no business over there anyway!" her mom said with no heart. "That is so classless for you to be with those ghetto girls! Bye Fah'ry!" her mom said in disappointment as she hung up the phone.

Fah'ry just looked at the phone and started to cry. She went in the bathroom to try and shield her tears from the rest of the girls before she went back into the kitchen. *She didn't even ask me if I was all right!* Fah'ry thought. *I mean, did she really have to say that? Even if I am not supposed to be over here. I would think that her concern would be my head and if I am OK. She doesn't even know if I was at the hospital or anything?* she thought in anguish with a hurting heart.

Make Me a Ghetto Girl

Fah'ry went in the kitchen with the girls and sat with them as they smoked marijuana. "You good G?" Lexis asked as she blew the marijuana smoke out of her mouth.

"Yea, I'm ok," Fah'ry said. *I wish that they would stop calling me G!* she thought. *I am not a G. Ugh!* Fah'ry held the ice pack to the back of her head as long as she could. *I know my mama is going to get me for being over here when she gets back. Well, at least she doesn't know that I've been spending the night,* she thought.

"B****! Pass the blunt!" Monica said with a humorous attitude. "You steady puffin!" All the girls start laughing with their low red eyes.

"Shut up!" Keke said as she laughed and took one last puff before passing it on to Kish. The kitchen was filled with smoke and chatter. "We be smokin dis kitchen out!" Keke said with excitement.

"Hahaha!" they all laughed.

"Fah'ry why you so quiet?" Keke asked. "You high ain't you?"

"Hahaha!" The girls laughed.

"Yup! She high off contact y'all!" Lexis said as she passed the blunt to Quana.

Fah'ry grinned. "No I AM NOT!" she emphasized. She sat back and enjoyed the marijuana aroma in the room as they all continued to hang out together.

"I'm hungry now y'all!" Lexis said. "Let's go and get some chicken."

"Yea. I need a foe piece!" Keke said as she got up from the kitchen table.

The girls took their routine walk to the chicken shack and went back to Keke's house to enjoy their meals at the table. Once they finished eating, the girls started moving around the house quickly and going through their bags.

What are they doing? Fah'ry thought as she watched Keke go into the bathroom with her purse.

"What y'all doing?" Fah'ry asked.

"I'm bout to go get me some!" Keke said. "I got my soap," she said as she put it in her purse while talking to Fah'ry. "I got my towel," she said as she put it in her purse. "And I got some clean underwear!" Keke closed her purse and left the bathroom and the other girls packed their purses.

"Oh!" Fah'ry said. "So that's all you taking?"

"Yup!" Keke said." Dis all we need. Hahaha!"

"Right!" Monica said as she put her purse on her shoulder and went to look out of the window.

"So y'all just gone leave me?" Fah'ry asked while sitting in the kitchen watching them walk back and forth preparing their purses.

"Yeah!!" Keke and Lexis said while giving a teased laugh.

"We be back tomorrow," Keke said. "So you gone have to hold the house down!" Keke advised. "I'm bout to have him screamin!" Keke said while laughing.

"Hahaha!" Monica laughed. "I know! I'm bout to be like . . ." Monica danced provocatively on the floor.

"Hahaha!" The girls start laughing loudly.

"You don't know nothin bout dat!" Monica said with a teasing laugh.

"Right!! Fah'ry you betta take notes," Lexis said. "Yo man gone want you to know how to dance," she said as she twirled, dropped to the floor with her legs open and gyrated her hips.

"Hahaha!" They all laughed. "And not the dancin she think!" Lexis said.

"Haha! She don't know nothin bout dancin!" Keke said. Fah'ry looked at them in amazement.

"Whelp!! I'm gone!" Keke said. She ran out of the house and got in the car with her boyfriend.

Wow! They are really leaving?? Fah'ry thought.

Lexis stood at the window waiting for her ride to pull up. "He betta come on!" Lexis said aloud. The sleek cars pulled up thirty minutes after another and the girls ran to get in the designated cars one by one.

"Bye G!!" Lexis said to Fah'ry as she ran out of the house holding her purse.

"Bye," Fah'ry said with a sad voice. *I can't believe that they left me!* she thought. *I mean, they are all gone! What am I supposed to do now?* She walked to the window and observed the dark and quiet neighborhood. *I don't see anybody.* She turned on the music to the love songs that the girls listened to all of the time. Fah'ry got in Keke's bed and tried to go to sleep. *I wish I had a boyfriend.* She started to think about Swerve. *Man! I can't keep a boyfriend for nothin! How do they get to keep boyfriends?? If I had sex with Swerve, would that make things better?* she thought. *I just can't do it. It just seems like nobody wants me. If you not having sex . . . You don't have a boyfriend. Chaston probably got him a girlfriend that has broken his virginity now. Ugh! I can't believe that he said that he wants to know what life is like without me.* Tears started to roll down her face. *They keep saying that I ain't on nothin. All because I won't have sex with them. Ugh!* Fah'ry cried herself to sleep as the sultry sounds played.

Fah'ry woke up to the sounds of gospel music. *Where am I?* she thought while trying to wake up. *That's the song that my mama plays in the morning while worshipping. Am I at home?* she wondered as she wiped her eyes and got up to follow the sound. She looked around and went to the window. *Where is that coming from?* Fah'ry started to remember all of the times that her mom would worship and pray. *Oh thank you God!* she said as she lifted her hands and started to worship and pray. *I miss my mom,* she thought. She went back in Keke's room and sat on the bed. She went to the window over the bed. *Oh! It's coming from the neighbor's window. I didn't even know that they were Christians.*

She started to look in her oversized overnight bag for clothes for the day. *It's so quiet in here. I wonder what time they are coming back,* she thought as she pulled out all kinds of expensive preppy clothes. *Ugh! I can't wear these. Obviously, this is not keeping Swerve's attention. I need something else to wear. Maybe, I should go where they go to buy their clothes and get some stuff like theirs. I hate the way that stuff look on Halsted though. It's so cheap. My mama never let me shop up there. But that's what all of the girls are wearing around here,* she thought as she went and took a shower. *Thank you God for this shower.* Fah'ry enjoyed her shower with no interruptions of other girls needing to take a shower.

She grabbed her purse and drove to Halsted, the neighborhood outdoor strip mall. She picked the most popular store for girls and started to look around. *Ugh! This stuff is horrible! Look at these cheap shoes! Ok, I have to find something,* she said to herself. *Ok, I have to find the most expensive looking thing in this store.* She picked through the clothing racks. *Ugh! Ok, what would Lexis wear? All of the guys are always trying to talk to her. Well, they be talking about her booty though.*

Ok! Here is something. It's khaki! I love khaki. Well, it's not the real kind but it's ok. Ooh, this material is so cheap. It's all stretchy! she said as she pulled the skirt. *I guess I'll get this. This thing is pretty short though. I don't know about this. Hopefully it won't be that bad. Now I need to find a top to match this skirt.*

Fah'ry went through the racks and found a matching tank top to the skirt with a brown butterfly on the breast area. She put both items next to each other to make sure that they look right together as far as color matching. *OK,* she said. *I think that this will work.* She smiled. *Now, I just need to find some shoes. Whew! I can't believe that people actually wear this stuff,* she thought to herself as she rambled through the picked over shoeboxes. *OK, what is this? This looks like it may match my skirt.* She said. *They are like a khaki color so they should work but this foam sandal is just ridiculous. This is so cheap!* She took her items to the counter and placed them in front of the cashier who had a weird pinned up hairstyle with red weave. *Why do they wear all this crazy looking stuff in their head?* she thought. *That's so ghetto. It's all packed to her head with all of that spritz and gel in it. That's so bad for her hair. It really dries the hair out. I wonder if they know that,* she thought.

"$30.15!" the cashier said.

"$30.15?" Fah'ry asked in surprise. "Yeah," the cashier said. "The sale is over honey."

"Oh, this was regular price?" she asked.

"Yeah," the cashier said. Fah'ry gave the cashier a $100 bill and paid for her items and left the store.

"$30!" she said as she got in her car. *That ain't nothing! Shoot, my nails cost more than that.* Fah'ry went to the beauty shop to see her beautician.

"Hey Kaydence," Fah'ry said.

"Hey Fah'ry," her beautician said as she set her at the wash bowl to wash her hair.

Ooh, this feels so good and I get to get that weed smell out of my hair, she thought. "Can you twist my hair up like in all of those little circle things?" Fah'ry asked her beautician.

"Yeah, I can," her beautician said. "Are you sure?" she asked as she stopped for a minute to hear Fah'ry's answer.

"Yea, I'm sure," Fah'ry said. *I think,* she thought with indecision.

"So, you're trying something different?" her beautician asked.

"Yea. I'm just trying something new," she said as she tried to convince herself in her mind. *Well, I really just want my hair pinned up like the other ghetto girls and I don't want it to look like I have long hair,* she thought. Fah'ry's beautician finished styling her hair and turned her around to the mirror. *Oh my gosh,* she thought. *This is so ugly. It looks so ghetto. This definitely does not look like me,* she thought to herself.

"Do you like it?" Kaydence asked Fah'ry.

"Yup! It looks so pretty!" she said with a smile. "Thank you so much!"

Fah'ry drove back to Keke's house and started to pull all of her ghetto clothes out of the bag and placed them on the bed. *They still not back!* she said as she squeezed into the little tan skirt. She put the tight tank top on and the thick foamed wedged sandals on. Fah'ry went into the living room and looked in the full-bodied mirror. *Ooh yea! I know that Swerve will have to say something to me now.* She twisted and turned in the mirror. *My arms are out and all of my legs are out and I have on this short skirt and these tall sandals. I know that he'll notice me right away,* she thought with confidence. *And this skirt makes my booty look big. I know that will get his attention.*

Fah'ry went and sat on the porch in hopes of seeing Swerve drive by. *Man! Where is he at? I haven't seen him yet! This is the perfect time for him to come and talk to me on the porch. Nobody's around and the girls are still gone. We wouldn't have to worry about anyone interrupting us or saying stupid and teasing things.* Fah'ry continued to sit on the porch and watch the cars drive by. Diesel's truck continued to circle the neighborhood but Fah'ry did not notice.

Maybe, if I walk to the store, I might run into Swerve. She was done up with her little mini skirt and tank top on. She wiggled to try and pull the little skirt down but it would not do any good. *I feel so uncomfortable. I feel naked!* she thought. *I don't see how they do this every day.* She walked to the store and looked out the sides of her eyes to see if she saw Swerve without anyone noticing that she was looking around for him. *Aw man, I don't see him.* She thought with disappointment. Fah'ry went in the corner store and purchased some chips with cheese and meat with a soda.

As she was walking out of the store, she heard Swerve's voice. *OK,* she thought nervously. *There he goes.* Her heart started to beat fast as she walked past him. He never looked her way and continued with his conversation. "Hey Swerve!" Fah'ry said in a sweet voice.

He took a double look at her. "Oh, hey," he said, "Girl, I didn't even know that was you." Swerve continued to engage in the previous conversation that he was in with the guys. *Wow! That's all he gone say?* Her heart dropped to the ground as she walked back to the porch. *I did all of this for nothing! I feel so stupid! He didn't even look at my legs or arms or my hair or anything,* she thought in disappointment. *I really thought that he would have liked me like this. Ugh! I am so tired of not having a boyfriend. I hate being by myself.*

Fah'ry went in Keke's house and quickly changed her clothes. She kicked her cheap sandals off and pulled off the tiny skirt and threw the tank top on the floor. *Let me take this stupid ghetto hairstyle down,* she said as she pulled the bobby pins out of her pinned up hairstyle. Fah'ry looked through her bag for her regular preppy clothes with tears in her eyes. She got dressed and went in the bathroom to wet her hair to get it back to its normal curly pattern.

I will never do that again, she said to herself. *I just don't want to be alone. Everybody has boyfriends and stuff and I'm always by myself. My mama always gone. I just don't have anybody. Even Chaston tired of me. He doesn't even want me,* she thought. Fah'ry started to replay her and Chaston's last conversation. She started to cry as she went to sit back on the porch. *I can't be crying,* she said to herself. *I am stronger than this. I can't be crying. Dang! Swerve didn't pay any attention to me. I can't believe this. I went through all of that just for him to see me and he didn't say a word. Maybe I'm just not thick enough or pretty enough? I don't know,* she thought as she sat on the porch with a sad countenance. *Nobody wants me,* she thought to herself as a thick cloud of depression was over her. *I guess I'll just sit here until they all come back from with their boyfriends.*

An expensive tan truck with sparkling tire rims pulled up in front of Keke's house. Fah'ry saw Diesel get out of his truck but she did not pay any attention to him. He started to walk in the direction of the porch. *Oh gosh,* she said in irritation. *I hope he's not coming over here.* Diesel walked to the front steps of the porch and looked at Fah'ry.

"What you doin on this porch all by yo self?" Diesel asked with a big smile.

Destiny Distracted!

Did This Thug Say Jesus?

The girls continued to leave her alone every Friday or Saturday night to be with their boyfriends. Friday nights were the most popular.

"Yea, I'm sitting by myself," Fah'ry said to Diesel. "I'm alright."

"So what's yo name? I be seeing you all the time," Diesel said as he stood at the bottom step of the porch.

"Fah'ry," she said.

"Is Keke nem yo cousin?" Diesel asked.

"No," Fah'ry answered. *I hope he hurries up and leave,* she thought. *I don't want anybody seeing me on this porch with him. And, please don't let Swerve drive by. I don't want him to think the wrong thing,* she thought as she took quick glances down the street with paranoia.

"Why you look so sad?" he asked.

"I just got a lot on my mind," Fah'ry said.

"Why don't you pray about it?" Diesel said.

Did he just say pray? she thought.

"That's what I do," he said as he continued to stand at the bottom of the porch steps.

"Yea, I've been praying about it," Fah'ry said. *I can't believe that he is standing here this long talking to me,* she thought. *No one over here has ever talked to me this long. No one has tried to get to know me.* Fah'ry glanced down the street again in paranoia. *Ok, this conversation is going too long,* she thought.

"You too pretty to be having whoever it is make you be down like that," Diesel said.

"Yea. I know God will help me through this," Fah'ry said.

"God. I know all about God. I be going to Faith Church," he said. "I be puttin a lot of money in that collection plate.

He goes to church? Fah'ry thought. *He gives, too! Wow,* Fah'ry thought with a subtle impressed look.

"I be taking my boys with me sometimes too," he said. "I remember one time I had to tell dem what the collection plate was," he grinned. Fah'ry laughed.

"I'm serious!" He said as he laughed. "Dey was surprised dat the church was passing around a plate full of money," he said with a dramatic voice. Fah'ry smirked. "I'm foe real! I was like . . . 'Stop looking at da money like dat! They gone think we some thieves!' Haha!" Diesel grinned and Fah'ry smirked. "Oh, so I made you laugh, huh?" he said with a grin. "So can I take you to dinner?" he asked.

"Naw," Fah'ry said with a sweet tone. "I'm talking to Swerve."

"Swerve!" he said as his voice elevated. "He be talkin to me about dis other girl that he said he think he in love with."

Huh? Fah'ry thought. *I feel like a dagger just went through my heart. Who? What girl could Swerve be in love with?* she pondered with a hurting heart. "Oh, well, I'm not ready to go out like that with anyone yet," Fah'ry said to Diesel.

"Just one time?" he asked. "Let me just take you from over here foe a minute to get yo mind off of everything?" Diesel asked in a convincing tone.

Fah'ry smirked and stretched her legs out. "Naw . . ." she said to him. "I can't do that."

"But seriously doe," he said. "Swerve be askin me all da time, how do you know when you in love."

I can't believe this! Fah'ry thought. *I feel so stupid. Now what??? I'm not gone be nobody's girl on the side. Ugh! Why does this keep happening to me?*

Persuasion Invitation

Diesel's phone started to ring but he ignored the call. "So will you think about me taking you out?" Diesel said to Fah'ry. His phone rang again. "Hello," he said on the call. He started to walk towards his truck. He put the phone by his side and had the person on hold. "Think about it, ok?" he yelled to Fah'ry as he got in his truck while talking on the phone.

Fah'ry watched him pull off in his shiny truck with sparkling silver tire rims. *He is crazy if he thinks that I am going to talk to him.* Fah'ry thought. *He ain't even the kind of guy that I like. And he's not cute to me,* she thought. Fah'ry continued to sit on the porch for most of the day alone. *I can't wait until I go to college. It's almost here. I got like a month left. I can't wait to see what Brighton is like. I'm going to miss everybody. I can't believe what he said about Swerve. I have never seen him with another girl over here. I really thought it was just me. Man!*

One by one as the hours passed by, Lexis was dropped off by her boyfriend, followed by Monica, Keke, Quana and then Kish.

"What up G!" Keke said with a hyped voice.

"Hey," Fah'ry said.

"You all hypa! Monica said. "You done got you some and now you hyped like you had a bag of candy. Haha!"

The girls laughed as they sat on the porch. "So what!" Keke said. "Yo man must didn't do something right," Keke said as she twerked.

"Haha!" Monica laughed. "I ain't got to brag."

"What you been doing G?" Lexis asked Fah'ry.

"Nothing. Just took care of my college stuff." Fah'ry said.

"When you leaving?" Monica asked.

"August 17th," Fah'ry said.

"And you gone be all da way in California?" Monica asked.

"Yup!" Fah'ry said. "You know who just left from over here?" she asked.

"Who, Swerve?" they all said together while laughing. "Hahaha!"

"Naw, Diesel," she said.

"What he want?" Keke said with an attitude. "Looking for Kyasia probably."

"Naw, he probably was trying to holla at her," Quana said.

"Yeah," Fah'ry said with concern. "He asked to take me out to dinner," Fah'ry said.

"What you say?" Keke asked.

"I told him naw!" Fah'ry said as she elevated her voice. "I'm not trying to talk to him!"

"Why not!" Lexis asked. "It's just dinner G!"

"Right!" Monica said. "It ain't like you gone fall in love or something! It's just dinner!" said Monica in a convincing tone.

"Yea. You need to go out!" Quana said.

"Just talk to him!" said Keke with coersion.

"Naw," Fah'ry said as she shook her head. "I'm talking to Swerve. And don't he mess with Kyasia? I don't mess with all that baby mama drama stuff."

"Girl you ain't got to get serious! Just take his money! Have some fun. Swerve ain't going nowhere. You always tryin to be faithful! Dese n***** ain't sh**! I saw Swerve da otha day with a girl in da car," Keke said.

"Really!" Fah'ry said as her heart started to beat fast. "What she look like?"

"I couldn't really see her face," Keke said. "I just know that she had her hair twisted up in one of dose pin ups," said Keke.

"Oh!" Fah'ry said as she was left speechless.

"See, we keep trying to tell you!" Lexis said. "Treat these n***** just like dey do us!" said Lexus.

"Uh huh!" the girls said. "Just gone head and talk to him," they said.

"Yea! Cuz I get tired of seeing you walk around sad all da time like you lost yo dog!" Monica said. "Hahaha!"

Man. Fah'ry thought. *Keke could have told me that she saw Swerve with a girl in the car. Why didn't she tell me? I wonder what she looks like? Is she prettier than me? She probably thick? They always be all in the thick girls faces. Ugh! So maybe Diesel was right,* she thought. *Maybe Swerve is in love with another girl. Ugh! How did I not notice that? I can't keep a boyfriend at all. Everybody always chooses somebody else over me.*

"Let's smoke y'all!" Keke said.

"Where YO money at!!!" Monica yelled. "You always asking us! Hehehe!"

"I got money!" Keke exclaimed.

"Yea. Cuz you was trickin off last night!" All of the girls laughed as they sat on the crowded porch.

"I ain't gotta trick off! What you thought?" Keke said in defense. "Haha!"

"Naw, haha, here go my money!" said Monica as she grinned.

"Huh!" Lexis said as she put her money on the porch step.

Quana threw ten dollars down and so did Kish. The girls did their normal routine of smoking, laughing, talking and eating chicken afterwards. All of the girls left again for the night with their boyfriends except Monica.

"Girl I didn't feel like going tonight. Deese walls need a break," Monica said to Fah'ry as they sat on the porch. Fah'ry grinned. They watched the cars go by as their blue headlights lit up the street. "I love them blue lights!" Monica said with excitement.

"Yea," Fah'ry grinned. "They are nice."

"Oh man! Girl here come Diesel truck!" Monica said as she grinned.

"Ugh! I hope he don't stop over here," Fah'ry said.

Diesel's truck glided gracefully down the street and slowly pulled over in front of Keke's house. He got out of his car and walked towards the porch while talking on the phone. "Let me call you back," he said. "What up Monica!" Diesel said with a chuckle.

"Nothing. What up Diesel."

"I'm coming over here to see if yo girl gone let me take her out to dinner. Tell her to give me a chance Monica!" Diesel said as he stood at the bottom of the porch stairs.

"Haha! I can't tell her what to do," Monica said to Diesel.

"She gone make me beg huh? Just go out with me one time?" he asked. Fah'ry smirked. "I know you don't know me like that. Monica can come too. Ain't nothing to do around here. Let me get y'all off dis porch." Diesel's phone rang and he walked away to take the call.

"You should go G!" Monica said. "It's just dinner. You need to get yo mind off of Chaston and Swerve!"

"Girl no! I don't know him like that!" Fah'ry as she elevated her voice. "And he got a baby mama and stuff! And he not my type."

"Girl just go!" Monica admonished. "You never know what will happen."

Diesel came back to the porch. "So you gone go out with me to dinner?" he asked with a smile. "Ok, how bout

Monica come too?" he said as he held his phone in his hand.

"Uh uh! "Monica said quickly. "I'm not bout to be no third wheel!" Fah'ry just watched their conversation. "Come onnn Monica??" Diesel pleaded.

"She ain't even said she was going! How y'all gone put me in da middle??" Monica raised her voice.

"Who put you in the middle?" Fah'ry grinned.

"I just wanna take you out. Just let me take you out? Promise I'll bring you back!" he said as they all laughed.

"Come on Fah'ry! I'll go wit you," Monica said in a convincing tone.

"See!" Diesel said grinning. "She said she will go! Haha!"

Fah'ry laughed, "Y'all are crazy!" *Well, if I go, what will it hurt? I mean, I guess Swerve is in love with someone else and Chaston ain't called me. I guess he's moved on with his life. So why am I trying to be faithful?* she thought. *I'm tired of chasing both of them anyway. It's like nobody is paying any attention to me. At least he is trying to take me out to dinner. I just can't believe Swerve! Ugh! My heart feels horrible!* "Ok, I'll go!" Fah'ry said to Diesel and Monica.

Dinner for Three

Monica and Fah'ry got in the truck with Diesel and headed to dinner. *I can't believe that I just got in the car with him,* Fah'ry thought to herself. *Please don't let Swerve see me in this car with him.* Fah'ry kept her head turned away from the window to avoid being seen by any of Swerve's friends. *Please hurry up and get to the expressway,* she thought with extreme nervousness.

"What y'all wanna eat?" Diesel said.

"I don't know. It don't matter," Monica said.

Diesel looked at Fah'ry. "What you want?" he said with a grin.

"I don't know," Fah'ry said in a low tone.

"Alright," he said. "I know a place." He continued to drive a long distance to the restaurant. The ride was silent as they rode past the boats on Lake Shore Drive. He turned on his loud music and played a compilation of love songs. *Wow! So this is what it's like to be in one of these cars with them?* Fah'ry thought. *I can't believe that he's not listening to rap like the rest of them??* Song after song played and Fah'ry slowly started to enjoy the ride. *He's playing all of my favorite songs!* she thought and was quite impressed.

"Y'all wanna listen to something?" Diesel asked over the loud music.

"Naw. This is good," Fah'ry said.

"Yea. We good," Monica said from the backseat.

"If you get tired of the music, just let me know," he said to Fah'ry with a smile.

"Ok," Fah'ry said in a low voice. A new song came on. *Ooh! This is my favorite song, she thought. It helps me think of how to get over Chaston. He need to turn this up!* she thought. Diesel turned the song up and started singing the ballad. The girls started to laugh at him. *I can't believe that he knows the words to this song,* she thought. *I thought that they all listened to rap.* She looked at the screen. *That track is number five. He seems pretty nice. But Kyasia nem be telling some bad stories about how mean he is and how he treats her horribly,* Fah'ry thought. *Did he just read my mind and turn this song up?*

Fah'ry started to enjoy the music and let it soften her broken heart. They arrived at the elegant restaurant and sat down for dinner. Fah'ry started to scoot over on the booth as her feet swung under the table as Diesel waited for her to comfortably sit.

"Look at your toes!" he said.

"What??" Fah'ry said with concern and a confused look.

"Your little feet are pretty," he said. Fah'ry started to laugh. "I'm serious!" he said as he glanced at the menu. "Your feet are pretty. You know how some girls feet look all messed up! One toe be crooked or the big toe be too big! Haha! Your toes are perfect! They are made for sandals."

Fah'ry grinned. "Thank you." *I mean I always knew that I had nice feet and they looked cute in sandals but no body ever said anything to me about them,* she thought. *Chaston never paid attention to my feet and I've always worn sandals around him,* she thought.

"Oh God!!" Monica exclaimed. "Why did I come here with y'all?" Monica said with humor. "I should have stayed on da block!"

"Naw. You should have come just like you did," Fah'ry said to Monica in a funny tone.

The waitress arrived at the table to take the orders. "Hey Cing," Diesel said to the waitress.

He knows these Chinese people? Fah'ry thought. *He must come here all the time. He didn't even really look at the menu,* Fah'ry thought to herself.

"Do you want the same?" the waitress asked.

"Yea," Diesel said. "Just make sure you leave the shrimp out. I'm allergic to shrimp y'all. If I eat it, my face blows up really big," he said as he gestured with his hands wide around his face. "Haha!" They all laughed.

"So is all that your hair?" he asked Fah'ry. He smiled while waiting.

"Yea," Fah'ry said as she sipped her water with lemon.

"Dang! Haha! Y'all know most girls be having all that weave in their head. I hate when girls do that! Dat's unattractive." Fah'ry laughed. "I'm serious! Y'all think I'm playin! Why y'all keep laughin at me?" Diesel asked as he laughed with them.

"Cuz you funny!" Monica said.

"I just don't like all dat ghetto stuff! I hate when girls be wearing all dat cheap stuff from off Halsted."

Really?? Hmmm, Fah'ry thought.

"So!" Monica said as she popped her lips. "What's up with you and Kyasia?"

"Mannnn! She so bogus!" he emphasized. "They told me that they saw her at a party and Big C was all on her!" he said with emphasis. "I can't believe she would do me like that! Dat's my baby mama! It hurt but I try not to even trip."

"So you ain't talkin to her no moe?" Monica asked.

"Naw! I can't do that joe! I can't let nobody make no fool of me. I ain't stupid! If she wanna be out there like dat. Den she can gone head!"

"Oh ok," Monica said.

"I'm serious!" Diesel said in a convincing manner. "I just don't do that! I'm done joe!!" Diesel said as the waitress brought out the food.

"Thank you," Fah'ry said to the waitress as she placed the plate down. *It sound like he a little broken hearted himself,* Fah'ry thought to herself. She closed her eyes and prayed over her food. They continued to talk and eat as Fah'ry was very passive.

"Why you so quiet?" he asked while smiling at Fah'ry.

"No reason," she said as she held her fork in her hand. *He looks so grown.* Fah'ry thought. *Wow! Look at his beard. Chaston or Swerve don't have facial hair. How old is he? He look too grown. I'm ready to go,* Fah'ry thought. They started to finish their dinner and the girls put their leftovers in a takeout box.

"Y'all ready?" he asked.

"Yeah," they said.

Diesel stood up and left a hundred-dollar bill on the table for a tip. Fah'ry glanced at it in an effort that he didn't see her looking. *A hundred-dollar tip!* she thought. *That is really nice of him.*

They walked out of the restaurant and got in the truck and headed back to the neighborhood. Diesel turned the music back on and blasted the love songs all the way back to Keke's house. *I hope he plays number five again,* Fah'ry thought. *I love dat song. Ooh yeah!* she thought as she enjoyed every song that came on.

"Ooh Diesel I need all dese songs you got!" Monica said.

"I got you," he said.

"Really?" Monica asked.

"Yea," Diesel said as he smoothly pulled up to Keke's house. He looked over at Fah'ry. "See, I told you that I would bring you back."

Fah'ry smirked. "Thank you for dinner," she said as she stood with the truck door open.

"You welcome," he said. "You ain't gotta thank me doe!" he said with a slight grin.

Fah'ry closed the truck door and went into Keke's house. "He was cool," Monica said as she put her blanket and pillow on the floor to lay down for bed. "He was nice to you G. You should give him a chance," Monica said as she yawned. "I guess dem tricks be back tomorrow. Haha!"

"Yea. They stay gone now," Fah'ry said as she lay on her pillow. "Yea. Diesel was cool. Girl I was loving that music! He was playing all the songs!" Fah'ry said.

"I know!" Monica said with excitement.

"I'm just not trying to get my feelings hurt anymore." Fah'ry said. "I'm still trying to get over Chaston and I don't know what this is with me and Swerve."

"I feel you," said Monica. "It will take time but that don't mean you can't have fun. You really need it G! You got to get off dat sad stuff," Monica said. "Just give Diesel a chance. You never know."

"But what about him and Kyasia?" Fah'ry said to Monica. "I'm not trying to be in the middle of no baby mama drama stuff. And I ain't never gon be nobody's side girl," Fah'ry said as she yawned.

"Well, he said that he don't mess with her no moe. All you can do is believe him until you catch him up," Monica said.

"Yea, I don't know about that," Fah'ry said as she looked over at Monica and noticed that her eyes were closed. *This girl done fell asleep on me,* she thought. *I don't know about this Diesel thing. He is just not my type. I'm not even attracted to him. I wish Swerve was trying to take me out like this. I mean he's never asked to take me out anywhere. All we do is talk and kiss on the porch. And now he's ignoring me and Diesel said that he is in love with another girl. And Keke said that she saw him in the car with a girl. I just don't want to be stupid about this and keep letting people hurt my feelings. I'm not going back to dinner with Diesel though. I am not interested and*

I don't want him to think that I am supposed to give him something in return. I had a good time though. It felt good to get off the porch and ride on Lake Shore. I haven't been that way since my friends left for London.

Fah'ry started to think about the time that they were all on the yacht before they left. *I so miss them. I can't wait until college starts. They are going to be so surprised when they see that I am at Brighton. I am so glad that I decided to change my mind about Polk State. I definitely don't need to be there with Chaston. I need to get over him and being there definitely will not help. Ugh!* She started to see flashes of his face and started to reminisce on all of the good times that they had together. *I so miss him. But I can't keep letting him treat me like crap and I definitely can't keep chasing him. As much as I want to, I can't chase him anymore. I refuse to keep looking stupid or desperate. That ride in Diesel's truck was cool though,* she smirked. All of the love songs that he played in the car started to replay in her mind as she fell asleep.

Monica ended up going out for dinner every night with Fah'ry and Diesel for an entire week as they became acquainted with one another. They all spent most of the day and evening riding around with Diesel as he drove from one side of the city to the other.

Week 2: Just Us Two

Fah'ry and Monica sat on Keke's porch and enjoyed the summer breeze. They laughed and talked as they watched the neighborhood guys drive around the blocks continuously.

"G, I wanna smoke," Monica said. Fah'ry looked at her with a blank stare. They started laughing uncontrollably. "I'm saying it like you gone smoke with me," Monica said.

"I know!" Fah'ry said. "That's why I'm looking at you like, I don't know what you want me to do," said Fah'ry.

"Let's walk so I can go get a bag," Monica said. The girls walked to get a bag of marijuana for Monica. They sat on the back porch and talked while Monica prepared to smoke. "Girl look at that thing on da light pole," Monica said. "I think that's a hidden camera. I think they be watching us."

"Haha," Fah'ry laughed.

"I'm for real!" Monica said as she puffed on her blunt.

That weed does smell good, Fah'ry thought.

"G, here, hit the blunt!" Monica said as she held it at Fah'ry as if she were passing it.

"Girl naw!" Fah'ry said while grinning.

"Come on! Just one puff?"

"Nope!" Fah'ry said. "Get that out my face! I don't want no yellow teeth, black lips or burnt fingernails! Plus, it messes with your brain cells. I ain't trying to have nothing messing with my brain!" Fah'ry urged.

"Girl it's not gone do that on one time!" Monica said while smoking.

"So what! And I don't wanna be high!" Fah'ry said with an elevated tone. "Why would I take something that is going to alter my mind or make me do stupid stuff that I won't remember?" Fah'ry asked.

"Haha! It don't do dat!" Monica grinned.

"Yea ok!" Fah'ry grinned. "If you could see how y'all be acting!" They both started to laugh.

Should I though? Fah'ry thought. *Just one puff? What will it hurt? It's just me and her. I know she won't say anything to everybody else. I would like to know what it's like to smoke. Should I? They do be looking like they be having fun.*

"Ok, let me try," Fah'ry said to Monica.

"Here," Monica said as she passed the blunt to Fah'ry.

She tried to hold it in her hand like she saw the other girls do. *What if this stuff has some other drugs in it and I get sick? It be just my luck this one time.* She held the blunt in between her fingers like the other girls. *I remember somebody getting really sick off of this and almost losing their mind because it had some other drugs in it.* "Ouch!" Fah'ry shouted. "That thing burned my finger!"

"Haha! Girl, come on! You letting it burn out!" Monica said.

"Here! Take this thing!" Fah'ry said. "It burned my finger! I'm not putting that on my lips and it puts a burn mark on my lips! I'm good!" Fah'ry said.

"G, you over the top," Monica said. Fah'ry passed the blunt back to Monica. "G, I'm not going out with you and Diesel tonight," Monica said as she took a puff.

"Why?" Fah'ry asked.

"Cuz B****! I'm tired of being with y'all! Plus I'm going with Danny tonight!"

Did she just call me a b? Fah'ry thought. *I hate that! I don't know why they address each other like that. That is so disrespectful. Me and my friends never talked to each other like that. I know that they are not serious about what they are saying but still, they shouldn't say that to each other. Why would somebody want to be called that? Especially by their friend!*

"You good!" Monica said. "I been going out with y'all for a whole week. You should be comfortable with him now. I'm tired of tagging along with y'all!" Monica said.

"I can't believe you!" Fah'ry said. "What am I supposed to do now?"

"Just kick it wit him like you been doing while I was there!" Monica said. "G, you will be fine. You don't need me anymore," said Monica.

Oh gosh! Go out with him by myself? Fah'ry thought.

Monica's phone rang. "G, I'm bout to go. Danny outside!" Monica said as she grabbed her purse and ran down the stairs to the car. "See you tomorrow G!" she shouted.

"Bye," Fah'ry said with disappointment. She walked around Keke's house. *There is nothing for me to do. Here we go again. I'm all by myself. I hate being alone.* Fah'ry looked out of the window. *It's so quiet. I guess everybody with somebody. It ain't even late. The sun is still out.* Fah'ry went and laid in Keke's bed. *I guess I'll go to sleep. There's nothing else for me to do. I know it's still early but hey I'll feel better if I just go to sleep. That way I don't have to think about being alone,* Fah'ry thought to herself. She dozed off and her phone rang. "Hello," Fah'ry said.

"What's up pretty girl!" Diesel said.

"Hey," she grinned. "Stop saying that!"

"Why?" he asked. "You are pretty!" he said in a serious voice. "I'm about to come get y'all."

"Monica gone with her boyfriend," Fah'ry said.

"Dat's ok! We can still go out without her, right?" he asked.

"Yea, I guess so," Fah'ry said.

"I will be there to get you in about 10 minutes," he said.

"Ok," Fah'ry replied. *Oh God! How am I going to do this by myself? Please help me? Please protect me? I don't really know what I am doing. I don't want to keep sitting over here by myself though. I mean I have been having a good time. He has been a cool friend.* Fah'ry gathered her purse and keys and waited at the window for Diesel to pull up. She suddenly heard the door open and someone walking up the stairs.

"What up!" Keke said.

"What!" Fah'ry smirked. "What you doing here on a Friday?" Fah'ry said as she glanced out of the window.

"Girl, I guess he about to do something with his kids. So I just told him to drop me off because his baby mama gone be there," Keke said. "Where are you bout to go? You all at the window!" Keke said in a suspicious tone. "I'm bout to go with Diesel," Fah'ry said.

"Oh. You kickin it with him now?" Keke asked in and an inquisitive yet sassy manner.

"Not really," Fah'ry said. "We just been going out. Monica been with me too."

"Oh. So what y'all been doing?" Keke asked.

"Just dinner or sometimes breakfast or lunch or whatever and riding around with him during the day," Fah'ry said.

"Oh! Keke said with a surprised tone. "So y'all have been kickin it."

"I guess. It's been fun," Fah'ry said. Diesel called Fah'ry to let her know that he was downstairs. "I'm about to go," Fah'ry said to Keke as she walked out.

"Well, I won't be here when you get back and I am taking the keys," Keke said nonchalantly.

"Oh. Ok," Fah'ry said. She was caught off guard with Keke's response. *Why was she acting like that?* Fah'ry thought. *I didn't do anything to her! She was acting real funny. I mean, they go out all of the time and come back the next day. I don't understand what's the problem. So now I'm going to have to go home afterwords? Ugh!* She got in the truck with Diesel. "Hey," she said.

"What's up pretty girl?" he said with a smile.

"Can you stop saying that!" she grinned.

"You wanna go go-kart riding?" he asked.

"Yea. That's fine," she said.

"What's wrong?" he asked.

"What do you mean?" she replied.

"I know that something is wrong," he said.

"Well," Fah'ry started to talk. Diesel turned the music down to give her his full attention. "It's Keke nem. They are starting to act real funny towards me. I haven't done anything to them, they just are acting real strange. They are treating me different since I've been going out with you," she said.

"Man, don't worry about them! They are jealous of you!" he said.

Fah'ry looked at him as if she was listening attentively. "I'm serious," he said. "Why would they not be jealous of you?" he asked as he got on the expressway.

"No," she said. "I just never thought about anyone being jealous of me. Especially them."

"Man, you shutting every girl down around there. I don't even know why you be around there anyway," he said. "You pretty, you smart, you about to go to college. You have a lot going for yo self. You have a bright future. They ain't on nothing. They just wanna watch the neighborhood n***** and sit on the porch all day," he said. "Don't let that bother you."

Diesel turned the music back on and they enjoyed the summer breeze on the expressway on their way to ride the go-karts. *I really be loving this music,* she thought. He switched the music a bit and turned to track number five. *Ooh,* she said to herself. *That's the song.* She enjoyed it and asked him to play it again.

"Yea," Diesel said. "Why you like dis song so much?" he asked as he turned it up loud.

"Well," she said as she started to tell him about Chaston and how he broke her heart. He listened to her all the way to the go-kart track. They raced around the track all night and Fah'ry forgot all about her broken heart. *This is so fun!* she thought while quickly turning the corner in her race car as she tried to beat him. Her curly hair blew naturally in the wind as she hit the gas. They wrapped up go-karting and got in the car to go to dinner. Diesel turned on track number five.

"I like this song too," he said while smiling at her. "You know why?"

"No. Why?" Fah'ry asked.

He started to talk about how Kyasia broke his heart and how he believes that there is no such thing as loyalty anymore. "No one is loyal," he said as they walked in the restaurant for dinner. He continued to talk about Kyasia and their problems.

They ordered their food and enjoyed their meal. He noticed a family of five eating at the next table over from them. "Give me one second. I will be right back," he said. Diesel walked over to the family's table and placed money in the mothers hand to pay for their food.

"Wow, that was really nice," Fah'ry said.

"I just wanted to help her. They just look like they struggling."

"That's really nice of you. That's very compassionate," Fah'ry said while eating. He stared at Fah'ry while she ate. "What?" Fah'ry said.

"You just so pretty! Look at your hair and your nails! Your nails are real! You don't have on anything fake. You like the perfect girl," he said.

Fah'ry grinned. "Stop saying that!" Fah'ry said with a serious tone. "I am not perfect."

"Yes you are," he said as he continued to adore her.

Why does he keep saying that? she thought.

"I bet yo bath water is clean after you get out. Haha!"

"No. Diesel stop!" she smirked.

"I'm just telling the truth," he said.

I don't want him thinking that I'm perfect, she thought. *I've never had any boyfriend tell me that I was pretty or anything like that. Why does he keep smiling and staring at me*? They finished up dinner and Diesel left another one hundred dollar tip on the table for the waitress. *Ok.* Fah'ry thought. *I guess this is what he does. He tips everybody like this. Interesting!* They drove back to the neighborhood while enjoying songs about being broken hearted. He took her to Keke's house and she opened the door to get out of the truck. *Should I hug him or something?* she thought. *This has been fun and he's really nice.* Fah'ry said thank you and leaned over and gave him a quick hug.

"Wow!" he said as he shook his whole body in a silly manner. "Fah'ry just gave me a hug! Haha!" he said.

"Stop that!" she said with a grin. "I had fun though," she said as she closed the door.

"I'll see you tomorrow," he said. "We gone have some more fun!"

"Ok," she said. Fah'ry got in her car instead of going inside of Keke's house. She looked up at the window and saw all of the lights on and heard some of the girls laughing and hanging out. *Man. She felt a stabbing in her heart. I guess they are mad at me or something? What did I do to them?* She pulled off in her yellow IvyKennington and drove home around the corner. *I hope Diesel doesn't treat me like he does his baby mama, Kyasia. I would be stupid to think that he won't treat me that way though. I mean that's the mother of his child. Why am I liking a guy with a child anyway? Ugh! Here we go! I'm back here at this nasty house. Dang! I'm not gone be able to take no showa in the morning! Ugh!* she thought.

She walked into the hot and musty house, greeted by the sounds of rambling rats in the kitchen. "Ugh!" she sighed as she went in her small rectangular man-made room. Fah'ry put the broken door up to the opening and laid down on the blanket on the floor. She started saying her prayers and her phone rang. She was startled in hopes that it was Chaston. "Hello," she whispered.

"What's up pretty girl!" Diesel said.

"Hey," she said.

"I just wanted to call you. I had fun and I'm missing you already," he said. Fah'ry smirked. Fah'ry and Diesel spent everyday together without Monica. They drove around the city as he took care of minor business. Diesel made their common eating arrangements for breakfast, lunch and dinner at lavish restaurants in the expensive district of downtown Chicago. They went on fun outings at the movies, game rooms, go karts and walks on the beach. Diesel dropped her off at home every night and called her to talk until she fell asleep for the night.

Week Three: When Angels Cry

(The Ultimatum)

Fah'ry woke up to the heat of the non-airconditioned house. "Ooh! It is so hot in here! I am sweating!" she said as she looked at her shirt. "And I can't even take no shower. Ugh!" Fah'ry picked a pretty outfit from her duffel in the corner of her room. *Yeah! Dis cute!* she said to herself. *This shirt is really wrinkled though. I need to iron this!* she thought as she held it up in front of her. *I love this shirt!! It is my favorite!* She laid her clothes on the floor and prepared herself to get dressed for the day.

Fah'ry grabbed her green wash pan that was hidden in the corner of her room. She walked to her mom's room as her uncle's smacking lips greeted her. *Ugh! I don't even feel like it today,* she thought as she tried to ignore her other uncle masturbating in the chair. *Uhn! So gross!*

She walked in her mom's room to look for the gallons of water in the designated place. *Shoot! Ain't no water! I don't feel like going to the park to fill up no water jugs! You know what??* she thought as she walked out of the house and went to the corner store next door. She grabbed five gallons of water and placed them on the counter.

"10 dollars!" Abe said to Fah'ry. She gave him the money and went back in the house to go through her normal wash up routine in the green pan. "Ugh! I hate this! I miss Keke's house. I can't keep doing this," she said in a discouraging voice. Fah'ry finally got all primped and pretty for the day. *I guess Diesel will call cuz I ain't calling him. And I can't go ovah Keke nem house cuz dey ain't talkin to me I guess. And I'm not gonna chase nobody no moe!*

She sat on the broken chair in her room. She lifted up the rusted window to try and get some fresh air in her room. *Uhn! This window seal is so dirty! Look at all of these dead bugs!* She quickly let the window back down and dusted her hands off with a nasty look on her face. *Ugh!*

Fah'ry grabbed her fashion sketch book and pencil and started to add on to the previous design that she started in the car while waiting for Lexis at the clinic to ease her mind. She turned her music on and started to sketch. Suddenly, she stomped her foot. "Get out of here!" she shouted to the rat that creeped in her room. *Ugh! I can't get no peace in dis house,* she thought. Fah'ry threw her book down in frustration and went outside on her little front porch.

She sat down and turned on her headphones. *Well this porch ain't like Keke's. I only got three little steps. I can't even fit a chair on this.* Fah'ry sat on the small stoop style step, listened to her music and watched three times the cars around Keke's house pass by because of her house sitting on a Main Street. Fah'ry sat on the porch for most of the morning. *Man! I miss Keke's breakfast. Now I gotta eat some cereal or something. I'd rather have some chips with cheese and meat. Ugh! Fah'ry's phone rang.*

"What's up superstar?" Diesel said as he grinned.

Fah'ry smirked. "Hey."

"I'm bout to come get you," he said.

"Ok." Fah'ry replied.

"Aye! Can you bring that video of you on that smart people's game show?"

She grinned. "For what?"

"I wanna see it!" Diesel said with excitement. "Is that ok?"

"O-Kay," Fah'ry said with suspicion. "I'm not at Keke's house so you'll have to come to my house," she said.

"Where dat's at?" he asked.

Fah'ry gave him the address. "Oh. I know where dat's at! I'm actually closer that way anyway. Wait! So how you get home last night after I dropped you off at Keke nem house?" He said in a curious voice.

"I drove," she said.

"What you mean, you drove?" he said in an elevated voice.

"I have a car," Fah'ry said in a peaceful voice.

"Stop playin!" he said.

"I'm serious," Fah'ry said.

"Haha!" he laughed. "What kind of car you got?" he said in sarcastic humor.

"I have a light yellow convertible IvyKennington," she said to him.

"He** nawww!" he emphasized. "Dat was yo yellow drop top in front of Keke's house??"

"Yea," she said.

"So why you be sittingg ovah with them all day? I don't understand why you be ovah there! You don't even fit!" he said in an astonished voice.

Now he sound like my mama! Fah'ry thought. She smirked at his questions.

"Danggg! I thought that car was that rich girl's car that live next to Keke nem. You know da one who mama got money but dey don't nevah let her come outside?" he said.

"Yea. I went to St. Martin with her," Fah'ry said.

"You went to private school?" Diesel asked in amazement.

"Yea. I never went to the public school around here. I actually graduated valedictorian of my high school and eighth grade class," Fah'ry said.

"Wow!!" Diesel said. "So you a pretty, rich, smart girl!"

"Naw," Fah'ry said. "I'm just me."

"Can you bring yo graduation video too?" he asked. "I wanna see dis!"

She grinned. "Alright. Yeah." *I was just like that girl next door to Keke's house. My mama don't want me outside over here either,* she thought as she pulled her pink lipgloss out of her pocket and applied it on her lips. Diesel walked up to her on the porch while still on the phone with her.

"Haha!" He grinned. "You thought I was still in my truck!" Fah'ry laughed at his silly gestures as she sat on the little step. "You ready to go pretty girl?" he asked.

"Yea," she said as she stood up and walked to the truck.

"Aye. You can't be sitting on da porch like dat," he said with sincerity.

"Why? What's wrong?" she asked.

"People can see between your legs and size you up."

"Oh!" Fah'ry said.

"Especially with you sitting on dat busy street."

Oh! I never thought of that, she thought.

Fah'ry and Diesel got in his plush truck to enjoy the day. "So where the videos?" he asked.

Fah'ry laughed. "You serious huh?" she said as she looked over at him on the driver's side.

"Yea! I wasn't playin! I really want to see them," he said. She passed the videos to him and he loaded them into his internal movie player. He pulled out a stack of bills and started counting them and placed them on his lap as he completed a stack. He passed a large stack of money to Fah'ry.

"What is this?" she asked in confusion.

"We bout to go shopping," he said. "Dat's yours!" he smiled. "I am buying you new clothes. Dat shirt is dingy.

I don't want my girl to ever wear the same clothes twice," he said.

Did he just call my shirt dingy? she thought. *Dis my favorite shirt!*

"And you can buy whatever you want," he said.

"Naw. I can't take this. I'm good. I got money," Fah'ry said.

"I know!" he said as he made silly gestures like a girl. "Just take it! Dat ain't no money to me! I don't need dat! Please take it?" he asked with his hands folded in prayer.

"I don't need it," she said.

"Ok. Can you hold this for me den?" he asked. Diesel passed Fah'ry another stack of large bills that was on his lap. "Can you just put it in your purse?" he asked.

"Ok." Fah'ry stuffed both stacks of large bills in her purse. *What am I doing? Well, it's just money. It's not like I'm holding drugs or something?* she thought. *I don't think I can get in trouble for this? Can I?*

Diesel turned Fah'ry's academic game show tv appearance video up as loud as it could go. He was entertained and amazed at her hit the buzzer and give so many correct answers. "Haha! You really are smart huh?" She smiled as they drove. He made a quick turn on da block.

"Please turn that down!?" she asked as her voice rang loud on the video as his normal music sound system.

"Why?" he said.

"Cuz. I don't want people thinking that I got you playing this and I'm all on myself," she urged.

"Oh. I don't care about dem!" he said. "I want the world to see how smart you is. You're like Ms. America! Haha! Dat's it! I'm gone start callin you: Ms. America!" He laughed and turned the video up louder.

Fah'ry's voice on the video could be heard from blocks away as they briefly rode through the neighborhood. They approach the corner of Keke's house and the porch was full of all of the girls. Diesel honked the horn at them but he did not stop. "Watch when we come back. Dey gone be in da same spot doing nothin!" he said.

Wow! Is that what they be thinking about us sitting on the porch? she thought.

He turned the corner and headed for the expressway as they prepared to go shopping. They spent hours shopping at the mall as Fah'ry picked out new clothes and sandals. Diesel shopped in the men's section while she shopped in the ladies' section. He came over to her as she picked out her items.

"You should try some of these," he suggested. "Dis all I wear. Da girl Roxidescent is nice too," he said.

She looked through that particular brand's rack and started to like some of the clothes. She grabbed about 10 of the hundred-dollar T shirts and a pair of pants and shorts to match each tee. They continued to shop for hours and they went shoe shopping next for her sandals as he promoted the beauty of her feet. They finally wrapped up shopping and headed to the truck.

"Do you want me to take you home to change clothes?" he asked. "I would like for you to change into some new and fresh stuff," he said.

"I mean. I can," she said.

He turned on the video and switched it to her graduation portion instead of the game show. He turned it up loud as he watched her walk across the stage again as well as the valedictorian speech. "Wow! Dis is crazy! You are really smart!"

She smirked. "Thanks."

"Why you be looking so sad?" he asked. "You need to smile more." Fah'ry tried to smile but it just didn't come natural. He eventually dropped her off at home to change into her new clothes. "Call me when you are done and I will come back and get you," he said.

"Ok," Fah'ry said as she closed the truck door to go into the house. Fah'ry changed into her new clothes rather quickly and called him back. *Please let him hurry up and come back because I can't stay in this house,* she thought. *Ooh! I really like these Roxidescent tees!* She pranced around as she felt confident in her fresh and clean new clothes and shoes.

Diesel came right back and picked her up at her call. "You still playing this video?" she asked.

"Haha!" he said. "You thought I was playing. I was serious. I want everybody to see how smart and pretty my girl is!"

Fah'ry shook her head in unbelief while smiling. *I am trying to smile,* she thought. *Ugh!* Fah'ry and Diesel took a quick ride around the neighborhood before heading to their next destination. He made a couple stops on each corner to greet the guys on the corner.

"Y'all see my Ms. America!" he bragged. "She pretty and she smart!" he emphasized. The guys gathered around his truck to talk to him as they saw the graduation video playing.

"Dat's you?" they said to Fah'ry.

She grinned. "Yeah."

"Dangg!" they said.

"Aye! Y'all should see this other video she on. She was on TV, like a game show answering all the questions," he bragged.

"Yea! She really is Ms. America!" they said.

"We gotta go," Diesel said. "We will see y'all lata!" He took a quick turn on the next block and he slowed down as he saw Swerve. He let his window down as Fah'ry was lost for words.

Oh gosh! I wish it was a way that I could duck down in this seat right now. Did he really have to stop and talk to him? What is really going on? she thought as she pulled her pink lipgloss out of her pocket and applied it to her lips. Swerve glanced at Fah'ry in the truck. Their eyes met briefly but not long enough to show that they had a deep connection in front of Diesel.

"Aye. What you bout to do?" Diesel said to Swerve as he stood on the passenger side of the truck but he did not walk to the vehicle and had a quick conversation with Diesel.

"Nothin. What's up?" Swerve said. He had the most uncomfortable look on his face and so did Fah'ry while she tried to conceal it. "We bout to go downtown to eat. Wanna go?" Diesel asked.

Oh gosh! Her heart started to beat extremely fast. *Please say no. Please say no. This would be crazy,* she thought.

Swerve gave a weird smirk. "Naw. I'm good," he said.

Whew! Fah'ry said to herself. *This has to be a joke. This can't be real,* she thought. Diesel pulled off slowly and

Fah'ry and Swerve caught each other's eye in the passenger side rear view mirror. They stared at each other until they could no longer see due to distance. *Oh my gosh. This is your fault. I am supposed to be with you not him. You ignored me. What did you expect me to do? I didn't know what else to do. Diesel told me that you were in love with another girl. Did you expect for me to be your side girl? What about the girl in your car? I really love you. Why did this have to go this way. I promise, I really don't even like Diesel like that. He is cool as a friend but I wanted to be with you but you pushed me away. This is really not what you think,* Fah'ry thought as her heart communicated through her eyes as they looked at each other in the rear view mirror. During the remainder of the ride downtown for dinner, she was very quiet and thought about Swerve.

Diesel and Fah'ry started to walk downtown as they looked for the restaurant. "I half to talk to you. We need to go to a park or something this week," Diesel said with a serious tone.

"What is it? Why can't you tell me now?" she asked.

"Naw. I really want to have enough time to really sit and talk to you," he said as they walked and talked.

"Ok," she said as a man walking by stopped to ask Diesel a question privately. He answered the man's question with laughter and came back to continue to walk with Fah'ry.

"Dat's crazy!" he said. "Haha!"

"What?" she asked with a curious tone.

"You ain't gonna believe what he just asked me," he said.

"What is it?" she said as she laughed with him.

"He said . . . 'Where did I get you from . . . Because you look like you came from heaven.' I told you ! You Ms. America!" he said.

Really? Fah'ry thought. *Am I really that attractive? I mean, I know that I am pretty but I would never have expected a stranger to say something like that.*

They finally reached the restaurant after a long walk. They sat down to enjoy dinner but Fah'ry had a difficult time for a while trying to enjoy her meal as she thought about Swerve. Diesel and Fah'ry finished dinner and took a long evening walk downtown Chicago back to his truck. He turned on track number five and they went back to the neighborhood. He kept playing the song as he noticed her enjoying the ballad. They both started to laugh because of the many times he played the song. "I will play this song as long as you need me to so that you can get over him. And it's helping me too, to get over her," he said. "I guess we both are trying to get our hearts better." They took a couple drives around the neighborhood and he pulled up to her house to take her home. Fah'ry leaned over to hug him and he responded very dry.

What is wrong with him? she thought. *Why is he changing? Did I say something?* she thought in a very perplexed manner. Diesel paused. "You OK?" she asked.

"Naw. You playing games with me," he said with a serious voice. "If you ain't ready to go to the next level, don't call me know moe. I want you to stay with me tonight," he said.

Fah'ry sat in the truck in silence as she was lost for words and her heart started to pound as she tried to make a quick decision. She started to think about Chaston's words. 'You ain't on nothin.' Then she heard

Swerve's words. 'You ain't on nothin.' *Oh man. I don't know what to do. I'm tired of being by my self. I don't want to lose another boyfriend. I don't know what to say. Think of something really quick.* She thought about what life would be like if she decided not to go with him. *Ugh! I'm going to be back at that stupid house by myself every day. I can't do it. I can't be alone. I don't want to be alone. I don't think I can make it by myself,* she thought.

"Ok. I'll go with you tonight," Fah'ry said.

Diesel turned the music back up and changed back to his normal silly self.

Lord please forgive me. I know that I am so wrong. I just can't be by myself anymore. Please forgive me, she thought. *I know that I am supposed to save myself for my husband but honestly I don't think that I will ever get married. Clearly, all these guys want is one thing. It seems like that.*

Fah'ry took the ride of doom as he pulled up in a motel style hotel. *A hotel?* Fah'ry thought. *This place looks like a cheap motel. What is wrong with him?* she thought.

"I tried to stop at the really nice places," he said. "But everything is booked since it's so late. This is the only place left with rooms," he said to her.

"Oh," Fah'ry said. Diesel went to pay at the cashier's window and received the keys to the room while she waited in the truck. *Oh God. Please forgive me. There is no way for me to get out of this now. I am here now. Please forgive me. I know I am wrong.* Fah'ry's heart pounded and her stomach balled up in knots so bad that she felt that she had to use the restroom. He came back to the truck.

"Did you want to get something from the store before we went in?" he asked. "Like some chips or juice or something?"

"Naw," she said as her legs shook while walking up the stairs to the hotel door. They walked into the mediocre style room and she sat in the chair.

"Why you sitting over there?" he asked with a smile.

"No reason," she said.

"What's wrong?" he asked. "You been quiet for a while."

"Well," she said. "I've never done this before."

"Oh. It's Ok," he said. He started to take her clothes off as she tried to get into it but she couldn't.

Ugh! she thought. Fah'ry let out a loud yell as that which was dear to her was given to a man that was not her husband. Fah'ry looked up as he had his way with her. She saw angels watching. She looked closer at them and saw tears rolling down their faces as they put their swords up.

Fah'ry woke up to a sunny day. She took a shower and they prepared to leave for the day. Fah'ry glanced at the white sheet with the blood stain of her ruptured sacredness on it. *Oh God,* she thought. *It's gone. I'm so sorry. My heart hurts,* she thought as Diesel closed the door and locked it. Her tube of pink lipgloss lay right next to the blood stain on the bed.

The ride home was long and quiet for Fah'ry. *I can't believe that I did this. I have not even known him that long. I have went against every standard that I have. I slept with him in three weeks. It's only been three weeks that we've been talking. I feel horrible.* Fah'ry shed tears through her heart as she tried to shield the tears through her eyes.

"You hungry?" Diesel asked as they approached the stop light by her church.

Oh! It's Sunday! she thought as she saw all of the cars double parked around the church area and building. "Naw, but you can drop me off right here," she said.

"Right here?" he asked as her favorite gospel song played in the background in the truck.

"Yea," she said.

"Are you sure?" he asked. "How you gonna get home?"

"Yea. I am sure. This is my church. I only have to get on one bus and it will take me home," she said to him.

"Ok," he said as he pulled over on the side of the street to let her out. "Call me when you get home and I will come and get you."

"Ok," she said.

Fah'ry got out of the truck and went into church straight from the hotel. As she walked in, she placed her yellow polished nails in her pocket to feel for her pink lipgloss . . . Fah'ry took a deep breath in nervousness, *Oh my gosh, where's my lipgloss?*

Week Four: He's Hazardous to My Destiny

Fah'ry continued to spend her days with Diesel being adorned with expensive clothes, going to lavish restaurants, being driven around in his world and put on a pedestal as Ms. America. She spent her nights with him at the cheap hotel continuously submitting herself to his sexual prowess. Fah'ry continued with her request of being dropped off at her church on Sunday mornings as they took the same route from the hotel. She rarely stayed at home at night. The cheap hotel became her supplemental place to stay as they ended long days of outings and neighborhood stops.

Lord, I know that I am wrong for going to this hotel with him. I guess I feel like I have already done wrong by giving up my virginity. It's like I already know that you are mad at me. I just hate being at this house with all these roaches and rats. I can't take a shower or keep myself fresh or clean. I mean, I get to take a shower at the hotel everyday. I know that I shouldn't be fornicating and I'm sorry but I don't want to be alone. I want a boyfriend like the rest of the girls and it seems like I can't have one without having sex. I mean, what's the chances of me getting married anyway? I just felt like I would be waiting for a husband that would never come. Look how Chaston and Swerve treated me. It seems like everybody that I want, they don't want me. What's wrong with me? Am I not pretty enough? Am I not thick enough? Is it all because I don't wear short shorts and halter tops like the rest of the girls? Or tall stilettos? I just don't know. But Diesel is practically worshipping the ground that I walk on and treating me like a princess but it doesn't mean anything because it's not who I want.

I'm tired of arguing in this house with my uncles and not being able to eat what I want in the refrigerator. I'm tired of fighting over water and going to the park water fountain to steal water just so I can wash up well. My mama is always gone and I wish that things were better between us. She would probably never understand why I hang out at Keke's house. I know that she feels that it is classless to hang over there but it kept me busy and my mind off of Chaston. If I would have stayed in the house for the summer, my depression would have come back. I probably would have went through with the suicide. I know that we are not supposed to do that but I felt that no one would have cared if I died anyway.

Please help me God? I can't stand my uncle for molesting me when I was six or five. I don't remember. I hate the way that he smells. It makes me think of how he smelled upstairs in that room. I just don't understand how my mama can say that he only fondled me and there was no penetration and other people have had worst experiences. As if my situation meant nothing. That's why I am scared of the doctor. I don't want anyone making me take my clothes off or in my personal space. I feel just like I did as a little girl standing on that dresser upstairs with no clothes on. I know that it doesn't make sense when I'm having sex with Diesel every night but I feel like I'm not really there. I just let him do it.

Lord please help me? I really don't mean to do wrong. I love you and I know that my mama did not raise me to be this type of girl. She taught me to worship and live according to the Bible. I was raised in the church and I know better. I guess I am not as perfect as I thought, just because I know you and wasn't doing what all of the other girls were doing. I messed up. I know my mama has paid all of this money for me to go to private school and I'm acting like the public school girls. I'm supposed to be different. I know. Holy, smart and on my way to college to be a doctor . . . Please help me God. I don't want to do wrong. I belong to you . . .

Fah'ry waited for Diesel to pick her up from home for the day. She sat on her little front porch, listened to her headphones and watched all of the cars drive by. Fah'ry's phone rang as it sat on the burgundy porch step.

"Hello," Fah'ry said.

"What's up Ms. America!" Diesel said.

She gave her normal smirk. "Hey!" she said with a smile.

"I'm on my way. We gone go to the park and talk sometime this week. I got some stuff that I wanna talk to you about," he said with an urgent tone.

"Ok," Fah'ry said.

"Aye!" he said in a low voice. "Can I come in right quick? I gotta do something," he said.

"Um ok. You can come in the hallway. Will that work?" Fah'ry asked.

"Yea. That's fine. I just need to come in right quick."

"Ok," she said. *Why does he want to come in? He can't go any further than this hallway. This is probably the best-looking part of this house,* she thought.

Diesel walked up to Fah'ry on her porch.

"Hey," she said. She showed him inside of her hallway which was a small room at the outside entry door before a second set of doors and a second hallway before reaching a final door to get in the house.

"Ok. This is good," he said as he whispered. Diesel pulled out several unfamiliar items to Fah'ry. He knelt down and started to sort and weigh items.

She stared at him. *Oh my gosh! Are those drugs? Oh Lord. What is going on?* she thought as she watched him and watched the house door in hopes that no one would come in the hallway from inside of the house. Her heart pittered and pattered as she watched him.

"Dis right here," he said as he pointed to one of the items. "You can get ten years for this by itself," he said in a teaching tone. Fah'ry looked at him with no response. Diesel wrapped up what he was doing quickly as he counted and clicked the numbers on a calculator. He grabbed a piece of one of the items. "Aye. You still got that money that I gave you?" he asked her.

"Yea. It's in my purse," she said.

"Ok, hold on to it," he urged. "And can you hold this for me?" he said as he passed the item to her.

Huh? she thought. *He wants me to hold that. Where am I going to keep that at? This is crazy. But I guess I can? I don't want him to think that I'm not there for him,* she thought as she took the item from him. "Yea," she said.

"Just hold it for me," he said. "You ready to go?" he asked.

"Yea. Let me go and put this up," said Fah'ry.

"You know what!" Diesel said. "Let me go do dis and I'll come back and get you."

"Oh ok," Fah'ry said. She let him out of the hallway and went to her room to put the item in a safe place. *What am I doing? Why did I tell him yes? This is so stupid. I am smarter than this,* she thought. *I shouldn't be holding anything for him. Why would he ask me to hold this for him anyway?*

She sat and waited for him to come back and pick her up. Fah'ry called Monica to see if she wanted to hang out with them for the day. Monica was the only friend that was still seemingly talking to her from Keke's house.

Diesel picked her back up right away. They started to ride around and made a stop at his family's house. Fah'ry was introduced to everyone as they laughed and played while joking around with Diesel.

Why am I here? she thought. *This is not where I am supposed to be. This is not what my mama would expect for me. I should not be dating anyone like this. I don't belong here. Ugh! If I stop talking to him, then who do I have? I'll just be sitting in the house by myself and I don't want him to think that I am just with him for his money. I can care less about his money. My daddy gives me money. My daddy takes care of me,* she thought to herself.

"Diesel she is so pretty!" his cousin said in an elevated voice.

"Haha! That's Ms. America!" he said as he bragged. Fah'ry gave his cousin a smirk and a smile.

"Now don't you be hitting on her like you do Kyasia!" his cousin admonished him.

"Naw! She ain't nothin like Kyasia! I ain't gone do nothin to her. That's Ms. America!" Diesel said as he smiled and looked at Fah'ry. "She bout to go to go to college too!" he boasted to his cousin.

"Oh really!" she said. "What college?"

"Yes. I am going to Brighton University," Fah'ry said.

"Oh! The Ivy League school in California?" she asked with a curious voice.

"Yea," Fah'ry answered as she sat on the couch.

"Oh, so you're smart?" his cousin said.

"Yea! She graduated top of her class!" Diesel said as he interrupted the conversation.

"Really?" his cousin said in amazement as the rest of his family laughed and played in the kitchen.

"Yea . . ." Fah'ry smirked.

"Awe! Good for you!" his cousin exclaimed as she walked to the dining room table. Diesel smiled proud as he finished the conversation with his cousin. Fah'ry and Diesel left his cousin's house and continued with their day.

They started to drive through the neighborhood of his cousin as they approached the expressway. Diesel turned on the music to soothe their broken hearts and they drove while enjoying the summer day. They listened to track number five several times during their ride.

"I talked to Monica," Fah'ry said.

"What she say?" he asked.

"Nothing, she said she was just sitting around the house."

"We can go get her if you want?" Diesel suggested.

"Um. That's fine," Fah'ry said. "Let me call her and tell her that we are coming to get her. You know, I was thinking," Fah'ry said to Diesel. "I hope that you don't hit me."

Diesel turned to Fah'ry with a sincere and surprised look. "You think that I would hit you??? I wouldn't do that to you," he said with sincerity. "You too pretty for that. I care too much about you. You have a future ahead of you. That's why I always use a condom with you too. I don't want to mess your life up. I don't want to be a part of messing up your future," Diesel said.

"Yea, but if you hit Kyasia, you'll hit me," she said.

"Naw! That's different," he said in a convincing manner.

"Well, I just feel like it's not about how pretty I am, is just when and if I make you mad enough to hit me," she said.

"Naw! I am so serious. I will not hit you. I won't do that to you," he urged her in a serious voice. They continued to ride as he turned the music back up and stopped by Monica's house to pick her up.

"What up Monica!" Diesel said as she got in the truck with them.

"What's up y'all!" Monica said.

"Hey!" Fah'ry said as she put on her sunglasses. Diesel made a quick stop around the neighborhood. He stopped at the corner and double parked the car as the guys greeted him. They peeked in the truck window.

"Heyyyy Ms. America!" This was the repeated greeting as each guy walked past his truck and spoke to Fah'ry.

"Hey," she said. *I don't know how to feel about them calling me that. I guess it's a complement. So why am I feeling bad about it? It's nothing wrong with that? Right? I mean, I didn't make it up myself and call myself that. Someone else did. I guess it's like any other nickname that people have,* she thought to herself.

Diesel came to the truck to talk to them. "You can take a ride if you want. Y'all don't have to sit here and wait for me," he said to Fah'ry.

"Drive your truck?" she asked as she could not believe it. *They don't let anyone drive their cars around here. I know that these things are precious to them,* she thought.

"Yea!" Diesel said while standing at the passenger side window where she sat. "Gone head!!" he said.

"Haha!" The girls started laughing at him. "You are playing!" they said.

"Naw! I'm serious as a heart attack! You can drive my truck! I don't care!" he said. "Let me just show you how the security system works so that the car does not shut down on you." Fah'ry got on the driver's side and Monica jumped on the passenger side. *Should I be driving his truck? What does this mean? What if I get stopped by the police?* she thought.

"I'll be here when y'all get back," Diesel said to Fah'ry.

"You serious huh?" she said to him as she sat on the driver's side with her hands on the steering wheel while he stood at the window.

"Yea!!! Gone head!" he said as he laughed. "Ok," Fah'ry said. She put the truck in drive and rode around the neighborhood in Diesel's prized possession with Monica.

"Girl! You got him sprung! He let you drive his truck! Haha! H*** naw!!!" Fah'ry turned the music up and the girls enjoyed riding around alone in his plush truck. They finally came back to where he was and as they approached the block, there were a large amount of guys on the corner.

Oh man! Where did all of them come from? she thought. *It wasn't that many of them out here when we left. Please don't let Swerve be out here? OK, there is no way for me to hide now anyway.* She drove up slowly to the crowd of guys to pick up Diesel. All eyes were on her as she stopped the truck in the middle of the street. He smiled at her as if he was proud and all of the guys watched as they switched seats.

Diesel got in the truck, fixed the seat and turned up the music. They drove off and headed downtown for dinner. Fah'ry glanced at herself in the side-view mirror and noticed that something was missing. *I really need to find my lipgloss,* she thought. *I look so different without it. Ugh!*

Fah'ry, Diesel and Monica enjoyed dinner for the most part. They left dinner and started to ride around an unfamiliar neighborhood to Fah'ry and Monica. *I know that his phone rings a lot but it's been ringing all night. Ever since we left from on the block, his phone has been ringing like crazy. He think that I'm stupid, she thought. Every time that his phone rings and he answers with*

"YO", I know that it is a girl. He doesn't do that with everybody that calls him. I'm not dumb.

As his phone kept ringing abnormally, with his answer of "YO", Fah'ry tried to ignore it. They reached a stop sign and several guys on the corner stared at Diesel.

"What's up!" he said with a stern voice.

"What!" the guy said back to him in a confrontational voice.

Oh God! Please don't let anything happen. Please let us get from over here. Please don't start anything, she thought. The guy said some gang slurs and Diesel tried to be as calm as possible.

"Do you know who I am?" he said to the young guy who was being territorial and confrontational.

"What! I don't give a f***!!!" The guy said with a mean face as he stood confident.

Lord, Lord, Lord! she thought. *Lord, Lord, Lord! Please let him drive off! Please don't let him start to argue with this guy?* she thought in fear. Fah'ry looked at the guys on the corner as she sat up right in the truck. *I hope that they are nice enough not to shoot while girls are in the truck,* she thought. The confrontation was brief but seemed very long. Diesel pulled off slowly as he watched from his rear-view mirror. *Whew! Thank you, Lord!* she thought to herself in relief. Suddenly . . . Pop! Pop! Pop! were the sounds of several gun shots. "Ayyyyy!" Fah'ry screamed . . .

Week Five: Jealous Girls - Baby Mama vs. Ms. America

"It's ok," Diesel said to Fah'ry and Monica in a calm voice. "Dey just shot in the air. Dey ain't on nothin but they shouldn't have done dat. Dey just messed up. Dey ain't scaring nobody," Diesel said in an upset voice. He looked over at Fah'ry. "You alright?" he asked.

"Yea. I'm trying to be," she said as she continued to look in the rear-view mirror as she had flashbacks.

"Monica, you ok?" he asked as he looked in the backseat.

"Um yea," Monica said as she sat quietly.

Diesel picked up his phone. "I gotta make a couple of calls," he said in a very serious voice. He completed his phone calls and continued to drive peacefully.

How can he be this calm right now? Fah'ry thought. *I mean, they just finished shooting!*

"I'm gone have to drop y'all off to take care of something. I'll come back and get you," he said.

"Ok," Fah'ry said in an understanding voice. *Lord, whatever he is about to do, please take care of him. Please don't let him get hurt,* she prayed to herself.

Diesel dropped Monica off first and pulled up to Fah'ry's house next. They sat on the busy street in his truck for a brief moment. *I am really nervous for him,* she thought. They started to see police cars drive past the truck.

"That's the same police officer that keeps passing us," he said. "They about to try and start something. I bet they are," he said with confidence.

"Well, let me go ahead and get in the house," Fah'ry said as she picked up her heavy purse from off of the floor.

The police officer pulled up on the opposite side of them. "Why you sitting on this busy street?" the police asked. "I should take your truck! That's a nice classic truck, ain't it?" he said to his partner as he laughed.

"Yeah. I think I want that," he said.

"Aw! Here they go!" Diesel said as he put the truck in park. "I knew it!" he said in frustration as two swat cars pulled up behind them as they sat parked on the busy street in front of her house.

Oh God. I need to go in the house. I knew I should have went in the house right away, she thought.

Her hands started to shake and she lost all sense of understanding for a moment as she tried to grab her purse. The police got out of their cars and the male officer went to Diesel's side and asked them to get out of the car. *Why are they asking me to get out of the car? I'm a girl? Shouldn't I be able to sit in the car while he gets out?* she thought. Fah'ry looked over out of her window and a female officer was standing at her door.

"I am going to need you to get out of the car," the female officer said while the male officer had Diesel on the car searching him.

"Ok," Fah'ry said. She got out of the car as the female officer watched her.

"You can leave your purse right there on the ground and put your hands on the car," the officer said.

Oh my God! I can't believe that this is happening, she thought as the blue lights from the cars lit up the entire street. Fah'ry looked up at her house and saw her grandmother peeking from the back porch. Their eyes met as she saw the disappointment in her grandmother's eyes as the female officer searched Fah'ry. Her grandmother shook her head and went back in the house. Fah'ry's head dropped as she saw the disappointment in her grandmother. The officer patted her down as her pretty yellow manicured nails lay flat on the truck and her legs spread apart. Fah'ry looked over at Diesel as the male officers taunted him. *Lord, please get me out of this? Please let me just go in the house,* she thought.

"You don't have anything in that purse, do you?" the female officer asked.

Oh man! Fah'ry looked over on the ground as her purse sat there standing upright because of its contents. *I forgot that I have all that money in my purse. What should I say? Should I lie? Should I tell her that something is in there?* she thought. *I don't know what to say. I'm just going to take my chances.* "No," Fah'ry said.

"OK, I am going to take your word for it," the female officer said. "You can go now."

"Thank you," Fah'ry said as she picked up her purse from off of the ground and went in the house. She peeked out of her bedroom window as the male officers continued to taunt Diesel before letting him go. He immediately called her once he was able to drive off in his truck. They talked on the phone until he reached his previously intended destination before the officers' encounter.

Fah'ry woke up the next morning to bright sunshine in her room. *Thank U Lord so much for keeping me last night. I probably would have got in lots of trouble for having all of that money in my purse.* Fah'ry got up from her make-shift bed on the floor and went to check in the place that she left the item that Diesel asked her to hold. She picked it up and noticed that it looked strange. She took a closer look. "What happened to this?" she said as she examined it. She noticed little holes in the plastic that seemed all too familiar. *Oh shoot! Dem stupid rats done ate a piece of this. Oh man!* she thought as she started to sweat and her palms started to get very wet while her heart beat faster and faster. *What am I going to tell Diesel? He is not going to believe me if I tell him that a rat ate a piece of this. This is so embarrassing. I don't even want him to know that we have rats. I don't want him to think that I did something to this either. Like I got some personal gain off of keeping a piece for myself or something. What am I going to say? He is going to be mad at me. He probably won't trust me anymore. I should have just told him that I couldn't hold this for him anyway,* she thought as she tried to fix the piece back to its normal look with part of it missing. *OK, it looks the same almost. The rats didn't eat too much of it.*

Fah'ry's phone started to ring. *That must be Diesel,* she said to herself as she picked up the phone. "Hello," Fah'ry said. *Think of something to say. I have to find a way to tell him,* she thought nervously.

"Hey," he said.

She took a deep breath and couldn't believe it. "Hey Chaston," she said.

"So, what's up?" Chaston asked in a sad voice.

"Nothing," Fah'ry said in a spunky voice.

"That ain't what I heard. I heard you got a grown man treat you like a princess and everything. So you getting everything you want now huh?" he said.

"I guess you could say that," she said with a smirk of confidence.

"Oh," Chaston said in a weird tone. The phone conversation went silent as Fah'ry did not spark any additional conversations. Her other line started to beep.

"I gotta go," she said.

"Oh ok. It's like that? That must be him?" Chaston said as he tried to keep her on the phone with him.

"I gotta go," she said as she clicked the phone over to the other line. *I don't have time for him anymore I will not let him think he can just come back in my life and I just put everything down for him. I'm done,* she thought to herself. "Hello," she said.

"Is Fah'ry there?" the woman said.

"This is she," Fah'ry said with suspicion.

"Well, I found your number in Diesel's pants pocket. This is Tasha. Did he tell you that he has a family? I don't know why he thinks he can be out here talking to these young girls and come home and think I won't say anything. I am his child's mother and we live together," Tasha said in a cordial tone.

Fah'ry just listened as she talked while she tried to gather herself. *I can't believe this! I can't believe he has another baby mama??? He could have at least told me. Man! This is crazy!* "Well, he never told me anything about you," Fah'ry said.

"Of course he won't, he wants to be out there playing and then come home afterwards," Tasha said. "All that I am saying is that you need to leave him alone. We got a family," she said.

"And you need to talk to him," Fah'ry said as she hung up the phone. "Ugh! Ooh!! Wait until I talk to him!" she said. *He been lying all this time. Wait! How could he have a family and he stayed with me at the hotel every night? This doesn't make sense. I mean, we are together all day and night. Breakfast lunch and dinner! What kind of family is that?* she thought to herself. *You know what though? I should have known. But I allowed him to keep answering that phone and I knew that it was a girl on the other line and I didn't know if it was Kyasia. I figured that she may have been calling to talk about their child. But another baby mama?? Oh no! I am nobody's side chick! And I won't be the other woman in anybody's life. My mom did not teach me to be that kind of girl. Ugh! I am so mad right now!!*

Diesel finally called Fah'ry to start their day. "What's up Ms. America?" he said in an excited voice.

"Hey," she said in a dry tone.

"What's wrong?" he asked with reservation.

"Nothing, we can talk about it later," she said.

"What?" he asked with concern.

"I will tell you. Don't worry," she said.

"Alright. Aye. Can you bring dat? You know, what I asked you to hold. I'm over on the block," he said.

"Alright. Here I come," she said. Fah'ry put it in her pocket and walked around the corner to the block instead of driving. She never thought twice about what she was carrying and its consequences. She met him and saw that another guy was waiting with him. She got in his truck and pulled the item out of her pocket.

"I be right back," he said as he walked to meet the guy on the corner.

"Ok," she said. *Yeah. Please hurry up because I can't wait to talk to you!* she thought to herself.

Diesel got back in the truck and they started to drive away from the neighborhood.

"So what's up?" he asked. "What's wrong? I know that something is wrong. You are acting different," he said as he tried to figure it out.

"Tasha called me today," Fah'ry said in a disappointed voice.

"What!! She did what!" he said in anger. "What did she say?"

"She said that you had a family and a home. She said that I needed to stop talking to you. She also said that you have a child with her," Fah'ry said.

"I can't believe her!" he said. "I gotta go. I be right back," he said in an upset tone. "I'm gonna have to drop you off but I'll be back," he said.

"Yea ok," she said. *It's whatever. I don't really care. I don't have time for all of this baby mama drama,* she thought. *This is why I didn't want to talk to him in the first place. One baby mama is enough. Now there's two! Ugh! I really don't have time for this.* Diesel dropped her off at home. They hugged and he insisted that he'd be right back.

Fah'ry waited for Diesel to come back. Hours passed but he never showed up. *That's weird. He never takes this long to come back and get me. It's almost bedtime and we normally go to dinner every night. I don't like calling guys but maybe I should try and call him. I just hate calling guys now,* she thought. Naw. I'm not going to call him. I'm not sweating anybody. *Maybe he's with his baby mama. Maybe they are making up or something. He calls me any other time. We spend all day and night together. Maybe he just got busy. I don't know. I do know that I won't be calling him. I just can't do that anymore with any guy*. A couple of more hours passed and she still had not heard from him. *OK, maybe I should try and call. It's getting really late. This is weird. I'm starting to feel like I did when Chaston started dodging me,* she thought to herself.

Fah'ry called Diesel several times but it went straight to the voicemail. *So he turned off his phone? Really? His battery never dies.* Fah'ry laid down and went to bed to try to ease a familiar pain. A few hours passed as she slept and the phone rang. "Hello," she said in a raspy voice.

"You have a collect call from . . ." the automated voice said, and then there was a pause that allowed diesel to say his name. "Will you accept the charges?" was the next statement from the automated voice.

"Yes," Fah'ry answered and the call was connected.

"Hey," he said in a low and sad voice. "Mannnn. I'm gone, Joe. I'm gone," he said in disbelief.

"What do you mean?" Fah'ry asked as she sat up on the floor to hear his answer.

"Man . . . I'm locked up," he said. "I'm gone. This is what I wanted to talk to you about at the park. All of that stuff. Even the baby mama stuff," he said. Suddenly, the phone started to click and the voice recorded system alerted them that the call was about to end. The phone disconnected and went dead. She spent several days alone as Diesel was in jail. She sat on her porch, listened to her headphones and watched the cars go by as she counted down the days for college. *Man. It would be nice if I could go hang out with Keke nem but I am not chasing anybody. Obviously, they don't want to hang out with me. They haven't called me at all,* she thought. *Maybe Diesel was right? Maybe they are jealous of me?* As the day grew closer for her to go to college, she took care of minor business with Diesel's attorney regarding his court case. The days and nights grew longer and became more boring as she had nothing to do every day.

One more day before Brighton! Fah'ry said to herself as she sat down on the porch. She finally had time out of her day as it was filled with meetings with Diesel's attorney. She sat on the porch for the remainder of the day until it got dark. Her phone started to buzz on the bottom step. "Hello," she said.

"Hey, what you doing?" Monica asked.

"Nothing," she said.

"Why don't you come out tonight? We about to go to a party around the corner. It's your last day before you leave for college. Come to the party," Monica said with a convincing tone.

"Naw," Fah'ry said. "I don't need to be around there. I haven't talked to anybody over there in weeks," Fah'ry tried to explain.

"Girl, ain't nobody mad at you! You need to come out and kick it!"

"Naw. I'm good. I have to finish packing."

"Come on, G! Dis yo last night before you go to college. Just come for me? Please?" Monica pleaded.

"I don't know. I'm just not sure. I don't really want to come over there," Fah'ry said to her.

"G, you don't have to stay long. Just come for a little bit? Then you can go back home," Monica said. "Come on!"

They sat on the phone in silence as Fah'ry tried to make a decision. "Ok. I'll come for a little bit. I'm just coming because it's you Monica," Fah'ry said in a serious voice.

"Ok. We on the porch. We just waiting for you so that we can walk to the party," Monica said to her.

"Alright," she said. "I'm on my way." *Ugh! I don't really want to go. I mean, how can I go be with them and act like they didn't just stop talking to me for weeks. I don't feel like being all uncomfortable around them. I hate that feeling. I can't stand fake friends. Ugh! I feel like I really shouldn't go over there. Something doesn't seem right.*

Fah'ry walked around the corner to Keke's house. She arrived to a large group of girls on the front porch drinking and smoking as they prepared for the party including Kyasia. *Oh, I guess everybody's going to this party?* she thought. The girls started walking to the party. They did their normal routine of singing and provocative dancing in the streets. This time, instead of Fah'ry walking behind them as they danced, she walked in front of the crowd. She gave a brief laugh at them. *They are so crazy.* She felt someone running behind her and she quickly turned around.

"Fah'ry why you messing with my man?" Kyasia said with a large smile on her face and her hands behind her back.

"What!" Fah'ry said with an attitude. "Girl, I don't care nothing about Diesel!" she said with her face twisted in a upset manner.

"Yeah! Why you keep messin with my man!!"

"Kyasia! I don't . . ." They started to raise their voices as they argued. All of a sudden, Fah'ry felt a heavy blow to her head. The girls started to run towards them as Fah'ry and Kyasia started to fight. *Did she just haul off and hit me in the front of my head with a alcohol bottle?* she thought as they fought. Fah'ry's pretty hair was flying all over the place as they swung several times at each other. Kyasia's main goal was to go for Fah'ry's hair and face.

"Why did you hit her with that bottle Kyasia?" Some of the girls started to shout as they broke up the fight. "You bogus for that!" they said to her as she ran while the girls were checking on Fah'ry's head. Fah'ry felt the gash on her forehead that had a large knot and blood running down her face.

"I need to go to my cousin's house. She lives right here at the corner. Let me go get my cousin," she said.

"Naw! You don't need yo cousin! You got us!" some of the girls said as they grabbed her arm to pull her in the opposite direction of her cousin's house.

"I'm just gonna go home," she said.

"Naw! You gone fight her! We gone find her! She hit you in the head with a bottle! You have to fight!" they said. They all started to walk back towards Keke's house to look for Kyasia.

I don't want to fight. I've never had a fight, she thought as her legs shook and her hands trembled. *And this girl is way bigger than me.* As they got closer to the house, they started to see many of the guys out on the corner.

"Have y'all seen Kyasia?" Fah'ry asked.

"Naw," the guys responded in a calm voice.

Fah'ry went inside of Keke's house to find a scarf to wrap her hair up in an effort to shield her hair from being pulled during the fight. She looked in the kitchen drawer and grabbed a large knife. She heard a voice say, "Put the knife down" She stopped and took a deep breathe. *Naw. I need to put this back. I don't want anybody getting hurt like that,* she thought. She put the knife away and started to go downstairs as she heard the crowd outside of house. The girls ran behind her as she headed outside for the fight. On her way out, she saw a large bat sitting at the door. "Y'all please don't let me get beat up in this fight," she said to her friends. "We got you," Keke said in a reassuring tone. *OK,* Fahry thought to herself, *I feel better now. They won't let anything happen to me.* Fah'ry grabbed the bat and walked onto the porch.

She was greeted by the entire neighborhood watching and waiting. Kyasia pulled up in a car and got out of the passenger side with a bat in her hand. *How interesting is that? She has a bat?* Fah'ry thought. She walked in the middle of the street to greet Kyasia. She held her bat like she was about to hit a ball. She suddenly had glimpses of her summer camp days when she learned how to hold a wooden bat and focus on the fast ball coming toward her. Kyasia smiled and did the same. *Aw man! I am going to have to knock her out with this bat. If I don't, she is going to get the best of me because she is too big,* Fah'ry thought. Fah'ry took the first swing as hard as she could and hit her a couple times in her back with the bat. Shortly after, both of their bats clung together and fell to the ground.

They started to fight with their fists and suddenly Fah'ry's scarf came off and Kyasia went straight for Fah'ry's hair. They continued to fight but Kyasia had a strong grip on Fah'ry's hair. They tussled on the ground for awhile. Fah'ry punched, kicked and even tried to bite into Kyasia's fat rolls on her stomach to get her to release her grip on her hair. *I am getting so tired. This is the longest fight ever.*

Kyasia loosed her grip on Fah'ry's hair for a brief moment but only in an effort to sit on top of her. Kyasia sat on top of Fah'ry and started bashing her head against the concrete.

Uh! Uh! Uh! These were the sounds that Kyasia made each time that she attempted to push her head to the ground. Fah'ry used all of the strength that she had in her abs to keep her head up from hitting the ground. Her posture was as if she was doing sit ups or crunches on the ground.

Fah'ry took a brief look up and noticed that they were fighting right in front of a church. *God, I feel like I am fighting for my life!* she thought. She took a second look up and saw all of her friends standing around watching.

She took a look at Keke and saw a weird look in her eyes. Something similar to . . . 'Yeah! Get her!' *What is that? Why is she looking like that? Why haven't they stopped this fight? Maybe I need to ask for help?* she thought.

Fah'ry took a third look and saw Monica standing over her head hollering. "Beat her a** Fah'ry!!" *OK, it seems like somebody is on my side,* she thought.

"Monica! Get her off of me!" Fah'ry yelled out but no one moved. All of the girls stood and watched along with the rest of the neighborhood. Fah'ry yelled again. She looked up at Monica and said, "... Monica get her off me!" None of her friends moved. They continued to watch the fight and ignore her cries for help.

One of the guys in the neighborhood who stood watching yelled, "She said get her off of her!"

But none of her friends moved and they continued to watch Kyasia attempt to bash her head against the ground as they fought in front of the church. Out of nowhere, a lady whom Fah'ry had never seen came in the middle of the fight and broke it up and quickly disappeared. *Thank you, God. I am so tired!* she thought to herself. *I just want to go home . . .*

Rebellious for Love:

College-bound or Prison-bound

I can't believe them! Didn't none of dem help me. They just stood there and watched me get beat up. They saw that I couldn't handle her. She was just too big and all of my hair was wrapped around her hand! Shoot, I couldn't swing as much because I had to protect my hair and face! I spent most of the time trying to pry her hands off of my hair. Ugh! What did she have to protect? Her hair isn't long. I guess I just didn't have the type of rage and hatred in me that she had, Fah'ry thought as tears rolled down her face and she laid on the floor for bed.

I am so glad that I am leaving for college tomorrow. How interesting is it that she waited for Diesel to go to jail to fight me? Wait until I see him tomorrow! I hope I don't have any concussions from that bottle or my head hitting the ground. Cuz this knot is big on my forehead. I hope that no glass got in this cut. How am I going to tell my mama this? What am I going to tell my dad when he picks me up to take me to college? I got this big ole cut on my head and it hurts like crazy. Ouch! Fah'ry said as she touched the knot and cut on her forehead.

Ugh! I don't even know what to pray. God, thank you because this could have been worse. Lord, please let me wake up because I really don't know the damage that the bottle did to my head. Fah'ry wiped her tears and put her hands on her wounds and prayed for healing before falling asleep.

Fah'ry woke up to the sun shining brightly in her face. *Geez! I guess this why they call this room the sun parlor!* she said while sitting up on the floor on her blanket. Fah'ry grabbed her mirror out of her purse and took a look at her face. *I don't even want to look. My face probably messed up! Ugh!* She looked in the mirror and started to examine the wounds on her face. *Oh my gosh!* she said as she moved the mirror from the cut on her forehead to the numerous deep scratches on both sides of her face. *This is horrible!* she thought as she started to pout. *She scratched my face up! Look at all of these red marks! And look at this knot on my head! I hope dese scars go away. I can't be walking around with no messed-up face like dese ghetto girls. I don't even wanna look no moe.*

She put the mirror down and started picking out her clothes for the day and packing her last clothes for college. *It's Sunday and I really need to go to church. How interesting is it that his visiting day at jail is on Sundays? The day that I go to church! I never miss church. Ugh! And he is asking me to only come in the morning? Why? It's at the same time as church. God please understand? I have never been to a jail before. I've never visited anyone in jail either. I don't know what this gone be like? Am I going to be talking to him through some bars or something?* she thought as she set out her green wash pan to wash up. *Last day for this and I am so happy.*

Fah'ry got in her yellow convertible IvyKennington, turned on worship music and headed to the jail to visit Diesel. *I need to stop and get some peroxide and cocoa butter for my face. Ugh!* she sighed as she glanced at her face in the car mirror. *I don't know how long this will be but I gotta hurry up back before my dad gets there and is ready to get on the road.*

Fah'ry started to get nervous as she approached the jail grounds to park. *Wow! Look at these buildings! Look at these barb-wired gates! It looks just like it does in the movies.* Fah'ry walked through the secure automatic gate with the crowd of women that were waiting at the gate for the first round of visits at 9:00 am. *I have no idea where I am going. I'll just follow them. Naw, let me ask somebody,* she thought.

"Excuse me. Is this the right way to Division 10?" Fah'ry asked the lady walking in the crowd.

"Yeah," the lady said as she walked quickly.

"Ok, cuz this my first time," Fah'ry said as she walked faster to keep up with the lady.

"Oh ok. I will show you where to go," the lady said.

"Ok thanks," Fah'ry said.

"Girl, we have to hurry up and get inside. They only take so many in the first round at 9 o'clock. If we miss it, we have to wait a whole hour for the next round while everybody is up there visiting," the lady said.

"Oh," said Fah'ry. They finally entered the first set of secure doors.

"Next time, leave your purse in the car. The only thing that you need is your ID. It is better that you leave everything else in the car or something. It just takes a longer time for you to go through the metal detector and all that. Cuz it get crowded in here real fast," the lady said as she walked up to the counter with her ID to check in as a visitor.

"I need you to put all purses, belts and everything else in this basket!" the jail officer said in a loud in mean voice.

"Um, so I have to leave all of my stuff down here?" Fah'ry asked.

"Naw, dey just gone check it and you should be good," the lady said.

"Oh ok. So, do I walk over there?" Fah'ry asked.

"Yeah, just give her your ID and his name and if you have his ID number, you can give that to her too," the lady said as she instructed her.

"Ok." Fah'ry walked up to the tall concrete desk slowly. "Hi. I am here to see Derrick Willis," Fah'ry said.

"OK, I need your ID and you can sign your name right here and put his name and ID on the sheet," the check-in officer said as she moved around quickly with no sensitivity to the people visiting.

"OK, she said as she filled out the sign in sheet. *I am glad that he told me his real name because otherwise I would not be able to see him. I probably would have never asked him his real name. I was scared to,* she thought.

Fah'ry sat down on the hard marble bench next to the lady and waited for the next set of instructions. "So, how long does this take?" Fah'ry asked.

"Well, usually it takes about 30 minutes for everybody to get signed in and sometimes even an hour. But once that is done, they will call us to get ready to go up there to see them. We can visit them for about 30 minutes, but if the guard is nice, sometimes they will let us stay over for about 45 minutes if it's not crowded down here," the lady said.

"Oh," Fah'ry said as they watched the television screen that replayed the tour of the jail and the sheriff greeting on video. *This is ridiculous. They could at least have real TV on,* she thought. "So how long have you been coming here?' she asked.

"Girl, he been in here for a year fighting his case. I will be glad when he go downstate or whatever is going to happen. I doubt if he's going to get out. I've been talking to his lawyer and the best thing he can do is get ready to go down to one of the good ones downstate. It's cool down there dough. You get to visit them as long as you want. There is no timeframe. You can stay all day. And you get to eat with them and everything. It's much better then visiting here. You know, talking to them behind a glass and everything. You don't have to do that. They have tables where you can sit right across from them. You can hug them and all of that," the lady said.

"Oh ok, well he just got here. So, I don't know what's going to happen with him," Fah'ry said.

"Oh. Girl, I see so many women come in and out of here visiting their guy. I been doing this for too long. After a while, you see the same people come at the same times to visit. Look at her over there. She been coming at 9 o'clock for a while too. Her, her, her, and her. They all come at 9 o'clock. It get real crazy around here after the first visit. This is the best time to come," the lady said as she watched the guard.

I wonder why she keeps looking at the jail guard like that? Fah'ry thought.

"Girl, I will be watching these guards because as soon as they are ready for visits, everybody be walking fast to get in the first round so I have to pay close attention," the lady said. "See, when he start moving over towards the door, that means he is about to let us go upstairs."

"Oh," Fah'ry said. Before she could get another question out, the people started to migrate towards the large metal door.

"Come on, see, it's time to go upstairs," the lady said as she continued to help Fah'ry. They walked through to metal doors and got on a large elevator.

So I wonder if I am going to see him in jail bars and stuff and all the striped black and white jail clothes? she thought. They walked into this well lit, small rectangular room with steel chairs and a glass window with a speaker hole in it. *What in the world?* she thought to herself as she tried to sit on the hard, small seat. "So where are they at?" she asked the lady.

"They coming. Sometimes they be still doing other stuff," the lady said. Fah'ry sat at the glass window and waited for Diesel to come out. One by one, the inmates started to come out to the visiting room and sit at the glass window to greet their visitors. *Oh, there he goes,* she said to herself. *Wow, what does he have on?* Diesel walked out with a somber face and a brown suit with the letters D.O.C. on the back of the shirt.

"Hey," he said as he sat down and spoke into the small round speaker on the glass window.

"Hey," Fah'ry said.

All of a sudden, he made a weird look on his face of amazement. "What happened to your face?" he asked her with extreme concern.

"I was fighting Kyasia last night," Fah'ry said as she leaned closer to the window.

"What?" he said. "That's crazy! What happened?" Fah'ry started to tell him the full story of what happened. "Man! They set you up! Ain't no way they call you asking you to come outside. They knew what was about to happen. They know you on your way to college. They set you up. I told you that they are jealous of you! They ain't been talking to you. Why did they want you to come outside last night?" Diesel said in a convincing tone. "Man! Look at your face. Make sure you get some cocoa butter to put on that and make sure you keep that cut clean," he said. "You know what! Here go her address! She leave for work at 5 o'clock in the morning, you can catch her when she leaving on the side of her house and knock her out."

Fah'ry looked at him with a sad face while he talked more than she did during the visit.

"Man! I got to get out of here, Joe!" he said. "My bond is not that much. I can get that money real fast. I got to get out of here!" Diesel said as he watched the guard that was keeping time. "I think it's almost time for us to go," he said as he looked around. "Man! You coming back next week?" he asked. "Just make sure you come at this time again because Tasha be coming later in the day," he said.

"Well, I'm leaving for college when I get back but I will try to get a plane ticket back next week to come and see you," Fah'ry said.

"Oh that's right!" he said. "I forgot you was leaving for college today. So, how I'm going to talk to you?" he asked.

"Just call my house, my grandma will call me at my dorm," she said.

"Man, she gone except my collect calls?" he asked.

"Yea," she said as the guard yelled out to indicate that the inmates had to leave.

"Man, I gotta go!" he said as he looked at all of the inmates leaving out. "Stand up, let me see what you got on?" he said as he smiled.

"I got on Roxidescent. I am so mad because I had on Roxidescent last night when we were fighting and it is all messed up. It's dirt all on it from us fighting on the ground," she said.

"Man, wait until I talk to her. She bogus!" he said as he got a last call from the guard that it was time to leave. "OK, they callin me now. I got to go. I'm gone call you as late as I can. Hopefully by that time you would have made it to school," Diesel said.

"Ok. Talk to you later," she said as she watched him leave out of the visiting room in a single file line.

So, Tasha is coming to visit him too huh? Now he gone have us visiting at two different times a day so that we don't run into each other. I don't know if I can deal with this. And he's bold enough to tell me that she is coming to see him. How stupid can I be? That's his baby mama, she thought as her heart beat fast and she felt betrayed. *Ugh! I am so tired of this already! It's just too much. What did I get myself into? I am glad that I am about to leave. I'm leaving all of this stuff right where it is and starting my life over,* she thought as she walked out of the jail and towards her car. *I am so mad that I missed church. God, I am so sorry.*

Fah'ry drove home as she listened to worship music and had a lot on her mind. *Man, I can't even say bye to Keke nem. Maybe he is right? Maybe they did set me up? It just doesn't make sense. Why did Monica call me asking me to come outside? She probably knew too! I don't trust none of them now. Ugh! I feel so betrayed,* she thought as she wiped the tears from her eyes.

She started to think about all of the fun that Diesel and her had together. *How am I going to visit him every week all da way from California? I mean, he did say that his bond was easy to get. Maybe he will be getting out soon? He said dat he got a good lawyer that has been helping him for years. Who's gonna talk to his lawyer for him? He looked so sad in dere.*

Maybe I should stay in Chicago and go to UC. I mean, I did get accepted dere too. It's prestigious just like Brighton, it's just here in Chicago, Fah'ry thought to herself. *Shoot, I don't want to leave my boyfriend annnd I'm gone be spending so much money going from Cali to Chicago. If I stay here, I can make all of his visits, help him with da lawyer stuff and save money. Cuz I'm gone be spending a lot of my money every week to see him. The only other thing is fuh me to go ahead to Brighton and visit him when I can. Ugh! But I just don't wanna leave and lose my boyfriend,* she thought to herself while driving past all of the jail fences and buildings.

I think I'm gonna just stay here. That way when he get out, we can go back to hanging out and I will still go to a dope college. Yeah, imma call UC tomorrow and accept their offer. Yea, I think this will be so much better! Annnd I can live in da dorms at UC! Ooh yea, she thought and started smiling. *Dat would be supa nice living in Hyde Park! Yeah, dats what I'm gone do!* she thought with excitement. Fah'ry sat up in her car seat while driving with a new confidence. *I ain't trying to go all the way to Brighton with no boyfriend!*

She turned up her music in her car and started to listen to the worship music. She glanced in the mirror and saw the big, long and red marks on her face. She gently touched the large knot on her forehead. "Ouch!" She whispered as the cut from the glass bottle started to sting. Tears started to roll down her brown cheeks. *Man, I can't believe my face is messed up like dis! Why was I even ovah dere?! My mama told me that I was different and I guess she really was helping me by not letting me go outside and hang around da house. I can't believe Keke nem! Ugh! Did they really set me up like Diesel said? Not Monica? She's my friend. Right? Shoot, I don't know what to believe. I don't know who to believe,* she thought as she wiped the tears from her eyes.

Maybe God is trying to say something to me? I mean, how could all of this just happen right before I go to college? How could I just give up my virginity like that? I mean, man! It was only like 3 weeks or something and I gave it up. That's not me. I don't do that. I was supposed to save myself for my husband. How could I do this to myself? Ugh! I don't even like him like dat. He's not even my type and he's not even cute to me. Why did I do that? I'm not a good girl anymore. Am I? I'm just like these other girls now. Somebody in the neighborhood can say that they slept with me. Am I a hoe now?

Why couldn't I just have told Diesel no? I should not have said yes and went to that motel. I mean, it was a cheap motel, not even a hotel! Fah'ry shook her head in disappointment. *He got all dat money but he took me to a motel?? Well, we did stop at a couple of places that night and everything was booked. I mean, but still, they were all cheap hotels. Why didn't he take me downtown somewhere on Michigan Ave? My mama is gone be so mad at me if she finds out. I wonder if she will be able to tell like they say?* She sighed.

I have messed up. Man! Am I ignoring God? Did I ignore God? Am I rebellious like my mama said? Now, Diesel goes to jail and we was only talkin for a month. Keke nem start acting funny and den this fight?? Maybe I should just gone head to Brighton and start ovah? But what about Diesel? Maybe God wants me to move on? How ironic is it that Diesel went to jail right before I leave for college in California? Ugh! I just don't know. I mean, what am I gonna do without a boyfriend? Fah'ry thought as the worship music continued to play and she pulled up to park in front of her house.

Ok, she took a deep breath. *My dad will be here in ah hour to take me to Brighton.* Fah'ry reached in her pocket for her pink lipgloss but was quickly reminded that it was gone. *I don't know where I could have lost my lipgloss, it's my favorite.* She took a deep breath again and blew all the frustrating air into her bubblegum and made a huge pink bubble. She stared at herself in the mirror. *What am I going to do? What is wrong with me? Don't be stupid, Fah'ry! Huh!! Do I go to Brighton in California or stay in Chicago and go to UC and wait for Diesel to get out?? Ugh!!*

She looked over at the front seat next to her and saw a huge pink and green cobra standing in an upright position with its mouth wide open. Fah'ry jumped in fear. *Oh my gosh! What was that???* she thought to herself as she took a second glance and the cobra disappeared.

If you would like to purchase Preppy Gyrl merchandise, visit our Country Club's Bubblegum Pink Smart Girl Shop @www.preppygyrl.com

If you would like to chat with us, visit our Country Club's College Dorm Diaries hangout.

www.ingramcontent.com/pod-product-compliance
Lightning Source LLC
Chambersburg PA
CBHW020930310726
48980CB00007B/714/J

* 9 7 8 0 6 9 2 9 1 7 7 5 6 *